THE ATLAS DYSTOPI
BOOK 1

XANDER CROSS

ISBN 978-1-7342142-1-5 (eBook)
ISBN 978-1-7342142-0-8 (Trade Paperback)

Library of Congress Cataloging-in-Publication Data has been applied for.

This book is a work of fiction. Any resemblance to persons living or dead, events, businesses, corporations and secret oligarchies is entirely coincidental. Names, characters, and places are products of the author's imagination.

Front cover image by Abi Grey
Cover Design by Emily's_World_Of_Design
Interior by Dreams2Media

First printing Edition: November 2019

xandercross13@gmail.com

To my darling spouse
and my friends in the writer's community on Instagram:
Thank you for turning a dream into reality.

And for yōkai lovers everywhere.

Author's Note

As readers progress through the first chapter, they will find the use of present tense breaking in on past recollections. "What's that about?" I've been asked by editors and beta readers alike. Please allow me to assure you this is not in error. The following presentation is a memoir, and if a supposition remains true in the main character's future timeline, it will be considered present tense.

CONTENTS

There are two worlds. One that is bright and solid, which most think of as reality. But there is another world that exists beside it, beneath it, and all around it. This is the Shadow Realm, the dark universe, a terrifying place of horror and madness.

The way into it is through the shadows that creep wherever light casts them, the dark spaces between buildings and at the end of lonely corridors, in corners and under furniture, always stretching, seeking... These places are the portals between the worlds of light and darkness. And this realm, too, has its denizens who live and dwell among the shadows.

They lurk in these unsanctified spaces, the hungry eyes that watch, the arms that grab, reaching out to snatch prey back into the darkness. The unfortunate go missing year after year without a trace. It is instinctual to feel it, the unease which shivers up the spine, serving as an early warning that an intruder stands at the threshold between the worlds.

Everyone knows this is where monsters live, regaled in the folklore of all cultures since time immemorial. In the domains of the farthest East, these beings have been called many names: ayakashi, bakemono, mononoke, and yōkai. Call them spirits, or demons, or even a type of faerie, for thousands of years these otherworldly creatures have existed alongside mankind. And whether benevolent, malevolent, or neutral, all such encounters are generally not recommended. Yet that does not stop the blurring of the worlds at the edge of twilight, and for those humans and yōkai who are forced to live together, virtually impossible.

Take, for example, those who live in the great urban centers, from the olden days of Edo up through the dawn of the

22nd century. As climate change and rising sea levels altered the landscape, humans conglomerated in the megapolises to survive the poisoned world they had made. Thus the shadows of the great cities became the perfect underworld playground for demons and monsters to seek their prey.

It was the Dragon's Law that such creatures should no longer be seen, except by true-believers, magic practitioners, and wishful thinkers. There were those in the know, whose businesses or situations directly touched the yōkai world. These mortals were called "The Sanctioned" and they could be found at all levels of society, from the poor noodle shop owner who spied the tofu-kozo across the street, to the wealthiest man in New Tokyo who tithed The Dragon directly.

The year was 2099 by the world calendar. It was a place of dark and forbidding oppression, of perpetual gloom and dank misery, with extremes in temperature and wealth disparity. In short, the world was a feast for demon-kind to prey upon the counted misfortunes of the mortal, who brought it upon themselves through greed and exploitation.

But opportunity is where you seize it, of course, a fact no yōkai can deny. I certainly could not. Who am I, might you ask? My name is Hayate, and I am of the white fox clan Daisuke. And this is where my story began a long, long time ago…

Chapter One

The Wounded Fox

I came to in the woods, prone, groaning. My head pounded fiercely. Trunks of trees swam in and out of focus. The world was grey, vague, and the air smelled foul.

"Wha-" I put my hand on the back of my skull and winced at the pain. Wet stickiness matted my hair. I looked at my hand, otherwise pale white save for my blood. Each fingernail ended in a razor-sharp claw. I stared in fascination that I should have a hand at all.

Where am I? I wondered. More to the point, Who *am I?* I could not recall.

I suddenly became afraid. Amid a wave of panic, slowly I began to remember. I was kitsune, a Divine Messenger of Inari OKami. Yes. That was who I was. I had three tails, placing me somewhere between two and three hundred years old. My hoshi no tama tinkled softly when I tried to move. Thank goodness. I had my soul and my tails. I was still zenko.

I forced myself up onto my hands and knees. I did not

want to move, but I knew I could not stay in this wretched place. My furred ears twitched, trying to distinguish sounds. The only noises I heard were the ones I alone was making.

My long white hair spilled around my face, pooling on the forest floor. White. Yes. I was born a white fox. You might call me leucistic, a term that refers to a milder form of albinism. My skin was snow white, my fur and hair, too, except for the black rim that immediately surrounded my eyes, a distinguishing feature on any shirogitsune.

I whined and whimpered like an animal when I attempted to climb to my feet. My head thrummed with intense pain and I nearly fell down again. The little bell that was my soul ball, tethered to a braid in my hair with a red and white twined cord, chimed sweetly in my ear as I collapsed to my knees. The world spun round and round so that at last I was forced to sit. I needed water and time to heal. I had neither.

The acrid fog stank and choked, scorching my lungs with every breath. Leaves fell grey and spotted around me. Everything in this world was dead or dying. Only vines thrived, and they appeared leprous, deformed.

I saw a little pond not so far away and crawled toward it hopefully. My three tails dragged through the desiccated leaves behind me, collecting detritus as I went. But as I put my face over the lip of the bank, I smelled the foul vapors more strongly than before. The fumes stung my eyes. I looked up across from me to see a huge pipe spilling tainted chemicals into the pond. Worse, all around me were the half-buried bones of little fish.

I backed away from the edge in disgust, gagging. My belly was too empty to vomit. I turned and crawled away, nearly colliding into an old metal storage drum. It was corroded and slimy with fungus.

What is this place? Where am I? How did I come to be… here?

I was alone and had no idea where I was. I had never been to this gloomy, putrid place before, I was certain. I strained my ears, which were large and vulpine, set higher than men's, for they began near my cheekbones, not my jaw. I rotated them independently atop my head, but still I heard nothing. Not a bird or small mammal. No insects, either. The forest was deathly silent.

I could not stay in this forbidden wasteland, hideous in every way. It was no wonder there were no living things! Nothing could survive here. I had to find my strength and leave this place, or it would claim me, too.

Groaning, I forced myself to my feet through sheer strength of will, cradling my sore head with one hand. I told myself to pick a direction and get moving. Anywhere had to be better than here. I stumbled awkwardly, confused. I could not feel the presence of my kami. I was separated, cast adrift. Lost. This was not my world. My god could not hear me, nor I my god. I was completely and truly alone for the first time in my life.

My heart wrenched as the weight of that knowledge descended on me. All I wanted was… *Home.*

I remembered forests that went on into eternity, wide grasslands and flower-filled fields. My people ran in them, and I with them, or else we flew over the trees from above on the wind, those of us who had more than one tail and so acquired the gift of flight. There were majestic mountains and the air was as sweet and pure as the mountain streams. Our sun-star filled the glades with golden warmth, and the stars shone in dazzling array at night where nearby worlds and moons glowed omnipresent above the horizon. There stood the great shrine of Inari, where I was trained…

I wanted so badly to be there. I had family, friends, and a mother. I imagined a beautiful white vixen with the most startling aquamarine eyes and nine tails tipped in molten gold.

"*Hayate*," my hazy memory of her voice said to me in an autumn glen.

That was my name! It meant the sudden sound of the arriving wind. Appropriate, for I ever loved to fly as soon as I grew my second tail and was granted the privilege of flight. I was a child of the wind, beloved by my god. I had been chosen, called to serve.

"Hayate," I said aloud, just to know I could speak. "I am Hayate. Of the lineage... Daisuke." That much brightened me. I knew my name!

But I still did not know where I was or how I had gotten here, wounded no less. Doubtless I had been struck from behind, but why, and by whom? Why was I dumped *here*, left for dead? I wished I could remember. It was all blank, another gaping hole in my patchy memory, and somehow, I had this horrible feeling I might never know.

I turned to look about, and the world went around and round ferociously. I nearly fell over. I felt nauseous. I staggered on. Painfully, I looked up through the mist to the mountain above me. If there was pure water to be had in this unforgiving world, it would surely be there! Perhaps I could get a lay of this land on higher ground. It was better than moping, certainly. I felt a thorn bite into my unprotected foot and picked it out, hobbling along as I left a dotted trail of blood behind me.

Holding onto the decayed bark of dying trees and vines, I navigated along the base of the mountain. Bark often dissolved under my hand like ancient dross. The going was treacherous. The air stank so foul that I had to put the sleeve of my robe up to my mouth and nose. When my burning lungs and scorched throat coughed, my head felt it would split asunder.

This was not like the forests of *my* world. Here the growth was thick, and trees lay where they fell, covered by detritus, fungus, and moss. It was hard to walk, for there were no paths, just rocks and roots and dead trees. What looked like solid ground was a slippery morass of leaves and branches that had built up over time and created the illusion of solid earth. But it was easy to sink into the unseen holes, to trip and twist an ankle. With my next step my leg sunk past my knee, the dead trees scraping my skin. I had to fight to extract myself, causing more damage to my calf and shin.

There was nothing for it but to persevere. In this way I shambled onward through the grey mist, trying to be careful of every step despite the uneven terrain. This forest was evil, the miasma thick, cloying. I could feel the wicked eyes all around me, peering from the shadows. Most were kodama, tree spirits, twisted when their trees became diseased, and formerly benevolent animal spirits turned hateful.

Yet none moved against me. I was a zenko kitsune, trained to kill yōkai. No matter how ill I felt, I still had some of my powers, and the lingering grace of my god was as yet upon me. Weak as I was, they did not dare risk a confrontation with me.

After an hour or so of struggling and barely getting anywhere, I succumbed to my weariness and sat on a fallen trunk. "Please, sacred and divine Inari, hear me! I *need* you! I am lost!"

There was no answer, not even a twinge. I prayed fervently in this manner for several minutes and still I could not feel my god.

"*Inari-sama!*" I cried out at last.

Nothing. No brush of warmth and light that was the gentle life force of my kami. The forest was so dense there was not even an echo of my own voice. "Please! I beseech Your Grace! Hear me, I beg! Where am I? Why am I here? Help me! Have I been cast out?" I shuddered. "What happened to me? What did I do to displease you? Kami-sama?"

But my prayer went unheard, I could tell. There was a wall of separation between us. "Why can I not hear you? Why will you not answer me? Where *are* you?" I asked at last. I choked back a sob.

I sat there for a long time, hoping against hope that something would happen. Nothing did. At last I conceded defeat. With a weary sigh I got to my feet, not without difficulty, and kept going. I was not going to simply lie down and die in this grey, dead world that was rotted, miserable, and cold. Granted, it was a never-ending nightmare from which I could not awaken, but that did not change my need for water. I was parched. Water became my singular driving thought.

I meandered slowly toward the mountain, until I stumbled into a clearing. I was so lost in my misery, and the forest too dense to allow sound to carry, that I failed to hear them. In the center was a long, silver thing, like a house, but with wheels, except those wheels were broken somehow. Deflated, dented, and bent in at odd angles, the sides scarred and rusted.

Outside this battered shelter sat a group of dirty creatures that smelled terrible. They looked up as soon as I appeared.

I stood frozen. These beings were not like me. They had little round ears like monkeys. Their legs were longer than their arms, like me, but their hair was black, their skin bronze beneath the dirt. They all had black masks on to breathe through, the sound of their air sucking and strange.

"What the hell? Hey, Kyo, what do you think that is?" One stood up out of an old, grimy chair and unlatched his mask. This was a creature called a human.

"Some kind of idiot? What's he doing? Or is it a he? Kind of pretty, ain't she?"

"I think it's an ani-vid cosplayer, I bet. Hey, are you a designer mutie got lost from the big city on a field trip?" He laughed at me. "Go back home, you stupid twat!" I did not know what a "twat" was, but I knew an insult when I heard it.

"To Hell with that! Maybe we can keep her... him... it. Could be fun to fuck and I'm tired of shagging Junko's sad ass over there, the broken-down hag."

"Heh, yeah," the one called Kyo said. "Come 'ere. I got something for ya, mutie."

I wrinkled my nose in disgust. What vile creatures these things were! I wrinkled my nose in disgust. What vile creatures these things were! I could smell them from where I stood, although the toxic air sought to drown their odor out in its sharp acridity.

"Hey, we're talkin' to *you*. You stupid or something?"

"Gotta be. Dressed up like a damned yōkai out here? Who fucking does that? 'Specially near those superstitious village jerks!"

"*Yōkai?*" I spat angrily. I was no damned spirit or demon! *I* was the messenger of the divine Inari OKami!

"It speaks!"

I felt my lips draw back and snarl at them. My tails lashed in anger.

"Fierce, too! We'll have fun breaking this idiot's expensive face." The two men stalked toward me while the third, a scrawny female, cowered back in her rags.

"Break *this*!" I summoned my kitsunebi in my hand. Blue flames called fox fire engulfed my white fingers without burning me.

They stopped at once, astonished. "Holy shit! It really *is* a yōkai!"

"I am *not* a *yōkai*!" I yelled. The effort hurt my head, but I was too angry to care. I flung the fire at them, which split into two balls as my summoned fire spirits sped towards each male. The derelict campers fled – even the woman, who ran off screaming incoherently in a different direction.

Annoyed, I went off to navigate my way up the damned mountain as before. Now that my adrenaline was winding down, my dizziness and nausea were back stronger than ever. And soon thereafter twilight fell. The forest came alive with *real* yōkai then. They were all small, lesser demons, creatures that could not really hurt me even in my weakened condition. None of them dared to come near me.

Finally, I knew I could carry on no further that night, and although my eyes could see in relative darkness, the terrain was far too dangerous to make the attempt. I laid down in a ditch, covering myself with rotting leaves and curled into a tight ball, my tails wrapped around me for warmth. I did not expect to sleep, save to lie there and doze while listening to the sounds of the alien forest. Such noises were few and far between, however, and with my injury and exhaustion, I fell into a deep, dark sleep in spite of my intent.

I AWOKE THE NEXT MORNING WHEN I HEARD THE SOUNDS. THEY were not far off and coming closer. Something – no, *several* bipedal somethings – were heading my way! Should I stay or run? I was not sure. By leaving I might get their unwanted attention. But if I stayed...

I peered out of the leaf filled trench. I saw nothing except the grey mist that hazily concealed the trees. They were coming closer and closer, and I knew they would stumble right on top of me if I did not move! I resolved to crawl away. That was when I accidentally came face to face with a group of young men. I had misjudged how close they were and from which direction they were approaching!

We stared at one another for a long moment in startled silence. I could see only their eyes above their cloth face masks. Unlike the fools in the clearing, these humans knew *exactly* what I was. They were afraid, but the pack stood their ground.

"*Kitsune!*"

"Back, vile demon!" one commanded me.

"Kill it! Kill that Wild Fox before it eats us and rapes our women!" cried another to his compatriots. And I knew then that no words of mine would sway them.

I meant to summon my kitsunebi, but I was dizzy and had no energy. As I struggled to gather my chi for such a blast in spite of my injuries, just to scare them off, they began pelting me with rocks. My concentration shattered. Most of the stones hit my chest and arms, but the next stone struck my left hand as I lifted it to shield my face, opening a huge gash across the

11

back beneath the last three knuckles. The hit stung and blood welled up immediately. I felt it run down my wrist.

I was far too wretched to fight. Without the divine light of my god in radiantly abundant supply, my powers were limited, leaving me as weak as a kit. I was more like to fall over than win this battle. I could not fly away in this foul air, it would choke me. The way my head spun, I did not think I could even get off the ground!

So I did what any fox would do. I bared my fangs at them, turned tail, and fled. And like a pack of hounds, they pursued. How long they gave chase, throwing things and howling at me, I do not know. There was only the beating of my frantic heart and the tinkling of the bell I wore, my soul ball in disguise.

Trees blurred past, the shouts of the men never far behind. It seemed I would never be rid of them! But I must have crossed some invisible border, for they stopped and turned back.

I did not! I ran up the mountain, bent low, while the bare tree limbs snagged my clothes and hair, whipping at my skin. Something sharp pierced my foot again, and then again. I gasped and wheezed, the poisoned air burning my lungs raw, but I could not stop. I felt crazed with fear, the pain a distant thunder as my adrenaline pushed me toward escape.

Eventually it wore off as exhaustion and my wounds made me stop. One moment I was running, the next I could not go on. I had run into an invisible wall.

After some indeterminable time of panting and swaying on my feet, I found I was standing by a moss-covered log. I felt tears leak out of my eyes and gave no heed to stop them. I was entirely lost. I could not feel my god's essence. I was wounded in an alien world, hounded by a violent alien species.

At any moment the humans could find me, and given enough of them, they would take my life. Starving, thirsting, I was utterly alone, and I had the impression no one was coming to rescue me.

Without my kami, what was I but a fox after all? Sooner or later I was going to turn yako if this kept up. Already I was beginning to feel tainted by the land around me and its dark miasma, that sensation of persistent gloom which makes a place seem haunted or a person not *feel* right. Demons and ghosts emit it, and the darker, more intense their emotions, the stronger the miasma they generate. Gradually, this and my growing depression were infecting my spirit.

I saw no reason to stop the tears. I simply no longer cared. I sat on the log and licked the blood from my hand as if it were a paw. There was no other way to clean it.

"Hey there," a soft voice called. Male. I lifted my head from my wound with an indrawn breath and start of fear.

Another human!

I had had enough of these creatures! I bared my teeth, fangs and all, and growled my warning deep in my throat. My ears lowered into an aggressive position as the man came into view. I had begun to turn feral in that moment, frightened and angry. I just wanted to be left alone. I could not flee. I had nothing left. If I could not scare him off, he might slay or capture me. If this was a kitsune-mochi, a fox witch, he might hold my hoshi no tama hostage to his will.

"Do you need help?" the kindly voice asked. The man was an older specimen, middle-aged, or so I suppose by his people's life span. He was dressed in a kimono and hakama, traditional clothes. His black hair was streaked with silver and receding, the scraggly length knotted atop his head. His face, weathered and lined, held only sympathy for me. He held up his hands as he approached very slowly and cautiously.

"Hey, now. I won't do anything, I promise," he said calmly. "Shhh... shhhh..." he hushed in mollifying tones. "It's okay. I'm not going to hurt you. I just want to help. You look like you've been wounded. Can I see? At least let me give you some water and clean those cuts out, yeah?"

I stared at this man in fear and fascination. I cringed back, wanting to run, but his soothing tone and non-aggressive body language gave me pause. I wanted to believe him. I whined piteously as he knelt in front of me and held out his hand.

"Can I see?"

I found myself hesitantly putting my damaged hand into his. I was shaking, from fear or exhaustion I could no longer tell. He smiled and gently looked over my wound. "My name is Kazuki," he said.

"Hayate," I croaked, amazed I could talk.

"So you speak? I have never seen anything like you before, Hayate-san, and I've seen all kinds of things. Kitsune, yeah?"

"Hai," I rasped, too parched for words.

He handed me his water bottle and I drank. The tepid water had a distilled tasted to it, metallic and plastic. I did not care. It was with great effort I made myself stop before I rudely drank the whole thing.

"Thirsty, huh? Go on then. No water that's pure, not even in the village. Their well's turning foul thanks to that damn corporation that owns the land on the east side of the mountain. Sadly, it is little better up here with the acid rain. But I have a distiller and a deep underground well. Anyway, wow!" He

14

peered at me wide-eyed with astonished wonder. "Like I was saying, you are the first kitsune I've ever seen."

"Until yesterday, I had never seen a human before," I told him.

"Treated you rough, eh?" He sighed and shook his head. "People are cruel, white fox. Especially when they are afraid, and people are very afraid in *this* world."

"What happened here?"

"That's a long, sad story. What you see is the result of man. The gods abandoned this world, and so too did creatures like you. It is a dark and terrible place now, our earth, polluted and unsuitable for living, ruled by those without hearts or souls." He sounded sad and weary.

"First came the droughts, then the floods by turns, famine followed by plague. The fat bastards choke our air, lay waste to our crops, and poison our water, then put us in debt for the cures and make us their slaves. And yet they *still* will not stop. There is too much profit to be made from suffering," he said bitterly.

I looked down and watched as he tended to my hand. "Inari-sama..." I said, almost a prayer. Still no answer. I feared I would never hear my kami again. "That is terrible."

"People will stab one another over a few yen; not hard to imagine what they'll do for millions." He sighed as he let my hand go. "I have no antiseptic with me and this needs treating. Your other wounds, too, I think." He looked down at my skinned shin. "You're in bad shape, kitsune. What happened to you?"

"I do not know," I blurted. "I cannot remember." I put my good hand against the nape of my neck below the head wound. It was tender and I winced. He stood and moved my hair aside, whistling as he saw the worst of my trauma. I supposed it did not look good to elicit that reaction.

"Nasty hit that," Kazuki confirmed. I nodded and instantly regretted it. I nearly pitched over from the pain and vertigo. The kindly man steadied me with a warm hand on my shoulder. His touch was exceedingly gentle. "Easy there. Come home with me, zenko. Do not worry. I am no kitsune-mochi. I won't trap you. And you really do need the help. At least let me tend to those cuts and feed you, poor thing."

I was in no position to decline his offer. I found myself standing with his help. He was more than a head shorter than me, but he put my arm over his shoulders. I hobbled with his aid wincing at the thorns in my feet with every step.

"How did you know I was zenko?" I wheezed.

"Your tears are water, not blood," Kazuki answered. "You are no Wild Fox, Three-Tail, and I'll wager my life on it now. Else, why would you say the name of Inari?"

It took a while at our hampered pace. The old hermit lived in a modest cabin by himself on the mountainside, but it was clean and comfortable. There, he pulled the thorns from my feet and cleaned my wounds with stinging water that smelled sharp and hurt fierce. The wound on the back of my head hurt most of all. I remember gasping at the pain and Kazuki telling me to take it easy. Afterward, he let me bathe in his tub, bandaged my wounds, and gave me a clean kimono to wear.

Most of it was a blur. He fed me porridge and gave me more water. Then I settled on a tatami mat, barely aware when he put a cover over me. I fell asleep instantly, no longer caring if I would be killed in the night. The truth was, I thought it might be a mercy.

Chapter Two

The Kindness of Kazuki

The next morning, I awoke to the mouthwatering smell and sizzling sound of food. Kazuki was cooking eggs over a little grill, and I found he had been no dream.

"Ah, kitsune-san!" He called out to me when I sat up groaning. "Awake at last?"

I crawled off the tatami mat and over to his table. He left a woven wicker pillow out for me to sit on. I stared at him curiously, still wondering why this man would deign to help me. Was there something he wanted or needed in return? Debts and obligations were the coin of non-human entities, and that was certainly true of kitsune.

"How are you feeling today?" he asked me as he set a modest plate of eggs before me. I was so hungry I had no manners. I ignored the sticks he gave me and grabbed the food with my fingers to cram it into my mouth. I had no control. Only when I had eaten it all did I realize what I had done. It was rude and uncouth. I was a shrine fox, raised better than this! I dropped my gaze in embarrassment, wiping my lips and chin.

But Kazuki only laughed. "My, my! Hungry, yeah?"

"I do not remember the last time I truly ate. I barely know my name."

"Hayate, right?"

I nodded, then as pain blossomed and a wave of dizziness passed over me, I remembered why I should not do that. He fussed over my head wound at once. "No, no, it's better. You heal faster than we humans do, that's for sure. But you're probably concussed, and that takes longer."

"Con... cussed?" I asked. *What does that mean?* I wondered.

"Knocked hard enough in the head that your brain is bruised. Must be terribly disorienting for you, especially in such an unfamiliar place."

"Yes."

"You'll be fine in a few days. You should sleep a lot, though. And drink plenty of water." He gave me a ceramic cup of it. It was just as tepid and metallic as yesterday. Yet it was drinkable, and therefore good, so I thanked him for it and drained it at once.

"I do not remember much of anything at all. My life, my memories... it is all blank."

"That can happen. Once had a student take a blow so hard to the head, he forgot his name for over a week. It's called amnesia. Sometimes you get your memories back, and sometimes you don't, sorry to say. It just has to take care of itself."

I sighed at the news. "Thank you for your help," I said. "I must repay you for your kindness."

"Nah, don't bother over me. I hate seeing anyone hurt,

wouldn't harm a vegetable or eat an egg if I didn't have to. Wasn't always like that. Didn't have much in the way of empathy when I was young, father beat it out of me. But my wife..." he choked and stared off. It was not hard to conclude she was dead.

"I am sorry," I said, and laid my bandaged hand on the back of his. I pulled back an instant later, startled by my own reaction, that I should invade his space so.

"It is ancient history. Do not fret." He patted my shoulder and smiled, but it did not meet his eyes.

I could not blame him. I had just lost my world, my people, my kami, everything I held precious and dear. My shattered memories did little to explain to me who I was or how I had gotten here, much less how to get home. However was I ever to do that? It seemed too impossible a task. And then it was my turn to look away, crestfallen.

"Hey now! Don't start that. Almost everyone here has lost something big. But there's still life to live, yes?"

"Yes," I sighed. "It does not stop it from hurting." My heart felt broken inside my chest.

"No," Kazuki agreed. "Never let anyone tell you it gets better. It doesn't. But you *can* survive it. What's the alternative?"

I blinked in place of nodding to show I understood.

"Wasn't always like this," Kazuki said softly as he took my plate away and methodically cleaned it. "Oh, there was always suffering in some form or other. That's just the price of living. When I was a child it wasn't quite as bad as it is now, and I have seen history vids of what this earth looked like before that. There was a time our world was quite beautiful."

"You said yesterday that there were catastrophes – drought,

19

famine, plague…" I prompted. I did not really want to hear it, but I needed to know as much as I could if I was going to survive here long enough to get back home.

Kazuki nodded. "Hai. Long story."

He was silent for a while, and I was not sure if he would elaborate or not. I decided not to press and passively gazed at the one room cabin. It was rather small, but orderly, and there was a rustic sense of 'home' to the place. Everything was in the place it was kept, the floors swept, his sleeping mat rolled up neatly. The only mess to be found was the one I had made when I left the cover behind me to eat. I was too much in a stupor to try to fold my blanket, although I felt badly of my mess, and said so.

"You should go back to sleep soon, Hayate-san. You are not recovered. Here," and he poured me another cup of water. "Stay here as long as you wish."

"Arigato gozaimasu," I said. "As soon as I recover, I need to find my way home. I do not belong here."

"No, kitsune, you do not. This world is too impure for you."

When he was done cleaning from breakfast, he sat at the small table with me. "Before you leave, there are things you need to know. You have seen only a little part of a greater catastrophe. I do not know how it is anywhere else, but I know what it is like in Japan. The rain is filled with the poison that comes on the smoky air. It is oily and stinging. Smells bad, too. Humans pumped a lot of crap in the air. Heated up the atmosphere and made most of the ice melt. And that's when it got really bad…"

Kazuki went on to explain that the unstable weather and

hotter summers spurred vicious wars over ideology, funded by a military industry to the profit of a bare few. Dictatorships funded by oligarchies and corporate interests sprang up globally. Wars made for refugees, which in turn gave birth to reactionary terrorism. Meanwhile, natural resources were used up until they ran out. Infrastructure in many areas broke down at the same time natural disasters increased, adding to a number of oil and chemical spills in the early to mid-twenty first century when pipelines broke, and storms tore through hazardous sites.

"Sea levels are rising along the coasts and the storms get worse as the weather becomes more unstable. The oceans are dead and choked, the ecosystem's collapsed. Now the Pacific is green from all the algae blooms, and there are giant islands of plastic tangled in it." I stared at my host in horror. "It's radioactive, too," he added.

I had no idea what most of that meant, but it sounded terrible.

"And then there are the plagues. The worst, the most gruesome one, was something they called Exploding Ebola," he said grimly. "Came from Antarctica in the early twenty-fifties. Group of ice core scientists went home with it. Virus ruptures your body while it liquidates your organs violently. Anyone your blood touches gets it, no matter how small a droplet. You don't even know you have it until the sweats and convulsions begin. The first one blew up in a public shopping area, and too many scattered before they locked a quarantine down. Within days it spread over a lot of North America and the New Soviet Union. No cure for it, but they made a medicine that can arrest it, if you diagnose it in time.

"But you, my new friend, should worry more over Black Vein. Rumor has it that one's a yōkai disease that jumped species. Turns your blood dark blue, makes your veins look black, like indigo ink. Kills humans. The other bad one is a kind of Spotted Fever. That one claimed my wife and son. The cure was new and… we couldn't afford it." He said it numbly, but I could tell it affected him deeply.

"There was a big earthquake up and down the eastern coast in 2068. Hit places like Tokyo real hard. They had flood gates and underground run-off caverns, but the quake just leveled it all. I was at a tournament in the megapolis of ŌsaKyoto at the time, not back home. Might have died if I had been. They built the Greater Metropoplex of New Tokyo out of the rubble during the 70s through the mid-80s. This is the year 2099.

"When you leave, you will probably find a lot of abandoned towns and small cities. The survivors of plague, Climate Upheaval, and the Great World Depression had to go where work and food are, so they left a lot behind when they moved to the large metropolises. There are feral animals scavenging out there, too, and I am sure yōkai are in proliferation. Derelict humans are all over the place, and a few communities, like the village at the foot of the mountain, are out here, too, and they know to fear what lurks in the dark. So be *especially* careful, Hayate-san. There are also those like me, clinging to life off the grid when life Inside got too much to bear."

"How long have you lived here?" I asked softly.

"Twenty-three years, six months and five days. No, I don't miss it. Some days are hard, getting harder the older I get. But I like the peace and quiet. It was better before everything started dying and the air got this choked."

"I have only been here a day," I said forlornly. How could I bear more? I was so miserable. I just wanted to go home.

"One day or a hundred, Hayate-san, you will bear it. You are strong, I can tell. Now sleep and recover that strength. When you wake again, it will be time for dinner and you'll feel better, yes?"

I let him guide me back to my sleeping place. I was afraid I might have nightmares of plagues and floods and earthquakes. But I did not dream at all from the moment I closed my eyes until Kazuki woke me for supper.

AND HE WAS RIGHT. I DID BEAR IT, AS I FOUND IN THE YEARS THAT followed.

Twenty times did the seasons turn in their yearly wheel, such as they were in this unstable place. The summers were burdensome hot, the winters could be stormy and cruel. We had to take shelter inside when the rain fell, for it stung the skin. The sky was often overcast, not by clouds, but by pollution. The air smelled awful. There was no soaring through that oily, dark, toxic brew! I was grounded.

Yet that did not stop me from trying to find my way home. I went on journeys, usually disguised as a white fox with one tail. I tried to find a ley line, a Way Gate, some crack in the Veil by which to return. I never did. It was like they had all dried up. I was shut out, imprisoned in this hazy purgatory.

I went to Inari shrines, but all of those remaining in the countryside were dilapidated and abandoned. Of my kami there was no sign, not a breath. No matter how hard I prayed, I could not make contact. The only foxes around were the animal variety, scrawny survivors barely hanging on. Of any other kitsune, there was no evidence – not zenko or yako. By that point I knew I was not capable of killing another of my kind unless I had to. I was too lonely.

At first, I ran off the yōkai I found nesting in the former holy places where gods no longer dwelled. But there was no way to keep them out once I left, and no reason to return to an abandoned shrine just to exterminate pests that were not really harming anyone, as no one visited to be harmed. Eventually I stopped altogether. This was their world, not mine. Why should I bother them?

I did a good job of staying away from humans for the most part. I did not come across many, and I always kept a wide berth. Alas, that first run in with the villagers at the foot of Kazuki's mountain was not my last. Anytime the villagers caught sight of me passing through, they shouted, threw stones and sticks at me to run me off. Sometimes younger men and boys gave chase, and once they even turned their dogs loose on me.

From that moment on I knew they truly wanted to kill me. I stayed well clear of that village at the foot of the mountain ever after and refused to pass through their boundary of woods for miles around.

I had not Fallen to yako, whatever the villagers thought of me, but now that my god's will no longer bound me in celestial light, I was susceptible to temptation. Fortunately, I had no hunger for human hearts, nor did I understand such a thing as lust. In my hubris I congratulated myself for my exultation above that which I could not comprehend.

But this world was steadily driving me toward degradation. A creature such as I could be tainted by the environment I found myself in, and without the divine light of my kami, it would eventually consume me. If not for the kindness of Kazuki, it would likely have happened that second day. I was growing harder, colder, and more desperate with every passing year.

So, I developed a kind of moral code, concocted of what I remembered my life's purpose to be. *Do not harm innocents. Help those in need. Protect the weak. Retain empathy.* Sometimes I recited it to myself like a mantra.

Try as I might to resist it, the darkness kept creeping in. My life was a ruin, and as the years passed it was clear there would be no rescue. Either they did not know where to find me, or I was not worth the bother. I was stuck until I found my own way back. It hurt, this abandonment.

The worst was not knowing *why*. My heartache and grief eventually gave way to rage. I was angry that I had not meant enough for my kami or my people to try! Did they even grieve for me?

These were the cracks that tore at my heart and allowed the shadows to gain a foothold into my soul. There was but one place that I felt reasonably safe and genuinely cared for. It was my only sanctuary in this unforgiving world. The gentleness of that one person pushed back against the dark thoughts and feelings that threatened to engulf me time and again. Sooner or later, I always ended up at Kazuki's door, my head hanging in defeat.

"No luck?" he would say, that sad smile on his face that told me he felt badly for me.

"No," I would answer with a small shake of my head that made the lonely bell chime, my ears drooping. He would reach up and pet the top of my head.

"Come in," he would tell me, and I always did. I had

nowhere else to go. The cities and towns with populations were not for a creature like me. I was not human or yōkai. Neither did I have any business in the villages where hangers-on lingered stubbornly. The world of the human was not for me and I wanted nothing to do with it.

One day I stopped leaving Kazuki altogether. I supposed that if my kami wanted me, being a god, Inari-sama would find me. Perhaps I was being punished, but for what I did not know. Had Or had I failed in whatever mission I was sent to perform? Was I exiled? Did I commit a crime? I felt if I knew, perhaps then I could accept my fate better. But my battered memory never got better.

And thus, I stayed with my only friend for the remainder of Kazuki's life.

I WOKE UP ONE MORNING TO WATCH KAZUKI TRAINING IN HIS daily discipline. As it turned out, he had been a martial arts instructor in his life "before".

"My father taught me. I used to go to the tournaments, but eventually I stopped fighting in them after my son was born and let my students take the mat in my stead. We had a good life in Tokyo back in those days, even after the quake. But then the outbreak hit The Sprawl, and my Chou got ill... and the cost... then my son at the same time..." He could never speak of them beyond that.

"I have no one to teach now, no one to pass my knowledge onto. Most of my students went into the gangs to make quick digi-cred." He grimaced. "The ones that didn't die should have."

"Can you show me?" I asked.

Kazuki brightened. "Hai, Hayate-san. If you wish." There was nothing else to do anyway, except forage and hunt to survive.

Early on I learned that I had excellent instincts for combat. I picked up whatever I was taught with ease. Someone had apparently gone through the trouble to teach me how to fight and fight well over a long period of time. In service to my god, 'to do battle against yako and other yōkai,' I seemed to recall. I did not remember who my teachers were, yet my reflexes were astonishing.

Kazuki taught me more. He knew many styles of martial arts. Aikido, Kendo, Tai Kwon Do, Kung Fu, Karate, and so on, including how to wield medieval Japanese arms. Since guns were illegal for the average citizen in New Tokyo, martial arts and ancient weapons were a way of life for the gangs. Those were always on the lookout for angry young men of modest skill yearning for a brotherhood that they were willing to throw their lives away for. Or the poor youth trying to pay for grandmother's ridiculously overpriced, jacked up medication.

More than one of Kazuki's former students ended up in such circumstances. He confirmed the identity of one boy too many, and those after the deaths of his wife and son. It was no wonder that Kazuki chose to live off the grid on this plot of land his family owned.

Kazuki's instruction became our daily routine. We would wake, eat lightly, and then Kazuki would teach me until the early afternoon. I meditated to build my chi and keep my feral instincts at bay until dinner in the evening. After, I would practice using my chi to generate kitsunebi through focused martial poses.

"Impressive, Hayate-san," Kazuki would say from time to time.

And I would smile. "The better to smite yako and other yōkai."

"No yōkai comes near my cabin when you are here."

"Nor will they," I promised. If only it were so with the children of the village.

SOMETIMES BOYS WOULD COME UP AND THROW A STONE AT KAZU-ki's cabin in the dark. They would run off giggling or screaming into the night. Sometimes they chanted "Fox Witch! Fox Witch! Kitsune-mochi! Show us your white fox, old man!" But whenever Kazuki opened his door, they scattered like leaves.

One night they hit the window and I awoke to the startling sound of shattering glass. There was no way to replace the window, no glass smith or anyone to order a new set of panes from, certainly not for an old cabin like this. It would have to be boarded, our daytime world made dimmer by the lack – as if we needed more gloom. It made me incredibly angry at the unjustness of it, that these brats could get away with their vandalism!

"You should let me prank them," I told Kazuki bitterly as we swept the glass from the floor. My voice was cold with fury. "Teach them why they should be in bed asleep instead of roaming the woods late at night. A little fox fire to chase them off." I grinned, a shade wickedly at such an appealing idea, showing my fangs. "Maybe give them a bit of a *singe* to remember the lesson by," I hissed, ears flattening. My eyes narrowed at the direction the village lay in.

I meant every word of it, too. I was too angry to care that I had let more darkness in the form of helpless rage into my heart. The truth was, I wanted to hunt them down that very night and wring their necks!

Kazuki looked at me with worry. "Oh, Hayate-san, I forget sometimes how much of a fox you truly are."

28

"Well, better *that* than they end up dead in the belly of a *real* yōkai!" I snapped. "Or what if they fall into one of those ditches and break something in the dark?" I defended hotly. "Likely they will blame *that* on you, too! Does it truly not bother you that those stupid humans think you are a Fox Witch?"

Kazuki sighed and shook his head. "No, because I am not one. But if you go after them, I become one. Do you see?"

I sniffed sulkily and continued to sweep glass.

"It is a rite of bravery, nothing more," Kazuki said. "All boys need such, and some girls, too. They will grow out of it."

"But what if they do not? Kazuki, they could really hurt you! What if the game stops being, 'Let us throw rocks at the kitsune-mochi's cabin!' and becomes 'What color does he bleed?'" I argued.

"Oh, Hayate, for pity's sake! They're just children!"

Maybe. But I was not so sure. Children grew up. Adults remembered. And humans were cruel as yōkai by nature. That was a lesson I never forgot.

Chapter Three

The Broken Doll

Then one fateful day two children stumbled into our patch of woods. These were quite unlike the hooligans that snuck up from the village below. They came in broad winter daylight and walked as two who were aimless, moving for the sake of having to do so with no clear idea of a destination.

The boy was a young teen, his dark blue coat frayed open to reveal the dirty lining underneath. His jeans were so filthy they were more black than blue. His scowling face was filled with a curious mix of resentment and determination. His shoulders hunched, but his hands were balled up into fists, as if he were ready for a fight.

The girl trailing behind him was a year or two his junior, obviously his sister by her appearance. She was short, so small as to look younger than she was. Only the barest hint of breasts showed she was in the early turns of puberty. Where the boy's hair was longer and pulled back into a ratty tail, the girl's was sawed off raggedly around her jaw. Someone, her brother most like, must have taken a dull knife and hacked it off. She wore a pink coat, also ripped and dirty, covered here and there in old leaves from sleeping on the ground. Her pants might have been some bright shade of mauve, but both the knees were torn out and the rest was also dirty.

They were both malnourished and dehydrated. Their nails were encrusted black, and charcoal streaked their grubby faces. Neither of these two had seen the inside of a warm home in a long time. The boy wore an expression of sullen anger, the girl one of numb shock and depression. My sight caught the movement at a distance on that barren February morning. I alerted Kazuki at once.

"I see," he said when he stepped outside his cabin at my request. The air was bitterly frigid that day, I recall. For once the sun shone in the patchy sky, which it did not do very often. "Let them come, then. We'll give them some food at least. But you, my friend..." He looked me up and down.

I understood. A ghostly pale man with long white hair and fox features would look unusual, spooky. I nodded, resigned to the part I must now play. I transformed into a single-tailed white fox and waited by his side until the children drew near.

"Hey there," Kazuki called out to them gently. They looked up in unison, startled.

"Who the hell are *you*, old man?" The boy scowled to cover his fright at the sudden appearance of a stranger in the woods. They had been out long enough to be suspicious of adults, but they stopped all the same.

My friend smiled disarmingly. "I am Kazuki. And this is

Hayate." He smiled down at me. "We mean you and your sister no harm. Are you hungry? Thirsty? I can offer you food and water before you go on your way."

The boy seemed on the point of refusing, but the girl's stomach gurgled loudly. She placed her small hands over her belly. The boy sighed and rolled his eyes, even though he was obviously as starving as she was. The two were painfully thin and in desperate need of nourishment.

"What do you want for it?" the boy asked suspiciously.

"Nothing," Kazuki answered.

"*Every*one wants somethin', mister."

"Well, that is true. I want to feed you before you travel on. I had a son. If he were you, I would want someone to feed him a hot meal before he lurched toward an uncertain future. I will even leave the front door open, so you can run away if you feel afraid." He smiled disarmingly.

It was the promise of warm food that did it. Against their fear they came, and Kazuki did as promised. In spite of the cold, he left the door ajar. The children, who had been out in the wild for far too long, were warmer just for being inside the shelter. Kazuki cooked up some eggs from the chickens he kept, along with the leftovers of a few mice I had found and caught the day before. It was practically a feast in this time and place! Our strays ate eagerly.

Kazuki had to put my portion in a bowl. It was somewhat humiliating to eat in this way with my mouth alone. I had to remind myself sharply that I was supposed to be an ordinary fox.

"So what are your names?" Kazuki asked.

They looked at one another warily. After several uncomfortable seconds passed, the boy finally said, "I'm Ichirou. This is my sister Aiko."

"I am pleased to meet you both. Where are you heading?"

"To New Tokyo. There's nowhere else to go," the girl said shyly.

There was something a little off about her. Different. After my bowl was licked clean, I jumped onto the cabinet and curled up to observe unobtrusively. The more I watched them the more certain I was that the girl did not quite exist in this world. She had some great spiritual energy, a bright, shining light inside of her. It drew me in spite of myself. It reminded me of the divine light my kami once bathed me in, comforting and warm. Her very presence pushed back the darkness that had been threatening to overtake me, to the point that before she arrived, I had been actively plotting revenge against those village kids for breaking that window. Now, all such thoughts seemed absurd and beneath me.

Over the course of our humble meal I repeatedly drew her gaze, too. The otherworldly in her recognized the same in me. We were kindred spirits, she and I. Lost and alone in a cruel world that did not want us in it.

Her brother glared at her. "What did I *tell* you, Aiko. Don't tell strangers where we're going!"

"Do not worry, I will not stop you. Nor will I follow," Kazuki promised. "If you like, you can stay here awhile. Rest and eat. The journey to the coast is perilous, believe me – I know! I came from New Tokyo. It's not easy to get in if you're not a citizen. If you look sick, the guards on the wall will shoot at you."

"Yeah, right. You gonna be a pervert and diddle us in the night, old man?" the boy wanted to know.

"Gracious, no!" Kazuki said at once in horror. "Listen, I do not have much, but I have some sleeping bags, a hearth and a roof. If you want, take a day or two at least and prepare for what lies ahead."

"Oniisan," the girl entreated, eyes pleading. "I'm cold."

He sighed in a huff. "Maybe just tonight."

That night would turn into the next several weeks.

BY THE NEXT DAY KAZUKI CAJOLED THEIR STORY FROM THEM. These two had been living in northwest Japan until a light earthquake rumbled the houses of their town. The initial damage did not seem bad, although the quake itself had been a little frightening. It was the resulting tsunami that took their lives away. Ichirou had watched as people, animals, and things were swept away, including their father. The boy had been pouting in a teenage snit atop the roof where he was told not to be, but his disobedience had saved his life.

His mother managed to grab Aiko and hold on to a pipe on the side of the house as the water rose, but she slipped while imploring Ichirou to save his sister. He had a choice between them, which he resented bitterly. In the split second he had to act, Ichirou did as his mother bid before he lost her forever. It was obvious he held it against his younger sister to this day.

Aiko blamed herself, it was clear. Worse, Ichirou treated her badly for it. He was too young to become a responsible adult for his autistic sister. She was a burden to him, a reminder of all he had lost. He was bitter and angry with the world, but he could not vent his frustration on it. So he took it out on her instead.

I pitied her and found myself drawn to her. More than anything I wanted to help. Sadly, as a fox, my friendship was sorely limited. The best I could manage was to curl up beside her head in the night. Yet it was enough. She pressed her face into my fur, murmuring how soft and warm I was, and drifted to sleep with a smile.

"You have a beautiful fox, mister," Aiko said over dinner two days into their stay.

"Oh, Aiko-chan, he is not *my* fox," Kazuki explained. "Like you, he came here thirsting, starving, and very hurt. I pulled the thorns from his paws and cleaned his wounds, and he stayed. Hayate is Hayate's fox. That is why I call him my friend, for foxes are not true pets. We look out for one another. He hunts for me and I cook for him. He plays guardian and I give him shelter. But one day he will move on. Foxes are itinerant by nature. They invite themselves into your life, stay for as long as they please, then leave when it suits them."

"He's a smart, pretty fox. You can tell he really knows what's going on," the girl said.

"How's that?" Kazuki asked a shade nervously.

"It's in his eyes. He takes in everything. He understands even though no one thinks so. Like me." She looked at me in my new spot atop the cabinet.

I closed my eyes and curled up, sweeping my tail over my face and pretended to go to sleep when Kazuki frowned at me. "Yes, he *is* a smart fox. Too much for his own good sometimes." I could hear the worry in his tone. Without even trying, I was giving myself away.

"You're reading too much into it. He's dumb and ugly," Ichirou said with his customary contempt. "Stupid albino. They die fast."

I opened an eye and glared at the little hooligan.

"See!" Aiko giggled, pointing at me.

"Whatever." Ichirou rolled his eyes and mumbled about his sister being an idiot.

Kazuki laughed to downplay the tension. "He's not exactly albino, not in the classic sense, or his eyes would be red."

"What fox has green-blue eyes?" Ichirou asked disapprovingly. "It's a mutant or something out of Fukushima. Better be careful, old man, your pet could be radioactive."

"I promise he is not contaminated. Hayate is an exceptional fox, wherever he's from."

Ichirou snorted his derision and laid down in his typical irritated huff, turning his back to everyone. It was clear that the boy needed direction, a paternal hand to guide him. Kazuki tried to fill this role, but it was a trial from the outset. As he had once taught me, the old martial arts master tried to teach Ichirou to give him discipline, or at the least be better equipped to handle himself. So Kazuki spent his afternoons trying to instill his teaching into the angry young man.

In stark contrast, Aiko was dreamy and vague, always lost in her own world. Ichirou did not much care for what happened to her as long as she stayed quiet and kept out of his way. She wandered the woods around the cabin, smiling and humming to herself, touching trees that would glow afterward in my spectral vision. She was healing them. The land responded to her presence. This was not something that Kazuki or Ichirou could feel or understand. But I was not human. I saw. I understood.

I feared for Aiko, for a gift like that was sure to draw yōkai, who would want to eat her and devour her energy. I, an ex-Divine Servant who no longer had any mission – and thus no purpose – endeavored to keep Aiko safe. This much I could do. And secretly I hoped that this was why I was sent here, to protect Aiko and her powerful gift of life. At least that would give meaning to my meaningless situation.

One day she spied me following her trail. "I know you're there," she said. "You always come." I stepped lightly out of the brittle underbrush on four padded paws and cocked my head questioningly at her. "Come on, then," she said and walked away.

I barked once and bounded off to trot beside the girl. Together we meandered through the barren woods until she found a tree she liked. It was a cherry blossom tree, but it had not bloomed in years. Kazuki's great-grandfather had apparently planted it here long ago for his wife.

"Watch this, Hayate," she whispered, and she sat cross-legged with her back against it. She began to shine. The light flowed out of her and into the tree. I saw it glow gold and white, beautiful to behold. I could feel her power bring the tree back to life. It took my breath away.

I laid beside her under that tree while she sketched doodles in the dirt with a broken, old branch. "No one knows. They don't care, no one does. Why is everything so mean in this world, old fox?"

I wished I could answer her. My heart hurt for the lack of my voice. So I bumped the flat of my head into her arm to show her that *I* saw, I knew and cared. This world was too cruel for the likes of us. But maybe together, we could make it through.

I looked and saw that the lines she was drawing were not just random scribbles, but a beautiful rendering of a woman's face. I cocked my head at it and made a questioning whine in the back of my throat.

"That's my mom," she said. "She was really pretty. She used to tell me I was special. But she was wrong. If I was special, she'd still be alive."

I whined piteously at Aiko. How I dearly wished to tell her that her mother was right! She *was* special. She had a powerful magic inside of her. She was not 'retarded' as her brother called her, but one of those rare creatures imbued with sacred power, a true mystic. I was convinced she was the human incarnation of a tennin, an angelic being, and more specifically a tennyo - a celestial maiden. And nothing could have saved her mother, who sacrificed herself gladly for the child she loved. Whom she must have supplicated for, and *this* was the answer to that prayer.

But my voice was silenced. I could not speak save for what my body language and animal sounds offered. Fortunately, she seemed to understand. Aiko-chan was like that. She was an outlier and perceived what others were too shortsighted to comprehend.

She looked at me now, tilting her head to one side, then the other in mimicry when I did it. She giggled. "I know you're special, Hayate," she said with a smile, petting behind my ears. "You're not dumb *or* ugly. I see you. There's an old soul inside there. I know you wish you could talk to me. I wish you could, too."

I gazed up into her eyes as she looked deeply into mine. Yes, she could see me in this in this helpless animal form. And I saw her, the luminous being trapped inside of a maiden's guise. In that moment the illusion our bodies presented to this world faded away. We saw each other, truly, soul to soul, and something strange transpired between us. That ethereal light in her touched me deep inside, bathing me in radiant warmth. I heard the ethereal chime of my hoshi no tama ring out in the instant I felt the connection between our souls. Words fail me to this day to describe it. It was magic.

We stared at one another, her with an open mouth and wide eyes. A chilly breeze ruffled my fur and made her hunch into her coat more tightly. But though that miraculous second had passed, I still felt her presence, her light inside of me, and I knew I belonged to her forever.

"You're my friend, aren't you?" Aiko asked. I licked the tip of her nose in response and she giggled, wiping my fox saliva off with the palm of her hand. "Ewww!" But she petted my neck fur and hugged me, and from that moment on we were nigh inseparable.

Later that night when both children were asleep, I beckoned Kazuki to come out and speak with me. It felt so good to be in humanoid form again and have the capacity for speech! I dreaded going back into my pure vulpine state. I explained to my friend and former mentor what this girl was, *why* she was so important. I also told him of her talent with drawing.

"I see," Kazuki said when I was done my account. "I have some old paper sheets and charcoals she can use. I will give them to her tomorrow. I know with enough time I can turn Ichirou around. He's not a bad kid, just very hurt inside. But this is good! I will help him and you keep watch over her. At least we can give them this much."

"As you say, Kazuki-san." I did not tell him my intent. I looked at the hut instead, preparing to transform back into my temporary prison.

"And Hayate-san?" Kazuki called softly. "Be careful,

kitsune. I may not be able to bind you, but if she is what you say, *she* can."

I nodded. "I know," I whispered. But his warning came too late, for Aiko already had bound me to her that very day. When she left, I was going to go with her. I considered it my sacred duty to watch over her. I was far better equipped than Ichirou to protect Aiko.

OUR PATCH OF WOODS WAS NOT SO DEAD AS BEFORE, NOT WITH Aiko-chan here. So when we left winter behind into the earliest turns of spring, the first pale, wild green appeared. The weather grew balmy, and the sakura tree bloomed. It was on days like these that Aiko especially loved to go for our walks. While Kazuki taught Ichirou, we would visit the tree, and she would sit beneath to draw.

"Oh, Hayate," she said at last as she shaded a few charcoal lines on the page. "I wish he understood." I knew she meant Ichirou. "I don't mean to be a bother to him, really I don't! I hate that I am. A bother, that is."

I wanted to tell her that she was no trouble at all, that her brother was just kind of a shit. Kazuki *might* be able to gentle him, but I had my doubts and privately thought it was too late for the kid. I hoped Kazuki could help for both his and the boy's sakes, for he was fast looking on Ichirou as his lost son. Or perhaps he saw all those boys who died in the gangs that he could not save. It became Kazuki's mission to save this one, although Ichirou resisted as only a petulant youth could.

Yet, what could a simple fox say? Instead I laid my muzzle on Aiko's knee and whined in support. She ruffled the fur behind my ears. "*You* don't think I'm a bother, do you?"

I sneezed once and she laughed. "You're my only friend, Hayate. I love you." She leaned over and kissed me on the head.

I had grown to care deeply about this child. I truly did love her. More than anything I wanted to help her. Even in this limited form, I was her true friend.

Somehow that angered Ichirou. He did not like that she made renderings of landscapes on paper, or that a fox had become so close. Every night I slept in a ball next to her to keep her warm. He told her she would get fleas and ticks, but that did not change anything. Whenever I awoke, I would find her hand clutched in my fur, her cheek snuggled against me.

In spite of his irritation, Ichirou lived for his training. But discipline eventually lost out to youthful anxiety, and on that day everything changed. One morning Ichirou had a fit and tore up several of her drawings. He called her terrible names, all the while ripping the paper into halves, then quarters and so forth. He threw them at her, a storm of fluttering confetti.

"It's *your* fault, Aiko!" he screamed at her. "Mother is dead because of *you*!"

Aiko sobbed.

"Why the fuck are *you* crying? *I* should be crying! You're horrible! I got a raw deal. You're worthless! All you care about is that mangy old fox! I hate you! I *hate* you!"

I barked at the little bastard and he cuffed me hard on the head. I whined sharply, caught off guard by the ferocity of his attack. "Hayate!" Aiko screamed, shielding me with her body. The only thing Ichirou had hurt was my pride. I hated him for abusing Aiko so, more because I could not bite him or properly protect her against her older brother's verbal onslaught.

Kazuki later confided the boy had a bad dream in which he relived the day his parents died. I still thought that was a terrible excuse for his behavior. The effect of his diatribe on Aiko was immediate. She ran out of the cabin in tears, not watching for where she was going. I scrabbled after her in panic.

The cherry blossom petals were falling gently in a soft scented rain of their own making. For the first time this world was becoming beautiful to my eyes. That was Aiko-chan's doing. But the horrible pain she was in broke my heart to pieces! I wanted to reach out to her, to dispel her brother's poison. She did not deserve his abuse. I cursed my futility.

I barked at her, hoping to make her stop, which she did.

"Hayate!" she yelled at me in tears, snot running out of her nose when she turned her head. "Go away, you silly old fox! Leave me alone!"

I trotted behind her doggedly, determined to keep an eye on her no matter what she said.

"NO! I said *go away*!" She threw a pebble near me, not aiming to hit, but startle me. I whined when the stone whizzed by and slunk away while she melted to the ground and cried against her drawn up knees, rocking as she keened.

"I don't deserve to have anyone!" It came out as a choked screech.

It was only a matter of time before she started scratching herself. I had seen the marks on her forearms. It was her way of punishing herself for her brother's words, self-hatred made manifest. I was terribly worried. I could not bear to see her wound herself for his malice.

"I'm no good, I'm no good, I'm no good…" she chanted over and over again, fingers ripping at her hair.

I transformed behind the wide trunk of the cherry blossom tree and peeked around at her. I was helpless. I could not approach her like this, the only form that could get through to her. But how could I leave her in this wretched state? I wrung my hands in distress.

I was locked in these thoughts, trying to figure out what I should do, when I felt a sudden gust of wind pull at my hair and kimono. The little bell chimed softly in the breeze. My very soul had given me away. In that instant she turned her head, and even though I whipped myself entirely behind the tree, I knew Aiko had seen the flash of silver-white hair. I heard her gasp and I silently cursed myself for a fool as I pressed my back into the trunk.

"Who-who's there?" she asked cautiously as she came toward the tree. I heard her footsteps draw near.

I should have turned myself back into an animal and played it off as a figment of her imagination, but instead I ducked and flattened myself against the tree. I heard her small feet rustle the brittle grass and begin to round the trunk. So I moved silently to keep the tree between us. Again, I heard her approach, this time from the other side, so I crept back in the opposite direction. Then I heard a sudden scuffle and felt my three tails bump into a small form behind me. We both whirled to face one another in the same instant.

She stared into my teal green eyes with her wide, dark human ones. In the daylight, my pupils were dagger slits. I did not know what to do or say! I could not breathe. For a long moment we stood transfixed, girl and kitsune. Then I blinked and that seemed to shatter the spell. She saw me, like the day she had bound me to her soul.

"Hayate!" Aiko threw her skinny arms around my waist.

I smiled and tentatively returned the embrace, my ears flattening down. "Hai, Aiko-chan," I said softly. "I am your fox."

"It is you! Are you a kitsune?" she asked, looking up at me in wonder. "The magic kind?"

"Yes," I replied.

"The good kind or the bad kind?" she asked, scrunching up her face.

I smiled. "I am one of the good ones. I serve Inari-sama. Or I did, before I got lost and wounded. I cannot seem to find my way home." I sighed sadly. "Kazuki healed my wounds and took me in."

"He's not a fox witch, *is* he?" she asked me suspiciously.

"No," I said, shaking my head. The little bell chimed. "He is just a kind man who wants to help people. Like I want to help you." I knelt down so as to not loom over her.

"You've been watching out for me all this time."

"Of course I have," I said gently. "You are my friend. Unless... you do not wish to be?" I asked hesitantly. The idea of that was shattering to me. But what business did a nearly three-hundred-year-old fox have being friends with a thirteen-year-old human female? Yet my intentions were pure. We shared a bond. Whatever may come, I could not bear to lose her.

Her response was to hug me fiercely. "I am your friend forever, Hayate! I *love* you!"

"I care for you very much as well." I smiled happily, basking in the radiance of her pure and holy light. "You must say nothing of this to your brother... and best not to mention it to Master Kazuki, either. He would not approve that I showed myself to you." I felt like I was doing something wrong to keep this a secret, and worse to make her complicit. But at least her tears had dried and she was no longer in pain.

"I won't say anything, I promise! This is our secret friendship, our pact."

"Yes." I nodded. We sat together beneath the sakura tree on the side facing away from the distant cabin, in case anyone approached.

"I am sorry for what happened to your pictures," I told her earnestly. "It made me very sad and angry. I wanted to bite Ichirou."

She giggled, and I knew she was seeing me as a man nipping her brother's ankle rather than a fox. "It's okay. Ichirou hates the things I make."

"*I* love your drawings," I said haughtily.

"You do? Oh! I bet you got Kazuki to give me that paper, didn't you?"

"I did," I said with a wry grin. "I think you have great talent, Aiko-chan."

She smiled. "Ichirou says they're a waste of time. I can't draw and I suck. But I can't stop doing it anyway. It's the only thing that makes me feel good, besides making things live."

"Ichirou is a jerk. He has nothing nice to say of anyone because he does not like himself," I said bluntly. "He takes his hurt out on everyone else because he is too lost in his own personal martyrdom. You have a great Gift he does not and can never have. Ichirou is jealous of you. There is a special golden light inside you, one that is bright and beautiful," I said fiercely.

"What light do I have?"

I smiled. "You have a power that draws lost souls and wayward spirits, yōkai especially. That is why I will not let you go into the woods alone. Most yōkai will want to eat you and steal your power. I will not let them, Aiko-chan. I promise. I wish to serve you."

"The darkness has always watched me, since I was little. Except I don't feel the eyes in the shadows when you're around, Hayate."

"That is because I will burn them to cinders if they come anywhere near you, Aiko-chan. I have been cast adrift, without a mission for twenty years. I think maybe if I help you..."

"You can go home?" she asked, such was the power of this child's insight.

"Yes! I feel closer to my purpose when I guard you, that I am doing my kami's work. I feel like myself again."

"You've really been here for *twenty years*?" Her eyes grew wide.

"Yes. A long time to be stuck, huh?"

"Yeah," she said softly. Then she looked a little sad. "I want you to go home and see your family, but I am selfish. I don't want you to leave. You are my only friend, Hayate-san."

"Do not worry, Aiko-chan. I cannot imagine I will be recalled anytime soon. I am here to keep you safe from the monsters."

"Promise?" she asked me with big, guileless eyes.

"I promise."

"Pinky swear?" She held out her littlest finger. I hooked it in mine and locked our fingers together. Mine was long, ghostly white, and clawed, where hers was stubby short and a light shade of sun-gold.

"Pinky swear," I solemnly swore. For just a moment, I thought I felt and saw a thin thread of light looped between us, tied finger to finger.

From that day forward, our friendship changed. I was no longer just a fox, but a secret friend and her guardian spirit. When we were alone together, she smiled and laughed. The closed, damaged child locked inside her skin opened up to reveal a burgeoning young woman with so much light and life that it infected everything around her with beauty.

Everything except Ichirou, that is.

We continued our afternoon sojourns. She would draw quietly for hours until suppertime, and I would sit with her. Sometimes, when I was in human shape, she would look at me a certain way and her cheeks color a dusky pink. When pressed on what she was thinking, Aiko's eyes would fall to the ground and she would become painfully shy.

I did not understand back then. I could not fathom the murky depths of human love, for I was a pure, celestial being, restored to grace by the divinity housed within my bond-mate's frail, mortal shell. I genuinely felt no lust or romantic interest whatsoever, but only a deep abiding affection born of my sacred spiritual link to Aiko-chan. I figured it must be the same for her, who was a divine maiden in human guise.

Yet, I was terribly mistaken.

Chapter Four

Bound

For three weeks my heart and soul were lighter than they had been since I awoke in this world. The celestial light inside Aiko mimicked that of my kami's, filling me with peace and contentment. I found myself grown increasingly loyal to my new friend. Once the very idea of being bound to a human frightened me terribly. But with this gentle child, it felt right. She was a powerful force for good in this world, one badly needed and in desperate need of protection, especially at her tender age. I could do that, and by so doing maintain my equilibrium as a divine servant and guardian.

Spring was only in evidence within a three-kilometer radius of the cabin. That was Aiko's power at work. Gradually her sphere of influence was spreading. I was certain that within a year it might encompass the whole of the mountainside. Privately it concerned Kazuki, as did my growing attachment to the girl. Sometimes he would stare at us with an expression of quiet anxiety. Yet he said nothing.

Ichirou did not even notice. Learning how to fight was all the boy wanted to do. And I had to grudgingly admit, Ichirou was beginning to calm down now that he had focus and a father figure. By this point Kazuki had grown as attached to Ichirou as I was to Aiko. I was convinced that my old friend saw in him his lost son. The old man indulged the boy accordingly, leaving Aiko's care to me.

But if we were left to ourselves, that was how Aiko and I wanted it. So while Ichirou trained every day, Aiko and her faithful fox would go on their adventures. Eventually I would take my human form, imperfect as it was without glamours to conceal my kitsune nature, and we would sit together under our sakura tree. There we would talk about anything and everything for hours. I learned Aiko's favorite color was pink, that she missed having longer hair and was envious of mine, which flowed past my knees since I had not cut it in over twenty years. She loved ani-vids and wanted to be a mangkata when she grew up. She was always making up stories and loved to draw beautiful characters. And if cats were her favorite animals, she allowed that foxes ran a close second, especially now.

I listened patiently to her concerns and offered advice when she asked for it. And every once and again she would ask me questions about myself. How could I not answer? There was so much I could not remember from my life before, much to my sorrow, but what I did know, I answered honestly. I could never lie to her.

"Why do you wear that bell in your hair?" Aiko asked me one day.

"It is my hoshi no tama," I replied. "Do you know how your soul resides inside you?" She nodded. "Well, most of mine, say seventy percent, is this bell." I closed my eyes and shook my head side to side to make it ring. There was an ethereal quality to that chime.

When I opened my eyes, I saw she was smiling dreamily and her cheeks had grown red to her ears. "Why?" she asked.

I shrugged. "There is this story, I think my mother told me, or maybe not. I do not remember. But I seem to recall something about how we all came from wild foxes. Then one day, a white fox, inspired by the greatness of Inari Okami, sought out the god with his mate and his kits. They went to the sacred shrine atop Mount Inari. So overcome were they by the kami's divine grace that they begged to enter Inari-sama's service.

"Seeing they were pure of intent and purpose, the kami accepted their request and changed them into divine beasts by bestowing this gift of empathy. My ancestors were given names and positions to serve, and from that day forward, we white foxes became the prominent Divine Messengers of Inari, born to serve."

"Oh," she said when I was done my tale. "So that's why you're all white. But why's your soul a bell?"

Again, I shrugged. "Well, 'tis not, not really. It is actually a ball of glowing silver-blue light in disguise." I placed my hand around it and at once it transformed in my palm. The brilliant orb chimed out, a pure crystalline tone in the precise pitch of the bell it appeared to be. Aiko ooohed, the light reflected in her eyes. When I took my hand away, it was only a small golden bell again. "See?"

"So pretty! That's your *soul*?"

"Most of it," I admitted, watching a cherry blossom petal float gently down to land in the open palm of my hand.

Before I knew what she was doing, Aiko reached up and tentatively touched the bell with her finger. I honestly had not expected to feel much of anything at all, as you might expect if someone touched your clothes. But with her extraordinary power, I heard that chime echo deep into my soul to resound throughout my physical manifestation. Her light momentarily infused with mine, golden bright with silver-blue intertwined.

It was confusingly intimate, and our bond strengthened accordingly. I stopped short with an indrawn breath, mouth parted, eyes wide in surprise. It was... unexpected, a bit like an innocent first kiss, but of the soul rather than the lips. I suppose she had felt it profoundly, too, for she gasped and turned red again. I looked down and cast my eyes away uncomfortably, embarrassed.

Aiko's brows knit in concern. "What if someone takes it from you? What then?"

"Then I must barter and trick my way into getting it back." I shuddered. What a terrible notion! But it had happened to kitsune before. "Otherwise I can be enslaved, and if I cannot retrieve my hoshi no tama, I will turn into one of the bad kind, a yako." A Demon Fox, a corrupted, lecherous vampiric beast that preyed on humankind.

"I don't want you to be a yako, Hayate!" she said earnestly, tears in her eyes.

"I do not want to become one, either." In truth, of all my fates, including death, I could think of nothing worse!

Suddenly she became more determined than I had ever seen her. "If that happened to you I would save you, even if it took a thousand years! *Three* thousand even!" She was quite fierce about it.

I smiled gently to reassure her. "As long as I am *your* fox, I will be gentle and good. I promise. Your light supersedes all else, just as my kami's once did." So long as that light infused me, my spirit was calm. But if I lost Aiko…

No, not 'if', it's when *you do!* I reminded myself sharply. *She is mortal, you are not. This cannot last forever, and then what will you do, white fox?* I would be devastated. It was a frightening thought. Her smile was fragile, her eyes filled with worry, and I could tell she was having troubling thoughts of her own.

"Here, watch this." To distract her I made a ball of kitsune-bi, the blue flame leaping from my palm. With a bit of will I sent it to hover before us, where it floated in midair.

"Oh! Wow!" she exclaimed breathlessly.

"This is fox fire," I explained. "It is more than just flame. It is a conjured spirit, a willow-the-wisp. It does not have sentience, not exactly. It is a construct of my will. If you listen, you can hear it." She did, and her face lit up with delight as she heard it croon. "Do you like it?" I asked.

"It's beautiful, Hayate!" She made to reach out to it.

"No!" By my will I pushed the ball of flame back. "It will consume all that it touches, except me. Only I can touch it and remain unscathed." I reached for it and summoned the wisp to my hand, where it danced on my clawed fingertips. "I can make illusions of flames that are harmless, of course, but *this* is the real thing."

"Oh," she said softly, gazing at the flickering blue light. "It's so lovely…"

I smiled. It was my greatest delight to make her happy.

"AIKO!" I heard Ichirou yell.

My blood ran cold in an instant. The flame wisp disappeared at once.

"AIKO! WHERE IN THE HELL *ARE* YOU?"

Before I could transform, Ichirou suddenly burst through the trees and saw us together. My heart stopped beating, then pounded in fear. My face felt numb as my limbs tingled, the blood flow redirecting itself in a rush of adrenaline. Aiko scrabbled to her feet, pressing back against the tree. I stood to my full height, looming over both children.

"WHAT THE *HELL?*" Ichirou should have been training, but here he was. And worse – he had seen me.

"Who the fuck is *this?* Why are you hanging out with a stranger? Get *over* here!"

"No, oniisan," she said defiantly, standing in front of me. "This is my *friend.*"

"You aren't to talk to strangers, Aiko! How many times must I tell you, damn retard!"

"I'm not a retard! And he's no stranger! I told you! This is my friend!"

Ichirou looked me over. "Baka! What the fuck are *you* supposed to be, anyway, you creep? Some kind of costumed nutcase? My retard sister has a retard friend from that shit village?" He sneered at me in teenage disapproval. "Kind of old to be pals with my little sister, aren't you, perv?"

I growled, a gekkering vulpine trill to its timbre, my three tails lashing. I had had enough of this angry child. My ears folded down aggressively, my eyes narrowed. "The only thing 'retarded' around here is *you*, Ichirou! By way of willful ignorance! You are selfish and cruel. I am sick of your behavior. Be a thug, if that is what you want! Run to the big city and join a gang! See how tough you *really* are! Go on! No one will stop you. And do not worry about Aiko-chan – *I* will watch over her from now on! You are not wanted *or* needed!"

Ichirou stared at me in shock. No one had spoken to him like this in a long time, certainly not kind, old Kazuki! For a moment his lip quivered, and I thought he would cry. Then his face turned uglier than I had ever seen it. He was free to do as I said. A part of him wanted nothing better than to dump his sister and go. But if he did not have Aiko to bully, to blame for his faults and his losses, what did he have?

"I love you, oniisan, but Hayate is right. I do not want you to hurt me anymore. You can go now. I know you want to. It's okay. I will stay with Hayate and he'll protect me. He pinky swore." Aiko stood up straight, her voice calm but confident. She had never appeared so strong to my eyes as she did then.

Ichirou stared first at her, then at me. "Hayate? Wait... no, no, *no*! You're not... You *can't* be!"

"Cannot be *what*?" I asked imperiously. "The stupid and ugly white fox with teal eyes that *might* be radioactive from Fukushima?" I shot at him.

His eyes grew wide. "Fuck *me*! Yōkai are *real*?"

I growled again. "I am *not* a yōkai! If I were, I would have eaten you already!"

"Come here, Aiko!" Ichirou demanded, but now his ire was colored with uncertainty and fear. "Hurry! Get away from that demon fox."

"No!" she screamed. "I won't! He's *not* a demon! He's good!"

"I said, *come here*, you little bitch!" Ichirou said viciously, lunging for his sister. I grabbed Ichirou's wrist as he reached for Aiko. He snatched his arm out of my hand roughly before I could fully grasp it. My claws grazed his skin. The cuts were deep and blood flowed. The wounds were certain to scar. I had not meant to do that. I felt awful.

Ichirou snarled at me, cradling his arm. His face was a portrait of pure, venomous hate. "Fucking yōkai!"

Aiko gasped when the blood dripped down her brother's arm. "*Oniisan...*" She whispered, horror struck.

"See what you did?" he shouted at her. "You unleashed your pet monster on me! This is another thing that's all your fault, Aiko!"

"She did nothing at all!" I yelled. "Apologize to Aiko-chan this instant! No brother should say such things to his sister!"

He grabbed for her again, and this time he caught her wrist painfully in his grip. I was too afraid of hurting him again in front of Aiko to stop him. "Big brother!" she squeaked.

He spun her away hard and stomped back to the cabin. She shrieked in pain. "Come on, brat! We're leaving!"

"No! I won't!" She tried to dig her heels in, but he dragged her until she stumbled after him.

"Aiko!" I yelled. "Bring her back this instant! *Aiko!*" I followed relentlessly.

We came out of the woods that way. The commotion drew Kazuki's attention immediately. He was horrified to see me revealed, stricken to see our quarrel.

"Stay away from her, you monster!" Ichirou called back over his shoulder.

"I will do no such thing!" I shouted. "I belong to her!"

"Ichirou! *Hayate?*" Kazuki cried out. "What is this?"

"Fuck you, old man. Almost had me roped in. What were you gonna do, give my sister to this wild fox? What was *I* supposed to be in your game?"

"I only wanted to help you both!" Kazuki declared. "I still can. Hayate is kitsune, yes, but he is not a yako! I promise he will not hurt your sister –"

"More of your lies! Just look what your white fox did to me!" Ichirou held up his bloody arm. "Well, fuck you and your shit, you old fox witch! We're leaving!"

"NO!" I yelled, filled with panic. "Please leave her! Aiko-chan!" I went to go after her, but Kazuki stood in my way and held me back.

"Hayate!" Aiko screamed as Ichirou pulled her away down the hill. "Big brother, please!" she pleaded. Her eyes were wide with fright when she turned around to look at me. "*Hayate!*"

"Kazuki, *please!*" I tried to get around, push past him, but the old human refused to get out of my path. "Do not let him take her!" *I cannot lose her now!* "Let me go to her!"

"*Leave it*, Hayate!" he commanded, so angry that I stopped fighting him. I watched as Ichirou left everything behind, even his coat. He would not step foot inside the cabin again for that much. He dragged his little sister away until they were lost from my tear-blurred sight. I still made to follow, but Kazuki held me fast. "Let her go!"

"I – I cannot..." My breath caught and I fought a sob as that beautiful light moved farther and farther away. I was near frantic with fear, for her, for me, for everyone! The bell in my hair chimed sorrowfully.

"Why, Hayate? *Why* did you do this?" Kazuki demanded in a rare fit of anger. "I was just getting somewhere with him! And now they are both gone!"

"I did not do it on purpose!" I was nearly hysterical. "I cannot let her go! I am bound!"

But Kazuki's eyes grew cold and he turned away. "I told you to be careful. Now you've ruined everything." He left me outside the cabin.

I sank to the ground and sat there for a long time in that sunlit wood, already growing colder and cloudier for her lack. Without her light to sustain it, the life she had restored here would soon wither. It felt the same with me. A profound despair came over me. I sat like that for some time, lost in my melancholy, gripped by doubt and terror. Hours passed while I stared forlornly at the ground.

Finally, by early evening, Kazuki came to me. "Hayate..." His words and manner were gentle once more.

I could not speak. I turned my face away from him in my anxiety and grief. What if something happened to her? I was certain it would without me by her side! It felt to me like I was already too late, that she was lost to me, and that made me sick with fear.

I already made up my mind to slip away and pick up their trail after dark, when I could safely sneak toward the village, the direction Ichirou had dragged Aiko in. It would have been my certain death, and likely hers, to have followed her there by day. When I found her, I decided I was going to take her away from her brother and protect her like I promised. I had sworn a bonded oath, a thing most sacred to one of my kind.

"I know you care about her..."

I frowned. He had no notion what I was feeling.

"Maybe it is best this way," he continued. "You became too attached..."

"*Someone* had to!" I protested. "She was scratching herself to blood, did you know that? And the light inside her... she is a feast to demon kind!"

"Hayate…"

"No! You do not understand! I gave my word I would protect her! I gave *my word*. She bound me, Kazuki, before you ever said anything. I belong to *her* now. The light in her… She is all I have to keep from turning yako!" My eyes were wild in my desperation.

Kazuki grimaced and sighed, sitting heavily next to me. Never had he looked so old and weary to my eyes. "I knew you had revealed yourself to her. I found the pictures she drew of you secreted under her sleeping sack when I swept up one morning two weeks ago. I should have said, but... This is my fault, too. I thought if I could help the boy…"

His admission made me feel worse. But that would not stop me from running off after her tonight. She needed me more than Kazuki did. It was my mission to protect and serve her, that she might do great good in this world. I had a sick feeling in the pit of my stomach that was growing stronger with every passing minute. There was no more time to spare. I stood, prepared to tell him I was leaving.

"Kazuki, I..." And that was when I saw the light – no, many lights! Fire! And it was marching up the side of the mountain towards us! "Kazuki!"

He turned and grunted. "Get my sword, Hayate-san. And one for you. Be quick!"

I nodded and ran into the cabin, grabbing katana and wakizashi for us both. We quickly bound the weapons in our obi sashes. There was no question where Ichirou had taken Aiko earlier. These were the villagers coming to confront the fox witch who lived on the mountain. Oh, the sad irony. Had he been a true kitsune-mochi, and I yako, none of their children would have returned from stoning our cabin.

I meant to transform or hide, but when I heard the rustle from the other side of the cabin I knew it was too late. They had flanked us downwind, distracted us with their torches, and surrounded us in the growing darkness. They saw me plainly, luminescent as I was. A few were older men, and although I did not recognize them, they certainly recognized me from twenty years before.

"There it is! The Wild Fox! We always knew this is where that yōkai fox got to, kitsune-mochi."

"I am *not* –" I began, but Kazuki held his arm out and gestured me to be quiet.

"We are not what you think we are."

"Shut up, old man. We've always known you were trouble. Our well wasn't poisoned 'til you moved back. Should've routed you out when you first came here, and that wretched fox of yours, too, when that thing turned up. Causing us only ill fortune to your gain! The proof is all around us! Our well is poisoned, our trees dead, our gardens withered! But this is all alive! You stole our livelihood for yourself, sorcerer!"

That was not true. The corporations which were poisoning the land had done that. Our woods were just as dead until Aiko came. There was not a child in the village that did not know that! If Aiko stayed, in time the green would have spread to them as well, the damn fools.

"But we know how to deal with a fox witch!" The human brandished his torch to highlight his words. "We took care of the girl the old way. Now it is your turn, kitsune-mochi!"

My heart stopped at the mention of her. What had they done to Aiko? The *old* way? *Oh, kami-sama! No!* The others behind him called out in primal justification of their actions. I smelled the scent of burning wood and turned to see that one of those behind us set Kazuki's cabin on fire.

"No!" I yelled. They closed in and surrounded us.

Kazuki touched my arm. "Back to back, kitsune." And so we stood as the fire lit through his cabin, the smoke black and heavy. Night was fast descending, but my eyes were made to see in darkness. The men were trying to pen us in toward the conflagration. We drew our swords and I sliced the head off a torch as it came near to scorch me.

They had no weapons save knives, old garden tools and their fire, but those things could still smite. Kazuki and I deflected their attacks, not aiming to kill them as they were us. The martial arts master was disarming them as they came on. I did the same. I was not a killer, although I had the innate instincts for it. I fought not even to wound.

I heard Kazuki's chickens cry out their alarm a second before one ran by me clucking and screeching. The crackling flames of the burning cabin were hot against my skin, the gusting wind buffeted the heat toward me. I decapitated torches left and right. Someone came at me from behind with a garden tool, screaming, "Die, kitsune!" He got a little too close and when I sheared the haft of his hoe, I accidentally took his fingers off with it. Kazuki kept his swords razor sharp.

The man screamed, eyes wide at his spurting stubs. That enraged the others. The attack went on with renewed fury as the maimed man fell back and away into the night. Somewhere off to my right a tree was on fire, but how or why that came to pass, I honestly had no idea.

I GOT SEPARATED FROM KAZUKI IN THE FLAME-LIT DARKNESS.

Shadows were shifting with the firelight. There was always another villager, usually at least two. They had the numbers, but I did not fall. They were only human, after all, and I was a healthy kitsune, not the confused and concussed creature some of them had met in the woods twenty years before. My sword made a steel cage around me. I thought about Aiko and my blood rose to the challenge. They had *hurt* her! My strikes hit more true, slicing into arms and legs with the intent of forcing my foe to abandon the fight.

And then I heard it. A grunt, rather like a sigh. How I heard this above the din of men and chickens and the roaring inferno, I do not know. I turned. Someone had managed to grab Kazuki's wakizashi from its sheath and buried it in his stomach to the hilt. A master he might be, but Kazuki was also over seventy years old and vastly outnumbered.

"KAZUKI!" I screamed. He and the other man stared at it, then at each other, as if in disbelief. Then Kazuki's legs crumpled beneath him. "*NO!*" my distraught voice cried out in the chaos.

When I saw Kazuki fall, I lost my composure. I ran to him and the man who murdered him. He looked up to see me sweep down with my katana. It was the last thing he ever saw with those astonished eyes. My blade flashed down, opening him from chest to groin. Something, not a memory but rather some innate gut knowledge, told me this was my first kill, just as Kazuki's had been his. I decapitated another nearby half a second later.

Now that I had finally killed, I could not seem to stop doing it. Kazuki was dead, or as good as! They had harmed my bond-mate! And now they wanted to kill me! I was wild with fury. Men scrambled back and away. The battle rage had me in earnest. I needed vengeance! All the training instilled within me for years came without hesitation. I was a dervish of silver steel and blue flame. I moved like the wind between them, warping space to disappear and reappear at will.

After I cleaved one man's arm from the elbow down, and swept another's legs out from under him, the men retreated. But all I could think of was the cabin, Kazuki, and my poor Aiko most especially. That sweet, innocent girl… my friend…

Rage and hatred built within, and suddenly a wide arc of blue fire emanated from me in a burst of chi. Every human it touched was consumed by it and reduced to ash, screaming briefly before he died. No one was spared. I sent balls of kitsunebi after those who were fleeing and felt malevolent satisfaction as each one was burned alive into nothing. Soon there was no one left. I smiled in dark satisfaction at my work.

Kazuki! I remembered. I looked around for him and found him lying on the ground near the corpses I had slain. "Kazuki," I uttered as I knelt. There was so much blood. His eyes blinked open. I was surprised he was still alive!

"Hayate…" His voice was distant, soft.

"I have to get you out of here," I told him, wondering how I was going to do that.

He shook his head. "I am dying, my old friend. It is alright. I am ready. I want to see my wife and son again."

"No! No, this is not right! You saved me. I have to…" *Save you*, I might have said.

Kazuki shook his head weakly. "Go after the girl, Hayate-san. Protect Aiko-chan if you can. Should have let you… follow her earlier. You… not to blame. I said wrong thing…

set him off… I let him go. Now…" Now Aiko was likely very injured and might also lay dying. Kazuki's eyes were burdened by the knowledge. "Go! Quickly! Before.. too… late…"

"Sayonara, dear friend," I said sadly, "I will miss you."

He nodded but was too weak to speak. He lay still, his breathing labored as his eyes drifted shut. I left Kazuki to die alone beside the burning shell of his cabin.

Chapter Five

Fallen

I flew down to the village below, for such was my terror and determination that I needed to reach Aiko swiftly! For a place that inspired terror in me, it was humble. The dwellings were not in the best repair, only one main street made of gravel with houses to either side. Somewhere nearby, a dilapidated torii gate showed the way to an abandoned, old shrine back in the woods.

The village appeared to be abandoned, the women and children hiding in their homes. Not even a dog barked to herald my coming and no lights shone in any of the windows. On a side 'street' that was more of a wide dirt path, a shiny transport vehicle was parked, obviously broken down and in want of repair. That was odd. What would something like that be doing in a place like this? Up on the mountainside above, I saw the flames where Kazuki's cabin and that tree still burned.

I looked around desperately. Where would they keep her?

I turned in place, not daring to shout Aiko's name. I sniffed the air and smelled blood. *Her* blood. With fear lodged in my gut and my heart in my throat, I followed Aiko's scent to a small storage shed. Alas, nothing, not even my worst imagining, could prepare me for what I found within.

I inhaled sharply before I could stop myself. My hand flew up to cover my lips as tears stung my eyes. She lay bruised and broken on the barren earth in the chill night air, her arms spread and wrists tied to tent pegs with stiff ropes. I could smell the blood strong now, and worse. I heard her wheeze as her chest rose and fell. Every inch of her skin was mottled and bloody, the bones broken in her skinny body, and... and... Oh, kami-sama, it was awful.

They had stripped the clothes from her and shorn her hair looking for the moving lump of the possessing fox spirit beneath her flesh, called kitsunetsuki or yakotsuki. There was no proper shrine nearby, and therefore no monks to perform the exorcism, called a kitsunewootesu. So the men had done it themselves, beating and burning her to drive the yako out. The result was an insult to life.

How could *anyone* do this to a child? But for fear of fox possession and witchcraft... I felt sick, disgusted. I wanted to vomit. They had gone through this sadistic ritual to exorcise *me*. It occurred to me then this was my fault! Had I been more careful, had I not shown myself to her in the first place, if only... I would have done or given anything to change this outcome!

"No! No, no, *no!*" I immediately went to her side, falling to my knees. "Aiko!" Her shadowed eyes flickered open, glassy and dull. Gradually she focused on me. "Aiko-chan."

"Hah-yah-teyh?" she whispered in a squeaky wheeze. Blood trickled from her nose and mouth.

"Shh.. shhh... I am here. I am here now, Aiko-chan." I had promised to keep her safe. I failed miserably. I touched her head, feverish beneath my fingers. They had not been careful when they shaved her with a knife, and she bled from the cuts they had made on her scalp.

"I knew you would come for me," she said, her voice barely above a whisper as she struggled to breathe.

I covered her nakedness with my haori. She was so cold. With my claws, I sliced through the ropes that held her wrists and took her hand in mine. Such a fragile little thing. How could they think there was any harm in her, those 'brave men' who had beaten and burned *a child*? The tears ran freely down my cheeks.

"I wanted to come sooner, but I was waiting for dark." What a fool I was. "But Master Kazuki and I were attacked by the men of the village just as the sun set...."

"Couldn't... stop them. I'm hurt," she wheezed. "Real bad."

I could see that, and smell it. It made me nauseous. So much blood, burnt flesh, the welts and bruises on her arms, legs and torso.

"Said you were bad. Told them you were good. Didn't care. Too mad." It pained her to talk, I could tell. Her chest wheezed and rattled with every breath, bringing up more blood as she drowned on it. They had broken her ribs during the beatings, and one had punctured her lung.

The sad truth was, the men did not do this because of me. They did it because in their helpless situation it was something

66

tangible they could fight, a way to vent their frustration. The men must have congratulated themselves for legendary heroes while they rowed themselves up to attack a lonely old man and his stupid pet fox. On the word of a despicable, spiteful lout who hated his sister for the crime of being saddled with her.

Except my claw marks on his skin were certain proof. The villagers had seen me go about as a white fox. Some of those I slaughtered this night had chased me twenty years ago in the shape I wore now. For them, our non-existent threat was very real.

I never hated humans so much as I did in that moment. I wept at the inexplicable horror of it all. I was such a gentle creature back then. I was certainly no demon, any more than Kazuki had been a sorcerer.

"Oh, Aiko-chan! Why did you not tell them what they wanted to hear? Why…?" *You should have lied to them! Then you would still be…*

"Because… I love you." And when she looked into my eyes, I saw the truth of that now plain as day. She had a crush. Oh, kami-sama… She could never deny me, not when she felt like this about me!

"I'm so cold," she said, then coughed. Blood spurted and speckled her chin.

"Please, *please* do not…" I gulped. "Do not die," I begged her. I shook my head in denial, my bell chiming mournfully. "I will take care of you, Aiko-chan! We can leave this place, you and I. I will fly us far away to a beautiful land, a clean one!"

Did such a one exist in this foul, polluted world? I wanted to believe so. I would make it so if I had to! At the very least, *she* could, given enough time. And if not, other worlds existed, and not all were dark and filled with monsters, human *or* yōkai.

"Then you can draw forever and ever, and no one will hurt you again! I promise! I love you, Aiko-chan." It was the first time I said it. She smiled briefly at the thing she most desired to hear. "Stay with me," I entreated pitifully. "Do not leave me in this world alone," I choked, my voice breaking. As if she could defy death.

She looked so sad. She knew she was dying. I could tell she wanted to speak more, but Aiko's face became listless, her eyes glazed over. Her voice, when it came, was from very far away. "... always... love... you, Hah... yah... teyh," she said with her last breath, blood pouring from her lips. Then all that made her Aiko was gone. No more pictures, no more smiles. Her laughter and her artistry were stilled forever, and the world became a darker place for it.

Mine certainly did. I watched the golden light of her soul arise, reach for me, then vanish. When it left, our bond was just... gone. The bell in my hair chimed of its own accord at the passing of my bond-mate. I was more alone than ever. The cold and the dark lodged inside of me.

"NO!" I clutched her tiny body to me, holding her as if that could bring her back. I felt the bones shift sickeningly inside of her. "'Tis not fair!" As if that could make everything all right again. Baka, *baka* kitsune. I wept and cradled her tiny corpse in my arms and my tails, rocking and keening my loss, my failure. No wonder I was trapped here, if *this* was how I succeeded in my missions!

My grief was a terrible wound in my heart. "Why, Inari-sama, *why?*" I called out over and over. There was no answer. There was *never* a fucking answer!

I knew I could not stay like this. Even if I had killed the

strongest men, eventually someone was going to come. I was determined to bury her with Kazuki up on our mountainside by dawn. There they both would be surrounded by the forest they had loved so well. With a heavy heart I kissed the top of her badly shaved scalp and forced myself to stand. I left the shed with her rapidly cooling body in my arms.

Once I was outside, I smelled him. I had wondered if that smarmy little bastard was lurking still around. "Ichirou."

"So you came for her, monster," he said, coming around the side of the shed.

I growled low and menacing. "Look at what you have done! How could you bring her *here*?" My words had an underlying staccato tremble.

"I was trying to *save* her, yōkai! From *you*! You bewitched her!"

"I was never going to hurt her *or* bewitch her! It is not in my power to possess a living being! Aiko was my friend! That is all!"

"Foxes and demons don't have friends!" Ichirou shot back. "You are both."

"I am no demon! I am zenko, a servant of Inari!"

"You are kitsune!" Ichirou shot back. "*All* your kind are demons!"

I growled at him again, my ears flattened back in my aggressive posture. "You are an ignorant fool, Ichirou!" I spat angrily. "And because you did this, Kazuki is dead!" The boy's eyes widened momentarily, as if perhaps he cared. "They killed him! All the men who went up the mountain are dead, too!" *Because of me.* "Aiko is *dead*!" I clutched her body in my arms, wet tears rolling down my cheeks.

"Don't you blame *me*, vermin! This is all *your* fault! And that old man's! He distracted me so you could seduce her. You both corrupted her to take her from me!"

"No!" I rasped. "*You* did this, you selfish, arrogant little fool of a human! You always hated her, blamed her. It was not *her* fault your parents died! All she wanted was for you to be her big brother. Instead you insulted her, treated her roughly, and cared nothing for anything she did unless you thought it made you look bad! You punished her for *your* feelings, you damned brat! She wanted to leave you!"

The boy's eyes turned ugly. "You lie! Vile thing!" Ichirou yelled defensively. He stood up to me, pushed me back, poked me in the arm hard with his finger. I felt my hold on Aiko slip under his onslaught. "She *deserved* it! She killed my mother! And she deserved what those men did to her, too! She tried to defend you, the little idiot! Her 'friend!'" He sneered. "A stinking fox!"

"Do you know what they *did* to her?" I threw back at him. Ichirou smirked. "Yeah, I know. I listened."

Horror flooded me. My body seemed to go numb. Aiko's corpse tumbled from my arms and I was helpless to hold onto her. The world narrowed to Ichirou's face as my blood roared in my veins.

"I'm glad they did it," he continued. Years of hatred toward the object of his mother's affections now exploded forth. "I always hated her! I just wish they would have invited me in to help! But they won't even bandage my fucking arm! All because I'm associated with that dumb old man and *you*." Ichirou was not lying about that. Unfortunately, anyone associated with a kitsune or a fox witch was shunned, and all their relatives with

70

them lest the contamination spread to the community. He spat on his sister's corpse in adolescent rage.

A tidal flood of my own raw anger finally destroyed my last precarious hold on sanity. The wildness I had withstood for so long, that Aiko's light had pushed away, flooded into me now that she was gone and I was confronted by this loathsome whelp! I felt a ruthless, contemptuous hatred unparalleled.

Nor was he in the least contrite. His face was a mix of raw hate and sheer sadistic arrogance. He enjoyed my pain at his sister's demise, and cared nothing that she was gone, save that he would miss beating on her! His smile was cold and cruel, and I wanted more than anything to rip his face to shreds with my claws…

And then he stopped. He looked at me in a state of shock, blinking in confusion. I stared at him, not understanding. *What?* We both looked down in the same breath. My hand was buried inside his torso. I felt it then, his heart beating against my palm. My hand spasmed, grasping that frantically pumping muscle, nearly crushing it. Something tore inside of him. I could hear it.

The dead boy fell back as I drew my arm out. I was overcome by the smell of hot blood and fresh meat, his heart clutched in the cage of my white talons. I drooled. I had been surviving on raw mice and a small portion of cooked eggs for years! And even those meager rations had been further reduced by accommodating the children. I was *starving!* This was hot, fresh meat!

Suddenly I was gnawing on that thick muscle, biting and worrying at it with my teeth. Hot blood spurted against my lips and spilled down my chin in rivulets. For all that it was tough meat, the boy's heart practically melted in my mouth like the finest delicacy. Nothing had ever tasted so fine, so *good*! I could not stop myself! I ate and ate, and then there was nothing left to eat. I was only half aware of what I had done, more animal than man as I licked my fingers clean.

Then the pain came. It started in my belly, debilitating cramps that doubled me over, followed by a fit of convulsions. The next wave of cramping sent me straight to my knees and I whined piteously, unable to stop such sounds in the grip of the pain. It was all I could do to remain conscious. To faint in this village was to die. But when the agony extended to my arms and legs, I wished I were truly dead!

The cord in my hair unwound itself and the little golden bell suddenly rang out of its own accord. As it floated free, it transformed into its true shape. I watched my hoshi no tama, that bright silvery-blue ball of glowing light containing most of my spiritual essence, dance before my eyes. I reached for it with the blood encrusted claws of my profane hand to snatch it, only to watch it flit back and away just out of reach.

"*No!* Nooo!" I cried out, devastated. "*Please!*"

Then it was... gone. *Fwoosh!* In a flare of light, it simply vanished up and away before my astonished eyes and I felt that beautiful part of my soul shred, ripped away from me as though it had never been. I leapt for it in a wild gesture of sheer, futile desperation! But it was no use. I shrieked in the pain of that horrible loss, feeling my celestial nature flee the manifestation of horror I was about to become.

The fires of Hell arose beneath me. I was thrust up into the air by an unseen force that burned cold. I struggled against it, but that was useless. I floated among the eldritch flames, two thin columns of billowing black smoke wreathed around me like the snakes of the caduceus. It struck at my eyes and my open mouth, and it was only then I realized I was screaming in torment. The darkness flooded me and invested me, my emotions cut off to be left behind by the cold, calculating cruelty of my id. I felt the insatiable power of hate, greed, anger, and lust, dark and *so* lovely. Miasma rolled off me in a tidal wave of cold evil.

The Hellfire alighted upon and burnt two of my tails off from tip to base, leaving only the one I was born with – and the excruciating pain of it! I screeched in agony and horror. My beautiful white tails, symbolic of my age, power, and wisdom were gone! Destroyed in mere seconds.

My pale skin took on a more ghostly hue; my tears became rivulets of blood. Four sets of claws turned charcoal grey and extended to a horrific length made for rending and shredding. I stared at my hands and wrists with wide eyes, watched them become longer, thinner. I felt the same thing happening to my legs and torso. My arms contorted, my shoulders dislocating, joints cracking, the arches of my feet elongated with sickening pops. Tendons tore and lengthened. I grunted and choked on the torture of the physical transformation.

Then came the worst yet.

My face felt like it was ripping apart! My jaw painfully extended, the teeth lengthening and sharpening, until my face became that of a hairless fox-wraith. My pained screams turned into a reverberating shriek. Pain became an exquisite ecstasy.

The wind whipped around me at my call. My body floated up higher in the Hellish vortex of chaos that swirled around me. I felt I was burning up inside, the fire within scorching me unless I released the power. At once a bright, blue flare of kitsunebi burst from me outward in every direction. I shrieked again, the xenomorphic sound shrill and deafening. It was the birth cry of a newborn yōkai howling for blood.

I had become accursed, the stuff of nightmare and legend. This was the reason the villagers had tortured Aiko to death and killed Kazuki, simply for the possibility I *might* be this thing. Ironically, that was exactly what they had turned me into.

I fell to the ground in a heap of shredded, bloody garments and windblown white hair. The children's bodies lay to either side like broken puppets cut free from a marionette. My body shook, but the remnants of pain slowly ebbed away. Terribly hurt and scarred, I grasped my upper arms and bent forward, whimpering and rocking. I was so terribly thin now. My fine white hair curtained my wretched, goblin-like face.

I heard the shift of gravel behind me, the step of a small foot grinding rocks into the dirt. I stopped. My head lifted and my ears perked, twisting backward. I sniffed the air. Her heart rate accelerated when I silenced and shifted.

I turned swiftly with gleaming eyes to see a frightened village maiden, no more than fifteen or sixteen years old. She held an old rake out before her, her breath misting the humid night air. She, too, was shaking, but in fright rather than shock. Yet she was bravely trying to stand against me. An old woman several yards behind her hissed in panic for the girl to get back and away from me immediately, frantically waving her hand in a 'come back' gesture that the girl could not possibly see. *"Kaori! Get back here now! Hurry!"*

"Get out of here, yōkai!" the young would-be heroine cried out at me, brandishing her rake. "Leave us alone and be gone!"

I inhaled her scent. Female, pure, young, mingled with stark fear. Sweat beaded and glistened on her brow. There was a slight tremor in her arms. *Prey.*

A hunger awoke in me of such intensity that I trembled, my baser needs screaming to be met. My demon nature wanted to despoil this virgin, to suck in her life force and rip out her heart! I felt the growl rumble in my chest and purr up my throat. My single tail lashed high in growing excitement. I crept forward on too-thin arms and deformed legs, enjoying the weight and heft of my new claws, made for tearing into soft flesh.

The girl froze while I skulked slowly toward her on all fours, my long lips and narrow jaw split into a bloodcurdling grin. My body made a rumbling growl-purr of pure desire coupled with extreme, slavering hunger. *"Sssssssooooo hungry..."* I heard myself say in a ghostly whisper, for I had not the mouth or lips to speak properly any longer. *"Sssssssooooooo pretttty...."*

And vulnerable. She was rightfully terrified.

"S-stay back!" She swung the garden implement at me in wide arcs.

How pathetic, I thought wickedly. I grinned as I rose up, floating before the brave maiden. I drifted slowly toward her. My thoughts directed my body easily. In my periphery, my hair, too, looked suspended as if I were in a pool of water and not flying through the air. I was part apparition now.

"I said s-stay – stay back!" She shouted in a note of hysteria, her voice rising higher with every word. She brought her weapon around to bear again. My hand swept up and shattered the rake's haft contemptuously.

The head and most of the shaft went spinning out into the

night in a cascade of splinters, landing with a thunk and sliding away. I chuckled cruelly. All the girl had was a bit of handle and in desperation she threw it at me, striking me on the top of my smooth muzzle. I brought my arm up to deflect, but was half a second too slow. I winced and flinched my head to the side at the impact, but it did not hurt near so much as I was expecting. My recent transformation had given me considerably more to howl about, and made me tougher in its aftermath, too.

I shook it off and looked at this girl with renewed cunning, for now she had no weapon and I could claim her for my own. It was my right! Was I not stronger, faster, a predator descending on easy prey? I growled my opportunistic pleasure, enjoying how it heightened the little rabbit's terror. She stumbled backward and landed on her ass, staring up at me with so much fear that I could taste it now as I hovered above her... reaching down for her with my long white arms and sharp, sharp talons...

"Mortal morsel. Lovely, lovely *maiden..."* Her pure heart and innocence would taste so sweet! All that youthful life force to drink in! Compared to that punk, this girl was a feast! My whispery cackle echoed in the air as I closed in, her face centimeters below mine...

And in her dark, wide eyes I saw my reflection. My skin glowed ghostly white, my expression dangerously lecherous. I was a terrifying monster.

I stopped cold, horror-struck. I touched my muzzle with my hands and whined. In sudden self-contempt I scraped my talons though the deathly white flesh, leaving three claw marks beneath my cheekbones. Tears welled, blinding me with their strange viscosity, so hot against corpse cold skin, and I saw in her eyes the dark blood of a demon's tears on a ghoulish face.

Suddenly I thought of Aiko. Had her eyes been wide like this girl's when they 'exorcised' her? *This* woman-child had done none of that, could not have stopped it if she had even known what was happening. And now I was what? Going to attack this little girl who was not quite a woman? Like they attacked my Aiko? What would she think to see me like this? Or Kazuki? Or my mother, my people, my kami?

I heard the girl pant heavily in her fear. I looked down at her with what remained of my zenko's heart and was disgusted with myself, deeply afraid of what I had become in a single moment of weakness – the very sort of beast I had been trained to kill! I was worse, for I had not been born this way, but had Fallen, the fate I secretly feared most.

I vowed to be better than this. A yako I might be, but I had been zenko. I did not have to descend to the worst of the worst. I denied the demon's hunger, and in so doing felt a measure of myself restored.

"Aiiiko," I whispered into the night air.

I drifted back, away from the girl whose terror became confusion. My ears folded down, I carefully gathered Aiko to my chest. How could I have dropped her like that? Guilt tore at me. I must have had some soul left, for the warm, thick tears flooded out of my eyes. My body changed back into its humanoid shape without willing it. I was only dimly aware that the girl and her grandmother stood there, watching me.

"I am so sorry, Aiko-chan. Please forgive me." I kissed the top of her head, her scalp cold against my lips. I clutched her tiny body to my chest, still bundled in my haori. She was so light, my poor, fragile, broken doll.

Please, I never meant for any of this to happen! I just did not want to be so alone. And neither did you. Now you are dead, and I am accursed. I swore to protect you, but I let you down. I let us both down.

I stood and cradled her earthly remains lovingly as I drifted backward into the shadows, something a zenko could not do. And before I knew it, or even how I had done it, I was back up the mountain with Aiko. Kazuki's hut was but a few embers glowing in the darkness by then, the scent of fire and burnt wood strong in the night air. I set Aiko down next to the old man. I closed his eyes and sang an old chant for them both. Once the cabin grew dark and cool, I dug their graves with a shovel one of the villagers attacked us with.

I buried Aiko next to Kazuki. The trees bore silent witness as I erected rounded stone cairns over each of them to mark where they lay. The smoky clouds were thick, my world turned grey again. I knelt between their graves, staring at those two graves for a long time. What was left of my heart and soul hurt sore.

I covered my face with my hands and let myself mourn one last time, keening and whining, all fox sounds. But this time there were no tears. I had run out of them. I curled up between the graves, wrapped my remaining tail around my body, and stayed that way for a time.

Eventually I stood. With the weight of my dead heavy in what little was left of my heart, I picked up Kazuki's prize katana and wakizashi, wrapping them in my obi in the old samurai fashion. That was a laugh though. I was a ronin without a master and no home.

"See? This is what you get, Kazuki, for taking in a fox," I said. "You should have known better, the pair of you." I meant it to be derisive, cruel even, but in truth I did not mean it at all.

Nogitsune. A Wild Fox. *Bakemono.* Shapeshifter. *Yōkai.*

Demon. *Ayakashi.* Evil spirit. I was corrupted and defiled, a Fallen shrine fox. Should I die, my spirit would plummet to the underworld where I would become something worse still! To avoid that fate, I was determined to be a ruthless, dangerous, sly and cunning beast.

Yet, without my hoshi no tama, I found I did not care enough to mind. An abiding coldness had lodged deep within and when I set out to find my fortune in this toxic world, I knew no fear. I was one of the monsters now.

Chapter Six

Journey to the Metropoplex

I walked for days and nights, how many I do not rightly know. It all blurred together. With the clouds and thick smog, it was never ending grey, darker or lighter as night and day gave way to each other. I scarcely rested, driven by my need to feed again. Disheartened and depressed I might be, but I could not bring myself to lie down and die.

I wrapped a scarf around the lower half of my face to shield against some of the pollution and shambled forward to nowhere. I saw no one as I made my way. It was like passing through the realm of the dead.

Several days had passed when I came across a town, or more specifically, the remains of one. It was deserted save for some pets that had gone wild when their masters either died or moved on. Many of the houses and shops had the kanji for death painted on their doors in white, a sign to stay away, plague had come. This town obviously had been nice once, the kind with stone tile streets and perfect Japanese-style houses, a quaint place where couples came to spend an afternoon shopping or taking tea in a cafe. Now everything was beginning to overgrow with moss and ivy, elsewise in stages of neglect and decay.

I passed a cat resting for the afternoon on a fence. It growled in warning at me, its fur bristling. I paused and turned, whereupon it hissed, spat and ran away. Its reaction startled me until I remembered. I was demon-kind now. Unnatural. Evil. The enemy of life itself. That's what they told me a yōkai was. I did not recall who taught me that, but I must have learned it in The Time Before. Before I lost my memories and wound up here. Before I Fell and became a yako.

At that moment the sun emerged from the roiling clouds. It fell full on me and I felt sick. My exposed skin became hot and stung. I did not erupt into flames or anything, but I skulked off into the shadows that fell between the buildings, and my relief was instantaneous. I was not a being of the light any longer. I belonged to the darkness now.

I felt sick all over again at the creature I had become, the loss of my precious tails. I was a traitor to my people. I had Fallen. If another zenko came across my path, it would come to battle between us. I would be put to death if I were captured. From this perspective, it seemed so damnably unfair. I only wanted to survive. Everyone and everything, it seemed to me, wanted to kill me or run away.

And in that sense, I was terribly alone. It was hard to hold my head up as I trudged along, my shoulders hunched inward. The little of my soul that was left was raw with despair and grief. And rage. So much rage.

Finally, weary of walking, I sat in the square on a park bench to ponder my existence, what had become of it... and me. The spring sun was setting, and the shadows grown long. In the center of an unkempt garden stood the statue of a human male with sightless eyes, staring out in relentless vigil. Whoever he was, whatever his uniform meant, he was no one now. The acid rain and hailstorms had taken its toll on the monument, pocking it, streaking the bird scat. Ivy strangled his legs up to the waist. I wondered how long it had been since anyone had lived here.

A dog bounded out from an alley with a woman's arm in its jaws. It was old, just bones covered in scraps of flesh. The cur stared at me, whined piteously, then turned and slunk away with its tail tight to its hind. It was a gruesome reminder that I would find nothing of value to me in the remains of this town. Only wild animals and yūrei lived here now, and perhaps a few lesser yōkai that did well to stay away from me.

It became increasingly clear I would need to feed again soon. Already I felt the early pangs signaling my depravity. To live, I must take from the living. I needed a human victim. I needed to move on.

Only I did not know where to go. I had no home, no place in this poisoned world. I was lost, alone, a stranger in a forlorn land that was naught but a dismal purgatory. I wondered if there had been any survivors from the plague, and if they had felt the same. Where did *they* go? In which direction had they pushed toward? Perhaps I was following in their wake. I decided to continue south and east to try my luck closer to the coast.

I was hoping something would present itself along the way. The gnawing feeling inside frayed at my nerves, brought my demonic instincts very close to the surface. I no longer had my kami to empower my chi, nor what sustenance I could muster from food, sleep, and the elemental earth. I had to conserve, or I would go completely feral. I might even die.

And so another couple of days passed with more grey. *This must be Hell*, I thought when my canteen of distilled water finally ran out. *Maybe I am in Jigoku or Yomi after all.* Yōkai I might be, but my situation was becoming increasingly desperate. If something did not give in my favor soon, I was going to be in real trouble!

Then early one morning before dawn I saw light glowing over the next ridge. *What is that?* I wondered.

Stretching across the horizon was a huge megapolis, and how it glowed in the pre-dawn gloom! The lights drowned out the stars, its buildings spiked high into the sky. A great urban Sprawl surrounded the glittering heart of the Metropoplex, for by its immensity I knew it could be nothing else. This had to be New Tokyo.

Atop the wall surrounding it was an electromagnetic shield. I could see the shimmer of it with my yōkai fox eyes. The bio-shield's ionizing properties seemed to keep some of the low-lying smog at bay, and no living thing was getting through it. I had walked through a veritable wasteland to approach it, and I saw no way inside.

The broken and the damaged, those who were too impoverished or ill to remain, wandered like lost ghosts outside the perimeter. They watched my passage with dim, suspicious eyes. No one approached me, most backed away. Here lingered the hopeless, the outcast, the untouchables either in some stage of disease, or mutations who were too hideous to look on comfortably. They were too wretched and unpalatable for my sinister intentions. They had not the life force to sustain me, although I knew it might come to that anyway if I could not get inside that great barrier soon!

It was the megapolis I needed, where healthier people abounded ripe for the plucking and the shadows lay long between the buildings. If I wanted to live, I had to get inside. But from out here, I could not find a way in. I tried to circumnavigate it, but it was far too large. The great wall with its razor barbed wire, guards and their guns made the city into a reverse prison.

It was as Kazuki said. Heavily armed and armored police walked the great wall that housed the bio-shield generators. The men did not hesitate to shoot at the remnants of tattered humanity on the outside of it to alleviate their boredom.

I had no identity, no identification from this or another mega-city to vouch for me. There was no getting in through the official entries, not with the guards and cameras watching. I had not the energy to sustain an illusion for long, nor did I know enough about the human world yet to trick my way in. I was too new at being a demon to understand how the shadows worked, but even that attempt failed. They were using magical methods to blockade the shadows and keep stray yōkai from passing through.

At last I had to concede that there was only one way in. The way the sewage came out. Something else, a yōkai most like, apparently had the same idea and had been strong enough to break in. My nose wrinkled as I peered into the tunnel beyond that newly broken grate, the only one in such disrepair near where the bay was creeping ever upward to swallow the old city along the coast. Water was gushing from the mouth of the sewer tunnel into a river, and from there it flowed out into the sea.

The coastal line of old Tokyo was already flooded with radioactive water from the disaster back in the early twenty-first century. Old skyscrapers and bridges were half submerged. The tide carried plastic garbage into the bay.

With nowhere else to go, I took a deep breath. I regretted doing so instantly and gagged at the odors that assaulted me. The chemical tang was worse than the shit!

Death is out here, I reminded myself sharply. *Life is in there. You are a fucking yōkai now, so grow a pair already and get on with it!* That little pep talk in mind, I wound my scarf tight across my face and ducked inside.

The sewers were flush with recent rain, so I kept my tail up. I did not want to touch anything in here, but I soon found that was utterly impossible. The ground was slick, some of the tunnels narrow. There was too much methane to light a ball of flame, nor did I want to attract unnecessary attention, so I had to rely on one of my new powers. I could see in absolute darkness. More than that, my eyes pierced into the Shadow Realm beyond. I can tell you that a lot of nasty things lived down in those sewer shadows, and that is all I have to say about that.

Some of the tunnel system was formed from the remains of the old city that had fallen during the massive quake and its successive aftershocks in the late 2060s. Accordingly, strange structures existed down here at random intervals. Dishearteningly, I occasionally hit a dead end and had to turn around. I did not know if I was working my way up or deeper down. More than anything I wanted to be out where the wind blew.

The stench was suffocating and stifling down here, the fetid air damp and cloying.

I was wondering if I had made a colossal mistake in attempting this escapade when I came to an open cavern. Suddenly I had hope! Too bad it was quickly dashed. A great waterfall crashed over the edge of a humongous cliff above and across from me into an endless abyss.

No, not a cliff. It had been a skyscraper once! The roar of the water was deafening and the air it created stirred my hair. Light was filtering in from overhead. It was sunlight! I shied away from it even as I delighted to see it. Somewhere above was the way out!

As I stood there looking at this strange, fantastic landscape, which might have been *almost* beautiful, I did not contemplate my danger. The rock was so brittle that it dissolved out from under my feet when I crept nearer the edge to get a proper look up. A heartbeat later I found myself falling, the rush of water gushing down around me. I might be able to fly, but I was too disoriented and confused at first other than to acknowledge my predicament.

I saw a precipice into another, lower tunnel. I reached for it as I went by and missed. But my claws tore into the soft, muddy wall and I slid, all four sets of talons locked into the earth until my velocity slowed and then gradually stopped.

I sighed in relief and looked up. I'd slid quite a way down. Perhaps I could float myself up... and I quickly concluded that I was too weak to fly. The energy from Ichirou's heart had nearly worn off. My body needed sustenance and damn soon! Sexual life force or a freshly taken heart, it made no matter.

There was nothing for it, weak as I was, my muscles

screaming at me. I had to make the long climb to that tunnel mouth above me and hope I could find a way out. Arms and legs trembling, I climbed my way up to the cave inch by tenacious inch. Finally, I heaved myself over the edge and lay flat on my stomach, breathing hard. I felt disgusting. I was covered in filth. I did not want to move, only to sleep. I nearly let myself.

I heard whispering. I looked up to see two children staring down at me, a little boy and a young girl. They were dressed in rags, filthy as can be. We stared at one another in astonishment.

"That strange man looks funny, Izumi. He's all white and got triangles on his head," the boy said. "Have you ever seen anyone like that?"

"He's a demon!" exclaimed the girl, slightly older, a sibling maybe. They both obviously lived down in this maze of tunnels. They were rank with the foul odors of sewage and chemicals.

"What kind of demon?" the boy asked.

"The bad kind," the girl asserted confidently. "*All* demons are the bad kind."

"No, stupid! I mean *what* kind is he? A cat? He got eyes and ears like a cat."

I growled, my ears flattening back. "I am a fox," I declared hotly as I forced myself to stand. The children gasped and backed hastily away from me. But curiously, they did not run.

"A cat, they call me..." I muttered to myself, checking on my katana and wakizashi. My daisho, at the least, were fine.

"Lookit, Izumi!" the boy said excitedly, pointing. "He got a tail, too! A big pluffy one!"

"'Course he does, brat. He's a fox yōkai like mom tells stories of when she wants to scare us."

87

I frowned at them. "Then why are you not running away?" I asked them, annoyed. "Go on. Shoo." I gestured at them to get lost. "Before I eat you."

"You won't eat us," the girl said. "Nobu's too small and I'm too quick. And anyway, we're both too skinny."

I glared at her. She was right, though. I would not eat them. I could never find it in me to eat a child of their years, not even these two insufferable brats. I had *some* shreds of my soul left. And I had to give the girl credit. She had pluck.

"Besides," the boy named Nobu said, "White foxes are the messengers of gods."

"Keep thinking like that, kid, and you really *will* get eaten one day," I told him as I wrinkled my nose down at my soiled state. My clothes were streaked with mud and toxic waste; torn, too. There was phosphorescent green slime all over me. I had lost my zori sandals and my feet were grubby, the black mud caked deep under all of my claws. It was gross. What a way to enter New Tokyo!

"Not all of us are godly, you know, whatever our color," I continued. "Yako can be white, too. Nature made us beautiful to lure in our prey!" I hunched my back and made creepy clawing motions at them, hoping that might finally run them off.

The boy gasped, but the girl glared daggers at me with her stick thin arms crossed over her chest. "Don't be mean to Nobu, Wild Fox. He doesn't know any better. He's just a kid!"

"Am not! I'm almost five and a half!" Nobu declared hotly.

"Well, *some*one must teach him," I told her as I straightened, ignoring him for the nonce. "There are worse things in the dark than me, you know – and as you pointed out, I am not one of the good ones."

"*That*'s obvious," the girl said, rolling her eyes. "You're down *here*, aren't you?"

"Not by choice," I told her with my usual sarcasm and wit.

"Ain't *nobody* down here by choice, Mister," the boy said gravely.

Well, that was certainly true. I opened my mouth to reply and found myself interrupted.

"Nobu?" a woman's voice called out, the sound of a parent seeking its young. "Izumi? Where did you go? You know it's not safe down this way…"

The woman emerged from the tunnel, stopping short as she saw me, her words trailing off. She stared at me in terror. I gazed back in resignation of what must surely come next.

"Nobu! Izumi! Get away from that man! It's not safe! He's a mutant, or –!"

"He's a demon, mommy," the boy child said. "A fox one. He even said so. See? He has a ploofy tail. And big furry ears!"

The woman grabbed her children and held them close. "Don't hurt us, kitsune-dono! Please, we have nothing! I beg you, let us go and leave my babies be!" She was as dirty and thin as her children, and so terribly afraid.

"Why would I? For the love of clean soil and green fields, woman! What makes you think you have *any*thing I want? Or that I should wish to stay *here*?" I asked her incredulously. She winced and cringed, but I was far too frustrated at my situation to care. "It is putrid! The very air is vile and assaults my nostrils! This whole planet of yours is a toxic mess! And will you look what this wretched hole has done to my kimono!" I gestured at my slime and mud-covered robes. "I have become *filthy*!" I threw up my mud stained hands in disgust. "Bother this and bother with you lot. I mean to find the surface. Which way is it to topside?" I demanded imperiously.

The woman stared at me and said nothing. Maybe she was shocked I was speaking so plainly.

"Hello?" I snapped my fingers three times to rouse her, but she only jumped and squeezed her eyes shut at the sound. "The surface? You know, above?" I pointed upward. "How do I get *out* of here?" But she just continued to look at me as if I would kill her and her human spawn at any second.

I shook my head, exasperated with these people. "*Baka!* Never mind. I will figure it out my damned self." I made to move past her into the deeper darkness, the only way it seemed I could go unless I wanted to climb again. I can assure you I did not. She cringed back against the wall, holding tight to her children.

"Wait, Mister Demon Fox?" the girl called out to me as I passed them. Her mother tried to shush her and hold her back, but she broke free. "You have to go straight down that tunnel," she said, pointing the way, "but take the first right. Then just follow up and up. You'll hear the sound of the trans-rails. They get louder the closer you get. The air gets better, too, and sometimes you can smell the food carts. We go up there sometimes to beg until the yellow-vest police chase us away with clubs."

"Izumi!" the mother said in horror.

"*Thank you*, young lady," I said to the girl, bowing to her traditionally and ignoring her mother altogether. "I owe you a favor in kind. One day I shall repay it." Such was the coin of my species. "Upon my honor as kitsune." And with that I went on my way.

"Bai-bai, Mister Demon Fox," Nobu called out behind me.

"Abayo," I waved to him in farewell, not bothering to look back as I walked into the deeper darkness. I hoped that child was in earnest with me. If she steered me wrong, I would have to repay *that* back in kind, too, unfortunately. As I said, such was the coin of my people, and the reciprocal obligations of yōkai, divine beings and gods.

Chapter Seven

New Tokyo

Several hours later I slithered out of a service tunnel near a wide street. The air was cleaner here, and so was everything else. Not even the alley I crouched in had a single stray piece of garbage. I peered out cautiously, careful not to be in full view of the well-dressed passersby. The buildings were huge, glitzy, all glass and metal lit by neon signs and bright streetlights. Above me there was a huge holo-screen upon which a professional young woman read the evening news. I heard the horn of the whisper soft speed-rail whoosh off in a rush of air nearby.

I used the rail tunnels only to find I might have gone *too* far. I meant to be in the poorer Sprawl, not the more elegant interior of the city. It would be easier to lose myself there and find deserving prey. I decided it might go down better if the heart belonged to a criminal. Besides, no one was like to care overmuch about a dead lowlife.

I had been wondering if I could bring myself to take another heart after I let that woman and her children go, but my rumbling stomach and the all-consuming hunger gave me my answer. I *needed* sustenance or my new demonic body would go on a rampage to see the task through. To keep the monster under control, I must feed, and soon.

But instead of the dilapidated houses and dirty streets I had hoped to hunt in, I found myself surrounded by sleek skyscrapers in the evening light. This was the Inner Metropoplex of New Tokyo, made for the wealthy by the wealthy, a beautiful kingdom within which to strive for power. It was not intended for me, certainly not in my current condition.

I pressed against the darkening alley wall. The ground was wet from recent rain and my footprints were still caked with residual sewer filth. I folded my ears into my hair as best I could and tried to keep my tail from sight under my kimono. It would not be enough. I did not have the energy to glamour myself.

Yet I could not stay here, either, and I refused to go back down. I was just about to pull out a broadleaf to try when the silhouette of a passing stranger paused at the entrance of the alley and turned to face me. Despite the growing darkness, he saw me very well.

"Hiding there shan't avail you for long, I'm afraid. You can come out. I will not turn you in. If you are what I think you are, I wish a better look at you." It was a man's clear baritone. His speech was very formal but laced subtly with a foreign accent.

Who in the Hell was *this*? He was bold enough, and in that way which he spoke I could tell he had no fear of me. I wondered if I should answer him or sink into the shadows, though

I was new to navigating them. Here the Shadow Ways were thick with my fellow yōkai, and until I knew more about the hierarchy here, it was best not to tangle with them.

If need be, I can always take this one's heart, I thought to myself. But when I looked at him, I knew that to be a lost cause. This creature was no more human than I was. His heart did not beat. He was... dead. Yet not. "Vampire!"

"As are you, just a different kind, kitsune. I drink blood, you eat hearts. You are yōkai, I presume, and not a divine animal? If so, then we both steal the life force of our victims through sex."

Sex? I had been chaste in this world. In truth, I was almost certainly a virgin! The idea of sex with humans had always been repugnant to me, and with the gentling guidance of my god's divine light, I felt no desire. Since I was breeding stock, a mate would have been chosen for me by Inari-sama. Except...

Now I was no longer fit to be bred. No zenko would mate with a yako, and if I had one, she would not want me back. The demon hungered for coitus in addition to meat. The bare mention of sex awoke a need I had not considered since the night I turned demon. Suddenly I wanted to fuck so bad it nearly hurt! It was disconcerting.

"I... have never purposefully fed," I admitted, and then cursed myself silently for doing so. I needed to guard my tongue, damned stupid fox.

"For true?" the vampire asked. "But... Or is it...?" He looked me up and down with those pale, wolf blue eyes. "Did you Fall?"

I said nothing and turned my face away, scowling.

"Yes, I suspect so. And quite recently, too. You must be starving."

"Who are you?" I asked defensively, disturbed by his acumen. How did a European vampire know so much about my kind?

"I am André Cagliostro, or so I go by now. I recycle the surname as it suits me. We shall speak more of that shortly. But come. New Tokyo is not safe for the likes of you."

"Where?"

"My limo. And then my suite. We will need to D-kon you, of course. Therefore, I would especially appreciate it if you sat on a blanket. It is my favorite limo, you see. Put your outer kimono over your head until we're past the cams. As I said, it is not safe in this city for a nogitsune to be seen abroad. If The Dragon sees you, you *will* be taken into captivity, and I shall have a great deal to answer for."

He signaled and a sleek, long, black car hovered above the electrified street at the mouth of the alley. As promised, the chauffeur spread a blanket for me like a dog, which I did not blame my strange benefactor for requiring. I was covered in sewage and filth, rank with it. I hurriedly climbed into the back compartment through a gull wing door. The vampire pressed a handkerchief over his nose and mouth as he sat across from me, and I did not blame him for that, either.

Dejected, I stared at my filth encrusted grey claws and said nothing. I was embarrassed that I stank, heartbroken by my losses, and filled with an insatiable hunger that was beginning to fray at my nerves. I had not felt so lost and demoralized since I first came to this world. Kazuki had been the instrument of my salvation back then. But who was this André? Why was he helping me? What did he want in return?

My host studied me. "You've been through hell, I'll wager."

95

I looked up. The neon lights of the city glowed across his pale skin in purple, green, blue, and other colors that were outside my spectrum to see. "If this purgatory of a world is Hell, then yes. I am in it now," I answered bluntly.

"It will not get easier," the Westerner said. "But it will get better."

I snorted a bark of derisive laughter. "How does *that* work?" This vampire did not understand my pain, my suffering. How could he?

"It does because the only alternative is death, and that makes this bullshit around us look like sheer Heaven. Besides, this sick world has its pleasures, my new friend. You will see. I shall give you a taste before I send you on your way, ...?"

"Hayate," I filled in the obvious blank. And, you know, for a vampire? This André was as good as his word.

The drive to his penthouse took twenty minutes. Using that blanket, the vampire smuggled me into a high rise via a bribe and the service lift. After that long, slow ascent, he took me to his very large and lavish suite, where he immediately had me decontaminated, or 'D-Konned' as they called it. When my naked body was scoured clean from head to toe with the sharp-smelling chemical treatment and hosed down with hot saltwater, I was then allowed to wash myself with the masculine perfumed soaps human males used to cover their scent. Thankfully the lather stripped off the lingering smell of garbage along with the astringent odor, which made me sneeze relentlessly.

Yet I felt wholly purified when I finally came out of the bathroom in a plush black robe. Even wet, my hair and fur were softer than they ever had been thanks to the high-quality shampoo and conditioner.

"Ah, now *that* is more like it!" André-san said, having waited for me. "But you will need new clothes. We had to incinerate the others, you understand."

I nodded. "My weapons?" I was almost afraid to ask.

"Your katana and wakizashi are being professionally cleaned. They will be ready for you by the time you need them.

"Why are you helping me?" I asked, unable to keep the suspicion from my tone.

"Because you *need* help. And one can do worse than to aid a nogitsune in crisis. Indeed, you may be able to help *me* before the dawn arises. Would you be so inclined?"

"It is not like I have a choice," I answered slyly.

André shrugged. "We all have choices, depending on how we feel about the consequences."

I crossed my arms over my chest. "That sounds suspiciously like blackmail."

"It is the coin of our world, yours and mine," he said smoothly.

"I suppose," I said, frowning. I was being cornered into a position of obligation. Yet he was right. I needed the help. I could scarcely pay upfront, so I would have to submit to the cost after the fact. I supposed I should be grateful anyone was willing to aid me for any reason.

"You are new to this life. I was once the same almost a thousand years ago. I was a Benedanti Stregone, a sorcerer trained to fight Maledanti – evil witches. But then something so horrible happened I thought I had no choice but to cut a deal. That did not go as expected, but when does it ever? My reason for doing so, while justified, meant nothing in the end. I crossed the line and became what you see today."

I blinked. Perhaps this vampire was right. We were kindred spirits of a kind. I was still haunted over my crime, the wound too raw to speak of. I wanted to kill Ichirou all over again. I was sorry I had ever done it.

André nodded. "Look in the mirror, Hayate-san," the vampire said to me.

I obeyed and flinched. Instead of *my* reflection, it was the monstrous Demon Fox that loomed there. My twisted soul reflected back at me.

"Do not run from what you are, kitsune. Embrace it, and you will find your strength."

I understood what he was saying, but it did not make it hurt less. Determined not to show more weakness than I already had, I closed my eyes and willed the mirror to show me as I appeared now. I squinted them open and sighed in relief when I saw the face I had always known.

It had been a long time since I had seen my reflection. How alien I was next to André, who appeared more human by far! It was not just the ears and tail that set me apart. Factor in fangs, dark grey claws, silver eyebrows… and especially those black rimmed, jewel-toned fox eyes. They were the only colorful thing about me, and appeared more brilliant for it. With my long white hair and skin tone? I was undeniably yōkai.

I fingered the front of my hair, holding out a lock over my left eye. "Do you have scissors?" I asked.

"I do, and I see what you are getting at, but let us have a professional attend to that, shall we? Trust me. Never cut your own hair. And I happen to have a consultant on the payroll." Less than ten minutes later, a tall, gangly man in an elegant suit arrived. I had not seen a dark-skinned human before that moment, and this one was pure ebony. I confess I stared at him in frank fascination.

"Ah, Rolfstein."

The man bent the knee at once, head bowed. "What can I do for you, my Lord?" he asked the vampire.

"Not me, *him*." André nodded at me.

The man named Rolfstein looked at me, curiosity turning to instant delight. "Oh, Signore!" He squealed in joy, my ears pinned at the high sound. "He's *gorgeous!*"

"This is our new friend Hayate. He is in desperate need of a makeover to begin his new life here. I can think of no one better for the task."

"Of course, my Lord. What a delight! And is he... *a yōkai?*" Rolfstein wore a sincerely hopeful expression.

"Yes. You see before you a rare breed of great demon: a nogitsune."

"Nogitsune?" he asked blankly.

"A Wild Fox. So be on your best behavior and treat our vulpine friend well. Mr. Hayate can incinerate you with scarce a thought, and he eats human hearts."

I realized this was true. I favored the dark-skinned man with a winning smile, sly and sinister. My beautician gulped.

"Oh, and make no deals nor offer any favors, however good it sounds," André continued. "Yōkai such as our friend here depend upon the system of obligation. They're like Faerie in that. Otherwise, have a blast."

The front of my hair was cut into irregular, M-shaped bangs that covered my white eyebrows and lessened some of the starkness of the natural black line around my eyes. The side edges framed my cheekbones and highlighted the narrowness of my face and jaw symmetrically. The rest was left long and trimmed even across the length of the upper thigh. It was flattering.

Then came the most annoying part. Finding the clothes to match. André reminded me that the first step to power was visual presentation, and I could not argue. I was dressed in a dark plum suit in the latest fashion with a silk shirt a dark sapphire tie. After that, the human spent an hour putting me into one costume after another. I suspected he did it for fun. I put clothes on, I took them off, and waited for Rolfstein to finally approve so we could stop this inanity.

At last he settled on a gorgeous traditional ensemble that complimented my eyes, complete with a peacock blue haori with a white fox embroidered on the back, encircled by three balls of kitsunebi. Apparently, there had been a wait to have it synthetically fabricated on premises. All the while Rolfstein cooed over me and fussed at my hair, which he secured into a loose tail with a ribbon just below my shoulders. When he was done, he looked at me as if he were in love.

"Very well done, Rolfstein. Perfect, I would say," André said upon his return. "Now I have private business to attend to with our friend."

"Of course, Signore. I shall leave you both to it." Rolfstein bowed, gazed at me longingly, and took his leave.

"Now, it is nearly time to attend feeding you," André said when we were alone. "I cannot offer you a heart *yet*, but the other sort of prey, yes. However, I beg you to heed my counsel. You do not have to take the entire life force to feed. The orgasm is the best delight and all you truly need. *You* choose whom to take down into death by draining their essence. You can go so far as to devour the soul! Or age your victim. But you do not need to do either unless that is your wish. The control of whom to take, how, and when, is yours, Hayate-san.

"I am telling you this because I have put in an order for tonight. Both of us need to feed for what we are about to face, and I would rather not have to explain to the company that one of their girls perished 'death by yako.'"

"And what precisely are we about to face?" I inquired.

"Ah, that. I want you to kill someone for me."

"Kill someone?" I tilted my head.

"I am going with you and I will help get you in. But I myself cannot do the deed. I must be able to say I did not kill this man and mean it. Yet that does not mean I cannot actively plot his death." André smiled cunningly. "Indeed, I intend to watch him die in terror. His heart is yours."

I confess I nearly slavered when he said those last four words. I was so hungry. The overblown id that was my demonic nature came to the fore immediately. The vampire smiled and I realized how I must look.

"In just a couple of hours, my friend. But first you must have strength enough to use your powers. And..." There was a knock, followed by feminine voices. "Ah! Our entertainment has arrived! Remember what I said. Do not kill her. It will be difficult, I know, particularly in your current state of ravenous need. Do try to persevere. Oh... and they do not know what we are." He looked me ears to tail and back again. "You might wish to conceal your yōkai nature entirely."

I nodded. "Give me a moment to compose myself and I will come out."

André nodded back. "Not too long, though. The night is wasting."

He left me alone and I stared at the beguiling creature in the mirror. I never cared much about what I looked like before, but I found myself pleased by what I saw now. Then, instead of glamouring myself to look more human, I let myself see the image of the monster within again, that I might remember what I truly was. The nogitsune was cruel and hideous to my eyes.

I was afraid of having sex for the first time, of hurting my partner or accidentally killing her. *Good*, I thought to myself. *Remember what you are, yako – and keep it hidden down deep for now. Unless you* want *to end up dead or in a menagerie!*

I pulled a broadleaf from an indoor plant. With that as my focus, I cast the Seeming of Mortality over myself. It was the most energy I could expend without collapsing. A short time later, I entered the huge main room of the suite, a wall of glass windows looking out on the city night to my right. My benefactor was speaking with two attractive women who were obviously our high-end prostitutes.

One of the ladies was a leggy, blonde, Russian girl. She was already sidling up to the raven-haired vampire. The other was looking around, mildly fretful of whom she might have to 'entertain' and jealous of her co-worker's good luck to score the handsome business mogul. That one was a pretty Asian girl who smelled of plum blossoms, and she was obviously meant for me. When she saw me, she lit up.

I smiled as I went to her, took her hands and brushed the back of them with my lips without knowing what I was doing or why.

"Oh!" she breathed. And now the blonde was a little jealous of her friend. That made me feel fantastic and I radiated the cock-sure confidence of the diabolical nogitsune. I thought it might be difficult to conjure, given my circumstances, but the opposite was true. I stepped into the role that nature had provided for me.

"Well, have fun!" André walked into his opulent bedroom with the blonde on his arm, leaving me with the Asian beauty.

"So, you are...?" she began.

I shook my head. "No names here," I said, leading her to the room next door.

"Oh," she said gravely, and I took that to mean she understood I was not to be discussed for both our sakes.

She studied me, assessing me. I wondered what she saw. Obviously, she was attracted. I could feel it like electricity before a storm when I took her in my arms, her body warm and soft, inviting. She smelled of soap, shampoo, and perfume as I inhaled her scent. Beneath, she smelled of woman and sex. I could have breathed her in all night.

She was not one for kissing, I could tell by how she turned her head shyly when I leaned forward. I nuzzled her neck instead. She melted against me and let my hands explore her body, disrobing her even as she brushed the haori and kimono from my shoulders. She also seemed to love my hair, for she untied that blue ribbon and sent it fluttering to the floor, burying her hands in the straight, white mass. I picked her up and carried her to the bed.

It was difficult to be gentle, but I managed it. I took André's advice to heart and made love to her, arousing her desire, her passion. I scarce knew what I was doing, yet the incubus side of me understood what was needed to seduce her. Although I must admit, there was vast room for improvement on my part. Regardless, she responded, her dark eyes filled with amazement that anyone should care at all about her pleasure, especially a man.

Overall, it was a wondrous experience. I did not know such pleasure existed, nor had I understood what the allure was until now. There truly were delights in this world now that I had acquired the appetite to enjoy them. And just like that, being a yako did not seem so dire a sentence any longer.

When at last she shivered in orgasm, I felt her energy leave her body and enter mine. It was intoxicating. I wanted more! The cruel beast within wanted to suck her dry and raged when I denied it. Yet I took only what was offered and felt it slake some of the thirst. When our copulation was complete, we panted side by side, her exhausted and myself energized.

"You have such beautiful eyes," she told me when she found her voice again. "I have never seen aquamarine eyes before. Are they real? And you're so pale." She ran her fingers over my arm, through my hair. "Even your hair is white as snow."

"I have leucism. It is a form of albinism," I explained.

"Oh," the woman said. "When I first saw you, I thought you might be a mutant. Not that I am prejudiced!" she explained quickly.

"Mutant?" I quirked a brow, wondering if I should be offended.

"Yes. Not one of the lab-farmed kind, but someone who could afford to, you know, bolster his appearance through genetic manipulation. You look too beautiful to be born this way."

I blinked at her and tilted my head, brows knit.

"You don't know?" she asked, confused.

"No," I admitted. "I am new to this city. People *do* that?"

"Sure! Those who can pay, of course. Hell, I'd do it if I could to make my breasts bigger! Sometimes it goes badly, though. The science is still kind of young in that field. Well, even if you come by it naturally, people are bound to think you've had it done, given how *you* look."

"And how do I look?" I teased.

"Like a gorgeous ani-vid villain, or maybe a fallen angel," she said as she brushed the hair from where it spilled over my right eye.

"Ah, but that would make me a demon," I said more mildly than I felt. We were hitting entirely too close to the mark.

"Yes, but a pretty one. Like a fox or something."

She hit the target and did not even know it. "Kitsune, eh?" I smiled devilishly. "And what do *you* know about such things?" I asked flirtatiously.

"Only the stuff on the shoujo ani-vids. The supernatural romances were always my favorite." She smiled dreamily. "If you were a yōkai, would you tell me?"

"No," I drawled honestly, as if bored.

"I know I shouldn't ask, but who are you? What do you do?"

I shook my head and held a finger to her lips to forestall any further questions. "It does not matter."

"Please! I want to see you again," she said, a note of desperation in her tone.

I sat up and shook my head. "I should not even be here." I meant this world, but she took my words to mean the megapolis, or perhaps this suite.

"It is time," André said, poking his head around the sliding shoji screen door.

I nodded and stood. "I must go," I told her and kissed her forehead. "Thank you for a thoroughly enjoyable night." I kissed her lips, and this time she allowed it.

"I sincerely hope I get to see you again," she said as she watched me dress, her eyes widening slightly when I wrapped the newly cleaned swords into my obi. Perhaps then she understood. I was a warrior hired to do a job, for which her body and life force had been my partial payment.

I pulled on the blue haori with the white fox and blue kitsunebi flames on the back. Her mouth was open as I looked over my shoulder. "Sayonara."

"Fox yōkai," I heard her whisper to herself as I donned my new zori and walked out of the room. I do not think she really believed it, though. I never did learn her name, and to my knowledge I never saw her again.

Chapter Eight

The Job

With a hooded cloak draped over me to conceal my face and hair, André led me out of his suite and down the service elevator. All the cams, he assured me, had facial recognition software, and I would do well to keep my features hidden at all times. In the side alley, we approached a new luxury car. I sat in the passenger seat as he climbed in the driver's side. The engine purred to life, and the machine hovered above the road.

"I shall fill you in on the details on the way," he said as he pulled out neatly into traffic, a surgical style mask over his lower face in pretense of a common cold. "I might be gaijin, Hayate-san, but I am also a very wealthy businessman with ties all over the world," the vampire began. "I have a home in every major city, and my influence is felt everywhere behind the shadows. However, the megapolises of the Far East are akin to their own city-states. To maintain my place *here*, I rely on leverage, obligation, and cunning.

"A rival, who has a powerful influence with the oligarchic council, recently took steps in a power bid to buy out my shares of critical holdings here in New Tokyo. Should this succeed, he will destroy my influence with the reigning elite who rule this city, and with The Dragon himself."

"Who is this Dragon?" I asked.

"His name is Hiroshi. He is a true Asian dragon, a fire elemental, and he rules New Tokyo scale, fang, and claw. All the great cities of the East are ruled by a dragon, a member of the Council of Dragons, who in turn commands the oligarchies – *and* the yōkai underworld. Effectively, every major city in Asia is a mini empire unto itself, and do not let the modernization fool you. These creatures are thousands of years old and they keep to the ancient ways. I am afraid that by entering New Tokyo, my friend, you have subjugated yourself to the Dragon Hiroshi's Law. Do you understand what this means for you?" The vampire's tone was not unsympathetic.

"Life in bondage if I am caught." I frowned. We kitsune were rare and often ended up in the collections of kami, dragons, and superior great demons.

Granted, it would be worse to end up in the clutches of a tsukimono-suji, a hereditary human sorcerer who could bind nogitsune such as myself to serve and empower his bloodline for generations. Once I gave my consent and entered the contract, such a powerful fox sorcerer could force me to do whatever he wished, and I would pass from heir to heir, wife to husband if that heir were female, and through them to the oldest adult male of the family line. A yako without divine protection was especially vulnerable to captivity.

"Yes," he said. "And eventually you will be. New Tokyo is

under state surveillance twenty-four/seven. There are places without cameras, where the ultra-wealthy can hide their scandalous behavior. In the deepest alleys of The Sprawl, deals are made in the dark and sometimes not even The Dragon is the wiser. But you cannot avoid the hidden eyes forever. They look down on every street and watch inside every home."

Internally I felt disheartened. It was more dangerous here than I knew. Had I made the right call coming to the city? Horrible as it was, at least I had my freedom on the outside! I did not want to end up in a menagerie, a thing to be bought and sold, used and bred when it suited my master, sent to destroy his enemies, and otherwise pimped out as a shapeshifting prostitute.

"What would you advise?" I asked, the heavy pit in my stomach growing. My imagination spun the lurid landscape of my possible future.

"I will come to that when our business is concluded this night. As it happens, I believe there is a perfect solution for you."

That was smart. This maneuver ensured I would see the venture through to the very end after I slew his enemy. Once I did that, I was technically free of obligation to him. But my powers were his insurance policy out again. Damn the man, he was clever as a fox.

"We shall have to be stealthy tonight," the vampire continued. "You cannot reveal yourself as what you are before any cam. Not yet. But you are a shapeshifter and illusionist. The woman should have provided you with enough energy to sustain a few Seemings until you get a better meal."

I nodded, although her offering was meager compared to the hunger that raged within.

"Good. Then this is how it is going to be." And with that he outlined his basic plan. "Are you good with that?" he asked when he was finished.

"Yes," I answered, and to my own surprise, I was.

André pulled up to the curb a block away from the building we were infiltrating. The damn thing was like a fortress. Once set down, we casually left the vehicle and approached on foot. André wore plain dark clothes, a hood and sunglasses, the surgical mask neatly in place. I glamoured myself to look like a non-descript suit, one I had seen walking down the street a few minutes before. We had a clear view ahead of the tall skyscraper, made of reinforced steel, concrete and glass. It was locked down for the night with cameras pointing at every conceivable angle, moving and scanning.

It seemed an impossible task, but I was not alone in the magic tricks department. When we got closer, the vampire summoned eldritch fire in his palm and wove a spell. The darkness in me thrummed to his sorcery. Then he knelt under the pretense of fiddling with his shoe, but he placed his palm on the ground. There were a series of pops, the smell of burnt plastic. The surrounding neon and all the cameras promptly died, the streetlights dimming around us.

From our position, we could clearly see inside the huge windows of the ground floor. The interior building was still lit, the lobby glowing bright. The security guard inside was reading from a holographic pad and had not noticed the cameras going on the fritz.

"Now we need to get inside that door," the vampire said.

"I can get us inside," I said matter-of-factly.

"Oh?" he asked.

I smiled. I knew a goodly trick that would make that human open the door for me. "Just act scary, vampire. I will handle the rest."

I changed my form instantaneously to the female version of myself for the first time. Everything felt different, but not on the inside. The core of my personality was as male as ever. Still, I had to adjust to the physical body I had just affected. My balance was different, especially in the stiletto pumps I had chosen to go with the skin-tight, sultry mini dress.

"Nice!" André commented appreciatively.

I shrugged and pointed to the digital billboard a street over. "It's *her* clothes," I said, startled at the seductive feminine voice that purred out of my throat and past my lips.

I adjusted my breasts to their best effect and then ran to the building in those ridiculous heels as if my life depended on it. Wow, did boobs bounce! I banged on the reinforced glass doors in panic.

At the lobby desk, the guard looked up startled and shook his head. I pleaded desperately with my facial expressions and body language, looking over my shoulder repeatedly, my eyes wide with fright. Finally he hit a button on the console and the door buzzed. I quickly scuttled inside and closed the door behind me.

"*Arigato gozaimasu!*" I exclaimed breathlessly, pretending to be scared.

He looked me up and down with wide eyes. And a boner. "Um, ma'am, you can't be here…"

"I… I know," I quavered. "But there's a strange man following me…" I looked over my shoulder. On cue, André's shadowed silhouette drifted steadily towards the door.

The security officer was scarcely a kid, short and slim. He gulped when he saw the brawny outline of the vampire. He looked at me again, his eyes lingering on my face and especially my breasts. I was taller than he was, especially in heels, so I leaned forward to give him a better show of that deep décolleté.

"*Please?*" I implored with pouty, quivering lips. "I *can't* go back out there! I can't! He might, you know... Oh, *please!*" I sounded for the world like I needed a hero. And this fool fell for it hook, line, and sinker.

"I gotta call this in, ma'am. Just a moment."

"O-okay. Whatever you do, don't open that door until the police arrive!" I begged him.

My pretense of panic slipped the second he tapped his earpiece. The human turned away to make his call, as if his back to me would make his conversation more private. I grinned malevolently and knocked him on the back of the head with one of my heels before he could tell the computer who to call.

"Sucker."

I went around the desk and pressed the button that was conveniently labeled with the kanji for Front Doors. André came in at once. "Effective."

I knelt down and yanked out a few strands of the guard's hair. I could use this to get farther, the DNA providing a detailed enough illusion to fool a retina scan. Or so I hoped. With a broadleaf, I virtually turned myself into him. I sighed in relief to be male again. Seriously... those heels were a bitch.

Once in the corridor, André conjured a spell and the whole building went dark. So did the surrounding power grid for several blocks. Now it was my turn to be impressed. We made a good team, this vampire and I.

Our objective was at the top of the building, and if we had been ordinary human beings, the ascent would not have been possible. Now that there was no power, we had to wait a moment for the emergency generators to switch on, which created stark white light intermittently in the corridors. A few of the cameras whirred back online.

"Why not send a professional hit instead?" I asked softly once we were out of range of the cams. "Surely you have the wealth not to dirty your hands."

"I do, but that would not be foolproof. Some of the events we set into motion require a personal touch. Besides, I want to be there to watch Takahashi die personally – and I want him to see me gloat."

I could scarce argue with that logic.

I tried my thumbprint on a stairwell door, but it only chittered in negative agitation. Access denied. This low-level guard did not have clearance to enter the building beyond the front lobby.

"Doesn't matter," André said. "Let's do it." He tried the door on a dark conference room, and we went inside. Except, I took the vampire's arm and we passed into the shadows instead.

It is hard to describe this borderland between worlds. The shadows were less an otherworld than a no-place. My demonic nature navigated it easily, intuitively, but if I let go of the vampire, he would be lost in this strange Void. André was fascinated by the Shadow Realm's double-sided corridor. He knew of it, but had never been brought here before. Vampires did not have the ability to traverse this realm or what lay beyond.

On the other side of the Veil sat a vast desert, a dark place I could see into as easily as I did the mortal world. There were great black spires and jagged mountains in that forbidding world where night reigned eternal.

My illusions melted away from the moment I set foot in the inky darkness. I was pure kitsune in the traditional kimono ensemble I had been given. Apparently, there were no secrets in the shadows. I was a pale and dangerous thing with glittering eyes, a beacon of demonic superiority and rare beauty. I reveled in a burst of pride I never imagined I could possess. Lesser yōkai scrambled out of my way like rats.

In this way we passed the human guards, who were sweeping the hallways in teams of two. But if the security personnel could not see us, they certainly felt my passage. I left a trail of cold miasma in my wake that bled into the mortal world. One uniformed man, more sensitive than the others, shivered and looked around warily, clearly spooked.

"What is it?" his fellow guard asked.

"Nothing," he replied, putting on a brave face.

"Don't let it get to you. Shit always gets weird when there's an outage. You know they call New Tokyo 'the Demon Capital of the World,' right?" He looked serious for a second, then cracked a grin.

The other guard laughed nervously and scratched at the nape of his neck. "Yeah, right."

We moved past their conversation. On the top floor I found the CEO's office, large and airy with an exquisite view of the city behind his enormous desk. André confirmed silently that this was the place and I stepped into that lavishly carpeted room, bringing the vampire in tow.

"So, this is your doing, Cagliostro-san," an older man's voice called out.

The chair behind the desk swiveled around to face us. In it sat a tiny, wizened Japanese man, obviously of superior wealth and influence. Takahashi-san wore an expensive suit, even at this hour. He had been working late into the night, and it was clear this was not a novel occurrence.

"It is," my benefactor said calmly, pulling down his surgical face mask as he stepped forward. "I thought we could have a bit of a private chat, Takahashi." He took his glasses off, those cold blue pupils alight in the darkened office.

"Did you? And you had to hire a rogue bakemono to see you in at this late hour?" The old man flicked his calm gaze to briefly consider me, but I stood too far back in the shadow-filled corner to be seen clearly. "You could have simply made an appointment, you know."

André smiled. "Would you have seen me if I had?"

"Perhaps, if only to disappoint you with my answer. This late night visit will not bring you what you wish, unless… is it to kill me?" He said it mildly.

André laughed. "Oh, Takahashi. You know I never leave anything to chance."

"So, you *are* here to kill me."

"Not personally, no. I am being quite charitable, in truth. I am giving you one last chance to back off and save face. Continue down this path, and I assure you that after your death, your family will know only dishonor once I've acquired your shares." The vampire smiled congenially, his voice smooth and unperturbed.

Takahashi's eyes narrowed, his voice grown hard. "I know who you are, *de'Medici*. And I know *what* you are."

"Then you should know not to play games with me," the vampire informed him.

The elderly human stood. "Your threats are wind, vampire! Kill me, then. I am old. I will not cave to such gaijin filth as you."

"Is that your final word on the matter?" the vampire asked.

"It is, but I do not believe you have the balls to murder me. The Dragon himself will oust you, and then it is *you* who shall lose face entirely."

"Ah, yes. That is always a sticky conundrum with you lot. But you see, I am not personally going to kill you. *He* is."

The vampire nodded his head sideways toward me. On cue, I stepped forth from the not bothering with any disguise. I walked toward Takahashi like a beautiful nightmare. The pale sight of me called the old man's bluff, the apple of his throat bobbing furiously.

"Wait! Wait, André-san! We can work this out, make a deal!"

"Oh, it is *far* too late for that, Takahashi," the vampire purred. "You should have been open to my proposal before. Instead you sought to humiliate me, trifle with me, oust me from New Tokyo entirely. I have lived for nearly a thousand years. Did you think I would suffer your insults and retreat without a fight?"

"It was just business! You would have done the same." His eyes flicked between the vampire and my steady approach.

"Perhaps, but with a far less heavy hand. I prefer panache." The vampire smiled at me as I stalked past him, my tail lashing, ears pricked forward.

"It is known the best way to deal with an enemy is to crush him entirely!"

116

"Exactly. You set yourself against me from the first. Perhaps it is because I am European? I remember when the Japanese first opened trade to the Portuguese in the mid-1500s. I had my hands in that, too. And when the black ships under the command of Matthew Perry demanded Japan end the Tokugawan *Sakoku* in 1853, I helped privately fund that operation through my American liaisons. I have a long game. Did you think one old fool would make me crumble in my resolve now, Takahashi?"

"I did what I had to!" My prey focused exclusively on me when I padded around the side of his desk.

"Yes, past tense. Now I am going to do what *I* have to."

The ravenous demon came to the fore within me, making it difficult to think clearly. I wanted this talking to end. I *needed* what had been promised. The miasma surrounding me intensified. I quivered, slavering, the undercoat along my scalp lifting to make my long hair full and wild.

André cast his eyes to me. "Hayate-san? I am done with him. Please enjoy your supper."

Yesssssss! the yako within hissed. My physical form shifted at once without any conscious control on my behalf. I floated above the ground, dark miasma drifting off my tattered sleeves and hem like oily smoke. I smelled deep and long the air around me. The scent of fear was undeniable, intoxicating. A resonating growl reverberated throughout my chest and my tail lifted high, my sharp teeth bared.

Silently, I glided across the remaining distance between us. Takahashi-san backed up against that UV protected glass that displayed such a magnificent view of New Tokyo. I reached out and stroked his cheek with my fingertips. He was scared stiff, shocked still. He trembled violently and the word *"Raaaaabbiiit,"* whispered through my feral mind and hungry maw. My breath echoed in that Spartan office.

"Oh, god! What is it?" Takahashi stared at me in disbelief. My eyes gleamed bright in the darkness, entrancing him. His terrified gaze could not look away.

"Ah, yes, allow me introduce you. This is my new friend, Hayate – a white nogitsune. Congratulations, Takahashi," I heard André gloat behind me. "You are about to meet a rare death by a rarer creature – a greater fox yōkai."

My maw grinned open at the scent of his fear.

"Shit! SHIT!" the soon to be dead man exclaimed, sweat dripping from his brow. "Where did you find –!" He looked at me in horror. I ripped his shirt apart to expose his chest. Buttons went flying. He screamed.

"Sayonara, Takahashi-san," André told him. "I will leave your family enough to survive, although perhaps not in the lifestyle to which they have grown accustomed. That way they can curse your name while they labor in The Sprawl."

I pressed my fingers together and drove my claws into the soft belly beneath his sternum. The old hare cried out when the air rushed out of him. I reached up through hot blood, past the lungs, searching for my prize. At last my hand closed around it. It was beating hard and fast in terror. I stroked it with a lover's caress and my victim's eyes rolled back.

With a vulpine grin I seized his heart in my palm, squeezing gently. Then I wrenched it in place, separating the aorta from the surrounding veins and tissue with my razor sharp claws. He went limp, practically sliding off my arm as Ichirou had done. I drew the heart to my sharp teeth and tore into it with relish.

From the periphery of my vision, I watched André smile. I suppose it gave him pleasure to watch a fledgling monster take those first awkward steps toward embracing its diabolical nature. When I was done, I flowed back into a man's guise once more. I licked my fingers clean, my lips sticky with blood. A burst of kitsunebi along my skin steamed the remaining blood away with a soft hiss.

The lights winked on.

"Well, fuck," the vampire said, drawing up his hood. "New Tokyo always was too damn efficient."

I turned myself into the likeness of the man I had murdered in the same instance the cameras whirred online. The body lay on the floor behind the huge desk. André had already run to the door and backed against the wall away from the camera. He put his shaded glasses and mask back into place. One of the guards began pounding on the door.

"Yes?" I opened the door. "What do *you* want?" I demanded imperiously.

"Your pardon, Takahashi-sama. Please forgive this intrusion, but you must know. It seems that there has been a break-in since the power went down. Two men, or maybe a man and a woman…"

"Then take care of it," I snapped in clipped tones, cutting him off. "I am busy here."

"It is being investigated, of course…" He looked past me to see the toes of the real Takahashi's feet sticking out from behind the desk. "Sir?"

I grinned and pulled him into the office, shutting the door. It locked with a click. Another guard must have been with him, because suddenly the door was being pounded on.

"What?" the man asked in shock when I revealed my kitsune eyes.

I kissed him full on the mouth. What made me do that, I do not know, but that same instinct made me reach down and grope his balls. Whether he wanted it or not, his body physiologically reacted to the touch. The spark connected and my feasting began. I did not need his pleasure to steal his energy, only the intimate contact. His eyes opened wide in shock and disgust that this old man was accosting him, prying his lips open with my tongue. Although he tried to shove me off, the human could not break away from my hypnotic gaze. I held him in an iron grip until his body went slack.

When I stepped back and let him go, a shriveled corpse fell to the floor. Me? I felt incredible! I smiled as I looked at my hand, glowing with auric light. A profane beast I might be, but I felt stronger than I ever had in my life!

The pounding on the door became more intense as the wall shook. They had a small battering ram, and in a matter of seconds, they would be in.

"I believe it's time to take our leave," André said.

"You think?" I grabbed his hand and dashed sideways into the shadows just as the door crashed open with splintering force. And that was when all hell broke loose.

I stepped into the darkness with my temporary employer to find that Mister Takahashi apparently had a few demons of his own on the payroll. Three of them stood before us. Where they had been before was anybody's guess, but they were here now. Ugly brutes, too, squat with giant mouths instead of proper faces. I had never seen or heard of anything like these mutant yōkai. Unbelievably long tongues reached out between serrated teeth to wag at us! I wrinkled my nose and sneered at them.

"Well, this is unfortunate," André quipped with perfect aplomb. Not much outwardly fazed the vampire.

"Nah," I said, grinning. Fierce the yōkai might appear, but they were not *my* caliber. These were dogs, lesser beings. *I,* however, was a great demon, recently fed. I held out my free hand and immediately a plume of blue flame erupted in my palm. I dispersed the flame toward them in an azure inferno, burning the alpha to ash.

The remaining servitors screamed their defiance and sought to flank us. I drew my katana and André pulled a gun. He shot one, I gutted the other. I had hoped that would be the end of it, but when my yōkai eyes pierced the darkness, I saw that it had not merely been three. No. There was an entire legion of the screaming bastards, and these had been just the front runners!

"Fuck this," I said. I lurched sideways into the Dark Realm on the other side of the Veil. At once we tumbled into a nightmare apocalyptic landscape that made our poisoned earth seem habitable.

"Is *this* the Dark Matter universe?" the vampire exclaimed in awe. "How can we see without a source of light?"

Demonic shrieks pierced the shadows behind us.

"Whatever! *Run!*" I urged.

And we did, over to a spire that was five times our height. I saw distant ripples from under the sand coming toward us. A huge predator lurked beneath the ground, sensitive to vibration. No doubt it had a mind to come up and swallow us whole. *Just wonderful.* As if we needed further complications.

But as the hellish mutant yōkai leapt out of the shadows on this side of the Veil to annihilate us, I had an inspired idea.

"Stomp on the ground," I told the vampire.

"What?"

"Just do it!" And I stomped the barren earth with my feet to show him how it was done. Fortunately, André was not stupid, quite the opposite. He spied the wave of sand, looked back at the army of lesser servitor demons, and nodded. Together we stamped upon the ground like two fools. The mutant yōkai loped toward our position over the sandy waste.

"Stop moving and hold perfectly still," I told him, pressing against the rock.

It was the hardest thing in the world to stand there motionless between the anvil and the hammer. My animal senses were screaming at me to flee! But as I hoped, the demons were making more of a ruckus in their bloodlust than we were, and they were too fixated on the vampire and me to notice their imminent peril. The thing beneath the sands veered sharply toward *them*, only to surface in a great rumble and deafening roar that shook the ground.

The creature surfaced. It was impossibly huge, with a tiger shark face and the body of a snake, but no eyes or ears to speak of. It glided toward them with maw opened wide and scooped up the majority of the things, swallowing them whole. It slithered past and dove back into the ground.

Unsure of where we would end up, I pushed myself and André into the darkness of the spire. We fell backwards out of that forlorn place, through the shadows, and into the building back in New Tokyo. Where there were guards on either side of the hall, blinking at us in utter confusion. One, quicker than the rest, aimed a cross bolt with laser sighting and pulled the trigger. There was a twang. I dodged sideways and the bold sped past me, straight toward the chest of the vampire.

To this day I do not know how I did it, young and disoriented as I was back then. Somehow, I saw the short arrow in time-lapse. My hand struck out of its own accord and plucked the damn thing out of the air mere inches from where it would have pierced the vampire's heart. André breathed out hard when he saw how close it had been.

"You owe me," I said. André nodded once.

Personally, I was elated. My debt to him, as it stood, was cleared. It was he who must repay me! But we were not done here. I charged into the security officer who had taken aim and thrust my sword up into him before he could reload. He was armored, but it made no matter. My force and the sharpness of my blade punctured the heavy vest, made to take rounds from a distance.

I whirled on to the next without pause, using the blunt side of my sword to force his gun up. Shots hit the ceiling. I twisted and cut his hands off at the wrists. The man stared in disbelief at his maimed stumps, screaming in wordless horror. Behind me I heard André fighting, too. I could not spare a moment to look and hoped he could hold his own.

Distantly I heard sirens. Alarm bells begin to blare in the building. A serene woman's voice urged everyone to keep calm and move to the exits.

"What *is* this thing?" I heard the next one utter before my claws tore out his windpipe. Blood gushed and flooded down his chest. My glamour had slipped entirely since entering the Shadow Realm. I would have to concentrate on reestablishing a Seeming when coming out of that dark place or risk exposure.

Great, I thought to myself sarcastically. *This just keeps getting better and better.*

And yet – I felt alive! My life was on the line, I was surrounded by enemies in *their* stronghold, fighting for every breath. And I *loved* it! Between the old man's heart and the younger man's energy, I was nigh invincible! Any hit I took felt distant, more like a passing graze from a mere child that healed almost instantly. Meanwhile, I was a ruthless dervish of claws and katana, and I tore through my opponents with grim relish.

When the last one fell, I turned to the vampire, who stood over his own latest kill. He nodded once and we took off running side by side, Kazuki's katana still in my hand. The elevator was ahead, almost within reach! The doors dinged and opened. The same female AI voice announced the floor number. Within the metal car stood a platoon twenty armed guards, looking out at us.

They trained their guns. I could hear their hearts beating, saw their fingers squeezing the triggers... I twisted and vanished, taking the vampire with me.

I had no time to get a proper line of sight on anything, so I concentrated on the sky outside and hoped for the best. We found ourselves floating in mid-air, and I saw the flashes of light from the police transport units far below. Heavy engines cut across the night wind. A police hover-copter was about to round the building. They would see us in an instant! I cast my eyes about desperately.

"Over there!" I heard the vampire say.

I saw a distant flat roof and twisted space as the nose of the police hover-port became visible. From our new vantage point, we watched the police crawl all over the building in swat gear, their strange machines circling the skyscraper with spot-lights. Had I not gotten us out, we would be trapped within, possibly dead for true.

I laughed. I felt giddy elation at the absurdity of having gambled my life and survived! "That was fun!" I wiped the blood from my katana with a cloth and sheathed my sword.

André chuckled. "Only a nogitsune would think so. Thank you, by the way. You saved my 'life.'"

"That is a favor you owe *me* now," I confirmed. I cast a Seeming of humanity about myself, turning my hair black and my complexion a normal shade for the humans in this city. It was time to leave this place before they widened their search. I stepped up on the concrete border wall and gazed fearlessly into the hazy night.

Chapter Nine

The Cage

Saving another supernatural entity's life is no small thing. By the obligation of reciprocation, André owed me *big*. He knew it and I knew it. This was not the sort of thing a new set of clothes or a high-end hooker could conveniently pay off, either. He owed me a life for a life. *His* life. And if he failed to pay the debt even when I called it in, I was within my right to try to extinguish him.

"Listen to me, Hayate," André told me before I ducked out near The Sprawl's Japanese Sector. A black limo picked us up the moment we touched down on the street.

"The Dragon *will* use you, lock you away, breed you, perhaps sell or slay you. You will spend your days a slave, your nights in a cage. Hiroshi-sama must *not* catch you.

"But there is one who can protect you from that fate if you ally with his cause. Lord Youta. He is a young water dragon, only six or seven hundred years old at most. He understands humans and yōkai as the others in their ancient ways do not, *cannot.* It is your choice of course, but I strongly believe Youta will welcome you, give you a place among his own once you prove yourself."

"Where do I find this Youta?" I inquired, knowing myself limited on options.

"He runs an underground yōkai club called Ori," meaning 'The Cage.' "It is deep in the Japanese Sector of The Sprawl, which begins across that wall. I have never been there, not being either local or yōkai, so I cannot advise you further from this point. Good fortune to you, Hayate-san."

"Yeah, I'm just *aces* in fortune these days," I said sarcastically as I opened the gull wing.

André laughed. "I bet. This is farewell then, nogitsune. For now."

"For now, vampire." I shut the door and the limo hovered down the street above the solar grid.

Now that I was topside, and my ability to disguise myself in Seemings re-energized, I found it extraordinarily easy to go where I wished. After a bit of exploration, I found a short, squat, little demon skulking in a dank alleyway, rummaging through piles of garbage. This little beast fed on filth and was known for spreading disease and ill-fortune among humankind. Keukegen were smelly moppets covered in long fur, like a head of hair gone matted and wild. They were lesser demons, shy and unassuming by nature, mostly just disgusting.

I grinned to myself. Before he knew what was upon him, I swooped the little yōkai up in my claws and vanished. I brought us to a rooftop in line of sight of the alley. I might be able to come and go like the wind, but bending space was not without its dangers. Two things could not occupy the same space without merging. If I warped myself into a pole, the pole would go through me as soon as I solidified around or into it. The same held true if I apparated in the sky and a bird just happened to be flying where I manifested. Nasty.

And, no, I could not just re-apparate myself to undo it. Once something was a part of me, it went with me. It was always safest to reappear where I could see, to minimize mishap. I did so now in the tell-tale rush of wind that came through the vortex I created.

I clutched the lesser demon's nonexistent neck and held him aloft so I could gaze levelly into his face. My slit pupils bore into those large brown eyes. "Well, well," I said nonchalantly. "Look at what I have here." My lips split into my most sadistic smile.

The demon squeaked. "My lord?"

My grin widened. I liked that, being called a lord. I liked the feeling of power, too, and how it made this base creature afraid of me. I found it a rush, his fear and my absolute control over him.

"I need to find Youta. Where is The Cage?" I asked politely in a smooth velvet voice.

"Great Lord, I do not know - urk!" He squeaked as I tightened my grip on his feigned lack of knowledge.

"Do not take me for a fool." I put a bite in my tone this time. "You lurk in these dark passageways on the fringe of the human world. You know *precisely* whom I mean and where to find him. So..." I pivoted and dangled the tangled mop out over empty air above the alley. I drew my face closer to his and bared my fangs. "Easy way or hard way?" I tilted my head inquisitively and raised a thin, arched eyebrow.

TEN MINUTES LATER I WAS WALKING THROUGH A PART OF THE JAP-anese Sector that few dared to tread, lest they were criminals or yōkai. Eyes watched me, assessing to determine if I were a seller, a client, a victim, or a threat. I moved with self-assur-ance and swagger, as if I belonged here. And I supposed I did. Although I maintained that human glamour I affected earlier, heads turned in curiosity and quickly looked away again. No one stared too long at anything on this dark road.

A set of short steps led up to a large, industrial steel door. No sign, neon or otherwise, marked this place. I banged on the metal outer door of The Cage. It boomed hollowly with my three heavy knocks. The rectangular peep hole slid open to reveal a pair of freakishly blue eyes.

"*Another* bakeneko?" a woman's voice inquired.

"Not exactly," I drawled with a smile, although I had to force it and push my irritation aside. Rare or not, I felt mildly insulted by her presumption. Why was everyone assuming I was a cat? Had no one seen a fox before?

"Password?"

"Kamikakushi." It meant to be 'spirited away'. That was another thing I had wrung out of the little yōkai before I let him go with the promise that, should his information prove in-accurate in any way, I was coming back. And I was not going to be so nice the next time. Now that I had his despicable scent, there was nowhere in this megapolis he could hide from me.

The heavy door unbolted and swung inward. I sauntered inside, feeling rather dashing in the emblazoned haori the vam-pire had gifted me. The door shut behind me.

"Unveil. It's the code." I did. Like the rest who would be

assembled here, we would be wearing our demonic aspects. This was not my *full* yōkai form, of course. That would have been overkill. But to judge by the horned kijo demoness at the door, anthropomorphic was in.

She blinked at me in surprise, her mouth parted open. "Kitsune? *Here?*" She stared at me.

My smile spread thin with a hint of the sly and the wicked thrown in for good measure. "In the flesh – *and* the fur." I swished my tail suggestively. "Am I your first?" I asked coyly, extending my chin.

She nodded, staring. "Go on in." She gestured to the heavy door at the end of a short hall. Muffled music vibrated hard against it, promising the loudness of a proper nightclub beyond the threshold. I steeled myself for that. My poor ears would be ringing within minutes, I knew.

There were cameras looking down on me from every angle. I brazenly looked back. Youta had to know I was here. I was too much of an anomaly for someone not to take notice and inform him. But would he want to claim me for his menagerie of upper tier yōkai? Ah, that *was* the question. Alas, Youta could just as easily turn me in to Hiroshi! This, then, was my gamble. I had to be prepared for anything.

I swaggered toward the door. Once opened, I was bombarded by the promised audio assault and more. There were holograms, neon, and flashing lights amid darkness. I pretended it did not affect me at all. To show weakness was to be prey. I had to prove my strength to these fiends and my heightened sensitivities be damned!

There was a bouncer on this side, a *huge* oni with a nail-spiked kanabo club. He sat on a stool about five sizes too small for him. His furrowed brows glowered at me. "No touching the dancers without permission or coin. No touching the wait staff. Period."

"Got it."

He grunted and that was the end of that.

I turned and faced a club filled with malevolent yōkai. There were demons of every stripe and flavor here. Neko girls were in abundance in the roles of waitresses and cage dancers, in addition to rabbit and young tanuki. To be honest, it was hard *not* to look at the eye candy. On stage, a beautiful long-necked woman, a type of yōkai known as a rokurokubi, was pole dancing in nothing but her incredibly long hair, winding her head about the silver bar as she spun.

Huh. Well, then.

There was only one way to play this they would buy into given my race. I had to be that curious combination of danger-ously wild and in perfect control of myself, to display superi-or confidence bordering on arrogance and sheer audacity. In short, I had to be a sleazy yako.

I looked with surreptitious coyness from side to side, play-ing up the kitsune image. Heads turned. Eyes appraised me from every angle. For the record? The neko girls totally loved me.

"Is that a kitsune?" I heard to my right.

"Worse. That's a *nogitsune*!" A futakuchi onna grasped food with her hair tentacles and shoveled it into the mouth on the back of her head.

"Holy Hell! Those things still exist?" The third member of their party asked, a woman with the appearance of a chunari hannya, that breed of horned female oni usually referred to as a kijo.

I moved past that table and heard another conversation to my left.

"I've heard of those, but no one's seen one in a long time."

"Seen what? What is it?"

"I forget how young you are. That is a white fox yōkai."

"Are they rare?"

"These days, yeah. Haven't seen any kitsune in nearly a hundred years, let alone a white one."

A particularly pretty cat waitress stared at me, fixated from the moment she saw me. I smiled flirtatiously and gave her 'the eyes,' as would be expected of such a lecherous beast. I walked straight past her to the bar, where I took a stool and ordered hot sake from the astonished bartender. The one-eyed yōkai – as in, he only had a single eye in the center of his forehead – demanded payment upfront.

I threw down the coin I filched off the keukegen. The human world might rely on digi-cred, but we demons apparently preferred hard currency among our own. The suspicious bartender made sure it was no illusion, for which foxes are admittedly notorious, then went to fill my order.

As I sat there, I felt rather... alone. I had not realized I was quite that rare. I knew my people had fled the toxicity of this world, that we were a hunted species, but the talk I overheard was beginning to disturb me. Was I truly the only one of my kind?

"The stories are true. They really are beautiful," I heard one of the waitresses whisper behind me with a drawn-out sigh of longing.

"And *dangerous*, sister," her fellow staff member said in chiding tones. "If he's here, he is *not* the good kind."

I looked up in the mirror behind the bar to see a waitress in a short skirt and fishnet stockings, complete with a little black halter top. Her sleek black hair fell over her shoulders and was trimmed into bangs evenly across her eyebrows. Ah, yes, the pretty one. She was speaking to a fellow two-tailed cat woman in a black blouse with a blue necktie and cummerbund, wearing feminine dress slacks and modest heels. That one glared at me as I smiled long, slow and sensuously, a gleam of the wicked in my jewel-toned eyes. I set my narrow chin on the back of my hand and tilted my head just so.

"There's a good kind?" the waitress asked innocently.

"Ehhhh... Just stay away from him. Never lose your head over a fox, got it?" the wiser one said, turning away. It was sound advice, but the short-skirted waitress with an empty platter stared at me longingly until another customer gruffly demanded her attention.

"Hey, babe! Instead of staring off like a friggin' moron, how about you do your job and get me another —"

I projected an air of disaffected boredom while I waited for my rice wine and tried not to look at myself in the mirror. Unfortunately, that was a rather hopeless cause. I could not avoid myself. I was the whitest thing in this place I had seen yet, and in a room full of yōkai, that was saying something! The cat girl was right, though. I *was* beautiful. I had never guessed how much before, since as a zenko I had never made it a habit to look at myself.

Seeing my reflection now, however, brought that truth home. My new demonic nature certainly skewed toward vanity. I was thoroughly infatuated with myself. This, then, was the first seduction of my new narcissistic personality. Sadly, it would not be the last.

My bartender came back and placed a little shuki set before me. He poured the first drink and walked away. I had only that first cup when two burly oni in suits that looked utterly incongruous on them spontaneously materialized to either side behind me.

"Boss would like a word," the one breathed with implicit menace.

"I rather expected he would," I said as if I had not a care in the world. I did not move. That earned me a glare.

"*Now.*" It was incredible how such a short, one syllable word could have so much weight and command attached to it. I sighed and stood with deliberate slowness, draining the rest of my tokkuri flask on the spot. I *had* paid for my cheap sake, after all, even though I had stolen the coin. Only then did I allow the goons to escort me to the uppermost deck that overlooked the club proper.

Sitting there among his chosen lieutenants, I knew who Youta was at once. He sported a thick, golden Mohawk spiked into dragon spines. The skin of his scalp was tattooed with blue scales, and he had two thin, long blond mustachios that hung down from either side of his lips to about mid-chest. The dragon's eyes were a fierce golden yellow, the pupils slit. I gazed into them serenely.

Six yōkai lounged around him, although he was the only one with a rabbit girl on his lap. He whispered into her ear and she stood up on heels that were almost as tall as her calves, and yet she still barely came up to the height of my chest. She swayed her fluffy tail out as Youta stood, circling around me. The dragon missed nothing. I could tell at once his perception was keen.

"Well, *well*. A white nogitsune. Where have *you* been hiding?" Youta drawled, a wreath of smoke wafting from his narrow nostrils.

I shrugged and otherwise stood perfectly still. "The mountains. My lord."

"Direct and un-elaborative," the dragon smiled at my cheek. "I suppose it does not matter. You are the only yako in New Tokyo, and recently arrived, too." I hated that term, *yako*.

"Hai, Youta-sama. I am." I accepted the insult and bowed my head deferentially.

"So, you know who I am." It was not a question.

"I do. And I know whose trust I would prefer to be in, my lord. Yours."

"*Trust?* Really?" an old tanuki with a robot leg sneered. Youta glanced at the raccoon dog and he fell silent immediately.

"Come to offer your services for my protection, have you? I want to believe you, kitsune-san, but your kind *is* known for deceit and treachery."

I sighed internally. This was always the rub. The problem was, they were not wrong. I did what I wanted when I wanted to, for my own reasons as I judged them to be in my favor. That was my yōkai nature. And yet, I was on the level just now. This was for my immediate survival.

"Perhaps," I answered. "Nevertheless, I come to you in good faith, my lord. I know how they treat Wild Foxes in the Metropoplex, and I know my worth as an asset."

"He's a spy, Youta-sama," the tanuki called out. He was obviously the oldest and least fit among the six, but he had guns holstered all over his person and I had no doubt he could use them. Else he wouldn't be here.

"Or an assassin," the oni offered. He had a bluish tinge to his skin and deep blue highlights in his long black hair.

The water dragon considered his underlings' words, then shook his head once. "No," Youta concluded. "If this fox were an assassin, he would not have come here like this. He would have come for me when I was alone or attempted to seduce me in female guise. I doubt Hiroshi would choose someone so flashy to infiltrate, hidebound as the old wyrm is.

"A nogitsune like this one is too rare these days. Hiroshi would rather make a slave of him and keep him locked away, a fate to which no Wild Fox would willingly surrender. Still," the dragon continued, "you must be tested if you would be one of us. No one gets in for free, kitsune."

"What would you have of me, Lord Youta?" As if I did not already know. It was obvious when the others stood and filed into the room next door. A room that was separated from the club by more than three feet of thick concrete and another reinforced steel door. No one would hear a thing.

"It's simple. If you are what you say you are, prove yourself. Fight the others and earn a place among my elite. Or leave. The choice is yours."

Chapter Ten

The Gauntlet

nodded and walked through that door. I was not stupid. If I tried to leave, they would descend on me anyway as soon as I walked out. I was free to go, but after that it was anyone's game. No one let a creature like me simply walk away. But I did not want to. I had come too far now.

The others fanned out around me in a semi-circle while Youta observed from the side. Each one was a different species of yōkai and powerful. All but one was male. But the female, a yuki onna, or snow woman, might have been the most dangerous of them all, next to that crow tengu. A daitengu, too, lest I missed my guess. He had come down from one of the mountains and had the manner of a monk. This was no lesser kotengu, certainly.

As the six stood facing me, the big oni transformed into his full demon aspect. There was even a devil bear in this company! Whatever their species, they were all formidable great yōkai.

Youta smiled benevolently. "All you need do, kitsune, is survive."

I grinned malevolently, my tail lashing in excitement of the battle to come. My fur bristled, ears flat back in clear aggression. My hands curled into claws.

"No sweat," I said. I tilted my neck to one side, then the other to crack the vertebrae and loosen myself up for the exercise. I stood at the ready.

I suppose I should have been more afraid. Yet, somehow, I only felt a wild joy singing in my veins. I did not care if I got hurt. I wanted to fight! If they thought their numbers would intimidate me, they were very much mistaken. One or two looked at each other in sudden doubt. It was writ plain on the monkey demon's face.

There was no signal. Suddenly it was on. I poured out blue flame toward the yuki onna as she hurled several rapidly formed icicles toward me. She fell back from my fire, her ice daggers turning to steam upon crossing that wall of kitsunebi. I turned and used the training that Kazuki instilled in me as the horned blue oni and a huge bear yōkai, the muscle of this operation, rushed at me. I backed out at the last fraction of a second, so they collided with one another instead of crushing me between them as intended.

That did not stop them, however. I found myself doing several combinations of martial arts styles to hold them both at bay, and barely at that! I mean, come on, they had an *onikuma*, for pity's sake, and he looked like a sumo wrestler on steroids! If that devil bear got a grip on me or a well-aimed swipe with those claws, I was done for! I had to dodge and dart around his attacks, striking where and how I could. My blows did not faze either the bear or the ogre much, but it felt good to hit them anyway.

After a minute of this, I resolved that this lot was *good*! They would have to be, else they would not be Youta's lieutenants. And yet, bravado notwithstanding, I was somehow managing to hold my own! Thank goodness Kazuki and I passed the years in martial arts discipline. His Bushido Way, however, did not apply among yōkai. These creatures were every bit as underhanded and dangerous as I was. Honor among yōkai was bound by the system of obligation, not chivalric code or social etiquette.

While I was trying not to get crushed or smashed to death, the monkey demon grabbed hold of my tail, his hands clutching painfully in tufts of fur. I swung my tail in an arcing lash, using the momentum to fling him off me. As he tumbled in the air, feet hitting the wall to launch himself at me again, I sent an arc of lightning at him. The sarugami fell to the ground, twitching and smoking.

One down. Five to go.

I heard a whistle cut through the air toward me and ducked my head to the side. A large snowflake with razor sharp edges flew past. It was that damned ice wench again, and she nearly took off the tip of an ear, too. Had I not moved in time... My lips twitched into a frown. I maneuvered the oni between us, him being the bigger target. He grunted when an ice shuriken embedded itself in the meat of his back. The woman cursed.

Movement caught my peripheral vision. I saw the fat tanuki pull a gun and take aim at my head. There was genuine hatred in his beady eyes, and I had no doubt he was aiming to kill. I vanished at once and reappeared behind him, twisting his arm painfully. The shot rang out and hit the wall, chipping a chunk out of it in a spray of grey concrete. He cursed, but I forced him to drop his weapon. I grabbed before it hit the ground and used the butt of it to whack him in the back of the head. That was two.

More ice objects came hurtling at me in lightning quick succession. I ducked and tumbled into a roll, the ice breaking into a spray of frozen water crystals when they struck the wall. The beautiful snow woman stood before me in a cloud of vaporous miasma. A katana of hard blue ice formed in her white hands.

I had a choice here, but I had to make it fast.

I stared into her arctic blue eyes. The tell came as she made to lunge for me, a slight narrowing of her eyes and tensing of the jaw. I jumped back, the blade coming within a hair inch of disemboweling me. I might have drawn my own sword, but I had a better idea. With a wicked grin I conjured a wisp flame. My kitsunebi melted her sword. She shrieked in wordless rage, turning into a more alien, hag-like demoness while my summoned fire spirit attacked her of its own volition.

The bear and the ogre used that moment to jump back in. The onikuma transformed into his full yōkai state, a ferocious giant beast with mighty, black claws. He opened his slavering maw and roared at me. Not only did his breath stink, but the sound was deafening!

I answered in kind to that threat. My body rearranged itself into its demonic vulpine form. I floated, and the growl that reverberated from my chest cut through the space around me with a gekkering trill. I was feral and hungry for violence.

Youta clapped. "Oh yes. You *are* the real thing!"

I shrieked and flew at the oni, who was just then aiming to brain me with his heavy iron kanabo. Faced with me in this form, the ogre stumbled backward in surprise and landed hard. He swung his cudgel overhead at me, although I floated too high above it to take a hit. I reached down with my long claws and plucked the heavy iron object from the oni's grasp. Then I brained him with his own damn weapon. It takes a lot to put down an oni, but my demon body was more than capable. Metal hit thick bone with a resounding *WHACK!* The brutish horned demon slumped bonelessly to the floor.

That was three.

I held onto his weapon and vanished in a draft of cold wind, only to reappear behind the bear, who was standing up on his hind legs. I knocked him over the head with the thick cudgel, then up the side of his face. He flew sideways and crashed into the wall. The concrete cracked into forks of lightning under the assault. When he fell, he stayed down. I tossed the kanabo aside.

By then there were only two left, the tengu and the snow woman. I returned to my hybrid state and faced them, standing tall. They would not stop until Youta told them to, even if it killed them. If this venture proved a success, I would be one of them and subject to the same strict command. I had no sympathy for them, nor they for me. We were monsters.

I had shown Youta I could fight with my body and my ingenuity. Now I would show this water dragon that I could wield a sword like the samurai of old. I thumbed my katana in the scabbard, faced the tengu and waited. Outwardly I appeared calm, yet inside I was thrumming with excitement! I *wanted* to feel the resistance of flesh and bone against my blade!

As expected, the daitengu came forth to meet me. He was very proper and stately, his manner respectful, elegant. We bowed to one another and pulled forth our katana in unison from their scabbards with the light rasp of metal on wood. We took stance, then flew at each other, our raised blades meeting briefly in a flurry of blows.

We broke off, reassessing one another. He was good! I was enthralled. It was an honor to fight this man, and it was clear he felt the same. Ours was a dance, dodging and weaving as we sought to strike the other down. It was *glorious*! I could lose, but if I did, I would not go down to a lesser being.

Perhaps he felt the same, for I heard the snow woman circle behind me, but the crow goblin shook his head. I smiled. We tried each other again. Neither of us could seem to get through the defenses and attacks of the other. He was the closest I had found to a true equal!

But the cold chill on the back of my neck that told me the yuki onna was attempting to cast on me, contrary to her compatriot's desire. I held my katana in my right hand, blue flames erupting in my left hand as a threat toward the yuki onna. I prepared to dodge her and hope she did for the crow, who was too worthy an opponent to put down by treachery.

"Enough," Youta's voice cut through. At once I stood down, lowering my blade, the fire extinguished. The tengu sheathed his katana. The snow woman ceased her ice summoning magic. "He is perfect," I heard the dragon say. "Multiple disciplines. Ingenuity, adaptability, and that magic... breathtaking. You are a thing of rare magnificence. And I confess, I've always wanted a fox of my very own." He smiled appreciatively. "What is your name, shirogitsune?"

"Daisuke Hayate, my lord." I sheathed my sword.

The dragon's eyes widened slightly. The tanuki, who was just then coming around and rubbing the back of his head, looked up at me with a start, then sharply over at Youta.

"Daisuke, is it? Fortune indeed sent you to me, Great Help on the Sudden Sound of the Wind's Arrival. A winter gale, and that is what I will name you for. You are The White Wind. When I unleash you, my Shiroi Uindo, the death of our enemies shall be certain. What do you say to that, Hayate-*dono*?"

I looked at him in a start of surprise. He granted me the style of 'lord' and stressed it. That was an accordance of great respect, a promise of what I could become in New Tokyo if I played my cards right.

"Hai, Youta-sama." I bowed deeply. "Your greatness humbles me. It is my honor to trick, slay, and steal for you."

"Why, what excellent manners you have, kitsune!" I heard the amusement in his tone.

"Arigato gozaimasu, Youta-sama," I said, bowing still lower from the waist. I could see nothing beyond the white curtain of my long hair.

"But Youta-sama!" the tanuki exclaimed. "White or not, he *is* a fox! They betray as easily as breathing!" He crossed his arms over his chest. "*I* should know."

"Will you betray us, Hayate-san?" Youta asked me casually in his deep, calm voice.

I straightened and faced my new master. "Betrayal is not my intent, my lord," I answered honestly. "I only seek to stake my claim in this world, for there is no longer any place in the wild unspoiled enough for me. I have no skulk, no people, *no one*. I yearn for clan and fresh, human victims without the stench of disease." Indeed, after using my talents to fight these people, I wanted sex and to eat a mortal heart so bad that I was practically drooling!

Youta laughed. "There you have it, Katashi," he told the raccoon-dog yōkai. "Foxes adapt. It is their strength. So will it be with this kitsune, wild... or not."

The tanuki harrumphed and staggered out. I could tell the tanuki was hardly convinced, but I simply did not care. I wondered what his deal was. I had always been given to understand that my sort ran well with theirs.

"Come, Shiroi Uindo," Youta commanded. "Let's talk."

He led me back out onto the deck of the rowdy club where hot yōkai girls and pretty femme boys danced in go-go cages, while a large variety of demons drank whatever their choice of poison and leered at them.

"We have been waiting a long time, shirogitsune," Master Youta said.

"For what, my lord?" I asked as we looked out at the assemblage of yōkai.

"For revolution. Why else are you here, submitting yourself before *me* rather than Hiroshi? Because those several thousand-year-old dragons haven't caught up with the age they live in. Their lives are so long they have lost sight of the future. But our world is quite fragile. Many of us depend upon humanity for survival. The humans are mortal, after all, and they live their short lives swiftly. They adapt and change, create and destroy. Unlike yōkai, they are changeable.

"For over a hundred years I have told my elders this, but what do they care? If humans overrun and destroy this world, the great old beasts will survive it. The rest of us?" He tsked.

"I may be a dragon myself, Hayate-kun, but I am a water elemental, and behold the seas and oceans! Wastelands of algae, kelp, and plastic; dead, bleached coral reefs and a radioactive brew of toxicity that little and less can survive in. The food chain has broken. Demon-kind of the sea have been altered into worse horrors to adapt, and many are being driven ashore. They in turn eat more humans, who grow wise to being prey. And when they do, what then do you imagine will happen?"

I already knew firsthand. "I see," I said quietly, thinking of Aiko, and how the villagers came for me and Kazuki.

Youta sighed sadly, shaking his head. "Our success depends on a delicate equilibrium of absolute secrecy and legendary fear. That is why the Ayakashi Syndicate works in the shadows beneath the human world. The Council of Dragons has controlled the great cities of the Far East for millennia, using yōkai as their hidden arsenal and mankind their slaves."

Youta looked at me frankly. "But none of us will survive in this desolate world if things go on like this indefinitely. The old ways, while desirable, are not always the *best* ways. Civilizations end. Humans change things. It is their power, their gift and their curse."

"Regardless, the dragons will remain in power," I pointed out.

Youta smiled. "Yes. But over what sort of world? I do not know about you, Hayate-san, but *I* want to live in a better one than what we see around us. As a Wild Fox, surely you must wish the same, or why else are you here?"

I bowed my head. "It is as you say. I do not wish to live in bondage to the likes of Hiroshi."

Youta smiled again. "You are the key instrument I have

been waiting nearly a hundred years for, Hayate-kun. If you are all that you promise to be, you shall certainly become my most valuable asset. And you will do quite well for yourself in the bargain." He fixed me with those shrewd dragon's eyes. "Do you have fortitude for what lies ahead of us, Shiroi Uindo?"

"Hai!" I answered at once.

"Good."

My eyes panned out again. I saw the pretty waitress with the kawaii cat ears and bi-forked tail, the one who had told her sister I was beautiful. She caught my eye and I smiled down at her. She blushed and looked away, then shyly peeked back up. Oh, she *did* like me. My smile broadened seductively.

Youta followed my gaze. "Fancy that one, eh?" He snapped his fingers and an attendant rushed to his side. He whispered a word and the servitor demon ran down immediately. When he returned, the pretty nekomata was by his side, bowing from the waist.

"My lord?" she asked, never looking up. She was trembling slightly.

"Our new friend here is recently arrived from out of town. A charming woman such as yourself could acquaint him with our fair city. You may take the rest of the night off."

She stiffened upright and looked at the dragon with big eyes, then at me. It was plain what she was expected to do. She was being offered to me as a plaything for the night. But when she looked me over, it was equally clear she did not care so long as it was with me. "Hai, Youta-sama," she said meekly.

He smiled at us both. "Enjoy one another. Return tomorrow evening, Hayate-san," Youta said to me, already turning away. "We will finish the details of our arrangement then."

I looked at the two-tailed cat demoness before me and flashed my most winsome smile. "What is your name?"

"I am Ishikawa Chikako," she said shyly.

"Daisuke Hayate."

"So, you are from...?" she asked hopefully, attempting mild conversation.

"The mountains up north and west of here."

"Oh. Do you have a place to stay? A hotel... or..."

I shook my head. "This is my first night in New Tokyo."

"Oh. Well..." She bit her bottom lip, her teeth giving the swell of flesh a playful tug.

I wrapped my arm around the nekomata's shoulders, and she leaned in. We walked past the hostess, who scowled at me. That one thought I was vermin – and in a sense she was not wrong. What was vermin after all, but a highly adaptive and opportunistic survivalist? And really, what was the opinion of one nekomata to me? I was hungry and beautiful, the night was mine to play with, and so was this woman.

I pondered how my life had changed in so dramatically short a time. After years of that static life with Kazuki, now I was jumping from one transient adventure to the next! I began this evening covered in filth fresh out of the sewers. Now I was a yōkai samurai in the service of a dragon daimyo. Talk about one *Hell* of a night! Man, it was *good* to be a great demon.

Chapter Eleven

Youta's Seven

hikako and I started banging as soon as we got in the door of her apartment. She closed the creaky old thing and pressed into me, and I found myself kissing her lustily, hands entwined in her sleek dark hair. We found our way into her tiny bedroom before I got between her legs, but only just. And for the next hour or so she screamed her pleasure as we traded positions all over that cramped space. I am not certain how we managed it, honestly.

And let me tell you that cat girls can *yell*! Imagine a female cat in heat yowling its head off outside the window in the middle of the night. I think she must have awoken the entire building. Unlike the prostitute, the nekomata was by far more expressive and intense in her passion, and it brought out the masculine animal in me.

After mutual consummation, we laid together in her single bed, a tiny little thing barely wide and long enough to accommodate her, let alone me. But we kitsune are cuddly creatures by nature, and so are most nekomata. Chikako was no exception. She pressed into my side, her leg and hip draped over mine. Her head was a comfortable weight against my chest while her warm fingers idly stroked my skin.

"You are so *white*," she said, marveling at me.

"I am shiroi kitsune. We *are* white."

"Does that mean there are more of you sexy white foxes lurking about?" she teased.

I shrugged. "Not that I've seen in this world. I have not seen another kitsune of any shade since..." I lapsed off and turned my face away. I was not about to explain.

"Oh." Her tone became slightly more serious. "So how long are you staying in New Tokyo, Hayate-sama?"

"I haven't a clue," I answered truthfully. "Possibly a long time. Maybe not long at all. It depends."

"On what?"

"This evening."

"Why?"

I shrugged again. "Because that is when I will know if I have a job or not."

"Oh! You are going to work for Youta-sama then?"

"Perhaps."

"You are *so* vague!" She sighed in exasperation. "You don't like to talk much about yourself, do you?" She pouted.

"Now wherever did you get that impression," I said with a mischievous grin. That made her smile a little.

"Something tells me you're incorrigible."

"Of course! I am a *fox*, after all."

"Yeah, that you are. A gorgeous kitsune," she sighed

dreamily and played with my hair, the strands drifting through her fingers. I rolled onto my side and snuggled into her. She rolled over and pressed her back into me. I wrapped my arm and tail around her sublime feminine shape. I liked the smell of her, the way her body curved, how lithe and flexible she was. And those two tails…

Ah, nekomata.

I dozed more than I slept at first, this being a new place and I did not know this woman. Her snores were rumbling purrs, something I was not used to. But I must have passed out, because just as the first light of dawn penetrated her blinds, I awoke with a terrible need to piss. I blamed the rice wine. I reluctantly left our warm little nest and found the bathroom just across the narrow hall. If I thought her bedroom was tiny, the toilet was smaller still. Space was a luxury in New Tokyo.

On my return from passing water, I found the nekomata hostess who had originally warned my waitress off me waiting for me in the hallway. She wore a thick, fluffy bathrobe and a scowl, her arms folded under her breasts. Her eyes were filled with loathing, and all of it was aimed at me.

"This is where she took you. I figured as much." She spoke to me as if I were vermin. It probably did not help that I was naked and reeked of sex pheromones.

"So?" I blinked at her, wondering if I should just shove the cat demoness out of my way to return to that warm bed and the pretty lady who was lying in it.

"You listen to me, fox. That's my baby sister you've got in there. If you hurt her –"

"You'll what?" I demanded.

"I'll kill you," she hissed, her ears flat to the sides.

I smirked. "Then do it!"

She did not move, her frown deepening. I had the favor of Lord Youta, and he had given Chikako to me. In this, the old ways applied. We were all subjects of our master. I did not fear this woman. Nekomata might be more powerful than the average bakeneko, but she was younger than I and less powerful. Nor did she have the posture of one who had been trained to combat. I was fairly confident I could cut her down, and I think she knew it, too.

"No?" I goaded her. "Not even one swipe?"

Man, if looks could kill! "*Don't* hurt her," she said again, sneering.

I had to give credit to her resolve, yet her opinion mattered little and less to me. I smiled serenely as she stalked back into her own tiny bedroom, the fur of her twin tails bristled out nearly as thick as my own, and both of them lashing in agitation.

I crept back into bed and snuggled Chikako. She murmured something dreamily, then awoke with a start and a short gasp. Perhaps she realized there was a strange man with her. Her sudden surge of adrenaline calmed down when she saw it was me and remembered the night before. "Oh, it's you. Hayate."

"It's me," I assured her. "Go back to sleep, beautiful." I kissed her temple and she closed her eyes with a small sigh. I drew the coverlet over us and felt warm, and good.

"CHIKAKO!" A VOICE SCREECHED.

I jolted awake.

"For fuck's sake, Chikako, wake *up*!"

Chikako's elder sister came bursting in already dressed for

work. She glowered at me in hot rage as soon as she saw me. I sat up and rubbed my eyes. It was only when I discovered I had bangs and over a foot less of hair that I remembered the night before in any detail. I frowned at the woman who had disturbed my sleep.

"What's wrong?" Chikako asked, clutching the blanket to her chest and nearly pulling it off me in the bargain.

"It's late afternoon for one thing!" And I saw it was true. But it must have been partially cloudy outside, for the golden sun came in waves of intermittent obscurity. "For another, we have to go in early."

"What? Why?"

"Check your phone, Chikako! Have you had it in Do Not Disturb all this time?"

"What's going on, Hiroko?" she asked, a hint of anxiety becoming evident.

"Just *do* it!"

With an exaggerated sigh of sibling irritation, Chikako pulled a clear, plastic, electronic device from her nightstand and began working it. I had no idea what it was or how it was done, but it lit up as she stared into it. Suddenly she exclaimed, "Shit! Boss wants us in there damn early! An *hour*? But why?"

"It doesn't matter why! Get your shit together! We gotta go! And get that damn fox out of here before we leave, too!" she called back, flouncing off down the hallway. "I won't have him stealing everything in our apartment while we're at work!"

"Hayate..." Chikako began apologetically.

"Do not fret. I, too, must go. I shall be there this evening." I stood up and gathered my clothes.

"Oh, yeah! That's right." She smiled dreamily as she watched me don my kimono.

As soon as I had myself together, Chikako showed me to the door. We walked past Hiroko shoving her wallet into her purse in the living room. The other cat demon continued to stare daggers of hate at me. I took my pretty nekomata's hands in mine and gave her a long, sensual kiss, ignoring her sister. If anything, I made it more erotic just to piss off Hiroko for annoying me.

"I will see you tonight, beautiful," I whispered loud enough to be overheard across the room. I glamoured my yōkai form into a mortal's Seeming and left.

With nowhere to go and nothing to do until The Cage opened, I cloaked myself in the appearance of a wealthy man and explored the In-Met. None the wiser that there was a demon in their midst, multitudes of people drifted by me going about their evening commute. No one paid me any heed. I was just another bland face among the herd of my favorite prey animal, and they were far too concerned with themselves, their electronic playthings, and looking at other attractive human beings.

At the edge of dusk, I went to the top of the tallest building in my immediate vicinity by way of warping myself up there. I uncloaked into my standard preferred form and stood rebelliously on the topmost point. From this precarious vantage I took my measure of the lay of the land. New Tokyo was *huge*. There seemed to be no end to it! The city simply went on and on well into the horizon, vast canyons of glittering buildings with streets like well-ordered riverbeds between.

I began to do some serious thinking as the sun steadily set

on that magnificent view. Who was I now? What was I becoming? How was I to survive and stay *me*? I did not really know the answer to any of those questions. But I knew what I did *not* want to be, some damn common yako bereft of all conscience. I asked myself what my boundaries were, which lines I must avoid crossing if at all possible.

Then and there I composed my new, personal code of ethics, the rules by which I, a former zenko, would live. Accordingly, the list itself formed into simple sentences I could reach for as a mantra if I felt myself losing control of my demonic nature. I told myself if I descended completely into that beast, Aiko and Kazuki died for nothing when they defended me. Most important of all, my new self-imposed discipline made me feel better, stronger, anchored to what I had been and wanted to be again.

When the sun fully descended below the city horizon, I lifted myself up into the darkening sky, relishing the wind. How long had it been since I had flown so high? I did not know. The lights of the city started to glow in neon splendor, hypnotically beautiful. The fierce wind whistled shrilly past my ears and whipped my hair. It was cold up here, but I did not mind. I was the White Wind that promised death with a cold bite. The demon I had become loved this new name and embraced it.

Shiiiroi Uiiindooo… it hissed breathily within, pleased. Even as I was imposing a regimen of moral ethics to contain it, the Demon Fox of my unbridled id had been doing some plotting of its own. I had come into direct opposition with myself.

I decided to feed before I headed to Youta's club. In that time-honored tradition of nogitsune, I disguised myself in a woman's form to lure my lecherous prey, a balding, middle-aged

154

man in a cheap suit with booze on his breath. But it was the monstrous Shiroi Uindo that manifested before his terrified eyes and stole his heart away in that dark alley. Let other yōkai eat indiscriminately if they must. I preferred the sinner.

I WENT IN THROUGH THE BACK DOOR OF THE CAGE ABOUT AN hour after nightfall. No one questioned my entrance or my right to be there. But expected or not, the stares and whispers of staff followed me through the hallway.

"Hayate-san," I heard a voice. I turned to see the daitengu from the night before. I smiled congenially.

"Shi-rou-san," I returned. That was the way I said his name, Shee-Rō, with a slight pause between the syllables. I meant it to be friendly, and it seemed to amuse him.

"You are being initiated tonight," he announced cheerfully.

"Am I?" I asked casually.

He smiled. "Hai. In front of everyone."

I blinked and my aplomb faltered. "*Every*one?"

Shirou laughed. "Oh, yes. Youta-sama has been waiting a long time for one like you to complete our number. So come, Master Fox. We must perform our kabuki theater this night. The masses require a show of strength and fearlessness."

"*Wonderful*," I drawled as I followed.

I was to wait in the wings until summoned. Before me were a black curtain and a flight of steps beyond it. I could not see anything else, but I heard excited murmurs from the throats of a multitude of demons out on the main floor. I thought all this seemed a bit much. I was only entering the service of this dragon lord as his loyal henchman. Why the big deal?

I soon found out.

Music, elegantly Asian and thrumming with war drums began, and all voices ceased at once. A minute later, I heard Youta's voice boom out as only a dragon's could, clearly heard above that theatrical music.

"Comrades! Many of us have waited for this night, some of you decades, others, centuries. I rejoice to tell you that your patience has been rewarded at last! Tonight, we begin our bid for the reclamation of New Tokyo!" The crowd roared. When they quieted down, Youta continued. "Fate has at last grant-ed our humble prayers. The kami themselves bless our cause! Now, we go into action! The final piece has stepped onto the board, and so tonight our war begins in earnest!"

A legion of demonic throats howled their excitement.

Wait – war? *What?* I scarcely had time to think when a woman with a wireless earpiece urged me to "Go!"

I climbed the short flight of stairs with all the stately grace and dignity I could muster, daisho proudly displayed on my hip. The lighting and holo-vids made it appear we were standing on the terrace of an ancient temple, pimped out demon-style. The 'sky' was an angry explosion of color, like that of a storm preparing to break at sunset. And the crowd! So many yōkai! All standing shoulder to shoulder! Every eye in the house was locked on me.

Holy shit!

That quick peripheral glance showed me that everyone in the audience was on the younger side for demon kind. Five hundred years of age or less on average. Ahead of me the other six stood upon the stage, each one wearing the mask and costume representing his or her respective breed of yōkai. They fanned out in an eye-pleasing arrangement behind Youta, who was the most impressive of us all. In shimmering garments, his golden hair a wild mane, the water dragon looked like an emperor standing in our midst.

I walked to my boss with my head held high, falling to my knees center stage directly in front of him. With my back facing the crowd, I drew my katana and laid it at his feet. Only then did I bow, pressing my forehead to the stage floor in full supplication to my new master.

"Hayate, formerly of the clan Daisuke, do you foreswear all oaths made to any other lord?"

"I do, Great One." I mean really, what else was I going to say?

"Will you take up my cause and serve with honor and supreme loyalty, to smite my enemies and make my will known wherever you are sent?"

"Hai, Youta-sama."

Around my shoulders he draped a white fur hanten, a winter kimono. This one was like wearing a soft, fluffy coat that matched my hair and tail. Over my head he drew down a terrifying kitsunenomen, a white fox mask with red markings, black stylized eyes and, in the case of this one, a long vulpine snout with teeth bared down the length of the muzzle.

"Rise, Hayate, nogitsune, and be counted as a valued member among my sworn elite, White Wind of Youta clan. When I send *you* forth, my enemies will feel your bite and your claws!"

I sheathed my katana, stood, and took my place with the others. A spot was opened beside Shirou in his long-nosed tengu mask. There was a wind machine, apparently, and it gusted now so that our hair would blow dramatically to the side. It seemed ridiculous, but the mob below went wild for it!

In that crowd I caught sight of my sweet nekomata beauty, her eyes wide with horror as they locked onto me standing up there in my new costume. Ah, well. We did have one good night together. Too bad. She was fun.

"Together, you are Seven," Youta told us, holding up an open palm. "Under my direction, we act as One and are unstoppable." He closed his fist and turned to face his demon horde.

"Too long has the old Dragon ruled over Edo. Hiroshi scarce understands New Tokyo. The Dragon would have you starve and tell you only the fittest, the oldest should survive. I say that it is foolish to pit us against one another for limited resources! Or risk discovery as more yōkai are drawn to our city for survival! The old Dragon would cling to the past until we all die! I say unto you – death to Hiroshi! Death to the old regime! New Tokyo is *ours*!"

And what would you know? The crowd chanted that shit right back at him. "Death to Hiroshi! Death to the old regime! New Tokyo is ours!" Then the floor exploded in roars and applause. My eyes were wide in mild horror and I was glad of the mask that hid my face.

Fuck me! What have I gotten myself into? I thought as thousands of angry demons cheered. All but two nekomata, one of which I knew rather intimately. Chikako gazed at me in despair, while her sister scowled. Obviously, she did not really care all that much about the war effort.

After the ceremony, we Seven exited stage left and were pulled into Youta-sama's private sanctum, decorated in modest wealth and beauty. We sat around a long table with the dragon at its head, removing our masks and setting them before us. I felt like I had just joined a league of super villains. When Youta called out our code names, I knew I had.

He looked at each of us in turn around the table, starting with the tanuki. "Dead Eye. Blue Thunder," that was the oni. "Black Claw," the demon bear, "Cold Fury," our yuki onna. "Crimson Blade," the crow tengu, "Fire Fist," the monkey demon. "And White Wind." He favored me with a paternal smile. "You are the elite among yōkai, my chosen warriors, great demons all seven. Whatever quarrels between you or your species, they do not exist here." He fixed the tanuki with a long, hard stare. The raccoon dog stared back, agitated, but he dropped his eyes to the table first, although not without a quick angry glance at the mask set before me.

"Tomorrow night we make the first strike," Lord Youta told us. "I expect you to obey my commands implicitly." He looked long and hard at each of us, weighing and assessing our strengths, weaknesses, and, in my case, loyalty. I could tell Youta was not entirely confident of me yet, not that I blamed him given the reputation of my kind. So when he gave his orders, I knew I would be tested. And I was right.

"Hayate, Takeshi, Shirou, and Jūro will go to the dark port in the Korean Sector. A rare shipment of arms equipped with the latest technology is coming in for the upper echelon of the Yakuza. Let them put that shipment on a transport and drive at least four kilometers away from the warehouse. You will stop that transport and commandeer it by treachery and force. Under the kitsune's illusion spells, you will then drive to the Western Sector into an underground garage. There we will move the weapons onto three fresh transports for distribution to our own armories."

We four bowed our heads in assent.

"Fuyuko, Taro, and Katashi, you three will go deep into our Sector of the Sprawl to The Laundromat. It is there the weapons are supposed to be transported first before they are 'cleaned' and distributed up the chain. I want you to slay everyone in that place. Leave nothing breathing, not even a rat."

Youta nodded at the raccoon dog and continued. "Furthermore, I want you to use the tanuki's illusion magic to make it appear the members from one of the Chinese Sector gangs stole the guns and made the hit... at least on the surface. I want you to drag their overseer into the shadows so he disappears forever. Leave this behind, as if accidentally dropped." It was a traceless digi-cred stick.

"In Hiroshi's mind this will seem an inside job. I want Hiroshi to feel steadily under siege by his own before he realizes this turf war has far wider implications than simple greed."

For avarice could be understood, bartered with, made an example of. Ah, but the youthful zealotry of revolutionary idealism? That was another, many-headed dragon, one far harder to slay.

Our master briefed each team the individual details of our missions so we would be independent and ignorant of the specifics of the full plan. It was best that way if one of us got caught or was a traitor. The tanuki glared at me often and well throughout, for in his head I could be nothing else. I resolved to do the most flawless job possible just to stick it to that bastard.

When our orders were fully given, we were released. We stowed our costumes and masks neatly in our secret locker room hidden behind a false wall. The facility came complete with a shower area for washing off blood and evidence, a nice touch.

"Are you ready for this, Hayate-san?" Shirou asked me as we moved toward the door. I nodded, but deep inside I wondered if I really was. This was not just a revolution of ideas, but a full-scale civil war for dominance of the largest megapolis in the world! This was beyond anything I could have imagined when I snuck in a little over twenty-four hours ago.

Yet when I thought of my long walk to get here, of the fantastic cityscape I had just viewed from the sky above New Tokyo, and the rich hunting grounds? Not to mention the wondrous technology to learn and all the new things to know? The opulence of a penthouse suite like André's in comparison to Chikako's tiny, overpriced space? I knew I could do this. Hell, I *wanted* this. I would gladly steal and kill for a slice of this pie.

"Hai, Shi-rou-san," I said boldly, my ears perking upright in my resolve. "I am."

My team captain nodded. "All right. Tomorrow night then." And that was that.

By then I was on the upper deck that overlooked the main floor. The huge room was restored to its typical nightclub appearance, no different from last night. Using my illusions to appear in a sleek suit, I decided to explore my new turf. I glided down the metal grate steps to the floor and came face to face with Chikako. The beautiful cat girl stared at me with wide eyes. "You... you're..."

"I am." I saw no sense in lying to her about it. I was a thug.

"Iiroko was right!" She looked heartbroken.

Why the fuck do I care? I asked myself.

"Nogitsune," she said, her face stricken. But really... what else did she *think* I was? No fox would be remotely near a place like this if it was not yōkai! Her big amber-gold cat's eyes shone large, her triangular ears angled back in agitation. "I have heard stories…"

"I know," I told her, imploring her to see I was not entirely twisted, that there was something decent left inside of me. "I like you, Chikako. I enjoyed last night very much. But I –"

She threw her arms around my neck, startling me silent. I embraced her back gently, confused. I had expected her to tell me to shove off. I was not braced for the opposite. Somehow, for whatever reason, this woman accepted me. And she was hot, too.

Hiroko glared in sharp disapproval. I narrowed my eyes at the hostess and snuggled Chikako, resting my chin on top of her head. Hiroko's gaze turned blacker still. I might have gloated a little.

My lover was not let out from work early to entertain me that night, so I lingered up on deck with the others until her shift was done. To be honest, it was terribly dull. But from that night forward I was one of Youta's Seven. Incidentally, that was also the night the Ayakashi War for New Tokyo began. The next saw shedding of first blood.

Chapter Twelve

The Revolution Begins

The Korean Sector of The Sprawl was a dark and dismal place. The Japanese never had any love for Koreans, or vice versa, and that had not changed by the twenty-second century. Most of this district was impoverished and heavily industrialized. It showed here in the dilapidated, toxic wharf that was the entrance to high-end illegal trade in New Tokyo.

The cameras did not work so well along the waterfront, where warehouses and factories loomed silent and still in the night. It was put out that radioactive hot spots or gang sabotage were to blame for the lack of surveillance, but that was a smokescreen. This squalid port was where the ultra-wealthy at the highest levels of governance concluded their most obscure transactions. It was dark on purpose.

I crouched on an adjacent rooftop, watching as the boat bearing the ordinance slowly drifted into harbor. Guns were illegal for the average citizen of New Tokyo. Only certain security forces, police, and upper tier Yakuza had them. Advanced artillery and incendiary devices were supposed to be exclusively in the arsenals of the government.

Armed men waited below with the transport truck. A representative of The Dragon was on stand-by, a normal procedure for such a sensitive shipment. If they had bothered to scout the area at all, they might have realized they were compromised. Alas, it seemed they had grown indolent as time went on and no one questioned the regime. This was simply business as usual.

Jūro the monkey demon stood beside me. He was so short he scarcely needed to hunker down. The sarugami and I did not speak to one another from our observation point. Oh, he had been a little chatterbox on his way here.

"Fellow trickster, hey? Don't get ideas! Fried me good the other night, Fox. I still smell like burnt hair. Owe you for that. Ooooh! Shiny!" he said in reference to a store we passed with some bauble in the window. "I should steal that!"

"Shut it, irritant," Takeshi told Jūro in that great rumbling voice.

Takeshi was the huge blue oni, a horned and tusked ogre whose malevolent species was well known throughout China and Japan. I think Takeshi's muscles had muscles, and he was over seven feet of smash and kill. His wild hair appeared to be dyed a thick, shiny blue-black, but it was completely natural. In his full yōkai form he was like a giant muscle-bound blueberry with horns and fangs. When stuffed inside a business suit, the buttons looked like they would pop off and ricochet in every direction at his slightest movement.

And yet, Takeshi would surprise you. A lumbering ogre

he might be, but he had an expansive vocabulary and was intensely well-read with a deep love of history and literature. He was a whiz at Sudoku. Oh, and he had a collection of delicate china teacups, about which Jūro ragged him endlessly. I mean seriously, though. Who *knew*?

He stood motionless across the way on the metal catwalk of an old smelting factory, wearing a horrific oni mask, his huge iron kanabo in that gigantic paw of his. Somewhere nearby but unseen was Shirou. He wore a red tengu mask, the front of his hair bound up in an elegant top knot, the rest flowing free. In black kimono and hakama, he was invisible in the night.

The waiting was the hardest. For one thing, this port stank like rotten fish and floating dead human bodies, along with raw sewage and putrefying garbage. We could all smell it, so it was useless to complain. Except Jūro, that is. The little drama queen kept putting his hand over the mouth of his mask as if that could stop him from breathing in the foul air.

As soon as the boat docked, the guns were offloaded. Men and machines moved efficiently, while untraceable digi-creds were scanned from one shell account into another. Just another night in the dark port under The Dragon's rule. When the crates were all loaded onto the back of the heavy industrial transport, the vehicle lifted, hovered, and slowly drifted out to the street with an electric hum.

That was our cue. I nodded to the other two on the factory scaffold and vanished into thin air. I apparated low in the sky seven blocks away under a Seeming of invisibility and fried the lights and the cams in a burst of lightning. I learned that trick from watching André and it stood me in good stead for years.

As soon as I heard the transport's approach, I transformed

into the semblance of a beautiful young woman dressed in immodest clothing. Short pleather skirt, torn fishnet stockings, studded heeled boots, and a tight top that revealed a whole lot of bulging breasts. The Korean Sector had one hell of an underground club scene in the warehouse district. It was here that designer drugs and snuff-flick holo-vids usually circulated among a disheartened and angry youth population.

I acted like I was terribly hurt, possibly stabbed, holding my left side. It was not really that unusual in this quadrant of The Sprawl, where violence was commonplace. I stumbled and fell in the middle of the road directly in front of the approaching vehicle. They slowed and stopped very close, as if the driver contemplated riding over me. Most likely, he had.

I heard a voice projected from a loudspeaker. "Ma'am, get out of the road."

I flipped over so they could get a better look at me, my clothes and skin covered in blood. I pretended to be writhing in agony with a few anguished cries for effect.

"We're *not* riding over her," I heard as the door was opened. "Just give me a minute!" And one of the men got out. The guard walked over and knelt down beside me. I looked up at him with fear and desperation painted on my face, pretending I could scarce speak. "I do not understand…" He leaned down to hear me better, the poor idiot. His pupils dilated slightly as his eyes flicked unconsciously to my breasts.

I grabbed him and kissed him. At first his lips melted against my own. But as I began the energy transfer, his eyes opened wide in confusion. He tried to pull away, but I held him to me in an iron grip.

I heard the others go into action around me. The driver was

pulled from his vehicle roughly. He grunted as he was beaten to a pulp by the oni's iron cudgel. There were voices from the guards in the back, turned to shouts, then swiftly to silence.

When I stood up, the man I had accosted was a mummified husk of his former self. I left him on the road and transformed back into the traditionally dressed version of myself. The tengu walked over and looked down at my kill

"Effective," Shirou said, his voice hollow behind his long-nosed mask. "Gross, but effective."

Takeshi grunted, slinging his blood and gore encrusted cudgel over his shoulder. Behind him several dead guards littered the street, their limbs splayed at awkward angles and their skulls bashed in. Blood and brains were splattered everywhere.

"Ewwww! That is *so* nasty, Fox!" Jūro said.

I shrugged. "Get in the damn transport."

"Nah," the sarugami's grin was apparent in his voice. "I'm joining you up top."

"Wonderful," I drawled. I burned my victim's corpse into ash in a blaze of kitsunebi and pulled out a handful of green leaves from inside my sleeve. I placed a broadleaf on each of my compatriots' heads.

"What's this?" Jūro asked, frowning.

"Your disguise," I said, and I made Shirou and Takeshi look like guards with an illusion spell. Jūro and I transformed into the semblance of random goons for a generic Chinese Sector gang, as Youta instructed me. I did it just in time, too. No sooner had I sealed the spell than the lights from another transport turned down our street.

"Shit!" Takeshi said. "Go!" He dove into the passenger side of the transport, which rocked under his weight. Meanwhile

Jūro climbed and I flew to the top. The crow got behind the driver's console and the electric hum started as those lights drew closer, first at a steady pace, then faster.

I will say this for Shirou, that tengu could drive! He throttled the power and the heavy transport gained speed as warehouses flashed by.

The other transport was loaded with men and it did not bear the weight of cargo or an oni like ours did. The big metal truck sped towards us, swiftly closing the distance. There were pops and random bursts of light as guards in heavy gear fired on us from the sides and roof of their transport. Jūro and I ducked flat as bullets whizzed overhead.

"Awww, hell!" Jūro shouted. The other transport lunged so close it nearly crashed into us! Armed security jumped the gap and landed onto the roof of our vehicle.

There was no time to think. I was up in a flash, slamming the heel of my palm into the closest man's jaw in an upward sweep. I turned him just as I heard the pops again, and felt the vibration of impact through his body. I guessed they had armor piercing rounds, because the security agent slumped lifeless against me. I grabbed his arm in a lock and whirled the corpse into another guard, who vanished with a scream. I tossed the dead body out into the empty air to join him. Both disappeared into the night

Another man made to strike me, using his gun as a blunt weapon. I dodged right, then left before taking it from him when he made to bring it down on my head. He tried to pull it out of my grip, but he was only human. I ripped the gun out of his hands and smashed the butt end into his face. There was a sickening crunch as his nose broke and his eye protection splintered. He cried out, but one kick to the solar plexus knocked him off onto the windshield of the enemy transport. Then he slid off and disappeared into the street, too.

Jūro jumped onto the shoulders of another security merc and ripped the man's face off. I mean that literally in the truest sense. First, he bit the human's nose off and gouged his eyes, then tore out his lower jaw. And the monkey had the gall to call *me* nasty! Tchk...

And yet I felt nothing at all upon witnessing it. No empathy or sympathy, no pang of compassion or regret. I simply did not care.

As another guard trained his gun on the sarugami, I disemboweled him with my katana. He lay where he fell... until Shirou banked a hard left down a cross street. The guard's body flew off to the side and I nearly went flying with it! I flung myself down, hard, sliding until I found a hand grip. I kept a hold on old Kazuki's katana, but sadly I lost the gun.

The other transport arced wide and nearly slammed into a building, but it did not lose us. The driver righted its trajectory and it sped back onto our ass again. Fortunately, the motion did succeed in flinging two of *their* men off, which I thought most fortunate. One hit the side of a concrete wall, and I have to admit I found the crunch his body made on impact to be rather satisfying.

"Pffft - fuck this shit!" Jūro shouted as he leapt from our transport onto the other. "Come on, Fox! Time to take the fight to them!"

I quite agreed and followed, landing lightly beside the monkey demon. He had apparently seized a gun in the last struggle. Jūro threw down a small explosive ball that tore a hole into the top of the enemy transport. The metal boomed loud and hollowly. The transport shook and veered with a sickening lurch. Cries of surprise and coughing within were cut short by the gun burst Jūro fired down into them.

We waited a moment for the smoke to clear, prepared to do for the drivers next. But then there was a huge, hollow *thunk*, followed by another, and another, each repetition growing louder as whatever it was drew closer. A large, black, clawed thing thumped over the back side of the damn truck as something big and ugly climbed up, followed by a second claw-thing. Metal screeched.

What in the hell is this? Jūro and I both stared as a black, grinning nightmare with bull's horns and rows of sharp teeth popped up. It left powerful rents into the metal when it pulled its monstrous bulk up and over the side to join us. The body was almost spider-like, but its head was distinctly bovine.

"Ushi oni!" I yelled to the sarugami, who grunted and nodded grimly. Either the transport picked up this misbegotten thing on the waterfront, or it was in the service of The Dragon Hiroshi.

Either way, this was a dangerous yōkai. Often found by the sea, an ushi oni was known to rampage on towns for food, spreading disease and cursing the inhabitants who were not consumed by its relentless hunger. Its usual environment was on the western coast of Japan. But thanks to rising sea levels and pollutants, along with the decimation of the human population from disaster and disease, the ushi oni had begun to migrate.

This one licked its lips with its tongue as it looked at Jūro and me. It grinned and scuttled forward on eight legs, bellowing its bloodlust. Jūro unleashed a torrent of bullets, but they had little effect on it. He cursed as the gun emptied and threw the weapon at the beast, which glanced off its back. The sarugami then aimed a few of his explosive balls at it, but the thing lunged forward and the explosions went off in the air behind the transport.

I hacked off its foreleg at the joint with my blade, and that was enough to give it momentary pause. It roared in defiance and lifted its front limbs in aggression at me like a spider. I, however, never stopped moving. With adrenaline coursing through my veins, I hacked another leg off on the same side, destroying the ushi oni's balance. It fell hard onto its left side with a thump.

I hazarded a quick glance over my shoulder and saw that there was a slight increase in the distance between this vehicle and our stolen transport. If we did not get off this thing soon, we would be left behind. But we did not dare return to our payload until this transport was disabled.

"I'll take this thing, you get the dicks in the cab," I shouted to Jūro.

"Sounds great! Good luck, asshole!" Then he was gone.

The bovine-spider yōkai looked at me with pure hate. "Come on!" I challenged over the roar of the wind and the hum of the electric engines.

It crawled forward faster than I would have believed for its two missing legs. I held my ground. It breathed in deep, the better to blast me with its poisoned breath, one of the ushi oni's worst natural weapons. I called to the wind that was my birthright and blew that stinking cloud of acidic vapor away from me while I swung my katana. I cleaved the head from its body and kicked the remains out into the street below.

The transport lurched forward, and again I nearly lost my balance. I ran to the edge of the truck and did a flying leap back onto the one Shirou was driving – in the nick of time, too! The empty transport swerved recklessly. There was a crash of glass, and then Jūro leapt from the nose of the thing onto the back of our truck. He threw a few more explosives into the open windshield of the enemy cab. The transport veered off and crashed hard into the side of a building, blowing up spectacularly.

Now that we lost our pursuit, Jūro used a slingshot to kill off the streetlights and visible cams. I concentrated on my next illusion spell and made our vehicle look like a typical food transport truck. Shirou slowed as if we were merely on a typical night delivery drive. From there we obeyed the traffic laws so as not to attract attention.

Fifteen minutes later, Shirou pulled into an underground garage, the loading bay doors shutting us off from the outside world. I uncloaked us from my illusions and breathed a short sigh of relief. Jūro and I leapt down. The tengu and the oni climbed out of the front cab.

"*That* was *in-sane*!" Jūro exclaimed with a whoop.

I grinned and lifted my fox mask to the side of my head. We all stood together watching Youta's servitor demons offload the merchandise. I decided if this was the way my nights were going to be from now on, I was in for one hell of a gig!

"Think they knew we were coming?" Takeshi asked the tengu.

"No," Shirou answered quietly. "This was standard back up, extra insurance for the amount of weapons, I think. Why they did not follow right away and caught up with us after…" He shrugged. Suddenly everyone turned to stare at me.

I stared back. "What? You can look at me if you want, but I don't know shit about your Metropoplex." Boy, if that was not the total truth!

Shirou nodded. "The kitsune did not betray us."

Takeshi grunted.

"Doesn't mean he won't," Jūro said.

"Not tonight." They all glowered at me. "It was a *joke!*" I crossed my arms and turned my face up to the ceiling in mock petulance. "A fox gets no love, I swear."

"Who said foxes deserve love?" the monkey demon asked sarcastically.

The lesser yōkai ignored us, transferring the payday onto two separate vehicles, one marked as a moving truck and the other meant for delivering bread. They paid us no heed, pretended as if we were not there.

"Hey, I wonder how the other team did," Jūro said out of the blue.

AS IT TURNED OUT, THE OTHER TEAM'S EFFORTS WENT OFF WITHout a hitch. Lucky them. Katashi swore up and down I must have leaked information when we reported our fiasco, but Youta would not hear of it.

"That is standard practice. Of course there was backup for so sensitive a shipment, but they were likely delayed. Or they were tracking the vehicle and went to investigate when it stopped. That is all. Be glad of the shirogitsune tonight. His spells of deceit covered our tracks and maintained the illusion of an inside job aided by the Chinese syndicate. Otherwise *you* would have been sent to the Korean Sector in his stead."

That shut the tanuki up.

"For the next several nights, we will let Hiroshi stew on what happened to his cargo. He will run after the gangs in the Chinese Sector," the water dragon continued. "If we are fortunate, he will torture and slay a few of his own, thereby taking more swords off the street and doing some of our work for us. Now go."

I fell in line to file out with the others.

"Hayate, a word first?"

I stopped and stayed where I was. "Hai, Youta-sama." I hoped I was not in trouble.

I stood in the middle of his office while he studied me intently. I refused to flinch and stared straight ahead. The dragon waited until the door shut and we were alone.

Youta did not mince words. "You did a job the other night for an independent contractor."

Was that what we were calling it? "Hai, Youta-sama."

"A tad sloppy, kitsune. You left your telltale kills behind, as well as the cam footage."

I stiffened and swallowed. *Oh, shit!*

I was still very new to this world. Hell, I was new to being a yōkai! I really did not have the first clue what I was doing. I was learning as fast as I could since my survival depended on it, but I had literally jumped into this life baptism by fire!

"I spoke with he who employed you. I know the immediate circumstances through which you came into this city, and the obligation you were required to pay off. But you should know your presence in New Tokyo has not gone unremarked. Takahashi had influence with Hiroshi and the oligarchic council. The Dragon is aware a nogitsune is lurking somewhere in his megapolis."

My ears pinned back, my tail tight to my hind. "Hai, You-ta-sama," I said gravely. I felt terribly embarrassed and angry with myself.

"We all make mistakes, Hayate-kun. It is in how we recover from them that proves our mettle. I suggest you do more than change your hair color and skin tone when abroad if you wish to remain anonymous on the street. You are an intelligent yōkai, Hayate. Hiroshi is keeping your existence and the precise nature of Takahashi's death quiet for now. The official word is that Takahashi died of a heart attack in his office."

Youta smiled. It was not completely untrue. I had attacked Takahashi's heart on a night he was working late. "But you should know Hiroshi is hunting for you, and rather desperately, I might add. Will you let him catch you, Wild Fox?"

"Hell no, Youta-sama!" I meant it to the core of my being.

The water dragon smiled again. "I thought not. You may go."

I bowed and took my leave.

I had gotten back late, but Chikako apparently waited for me after her shift. She smiled when she saw me, relieved that I survived whatever task I had been sent to perform for our boss.

"I'm so glad you're back! I was worried. Did everything go well?"

I smiled confidently. "Yes," I lied before I let her take me home.

Chapter Thirteen

Debts & Obligations

A few final strokes and gasps of shuddering pleasure, and Chikako rolled off me to lay by my side. She panted as she looked up at the dingy ceiling of my apartment, a garage that had been converted into a one room living space. I had divided it with shoji screens and laid down tatami mats, but my furniture was rather sparse. There was always a quiet echo here because of it.

It was the height of summer, and in spite of my little air-cooling unit, it was stuffy in my place. The temperature was terrible outside, where the noon zenith passed forty-eight degrees Celsius, or one-hundred-twenty degrees Fahrenheit. Today was five degrees cooler than yesterday. On account of the terrible heat waves that baked the city, Chikako began spending more time at my den, where the concrete walls and ground level floor kept the worst of summer at bay. I had a feeling this place would be freezing come winter.

My phone/device/thing buzzed on the floor beside my futon and I groped for it. I was expecting to be told to come into the Ori before my next assignment, but no. This was something else. I smiled.

At last.

"I am so sorry, sweetheart, I have to go out in an hour," I told my girlfriend, for that was what Chika was to me, more or less. We did not really do much besides hang out and have sex, but I supposed that qualified.

"*Another* job?"

"Hai." This evening I was being sent to perform a nice, quiet assassination on a rival yōkai gang leader. He was loyal to Hiroshi and that meant he had to die. But I had another task to perform first, one that was rather personal, an obligation I needed to fulfill.

"That's not fair. Youta-sama runs you way too much," she said with a pout.

I shrugged. "If he wants the job done right..."

I had become proficient at the art of death since the spring. My early foibles in New Tokyo *had* been sloppy, as Youta informed me. I endeavored to become more circumspect, stealthy, Shiroi Uindo in truth. Aside from hunting, I slew as my daimyo wished. If my Lord wanted a kill to look like a suicide, I did that. If he wanted a professional human hit, I did that, too. More rarely, Youta would send me to kill as a yako, but when he did, I ripped the heart from my prey and relished the taste of hot blood on my tongue. Those were the ones I left as calling cards for Hiroshi, per my boss's instruction.

In a short time, I had become a master of murder. I could have taken a mannequin apart with the same deliberate

callousness I did my victims. Whatever empathy I once possessed as a zenko, it had long since been overcome by the darkness of my yako nature. The art of blood and death was my
domain.

Chikako was spared the gruesome details of my work. For
all that she was a cat yōkai, in many respects she was an innocent. She did not need to know how cold-blooded I really
was. The face I showed her was the cavalier lover with a grin
and a quip. And if Hiroko still hated me and knew me for the
monster I was, Chikako remained willfully ignorant. I wanted
to keep her that way to protect us both.

"Even so! He sends you out far more than the others. I
worry about you, Hayate."

"I promise I will be fine," I assured her. "I know what I
am doing."

"If you say so…" My nekomata lover sighed and traced
her fingers over the musculature of my chest. "Can I come
over later after my shift? That is, if you can spare a night from
your holo-vid studies…?"

If I was not doing Youta's bidding or spending time with
Chikako, I was studying. No subject was left untouched. Within days of entering his employ, Youta had me learning a variety of languages, including multiple variations of Chinese, as
well as Korean, French, and English. That way I could know
what was being said by anyone in New Tokyo without the need
for dubious third-party translation. To make certain I did not
slack, certain servitor demons would only speak and respond
to me in those specific languages. It was a pain in the ass, but
it made me learn fast.

I also devoured texts on history, technology, science, math

– anything and everything! I wanted to know it all! No subject was too obscure. I had even learned how to drive and handle a transport the way Shirou did.

"So, if you're not caught up in your damn books..." she trailed off again.

"I will happily spend my night *in you*." I grinned wickedly.

She slapped my shoulder. "You're awful!"

I laughed. "*Hai!*" I seized her and kissed her. Chikako melted against me.

"I want this to be over," she said, meaning the war. I think she had this foolish notion that once we won, *if* we won, I would take her as my wife, and she could live a life of luxury by the side of the new Dragon's right hand. I had no such intentions, of course. I was a young fox and wanted to enjoy my freedom. I did not cheat on Chikako, as that was one of the tenets of my spurious Code, yet I had no plan that we should stay together forever, either.

But those concerns were for the future. For now, we simply stole what time was available to us and I enjoyed living in the moment. Nearly every night was a dance with death, so in those days I embraced life. For me, that meant having fun, which was all about hunting, slaughter, and sex.

"I know you do, sweetheart. One day it will be." I did not elaborate that we might lose.

Reckless I might be by nature, but I was also careful lest all I was working for be stripped away. I had come to love my gadgets, my crummy apartment, this strange new life. This city was a neon jungle filled with twilight shadows, and if it was noisy with humans and the ever-present hums and high-pitched whines of the electric grid, it was also now my home.

Chikako kissed me and left the bed, and I watched with hungry eyes as her nude, slender body sauntered off to my bathroom. When the door shut, I got up, pulled on a pair of shorts, and put on water for tea. While I waited for it to boil, I did a few chin-ups on my salmon ladder in the corner reserved for my workout equipment. Exercise was another thing I did every day, to keep myself strong and sharp. I did a full bar jump up the ladder rung by rung, and back down again.

Chikako came out and whistled appreciatively at me, which earned her a devious smile before I let go of the bar and jumped the short distance to the floor.

"*Very* nice! I need to come over and watch you do that more often." She purred. "Sure you have to go out in an hour?" she asked me coyly. I could smell her arousal. She thrust her chest forward and her ass backward, her tails lifting in that tell-tale sign I had come to know so well.

"I do, but I can spare a few minutes for you." I grinned wickedly and drew her to me as she came within arm's reach.

"A few minutes, huh?"

"Something like that." I never did heed the kettle as we tried a variety of positions on my bench. Her undulating screams in rising tonalities pretty much drowned out the keening whistle anyway.

FORTY MINUTES AND A QUICK SHOWER LATER, I WAS DRESSED IN A light grey suit under the guise of an average businessman. The humans I walked past were miserable in the sweltering heat. While I cannot say I found it pleasant, I was not as bothered by the temperature as they were. However, my illusion demanded I pretend otherwise. Nothing quite says 'demon in disguise' as a man who does not sweat. I frequently mopped at my brow with a linen cloth and affected an expression of distress, mutually reflected in the countenance of every human I passed.

I had become a master of disguise and an actor *par excellence* in the past few months. Not even my landlord knew what I truly looked like, and I had rigged the cam on a loop to ensure my privacy. Mindful of the facial recognition software, I never assumed my true appearance on the street, or anywhere unless it was inside the club or my den.

When I made my kills as Shiroi Uindo, I donned the mask Youta gave me and a white summer yukata with matching hakama, the better to show the blood spatter of my victims when I hewed into them. My yako heart-taking assassinations were done deliberately and at random intervals, designed to throw Hiroshi off balance. I heard it was giving the Dragon fits to know a nogitsune was stalking his town, operating silently in the employ of a secret enemy wearing a friendly guise. In true kitsune fashion, I could be anyone, anywhere, at any time.

I was frankly surprised none of the yōkai from The Cage had turned me in. I was a valuable commodity, after all. Yet they all seemed committed to the cause. Unlike humans, who were strongest in their youth, a yōkai's strength and powers increase with age. So 'survival of the fittest' meant the Old Order, leaving those who were younger, say five centuries or less, at a distinct disadvantage. And as more and more country and sea yōkai infiltrated, the older generations were not inclined to any sympathy for our plight – not that demons have much in the way of compassion to begin with. The supernatural world depended on the system of debt and obligation to stay civil, not kindness or mercy.

181

During the time that the seven of us worked together, we built up cycles of obligation between us. Such comes with saving one another's lives, which was unavoidable in our line of work. In time, the concept of I-owe-you-tit-for-tat blurred. Like a beetle tethered to a screw, we became firmly bound to one another. Our combined existence depended upon it.

But on this particular afternoon, I had a debt of my own to settle. The first one I originally incurred upon entering New Tokyo. Back in early June I called upon one of Youta's servitors to aid me in a personal favor and make the necessary arrangements. This particular demon was a lawyer in Youta's employ, and so at my disposal upon request. Being one of The Seven had its perks. I outlined the specifics of what I needed, and he implemented everything flawlessly. Only when I was certain the requirements properly met my conditions did I send him forth to conclude the transaction.

Except that the recipients had been difficult to locate. Until today, that is.

The lawyer sent my communication device a message as soon as he found she who would receive my most generous offer, and he kept me updated. In truth, I was probably being a bit *too* kind. Yet I had done well for myself in this city. I made a goodly sum working for Youta, most of which I saved as any fox would, burying my gains for future use.

I had already scoped out the small apartment dwelling the lawyer had chosen. I saw it now as I journeyed deeper into The Sprawl. It was a modest tenement in the lower mid-Japanese Sector, but there were far worse neighborhoods to live in. The tiny two-bedroom was less than three blocks from the local school. It was not the best apartment in The Sprawl, but it was adequate.

I went into the building, nodding at the front desk man behind a huge plate window. He buzzed me into the security door, and I went straight down the hall. I ducked down a side corridor and into the cool arms of the waiting darkness. I emerged out of the shadows in the human glamour of my true self, adjusting my silk tie. The ears and tail remained hidden behind a Seeming when I emerged, but I left my eyes, fangs and claws visible. The cameras had not yet come online and I needed to do this as *me*, more or less.

The small family standing in a dazed clump between the kitchen and the living room looked up at me in shock. I smiled when I saw Izumi, her brother, and her mother in the modestly furnished room, furniture being one of the amenities I requested in advance. The three of them looked and smelled as rank as I remembered. So much for hoping they had already been D-Konned. Ah well. I made a point not to wrinkle my nose.

"Ah, Izumi," I said pleasantly. "And Nobu." I was fairly certain I recalled their names correctly. The children stared at me with open mouths. For that matter, so did their mother.

They had to be bribed with food to come out of their hole to this place, skittish as they were – and *not* without good reason. No doubt the mother was afraid they were being led to some form of human trafficking. Sadly, that kind of thing happened. The yōkai lawyer found them begging in the trans-rail port where I said they would be, but it had taken a few weeks to locate them. It was not every day they begged topside, and they moved from station to station. Today, however, they had surfaced at last, starving worse than when I had last seen them. They were not going to survive down there much longer.

"You!" the girl exclaimed, astonished.

"Yes," I told her.

"It's the fox man!" Nobu said excitedly.

"That's *kitsune* to you," I informed him snobbishly.

"I don't understand. What is this?" their mother asked, confused and suspicious. "Why are you doing this?"

"To repay your daughter my favor owed, of course." I turned to the girl. "Izumi, you directed me out of that nasty hole. More to the point, you set me on the path to the surface and a better life. By the Law of Obligation, I owe you. This, then, is the repayment of my debt. From this day forward, you no longer need sleep in the sewers. As you could not aid me once you pointed the way out, you will have to work to remain topside. But if you are strong and persevere, you can stay out of that pit and make something of yourself in the Metropoplex."

"You mean, we don't have to go back below?" Izumi asked hopefully, her eyes filling with tears of gratitude.

"No, you do not have to go back," I told her. "I did all this specifically for *you*, Izumi-chan." I smiled sincerely.

"For *me*?" She stared open-mouthed.

"I have already arranged tutors to get Izumi and Nobu up to speed," I addressed their mother. "Then they may attend the local school. The one here in the Japanese Sector of The Sprawl is not too bad and within reasonable walking distance. The lawyer will see them enrolled as soon as they are properly ready to join their class."

"We're going to school?" Nobu asked. He brightened. "Oh, Izumi! We're going to school! Just like we pretended! We're going to *school*!" He jumped up and down screaming this until his mother put a gentle hand on the top of his head and quieted him. Only then did I continue.

"As for you, woman," I did not know her name, "the lawyer will give you the address of the house you will clean to make your rent. The first six months are paid in advance including utilities, but thereafter you must keep yourself here. It is not the best job, nor is this," I gestured to the living space around us, "the best home, but it is affordable and beats those tunnels a hundredfold. You all have a modest ensemble of clothes in your respective bedrooms to begin, and I hope the sizes shan't be too far off. Izumi and Nobu will have to share a room, but they have their own beds to sleep in. Likewise, you now have a month's supply of groceries to get you started. Your tap already has a water filter on it.

"In short, I am offering you a way out, if you want it. Like my own path, it will not be easy. You will have to work hard to stay here, and harder to achieve more. But the opportunity exists if you want it. All you need do is accept." I knelt before Izumi. "Is this agreeable to you, Izumi-chan?"

Her eyes grew big and teary. She made to hug me, but I held up my hand palm out and stopped her in her tracks. "Uh-uh." I shook my head firmly. "D-Kon and shower first. Anyway, it is unlikely any of you shall see me again. I also advise you never to speak of me... or this," I gestured to the apartment, "to anyone. *Ever.* Safer that way for all of us. Yes?" I stood. No one in Japan wanted to be associated with a fox, especially for their sudden turn about in fortune!

"Hai. Thank you, kitsune-dono," their mother bowed to me.

"Thank your daughter, not me. It was she who made this

possible for a kindness granted with no expectation of reward. I consider my debt paid in full. Our business is hereby concluded. Now get cleaned up and eat, for pity's sake. Best of luck, you three. Sayonara."

"Sayonara, Kitsune-sama. Arigato gozaimasu," I heard Izumi say as I turned and walked back into the shadows, leaving the demon lawyer to finalize the details with them.

And you know? I felt rather good about the whole exchange. I did not have much of a heart left, and roughly only thirty percent of my previous soul, but I knew I had done the thing right, the kitsune way. It was of course my decision how to repay my debt. I need not have bothered this much. And yet I was glad I did. Better still, I felt relief that this obligation had been conclusively paid. I was free of the burden of reciprocation to young Izumi.

So it was with a light heart and a spring in my step that I went off to make my next kill.

Chapter Fourteen

Within the Shadows

s the summer progressed, Chikako continued to lament that I was sent out on so many missions. But in all honesty, I preferred it. I found it much better than lounging about on the upper deck of the Ori, with all the flashing lights from the holo-vids, the garish neon, the loud music, the raucous youthful demons and their smells. Altogether, the club was a painful assault on my vulpine senses.

The most action one could see in there is if someone got rowdy, and the bouncers handled that without we Seven needing to sully ourselves. It was our job to stand around and appear threatening while Youta conducted his business. When he had a use for one of us, we came forward and bowed to our master immediately, then promptly carried out his will.

Only Katashi seemed to prefer sitting on his ass on the upper deck to running the shadows. Otherwise, the rest of us found merely playing at henchman inane, and so in general we did not hesitate to take a mission gladly. *I* certainly did not! I preferred the thrill of the hunt, the stalk, that sublime moment of death, so much better than the thudding bass of the club. And on the nights I was sent to take a heart, mine to eat, it was that much the better!

Most of the time, my hits went off without a hitch, business as usual. I went, I killed, and I returned. It had become so routine I scarcely thought about it. It was play to me, a kind of sport. But then there were other nights when things took an interesting turn...

This was one of them.

THE SUMMER OF 2119 IN NEW TOKYO WAS ONE FOR THE RECORDS, even during Climate Upheaval. Day or night, it was hot and muggy, and generally awful. Over a thousand residents of The Sprawl died from heat-related illness that year. But by mid-August, at last the unrelenting heat wave broke. It was still hot, but at temperatures that seemed a shade less oppressive.

Somewhere between evening and true night, I stalked through the electron haze of the In-Met. The bright neon glowed around me, skyscrapers shining bright as I passed beneath their glossy shadows. The crowd bustled and jostled along in the humid night, noisy as only humans could be. I secreted myself among the multitude, one face among many.

In this guise I was a young man, twenty-two years old, stylish and wealthy; confident, someone from a good family. Accordingly, women appraised me as they walked by in their tight, spaghetti-strapped dresses and light tank tops, with shorts or skirts that left little to the imagination. It was far too hot for rigid propriety. The city retained the day's heat as the evening lit up.

At the next street over, I took a right turn into a trendy, glitzy district made for youthful indulgence. If you were under thirty and had a huge digi-cred account to play with, *this* area was the place to be at night. University students and young twenty-somethings at the outset of their cushy careers proliferated in swarms. Music boomed out of open doors while lines formed up to the bouncers, most of which met the stereotype. One was even dressed like a sumo wrestler. Gimmicks such as this were a digi-a-dozen in this district.

The venue I headed to was huge. Three levels, wider than the clubs to either side of it. It was swathed in neon, and giant holo-vid crimson and gold dragons danced above the sidewalk, proclaiming to those in the know whose establishment this truly was. Otherwise, its name was totally incongruous to all those undulating dragons.

It was called, Bang, Bang, Baby! – in English, no less – or Triple B for short. I know, right? I rolled my eyes, too. But it was also something more sinister than its catchy little name might suggest. This was one of those places that had a hand in the underground, illicit sex trafficking trade. Otherwise, why else would Hiroshi have his claws in this business? And sure enough, if you were the type of skeevy clientele who could afford it, there were rooms on the third floor where traceless cred was traded for drugged and docile pleasure.

As I drew near, I heard an announcer over a mic declare that it was now buy-one-get-one-free hour. The techno-trip music ratcheted up in a tumult of bright, flashing lights. Cheers and yells of delight at the news echoed, and a flood of people on the street were drawn by the spectacle. I pretended to be one of them. I disdained the line and went straight to the bouncer, handing my holo-ID card to scan. I was not just portraying a random 'nobody.' I had been given the card and DNA of someone who commanded more attention than mundanely standing in lines.

The bouncer grunted, handed my card back, and cleared the way. "Enjoy your night, Mr. Matsumoto." I nodded, grunted back, and proceeded into Bang, Bang, Baby!

The clientele were nearly all human except for a few yōkai like me, who were sophisticated enough to blend in and hunt among them. But we could sense one another's dark aura and underlying miasma, like perspiration under cheap cologne. And no wonder. I saw quite a bit of choice fare among the wholly human population, gorgeous women and evil men. The demon inside me purred accordingly.

I lost myself among the throng, moved past the dance floor with its bright flashing neon colors, where humans danced in tribal groove to the heavy beat. As soon as I found a place in a corner where the shadows fell over me, I allowed myself to be swallowed by Mother Darkness.

I navigated to the head boss's office up on the third floor. What I saw as I passed by was… horrifying. There was nothing I could do. Rescuing sex slaves was not what I had come here for. To help them was to botch my mission. 'Try not to harm innocents' was not quite the same thing as '*save* all innocents.' Some you could, some you could not, and that was just the way it was. I looked away and moved on.

It was with relief I found the office I wanted at the end of the corridor. There were too many of my hit's subordinates in the room to go in yet. The boss lady was having a meeting. So I waited and watched.

My target, Nishimura Shizuka, was clad in tight lavender leather that left nothing to the imagination, including the cleft at the juncture of her thighs. Her hair was dyed silver platinum almost as white as my hair. She wore hers in a straight bob at her jaw with a fringe of bangs above pencil thin eyebrows and cobalt blue sunglasses, which I thought odd considering how much metallic blue eye makeup could be seen peeking around them with flourished strokes and spirals. Her lipstick was space cadet blue to match.

However, it must be said Nishimura-san was a very, *very* attractive woman. Lithe and dangerous, she had cybernetic implants for strength and faster reflexes. Technology had begun to level the biological playing field.

Her associates were all suited goons, and they sat around on cushy sofas and recliners, or stood in the background, while my target leaned her shiny pleather thighs on her desk dominatrix-style. I swear to you she was wearing nine-inch stiletto boots. She stood with an air of authority and easy confidence. Sexy.

I was troubled. Not about killing her. The megapolis was crawling with gorgeous women who died every night. What was the death of this one added to it? No, what really bugged the hell out of me was that this whole group dynamic reminded me uncomfortably of Youta and our Seven. I grudgingly acknowledged and accepted the truth. Whatever my ideals, I was just the yōkai version of a plain old thug.

"How many boys and girls did we get tonight?" she asked Mr. Metallic Purple Suit.

"Eh… Two boys, one sixteen, other eighteen. And five gals, ages fourteen through twenty. Good stock tonight." He smiled.

I wrinkled my nose.

"Higher quality this time, right?" She demanded to know. "Not some used-up whores pulled out of the Western and Korean Sectors?" Ms. Shizuka sneered.

"No, no! Good quality, Shizuka-sama!" Metallic Purple Suit promised. "Pure Japanese! They're fresh!"

"Good. My best customers were starting to complain. And make certain our meat factory participants have the proper dosages this time. That stupid slut who almost got out last night bit poor Yori-kun." She looked pointedly at the man who had his ear badly bandaged. He looked miserable and perhaps a little feverish. Human bites are so nasty.

"And the agency is still angry that their flesh mattress got dinged up during the take down. Can you imagine? So, *no mistakes* tonight. *Got it?*" She pulled down her glasses and gave each one a death glare with those elaborate, liquid-lined eyes.

"Hai, Shizuka-sama," they said in unison like beaten curs.

"I don't care if they're drooling on themselves. Keep 'em dosed."

I watched the slight shiver go through Ms. Shizuka as I turned the full weight of my attention on her. She seemed to feel my presence. How odd. She was not yōkai. But she looked straight into the shadows right at me. I had been made.

"You have your orders. Dismissed," she told her people. Without a word, they filed out, some in better spirits than others. Yori-san, for instance, looked downright ill.

Shizuka stretched languidly, clicked a button on her desk, which turned off all the cameras, and then crossed to the center of the room with a deliberate sway in her stride. She made a catwalk show of turning her tight ass around. "You can come out now," she said to my shadow strewn corner. "I've been waiting for you." She smiled coquettishly.

Really? I thought to myself. But what the hell? *Why not?* I stepped out of the darkness a born predator.

"Well, well, well!" She took off her glasses and looked me up and down. She smiled, so I smiled back. "Look at what Ryoichi sent me! You *are* delicious."

"To your liking?" I answered back flirtatiously, still wearing Matsumoto's handsome face.

"I have to admit I wasn't expecting you to look like *this*."

"Really?" Just what in the hell was she talking about?

"Yeah. You're unbelievably hot." Her smile was lascivious as she swayed closer. "I was expecting someone brawnier for your species. But that's okay, sweetheart. I like *all* types." Her grin showed teeth. I hate to admit it, but I was instantly intrigued.

She came up to me and threw her arms around my neck. I let her kiss me, indulged in it briefly. I considered killing her by taking her energy, but that would go against the purpose of this hit. This was not supposed to be a yako killing. And if she was expecting another yōkai to show up soon, I could not linger.

"I can't wait to see those horns." She caressed my forehead. *Horns?*

She smiled. "Don't be shy, baby. I saw your vid-pic. I know what you are when you morph out. I like it. Let me see the *real* you. The yōkai you." She ran her fingers down my chest. Then she kissed me again.

She thinks I'm an oni! Heh. 'The real me,' indeed.

This was the strangest hit of my life thus far. She thought I was her yōkai hook up! I almost laughed in her face, it seemed so absurd to me just then. Not to mention surreal. Who did that? But then I thought about it and found I was not genuinely surprised in the slightest.

"Well?" she asked when she came up for air.

I supposed this was as good a time as any. "Honey," I said in a smooth voice, "you can't handle the *real* me.'" My eyes changed from human dark brown to fox-eyed teal.

She gasped and stepped back. "You're not... But... What are you? You're not the oni I arranged for."

I leaned in close. "Kitsune," I whispered into her ear, a sly smile on my lips revealing the barest hint of fang as I sniffed her skin. I could not help the indulgence. Her arousal made it impossible to simply ignore *that* scent. And her in such an outfit, too...

"Kitsune? But I put in for an oni." She blinked, confused. I only grinned. "I didn't even know that kitsune were on the menu, they're so rare... Except for..." Her eyes widened. "You're not from Ryoichi!"

"No," I answered calmly. Without the cams watching, I revealed myself. I was too curious to see how she would react not to.

Her mouth fell open as she looked me up and down, pupils big and black, and I knew at once she desired me. "You're *gorgeous!*"

"Think so?" I asked in a seductive drawl. I nodded to the mirrored wall across from where I stood. Yes, she was so vain to have such a thing. And there, reflected where I should be, stood the leering, hulking fox-wraith that was Shiroi Uindo. Meanwhile, I carefully gauged her reaction to the monster I truly was.

194

She flushed, her breath quickened, a slight quiver of the lips, her wide eyes darting between my demonic reflection and me. I watched fear and lust mingle into full erotic heat. Her nipples stiffened into tight kernels that beaded through the shiny pleather. Holy Hell! I could *smell* her sudden gush of wetness. I began to salivate.

And that was when I saw it for the first time. My prey's fantasy. This was new. But yes… the incubus in me knew exactly what she desired. She craved the suave man-fox right in front of her *and* wanted the big, bad nogitsune to ravage her! In fact, she longed for me to seduce her like this to begin, then change in the middle of the act and take her full force.

Such a kinky girl, that Ms. Shizuka.

Oh, I wanted to! Temptation like this was nearly overwhelming! Even the little upturn of her lips as she glanced at my erection tight against the suit pants I wore… The monster in me wanted to bend her over that desk and shred that shiny pleather off her with its claws! I could make her cum and cum as I siphoned off her lovely life force. And if it were not for Chikako, or her real hook up, who could be here at any moment, damn right I would have screwed her brains out before I capped her!

"You're him, then. The shirogitsune. They whisper about you on the street, say your name like a prayer. But why are you here?" It was a doll's voice. She knew well how to play up to a predator.

I was not fooled. Instead I pulled myself back from the brink and drew out the gun I was given for this hit. Her eyes grew huge and she instinctively backed away. Her lips parted, but no words came out of her mouth. Lust became outright confusion, then anger, transforming the nature of her fear.

"Sorry," I said with a pang of regret. "This isn't personal."

She gathered herself to propel her cybernetic body at me in a last-ditch effort to survive. I shot her in the middle of her forehead. The silencer effectively muffled any noise from the gun, but not so the hard thump of her body hitting the floor like a heavy sack of sod. I learned a new lesson that night: silence is not just the weapon, it's the entire package.

"Miss Shizuka?" Her bodyguard called through the door. How this asshole could hear anything with the club racket that pounded the walls and floor from below, I had no clue. Maybe he had cyber-enhanced hearing.

I slunk back into the shadows as the door violently banged open, skulking past the drugged sex slaves. I could do nothing for them. That was not my job, which was only to kill this woman and leave. Youta would have my hide if I broke them out! Again, I turned away.

Until one of the doors opened and a man came out, zipping his trousers with a snide grin. He smelled of sex and blood. Behind him a young woman lay staring on the bed, splayed and naked. The door clicked shut. He swaggered off down the hallway, ever so pleased with himself. There was a certain cruelty in his smile that I knew was similar to my own when I was at my worst.

Right then and there my conscience would not abide it. "Damn it," I cursed softly.

I followed the smug bastard down to the noisy first floor and materialized out of the shadows behind a group of wall-flowers. I took the guise of one of the men I had seen attending Ms. Shizuka when he dashed past. No one paid the slightest attention to me as the lights pulsed to the throbbing beat. It was all too easy to use the humans to my advantage and avoid every camera.

I tapped the rapist scumbag on the shoulder before he could get back to the bar. He whirled around defensively. I stabbed the asshole twice in quick succession in the gut, once in the ball sack. Blood poured forth as he feverishly tried to work out what was happening to him, so sudden and vicious was my attack. He desperately clutched at the wounds, his eyes wide in horror and confusion. A second later his legs collapsed under him. I moved past without a backward glance.

The spreading pool of blood created a wet slick on the dance floor, and some hapless young woman in high heels went down hard. Girls began screaming, men shouted. Before anyone could register I was there, I had already stepped sideways into the shadows and disappeared again.

I was inordinately pleased with myself. I critically injured the rapist, which not only felt fantastic, but my action would call the police in. With any luck, they would find the victims on the third floor. It would not shut things down permanently, but it might stop it for this one night. Strangely, I held onto the forlorn hope that this meant I was not so far gone after all, that maybe I was redeemable. I doubted it, but…?

Since I lost my glamours in the borders of the Shadow Realm, I took precautions to keep from being recognized lest Hiroshi discover and track my movements here. I wore a billowing cloak with a deeply cowed hood, lightweight but opaque. I was winding a scarf over my lower face when I stopped short. A large figure was coming toward me.

"Ah, what a rare and beautiful creature," I heard a deep, velvety voice say. I stiffened immediately.

Who in the hell is this? I wondered, before I decided I just did not give a shit.

He was taller than me, stood enshrouded in a grey cloak that rippled. It draped over his horns, of which he had several from forehead to the back of his skull. What I could see of his lower face and hands had a queer bronzy-red cast. Long, sharp black claws accentuated his fingers. His miasma and chi were considerable.

"Kitsune..." He smiled. "How long has it been since such as *you* have walked the earth? Or *this* realm?" His eyes traveled the length of my cloaked body, appraising me. I said nothing. "White, too." He sighed happily. "A former kami's pet *here*?" He gestured around us. "Yet your breeding is impeccable, I can tell. Oh, you just keep becoming more interesting by the second! I am on my way to an appointment, but..." This was Shizuka's 'suitor.'

He shrugged, then stared at me with leering eyes and a lop-sided grin that was far too reminiscent of one of mine when knew I had the advantage. "Bah, forget that mortal strumpet. Ryoichi will have to forgive me. You are the better prize by far!"

Well, that was true. No matter how you looked at it, it was simply a fact. In terms of pure market value, a kitsune was worth a hell of a lot more than a mortal female. But I was not an easy trophy to obtain. He knew that, and yet he was willing to give it a go. This was life in the shadows. Eat or be eaten. To take such as I by force was a matter of prestige. This oni welcomed the opportunity.

I placed my hand on my katana, calmly took stance and waited. There was no way I was not going to fight.

"Heh, you've got some balls for a kitsune. I am going to enjoy playing with you." Then he traversed the distance in the blink of an eye and stood in front of me. He was too close! I leapt back to give myself space and swung. He leaned backward, under my arc, then sprang up and rammed me in the side.

I flew sideways and landed in a bleak forest of perpetual gloom. The trees were thick and black and bore no leaves. It reminded me of the wasteland outside of New Tokyo, except the air was clearer. It smelled of dust here, not acrid toxins. This was the Dark Realm. I managed to keep my feet and spun to face him... Except he was nowhere to be seen.

"Shit," I grunted and teleported myself several meters away. The oni had been standing behind me in the act of bringing his fist down on top of my head. He was still in that stance when he looked across the space to where I had vanished... and smiled at me.

"Motherfucker!" I rushed him with my katana. He simply turned into grey-gold mist as I made to cut through him and rematerialized several meters behind me. I whirled.

"Don't you get it, fox? I was *born here*. This is *my* place. I'm not some meager earth-born oni! I serve my Lord of Shadows in this realm and have for a thousand years!"

Great, I thought sarcastically to myself. *How the hell are you going to get yourself out of this one, baka kitsune?*

Honestly, the odds were stacked against me. I thought about jumping into the shadows and back out on the other side into the mortal world, but he rushed at me with no tell, no warning. I saw the blur this time and plowed into his attack with my katana. The oni separated into mist around me and solidified behind me. I whirled, swung my sword at what should have been his midsection. His torso turned into mist and as quickly returned to flesh the second my sword passed through.

It went on like that for a while, but how long? I genuinely had no idea. All the while, he read my moves and learned my patterns. The worst part? He was going out of his way not to damage me, presumably to keep me unspoiled for when the real games began.

That pissed me off. I tried to step it up. Kitsunebi, lightning, a combination of martial arts styles... It made no matter. I could not touch him. And I knew he could have landed a deadly swipe on me whenever he chose. No one I had faced yet had ever been this much more powerful than me except Youta. This guy was in a whole other weight class, and as I became more desperate, I knew I was falling into the trap.

Generally, I did not mind combat, but found a strange joy in it, the freedom to make violence. I was pretty tough and I healed fast, so I had little to fear. I had not killed in hot rage since Kazuki was murdered. In my new life, I was a cold-blooded killer. Most of my slayings were either for food or an ordered assassination.

This was different.

For the first time since I had killed Ichirou, I became angry. I reached for my cunning, but my mind curiously came up blank. That in turn fed my frustration and fueled my rage. Shiroi Uindo howled within, scratching at the walls inside my mind to get out.

I have to kill him somehow! I refuse to be a slave! And I dare not flee and leave an enemy like this one behind me!

He laughed at me, the deep baritone chiding me. I growled, my ears flattening. "That's it, kitsune. Get angry. Give into your yōkai nature. It will make binding you easier." Oh, I did *not* like the sound of that! "And when I have, you will be mine for as long as it amuses me."

I understood. The more of a beast I was, the easier it would be to supplant my will. There are different types of bindings and different ways to go about it. His promised to be painful and lasting, a full subjugation of will.

Fuck him then! I stood straight and still, lifting my chin. I stilled my tail and held my sword at the ready with the regal bearing of one who had once been celestial.

"Well, damn! Look at *you*. Bred to perfection and brain-washed for hundreds of years, I expect. No wonder a part of you holds on to what you were. I will have to work long and hard to break you, my defiled shrine fox. And I will enjoy every sublime moment of it." He sighed like a lover. "You are already my favorite."

"Yeah, well, fuck you," I spat, fangs bared. "Take me if you can!" I was preparing to leap straight up, out of his direct line of sight, teleport and come out behind him to cut his stinking head off, or try, when...

A large shape rose up behind the red oni and brought a heavy iron cudgel down on the bastard's head. The demon went down, having been so fixated on me that he failed to notice the blindside attack. There stood the huge azure form of *my* oni. And never was there a sight more beautiful to behold!

"Takeshi?" I asked, stunned, lowering my sword several centimeters, but unwilling to sheathe it.

"Hai. None too soon, hmm?"

"Yeah... I mean, I had an attack in mind and all..." I walked over while Takeshi smashed some more skull and brains with the blunt end, squishing and grinding the bits into the ground. "But I have to admit that's good, too." I tilted my head inquisitively as I observed his work.

"Intel said there was a second attack at your assignment, a stabbing. Sent me to check on you. Boss wants us to start going out in pairs or groups only from here on out," he rumbled. "Including you."

"Yeah, I can see why," I said as I looked at the mass of broken skull fragments and chunks of brain. "Thank you, by the way." I might not like being rescued, but I *really* did not like the idea of being bound as a slave in the Dark Realm! And it never hurt to be gracious and polite in this type of circumstance.

"Hmm," he said as an affirmation. "This is a bad one. We both got lucky tonight. Time to get rid of the evidence and leave fast."

"Yeah." I sheathed my sword, then set the corpse on fire. We watched as the blue flames consumed the body.

We began the walk back immediately. At first, I figured it would be a silent trek to the Ori, since Takeshi was not generally one for idle chit chat. He preferred refined conversation over a cup of tea and shoji. Therefore, I jumped slightly when Takeshi's deep, rumbling voice disturbed the perfect silence. "Can I ask you something?" I could tell it was serious. His brows knitted as he looked down at me with a frown.

"Uh...sure," I answered pensively, wondering what in the hell he was about to ask.

"You were a shrine fox?"

"I..." My mind was racing for a quip to deflect the question. But he had obviously heard that part of the conversation and I could not exactly deny the allegation without being a jerk about it. I nodded instead and accepted the inevitable. "Yeah... I am. About that..." I scratched the back of my neck and looked away. "I'd appreciate it if you didn't tell anyone. Please? It's kind of personal."

With Takeshi, the direct route was often the best one to take. He considered my words and body language for a moment, and finally nodded. "I suppose it would be. Can't imagine what that must be like. Anyway, not my business to go tell."

"Arigato," I said softly.

There was another minute of silence. Then, "So what was it like? Falling?"

That was a strange question. "Well..." I paused. "It hurt. A lot." I looked into the past, and unconsciously clutched my hair where my hoshi no tama had hung. For a moment I choked as I relived the memory of losing it, one of those foxish whines stuck in the back of my throat as I sought to clamp down on it.

Damn it! I thought I was over this! I closed my eyes and caught myself, shoved it down deep and cleared my throat. I managed a weak smile that was doubtless a million miles away from my eyes. "Worst night of my life."

"Sorry," Takeshi said at last. I could tell he meant it, too.

"Yeah," I whispered.

"Did you serve the blacksmith rice kami?" He meant Inari-sama.

"Yeah."

"You're the only one I know who used to be one of the heavenly types."

"Divine Messenger and Servant," I said with half a laugh. "Not anymore, though," I whispered.

Takeshi nodded and we did not speak the rest of the way. Fortunately, I had fully composed myself by the time we returned to Youta.

As it turned out, Bang, Bang, Baby! was shut down. During the investigation, a young female officer went poking around. According to the news, she was on her way to the owner's office when she heard a plea for help behind one those hideous doors. This resulted in multiple arrests on the spot and the subsequent rescue of all seven victims on the premises that night.

Since I went for the testicles, parameds discovered that asshole still had sexual fluids on him, including blood that was not his own. DNA would confirm it matched one of the victims being held incapacitated against her will upstairs. Because of the prominence of the club, the sensational stabbing brought the media, and they caught wind of the trafficking scandal along with the owner's death, obviously a professional hit.

The whole thing rocked New Tokyo for two weeks before it was downplayed and disappeared out of sight and mind. It took a few weeks for 'new buyers' to remodel and repackage the place. Within another month or so it was business as usual, without a doubt.

And no one, not even Youta, ever guessed the part I played in that. So far as anyone knew, I shot Miss Shizuka in the head and left, and any discrepancy in my time was explained away by my encounter with her hook-up in the Dark Realm. Until now, I never told another living soul about it.

Chapter Fifteen

The Dragon Hiroshi

So, my night was not starting out so well. The job was sensitive. Three of us were going in. It was to be one part robbery, one part butchery. Hiroshi hid sizeable portions of his hoard in secret safehouses all over New Tokyo, and tonight we were going after one of the particularly large caches that very few knew existed. We would not be killing in The Sprawl tonight. No, it was the Inner Metropoplex for us, a large estate with a well-guarded old-style Japanese mansion, the kind with outer corridors and sliding screens and luxury Zen gardens.

This was not going to be easy. For all its genteel beauty, a place like this was heavily secured. I needed to be clear of mind, sure of purpose. Alas that earlier in the day Chikako started talking about "moving in together."

Naturally, I balked.

"WHY NOT?" SHE ASKED, STRICKEN. "I PRACTICALLY SPEND ALL OF my time over here anyway!"

"Because I *need* my space! I'm a fox! This is my den!"

"But my moving in won't change anything! I already have clothes and a toothbrush here! What's the difference?"

I stared at her. "It's just different, that's all. This place is small, and you have an apartment's worth of stuff."

"It's not like I personally have all that much! Most of what's there is Hiroko's!"

"Then why do we need to change anything?" I asked. "I like it the way it is!"

"Yeah, well, do you want to know what *I* think?" she said, her tails lashing.

"Not particularly, but I am sure you will tell me anyway." As you might expect, that statement did not go over very well.

"You *ass*hole!" Her ears flattened, her tails fluffed and lashed harder. "*You* are afraid of commitment!"

That was not exactly true. I just did not want to commit to *her*. Or anyone in the foreseeable future, for that matter. Although it must be said I had never once cheated on my nekomata save for the random kiss of death. I filled my hunger with a combination of hunted hearts and Chikako's orgasmic energy. I maintained my Code as best I could, that threadbare remnant of my zenko honor. I was convinced it was the only thing that distinguished me from a born yako.

Part of that meant treating Chikako decently, although the emotion of love was out of the question. I simply could not feel it. Anyway, it seemed to me that whatever I loved died. It was better that my heart was cold.

"What I am 'afraid of' is you getting hurt – *physically*

– because of what *I* am!" The life of an assassin was not without peril, especially for the ones closest to him.

"I could get hurt *any*way!" she shouted. "I work at the club, for fuck's sake! I *sleep* with *you*!"

"It will be worse if they think you are more to me than a piece of ass!" I pointed out. Yeah, that did not go over so well, either.

She threw up her hands, claws unsheathed, ears lowered further in her feline rage. "Isn't that what I *am*, though? Just a free *whore* for your amusement?!"

"No!" I shouted back. "What? Where in the hell is this coming from?" I was bewildered. Just how did we get from 'moving in' to this?

"Hiroko said –"

"Ah, there it is," I said coldly, my own ears flattening. I crossed my arms over my chest, my own thick tail beginning to lash. "'Hiroko *said*.'" I bared my fangs. Chikako's sister was continuously trying to pry her away from me.

"She did! And you know what? She makes a lot of sense!"

"Does she?" I asked hard, now quite thoroughly annoyed with this whole thing. I despised fighting Hiroko *in absentia* through Chikako.

"She does! She told me you would break my heart, that I was nothing to you but a toy!"

"You are my lover! That is *something*!" Did it not count that she was my *favorite* toy?

"Oh, I see now! You know what? Hiroko was right! I *am* such a naive fool! You *are* just using me for the sex!"

"I am *not*!" I protested, although in retrospect that is exactly what I was doing. "I enjoy our time together!" Which was not untrue. I found her presence comforting.

"Doing what? Fucking!? That's *all* we ever *do*, Hayate!"

Well, that was true. But hey, she liked it as much as *I* did! Her appetites nearly matched my own, and who else could satisfy her like me? I, who gave her orgasm after orgasm! I hardly ever got shitty with her, never raised a hand. I was kind to her! Sometimes I even bought her pretty baubles to show my affection, such as it was. She was wearing the gold earrings I had given her just the other night.

"Well, what else do you want to do?" I asked haughtily. "Catch a cine-vid down at the 'plex? Play boyfriend and girlfriend? Hold hands and take an evening stroll?"

"No! Yes! Maybe!" She screamed in wordless rage and threw up her hands again. "I want us to be *more* than this, Hayate!"

And I did not. It was plain on my face. I was not even sorry.

"You know what? Screw this and *screw* you!"

"Does that mean you want to fuck now or that you wish to stop?" I tilted my head in genuine confusion.

She hissed at me, grabbed her jacket, and walked out. My ears furrowed back when the door slammed shut.

Well, maybe it was for the best. Better for her, certainly. And to be honest, I was not all that concerned. I would find others to warm my bed. In fact, I was now free to pick and choose as I would, opening the field to my feasting. But I would... miss her. I only realized it after she left. I was really going to miss having sex as myself, because even to buy a prostitute required a disguise in this town as things stood under Hiroshi's rule.

How disappointing. But so be it.

And I did not think much more about it, to be honest. That is, until I walked into The Cage after sundown. That bitch

Hiroko seemed happier than I had ever seen her. You would have thought she got laid! She wore that satisfied little smirk when she looked at me, the kind that said 'I won' without saying a word.

Chikako, on the other hand...

She would not even glance at me. Worse, glimpses proved she had been crying for hours. She looked miserable, fragile. Oh, boy. Somehow that was my fault, but what could I do? *She* was the one who left *me*! I never told her to get out.

A few of the dancers and other servers kept glaring at me whenever I caught their eye. Apparently, she had one hell of a support network at the Ori. Huh. All this time, and I had not been even aware she had friends. And wow, did they hate me. I hoped she would eventually get over our breakup, otherwise work was going to be awkward!

I'll talk to her afterward, I relented. *Just to smooth things over. Otherwise she might spit in my drink.* But that was not entirely truthful. I might not love her by any stretch, but I had no desire to bring her pain, either. *Besides, I need to get my key back, and she has to get her shit out. I should probably change my pass code, too, just to be safe...*

TWO HOURS LATER, TARO, JŪRO, AND I CREPT THROUGH THE GAR-den that surrounded the manse in the still of night. Our assignment was simple. Break in, kill as many as we could silently, grab the gold and get the hell out. We had to be careful of the shadows, since they would be protected and guarded. There was no way other yōkai were not lurking around. Or even lion dogs... something to guard against supernatural visitors.

And yet there was no whiff of any such thing. Not even a talisman barred our way. Instinctively, I really did not like it. But a job was a job, and no one was backing out.

The yard was quite beautiful, with carefully tended trees, shrubbery, and little stone paths. The maples had not turned color yet, and they rustled in the wind of that balmy September night. It was picture perfect, that garden. I remember it to this day. I kept expecting to be jumped by guards or yōkai outside, but there was nothing but moonlight and breezes. It was a gorgeous night, too, the kind made for running in fields beneath the moon. The wind was up, and so was my blood!

The mansion we stole into was like stepping across the threshold of time. Windows on all floors overlooked the exterior garden under the pale blue moonlight. Tree shadows writhed in the wind across tatami floors and painted screens. It was silent and warm inside. Yes, I remember it very well.

We bypassed the outer security and came across our first guard upon entering. He was looking out one of the windows with a bored expression writ upon his face. He jumped when he saw my kitsune-masked visage in the reflection of the glass. He turned just as I pushed my katana into his torso. Blood spilled from his mouth, then he sagged. He slid from my blade onto the floor.

The three of us fanned out, moving silently. Taro went to the left, Jūro to the right. I took dead center. Half a minute later I heard a sharp crack and a soft thump. Another guard down, Jūro's doing.

I kept expecting to be stopped by an armored guard at any moment. And here I was, in a white kimono and kitsunen-omen, long hair unbound, hand gripping my bloody katana. Surely there had to be more than a couple of paltry guards on duty! But for all I could tell with my heightened senses, the mansion was otherwise abandoned.

Save for *that* smell. Brimstone and musk. That was pure dragon. I knew from Youta's scent.

I told myself it was because Hiroshi's hoard was here. If he slept upon it, and recently, surely it might have his scent. But if that were so, it was stronger than I would have guessed. I frowned. I had that spine-tingling feeling, like I was walking into a trap. My gut fluttered, adrenaline surging. The lack of guards only increased my nervousness.

I thought about seeking out Taro or Jūro, but no. I did not wish to appear weak. The damn monkey demon would rag on me for getting squeamish. Besides, we were *sent*. You did not back out of any mission a dragon put you to. Not ever! Death before desertion and dishonor, to fail was to die. Youta said do, so we did, and that was the end of it. Trap or no trap, the only way out was through.

Just as I was about to give up and turn back anyway, there it was. Straight ahead of me, too close to simply walk away from. Hiroshi's cache.

Set beside the ceremonial tearoom was a short hall that led to an earthen vault for treasure, traditionally called a dozou or kura. Most Japanese homes had originally been built of wood, and fire in the olden days was always a disaster waiting to happen. The dozou was designed to protect a family's material wealth. This one was made to withstand everything short of a nuclear attack.

I crept forward warily and entered the dragon's lair. Coins from multiple eras of Edo and beyond proliferated, as well as statuary, fine art, precious gems, and all manner of such gleaming magnificence. It was truly a dragon's hoard! I walked in, starstruck by the sheer amount of golden opulence before me. It was staggering! And... well lit?

Oh, shit.

I knew at once I did not want to be here. There was no reason to keep the rest of the house dark and leave bright lights in *this* chamber! Damn it, where *was* Taro, anyway? He was supposed to catch up to me by now. On cue, I heard the roar of the great bear from somewhere above, on the second floor. He had transformed. The walls shook!

Well, that isn't good, I thought banally. Whatever was happening, as soon as I heard Jūro's explosive ball-grenades on the opposite side of the manse, I knew we were hosed. *Son of a –!*

I spun, ready to run to their aid, when a heavy steel door dropped across the entrance of the dozou! There were no windows here, and no other exit. This was a vault. I was trapped! "Fuck," I muttered savagely.

"Well, well, *well*..." His deep voice boomed in the echo of that room.

There stood a magnificent tall man with long black hair and mustachios down past his knees, his skin hued with a coppery cast. An attractive creature with the weight of great age in his manner, he wore vermillion robes, five-clawed dragons patterned across the outer garment in golden thread. His luminescent, gold, reptilian eyes gave him away as easily as his presence and his power. The Dragon Hiroshi was resplendent and arrogant as only an ancient dragon could be.

"I hoped if I baited the trap properly you would be the one to spring it! And here you are at last. Come, let me look at you, my beauty. You should feel honored. I have been waiting for months to meet you, after all," his smooth voice rumbled.

I stood straight and tall. I could smell the scent of my own fear strong in my nostrils. My hair and tail were thick and stiff with it! But I did not give into my animal instinct to back away and corner myself, in spite of that piercing stare. I swallowed hard, but I held my ground.

"I have been sending out feelers for months, trying this or that source. I have tortured and slain, trying to discover who is moving against me. Finally, I decided upon a different tactic. And now I know. It is Youta, eh? I had hoped not. He had so much promise, but far too much ambition," the Dragon said mildly disapproving.

I said nothing. What was there to say? Hiroshi had all the damn answers.

"The water snake is not half so clever as he imagines himself. Oh, he was smart to grab you up fast, but he should have made a gift of you instead of fashioning you into a weapon to use against me. A pitiable mistake, as he shall soon discover. But what to do with you, hmmm?"

I growled.

"So angry and afraid," The Dragon of New Tokyo purred. "You are bristled up so hard 'tis almost laughable! But you are not stupid. I have been watching you skulk around here, aware of the trap you were forced to walk into. You have been quite clever since that first night. I sought you, searched high and low. But then I concluded that it would be best to make you come to me, as you should have done the night you took Takahashi's heart.

"Take off your mask," he ordered. "Let me look at you."

I stood quite still. No way was I taking my mask off for *his* pleasure!

"No? Well, 'tis not as if I have not seen your likeness. I will see it again soon." He smiled, the bastard. "I could have given you a good life, kitsune. I still might consider it if you surrender to me willingly now. You might find I am more generous than perhaps you have been led to believe. I could use a strong warrior such as yourself. Anyone can see you are no ordinary yako. No, white fox. I know *Fallen* when I see it. And it did not happen so long ago, did it?"

My body stiffened at the mention of my great humiliation, my ears flattening straight back. He laughed at me, adding insult to injury. I was glad of the mask that covered my face. I am certain I looked like I had just swallowed shit.

"Oh, yes. You are one of Inari's specially bred little shrine foxes." My shame burned through me harder. "You know, I had a Wild Fox once. She was born yako. Her savagery was far less elegant than yours, and she held no scruples. But you do, I can tell. Ah, you have a code," he purred. "Fallen do, at first. It is the only way they can comprehend life after being cleaved from the divine light of their kami.

"You live by some kind of Bushido Code tailor made for your purposes, and tell yourself that adhering to it makes you better than a common field fox. But that is a bit of a laugh, is it not? How many times have you already changed that Code as you surrender to your new yōkai nature? It cannot be helped, of course. Whatever you were before, you are a bloodthirsty yako now. Since the day you Fell, that is all you will ever be."

I growled deep and long in spite of my fear. He had me pegged, that bloody old thing. How I *hated* him.

"Poor, broken Celestial lost and alone without a home to return to," he taunted. "Did you really think Youta could protect you, beautiful one? Tchk. He sent you *here*, did he not? Of course, had he known, he would not have. You are *far* too precious to squander, and yet perfect for such a task. That, you see, was the trap. It was made for *you*, my new pet."

I narrowed my eyes behind my mask, looking peripherally right and left for escape. But there were no windows and the only way out was opaquely barred to me. The shadows were useless in all this gleaming golden light. If I attempted to teleport myself out without a line of sight, I could seriously injure myself. I still had half a mind to try, casting about for where I could go that would be safe enough to make the attempt...

"By now you are frantically thinking of how you can escape. There is none, I assure you. You belong to me now, little Wild Fox. You can either submit, or I will imprison you to do with as I please. Torture will turn the most defiant creature, given years. Over centuries...?" Oh, that reptilian smile.

I shivered. He meant it! And once hidden away in whatever passed for a torture chamber and prison, no one would find me. There would be no rescue. I was so fucked.

But if that were so, I had nothing to lose. I resolved I would fight to the end rather than sell out my comrades for a cheap hope. Perhaps I could enrage him enough to kill me! Better a swift death than what Hiroshi had planned for me

To hell with that! I lifted my katana and bravely took stance, resigned to my fate.

He stared at me in surprise. If The Dragon was offended by my decision, it was hard to tell. But then Hiroshi laughed and clapped his hands. "Now that, I confess, I did not see coming. Most of your kind are vermin who will say anything to get out of a tough spot. But not you, ex-zenko. *You* would rather fight to your death than give in. I admire your spirit. A rare creature indeed, and such a waste." He sighed sadly and shook his head. "Yet, if that is your wish, kitsune, I will of course give you an honorable death by my own hand. I can do no less for one of your exceptional courage."

And then The Dragon transformed into a huge, serpentine monster straight out of legend. In a spiraling corkscrew of claws and scales, he lunged at me. I dodged to the side, but the monster's tail struck me and sent me straight into the wall, where I impacted hard. Chunks of rock exploded around me. I lost my breath, all the wind forced out of my lungs. I gasped for air until finally I sucked in that first agonizing breath and coughed. Oh, how it hurt! My ribs were cracked. I slumped to the floor in a state of shock. That expression about seeing stars? I saw galaxies! I just wanted to sink into the darkness... sweet, tantalizing surrender from the pain...

NOOOOO! the demon shrieked shrilly inside of me.

I looked up in a daze to see two big, red dragons coming straight for me. I felt the swipe of his large paw connect and I went flying again. I slammed into the adjacent wall and fell face first into a heap, my sword landing next to me with a metallic clang.

It hurt too much to move. I could scarcely breathe. I was broken all over. I did not know the extent of the damage, but I would guess nearly every bone in my body was fractured. My powers were already repairing the breaks, but it was taking most of what I consumed before the mission to heal the worst. I groaned and wheezed while The Dragon laughed at me. The world went around in lazy circles.

I had to get up! I was not done yet. I was still alive. Which begged the question...

Why is he toying with me? Why not the claws? He could just use his fire and have done. I supposed he wanted to play with his kill before he ate me. But one thing was for sure.

"I will die on my feet!" I declared defiantly. I gripped my blade and heaved myself up. The room spun a few times, but I stayed on my legs, pushing the pain back with sheer determination and force of will.

"Impressive!" The Dragon's great voice boomed in the confined space. "What else do you have?"

I was expecting the Dragon to cast a large enough shadow to disappear into, but that was a forlorn hope. Not in this room with its brilliant lights and glittering golden reflections. No escape. Nowhere to hide. I saw only one option.

I charged Hiroshi.

He blinked at me, curious. He had no fear that I could seriously injure him. So it was to his enormous surprise when one of his long mustachios fell shorn to the floor by the razor edge of my katana. Hiroshi roared in outrage. *That* got his attention. Man, was he pissed!

"YOU DARE!" That sulfuric breath blew my hair back. I grimaced against the Dragon's foul wind.

"I dare, Hiroshi-sama!" I cried out, my own voice a small thing compared to his. "For my daimyo!" I took stance and charged again, so certain of my demise that I felt wild with reckless abandon! I leapt up and brought my sword down on Hiroshi's head. The metal clanged against armored scale and I careened sideways with the impact. This time I tumbled in mid-air, landing in a crouch. Hiroshi swung his tail, but I jumped it. It was a near miss.

"Think that Youta is different from me, shirogitsune?" The Dragon laughed, turning his sinuous body to face me. I dodged a draught of orange flame, but only just. I rolled while he followed my progress across a room that was far too small with his length and size in it! And with fractured bones? The pain was unimaginable. I forced myself to breathe and kept moving.

"Maybe. Maybe not!" I yelled defiantly. "But I swore my allegiance regardless!"

"A loyal Wild Fox, is it? You will be a dead nogitsune tonight. Perhaps I will leave a piece of you, or three, to send back!" He drew in another breath to gather his flame. I managed to dodge the expulsion, although a bit of my hair got singed. "Your ears and your tail!" He lunged at me again. I leapt onto his muzzle and somersaulted between his antlered horns. I tumbled down his back as those writhing coils attempted to catch and crush me like a python.

The truth was, I did not have a prayer in open combat. I knew it, *he* knew it. He was too well armored in his scales. The dozou was too small. Dodging his attacks inside here was an increasing effort. Eventually my energy was going to run out, my injuries catch up to me, while his supply was virtually limitless. All I could do was take a beating for the sake of honorable mention and die promptly.

But if that happened, Youta's cause was dead. We both knew that, too, as we faced each other. The longer I was with Hiroshi, the more certain I was I had chosen well when I supplicated myself to Youta. My dragon trusted me. I would not fail him. I decided I was *not* going to die this night, and fuck Hiroshi!

Which meant I had no choice. I had to take the chance and bend space.

"Now to finish this!" The Dragon rushed at me and nearly crashed into me headlong with his maw opened wide. I leapt in midair, immediately warped the space around me, and disappeared. It was a better option than The Dragon's mouth! The only place I knew I could go was my own apartment. So it was to my home I concentrated…

But in my panicked and addled state, my calculation was off! I was thinking of my weight set as a visual guide when I felt a piercing, stabbing pain in my right side. I looked down and saw a metal bar sticking *through* my torso above the hip! I had materialized around my own barbell. I roared, utterly pissed.

I pulled my mask off and plopped it on the bench, tossed my sword to the floor. Man, I smelled like dragon. At first, I was not sure what to do, but I could hardly stay there all night and hope someone came here looking for me. I would be forced to explain how I ended up in this pathetic condition. There was no going to a hospital or calling authorities for help, either. I had to get myself out of this.

I was damn lucky my legs had not materialized into the bench, too. But hell, it was real close. Had I not been in a leaping crouch… I was badly shaken.

Resigned, I forced myself to slide up to the edge of the bar where it sat on the rest in front of me, pulling myself along its length with my hands. My body was so bruised and battered inside and out that every millimeter was an effort and I whimpered often. I did not know such pain existed! At last I discovered the end. Thankfully there were no weight discs on it.

Now the hard part. I took a deep breath and gripped the bar, pulling it up off the weight rest. I angled myself so that I could slide the rest of the way off while maintaining pressure to keep from ripping the wound further. I managed it out of sheer desperation, shaking as I forcefully slid myself completely off the bar. And let me tell you, it hurt. A lot.

Muscle and flesh tore, especially as I forced myself off the end. I let go and the bar clanged to the floor behind me. I almost lost consciousness then and there. I barely remember falling the distance to my hands and knees. One moment I was up, the next I was on the floor. Pain blossomed as the impact jarred my broken bones. The world went blinding white.

"Shit. Shit! SHIT!" I gasped. Blood soaked my white kimono. My arms were an increasingly disturbing shade of black and blue. I crawled to the kitchen sink nearby, leaving a bloody trail, my tail dragging painfully behind me. I grabbed a cloth off the counter and pressed it to the wound as best I could with my left hand.

"Fuck!" I cursed. I needed to eat, to heal. Worse, I had to get to Youta and report in! What had happened to the others? I had practically abandoned them. I felt like shit for that, but I had no choice. I could not go back for them now in any case, not in this condition. I was in danger of turning full yako in my demonic body's last-ditch effort to survive. Hell, it was possible I might even die here!

Things were more broken inside me than I initially guessed. I think my spine might have been hairline fractured down its length. I only now just realized my tail was broken in at least two places, probably when I hit that wall the first time. It had a sharp bend toward the tip that was locked in. I was definitely concussed. Every breath was a white-hot agony.

I heard the keypad punch and a physical key turn in the

lock to the front door. I crept back into the shadows of my darkened abode, pulling my wakizashi free of its scabbard, the only weapon besides my fangs and claws I had left! I held the shorter blade in both trembling hands and waited, fully expecting to die.

A feminine shape entered and closed the door. "Hayate? Are you here? I came to give you your key back. I could've at the club, I know, but I didn't want to leave it like this between..." Chikako stopped as she tapped on the lights. "...us." She gasped at the bloody trail. And then she saw me.

Her eyes widened at the sight of me. "Hayate! You're bleeding!" Obviously.

I looked down at my side. It was true. I was a bloody mess with a gaping wound front to back. I dropped my wakizashi on the floor.

"Your poor tail! What happened?"

"Chika... Have to... get... Youta," I told her. The world was becoming surreal, going fuzzy...dark around the edges... bright pin dots... nausea...

"You can't go anywhere like this! Shit!"

I forced myself to remain conscious. I had to make her understand. "You. Go to Youta, Chikako. Now! It was... trap." I swallowed, my burst of energy already slipping away. "Hiroshi knows. I fought him." An unbidden whine came out of me as the muscles around the wound spasmed. A burst of wet warmth stuck the cloth more firmly to my skin.

"Shit! Shit! Shit!" She ran her hands through her hair, looking very young and scared as I had never seen her before. The demon inside of me wanted to ravage and maul her to heal this body. What I needed most was for her to get the hell out of here!

"Please, Chikako," I panted, clutching her arm. I left a bloody smear. "Go to *Ori*. Tell Youta. I need you... do this." Things went hazy again and I could not power through it this time. "Please," I said softly, weakening. The world dimmed as I slumped over, unable to hold myself upright any longer.

"Alright." Then she was gone.

I might have passed out. Time did not seem to move. There was pain and darkness in bizarre intervals. Was this what it was like to die? How long would it take?

"Damn, my friend. You look like shit."

I blinked and smiled weakly. "Shirou…" Never had I seen a more welcome sight. "Yeah. Don't happen to have… spare heart on you, do you?"

"No, but I can take you to prey. Then Youta wants you."

"Hiroshi..."

"Youta knows. Jūro and Taro got out. Left a big hole in that place. They already reported back to Youta, who has been most anxious that Hiroshi got you until your girlfriend showed up. Can you stand?"

I nodded. "Think so." He helped me to my feet, wheezing and gasping. I was embarrassed I needed to lean on him, that he should see me in such a state of weakness. "Met him. Hiroshi." I grimaced as Shirou helped me to walk.

"And you're alive?"

"Barely."

"Could be worse. You just faced a dragon and walked away."

I chuckled, then winced as the contraction of abdomen muscles hurt sharply. "Maybe. There're a lot of broken things…" I panted for a second, "inside…me. Shit…"

"I've never had the displeasure of meeting his highness. What's he like?"

"He's a fucking asshole," I declared sourly.

Shirou chuckled. "Yeah, I bet."

"Knocked my ass for a loop, let me tell you." I used our conversation to focus and retain consciousness.

He took me to a back alley somewhere in the Western Sector. Of them all, this was the one in which trash floated around the streets and alleys. Westerners were generally regarded as stupid and foul smelling, but whatever their ethnicity, human still tasted like human to me.

"Got one good spell left in you, nogitsune?" the crow asked.

I nodded and cast the illusion of a pretty blonde woman in a short skirt standing at the entrance of the alleyway. It was a projected image, a bit like a hologram. The broken bones and the blood loss were taking their toll on me. But fortunately, sex sells, and it was no time at all before my beckoning maiden caught a likely fool. She backed down the alley, deeper into the shadows, sliding her skirt up her thighs with come-hither eyes.

The man who came after her was in his late twenties. Healthy. Strong. An especially good specimen. "Listen, bitch," he said in English as he closed the distance. "This is *my* turf, and you're not one of my sluts, so get this straight. Tell me who you work for so I can kill the punk, and you work for me. Or I slit that pretty throat. Either way you're getting fucked tonight. What's it gonna be, cunt?"

He made to reach for her throat, but she simply vanished into thin air. "The hell?" His eyes darted around in confusion. He shivered when I rose behind him in my full demonic state. It was the first time in months.

I could not hold out against it any longer, the desperation grown too great. I found that in this form the pain was far less. But the raw hunger was worse, maddening. I was *drooling*. It was all I could do to hold onto my sanity as the hair rose on the back of the pimp's neck. He turned and I struck. My hand tore into his flesh, my grinning muzzle leering in close to his, caught in shock and horror.

"*Cuuunnnnnt*," I called him in that whispery, evil voice. I floated before him, reached up higher into his chest. I consumed my prize with great relish. It always did feel good to me to slay one who so truly deserved it.

After another five of those, I was finally ready to see Youta.

Chapter Sixteen

Turf War!

I returned to the Ori an hour later, soaked through and encrusted with blood. I had soot streaks from dragon fire and was going to need a couple of inches trimmed off the singed ends of my hair. I *reeked* of blood, smoke, and dragon. In short, I was a mess.

Yet I held myself with pride and dignity despite the wretchedness of my appearance. A few workers and janitors still on premises at that early hour watched me come into the club with varying expressions of disbelief and mingled horror. I did not bother to look at any of them, preferring to see *through* them, my eyes leveled front and center with a warrior's intensity. I heard one of them utter, "Holy shit!" as I climbed the steps to Youta's office.

Chikako was still here with one of her bakeneko friends who danced in the cages. They were seated on the main floor, but it was her scent that gave her away. Chikako was more of a wreck than she had been before I set out on my calamitous adventure. Unfortunately, I could not stop to speak with her. It was to my master I must report first.

"He's fed," I thought I heard her say, but between the acoustics and our footfalls on the grated metal, I could not be entirely certain.

The other five and Youta looked at me like I was a yūrei when I stalked in beside Shirou. I was given up for dead. I could tell the tanuki had genuinely hoped for it. The tengu let them know just what kind of shape he found me in, a list of likely injuries I had sustained during my encounter, and how much it had taken to cobble me back together. It *was* rather impressive, to be honest, and more so that I survived at all!

The side wound and myriad injuries healed seamlessly after I properly fed. I had to break and reset my own tail so it would not heal with a permanent kink. How humiliating! *And* painful. But other than that, I was just peachy. The other six stood in attendance as I gave my deposition to our master. I left out how I had gotten the bleeder precisely, not wishing to reveal any weakness to my closest 'frenemies.'

But wanting to capture and torture me for centuries? And how he had been baiting this trap for months? I made certain *that* was in my narrative. I was clear on how I felt about the fire dragon, for now I hated Hiroshi almost as much as Katashi did! I also mentioned shearing off one of Hiroshi's long mustachios, too, of course. That earned me a pleased smile from Youta. It was spine-chilling, that deep draconic satisfaction.

That there would be retribution for this insult was beyond question. Mighty dragons did not suffer such from lesser beings, certainly not from little fox yōkai. If I had been hunted before, now Hiroshi was sure to redouble his efforts. Oh boy, were we in trouble.

On leaving, I found that Chikako scored a ride home. The entire place was cleared out. That was just as well. I was too weary to face another possible confrontation. Relieved, I returned to my apartment and cleaned it up, using ammonia to remove the blood. The sharp odor made me sneeze relentlessly, but it got the deed done. Then I showered and passed out.

I spent the next several hours asleep until nightmares about Hiroshi torturing and then devouring me made me give it up. The last straw was thrashing myself off the futon, tangled in my covers. I woke up when I hit the floor screaming.

I really missed Chikako then. Just waking up with her in bed beside me made things better somehow. After the trauma of last night, I needed that anchor, to feel cared for. She had been my constant since my first night in New Tokyo. I felt acutely alone. Man, yesterday royally sucked.

WHEN I WENT INTO THE ORI THAT EVENING, I FOUND I HAD BE-come something of a celebrity. My reputation had grown leaps and bounds since I slept. Word got around fast that I had faced Hiroshi in person, and in what condition I had returned. Demons looked at me with new respect because of what I had done.

Somehow everyone knew that I slashed off Hiroshi's mustachio, a mark of age, rank, and pride among dragonkind. I had not exactly taken that into consideration when I did it. I was just aiming for something I could cut, and that was the only thing available on a remarkably invulnerable monster. It was not like I was thinking clearly at the time. But no one else knew that. I have no idea who leaked the details, but I had become a legend within hours to do such insult to The Dragon of New Tokyo and audaciously get away with my life.

Thanks to Chikako coming in to inform Youta, and apparently having a few shoulders to cry on, they knew exactly what kind of state I had escaped in, too. That was an additional badge of honor in my favor, to have been tough enough to survive my numerous injuries. Sure, I had run away from that fight, but I had faced a dragon and lived! *The* Dragon! And foxes were never exactly expected to stand their ground anyway. That I had even attempted it was a big deal.

So when I lounged beside Youta that night, I did so with great pride. I was more than a worthy member of this Seven. The tanuki seemed to hate me more than ever, but whether because he did not believe I had not been turned, or because I had proven him wrong by staying loyal to Youta, I was not quite sure. There was no winning with that guy. I did not let it trouble me.

Eventually I saw my ex-girlfriend serving below. I asked permission from Youta to go speak with Chikako, to thank her for her part in saving my life, and the allowance was granted. Yōkai moved out of my way, staring at me and gossiping as I passed by. I have to admit, it fed my already enormous ego.

I came up behind Chikako in the precise moment a hairy patron reached out to pet her shapely behind in that tight, black skirt. I took hold of his wrist before his hand could besmirch her dignity. His leer turned into instant distress.

"Now that is *not* polite." I squeezed. I had fed well before I came in tonight, just in case someone targeted me for Hiroshi. I was full strength. Bones crackled and tendons popped beneath my grip. "I believe the saying at the door is 'Hands off unless you pay.'"

I crushed the demon's wrist and wrenched his arm in its socket as I twisted. I heard something tear inside his shoulder. He went down to his knees instantly. I was gratified by his sharp cry of anguish. "And that stipulation does *not* apply to the servers." I let go. It might seem like overkill, but as one of Youta's lieutenants, it was my duty to see my Lord's rules obeyed. And maybe it felt good to be tougher than someone after all those nightmares of Hiroshi, which honestly paled in comparison to The Dragon himself.

The yōkai backed away, holding his arm, his face a mixture of anger and fear. He wanted to curse at me to save face, but he dared not. The whole floor was watching, even the cage dancers. Two of them all but stopped dancing to stare. Chika-ko turned, gasped, and looked up at me with wide eyes.

"Hayate-sama! Where did *you* come from?"

This was something that happened a lot, not that I necessarily did it on purpose. Stealth was part of what I was, and sometimes it startled *me* when others jumped at my unexpected presence. I never understood how they could not hear me, smell me, or feel my breath. Yōkai at least should be more perceptive.

"Chikako-san," I began politely. "I want to thank you. You saved my life," I told her in earnest. I owed her. I felt the weight of my obligation along with my gratitude.

She flung her arms around my neck immediately, startling me. "I was so scared when I saw you like that!" Her voice was muffled against my chest. She started crying again.

I wrapped my arms around her slender waist and held her

in the middle of the club, ignoring the stares. I felt like I had just painted a target on her back. I cursed myself for not taking this somewhere more private before I opened my mouth. But I had to admit, I loved how her soft body felt clinging to mine.

"Hey now," I said gently. "I'm alive, in no small part thanks to you. You saved me." *You probably kept me from transforming into a rampaging monster with no conscience, saving innocent lives...* I owed her more than she knew, and I dared not tell her.

Chikako gazed up at me with hopeful tenderness shining in those bright, big cat's eyes of hers. "Oh, Hayate-sama..."

"I am sorry we quarreled yesterday." I surprised myself by meaning it. I had not liked coming home to an empty bed or waking up in one. "I enjoy spending my free time with you – and for more than just... you know..." Which, oddly enough, was true. Yeah, sure I missed the sex. But I also missed her idle prattle about inane things, the way she smelled. I enjoyed her. I decided I wanted her back.

She nodded her head. "I know. I'm sorry, too! I was angry, wound up..." Chikako sighed and stared at me longingly. She had missed me, too. "When I saw you like that last night... I guess you were right after all," she said, sniffling. "Maybe when this war is over, we can be more, but not now." She shook her head helplessly. "For now..."

"For now, this is how it must be," I said as I brushed a strand of hair from her glistening cheek. I cupped her chin in my hand and made her look deeply into my gleaming eyes. She complied at once, entranced. "My dearest one," I pitched my voice low so only she would hear. Her pupils dilated, lips parted slightly. I kissed my nekomata long and deep with the perfect amount of sensuality. And just like that, she was mine again. Oh, how she melted against me.

I suppose I should not have toyed with Chikako's emotions so, but I was not sure after my run-in with Hiroshi if I would survive this war anyway. The Dragon was certain to come for me sooner or later. Of course he would. I had defaced him! Instead I thought about holding her in my sleep, the warmth of her body beside me, the casual banter that filled the long silence, that beautiful smile when she gazed dreamily at me…

I had to stop, else I would have ripped her clothes off then and there and taken her on top of the nearest table in front of everyone! I pulled my face away reluctantly. Chikako looked so euphorically happy just then, her smile bright. To be honest, she looked drugged. She embraced me, clinging hard, and I held her in the safety of my arms. She was going to come home with me tonight, I knew. Would that I could take her home right now!

A quick glance showed me that we were the center of attention. Boy, was Hiroko *pissed*! A few of her friends looked a little uncertain about this, but I had her too firmly back in my clutches for anyone to rip her out of my claws now.

A great *BOOM!* violently shook the entire establishment! There was banging, smoke, shouts, pops of gunfire, screaming…

I held onto Chikako, who looked at me in fear and confusion. "Hayate-sama! What is –?"

I gazed over into the smoke, past yōkai running this way and that over those who had fallen to the floor, and saw a battalion of well-armed demons coming toward us in Hiroshi's livery. My eyes widened.

"Chikako, run!" And then I left her, drawing my sword as

I made to face the enemy. Damn I hoped she had the sense to get away!

Walking toward the danger far more calmly than I felt, I found I was not alone. Shirou was beside me. Then Fuyuko. The other Seven joined me on the front line where Hiroshi's battalion was killing younger, weaker yōkai indiscriminately. The more ferocious among those loyal to Youta fought back. All the while, the music blared on.

I stepped into the fray and cut down the first demon who rushed me. "Die, kitsune!" the oni shouted. He fell hard, dead a second later by my hand. I relished that.

How dare he? Invading our club like this? And with that thought, my bloodlust kicked in. There is no other way to describe it. The demon inside of me became… *me*, wore my skin.

Nor was I alone. In fact, other yōkai were morphing into their darkest aspects now that the battle raged in earnest! Taro was among the first, but it was his preferred form. I was convinced he would transform into a demon bear just to defecate!

The Devil Bear rose impossibly tall on his hind quarters, swiping enemy demons left and right with his huge paws. His deafening roar rattled what was left of our walls. Yōkai flew through the air in geysers of blood. One was ripped in half by Taro's long claws, his torso landing a meter from his legs. Man, onikuma will fuck you *up* in a straight brawl!

Three demons rushed me at once. I stepped into their advance with my sword, cutting the arm off this one, sweeping the legs out from under that one, stabbing down and then pulling my katana free to block a cut aimed at my head. I shoved that assailant back and ran him through. Another came at me and I shoved my hand into the kijo's face, summoning my kitsunebi to consume her skull! Flesh melted like tallow until her head ashed into nothing.

Peripherally, I saw Fuyuko let forth streaming gouts of ice, freezing four opponents at once. Her ice shuriken ripped through the throat of another. Then her ice ninjatō grew in her hand and she carved herself a bloody path over the frozen slick she laid down on the floor. Any yōkai who rushed her slid and fell at her feet. They looked like fallen tributes to the goddess of death.

Jūro jumped high in the air and unleashed his explosives into his opponents. Loud booms echoed as yōkai were blown apart. Limbs went flying in every direction, a few soaring past me! Then he was swirling among the rest with a short tanto blade, his small stature making it hard to get a bead on him. Meanwhile, his happy ass danced through their number, hamstringing and cutting arteries, taking the legs and loins from the fuckers. Jūro might be short, but he was extraordinarily strong, agile, and quick. And *vicious*!

Our great blue oni was also in full demon mode, and he was smashing creatures with his heavy kanabo. I heard the splintering of bones. Screaming yōkai flew through the air with every sweep of those muscle-bound arms of his! Takeshi brought his iron club down, and I heard a skull crack like an egg.

Every time I smote one, another took its place. There were so many! This was a decisive hit! Hiroshi was going all out to put us down, as well he might. The insult could no longer be tolerated. Now that he knew who we were, he had to act.

Perhaps it was my imagination, or maybe my ego, but I felt like I was getting a lot of attention. Granted, a lowly fox like me had shamed an old dragon by taking the symmetry from his appearance. It would take years for that to grow back. Until then, Hiroshi would not be making very many public appearances. Oh, yes, this was deeply personal. And boy, did it feel that way!

The ground shook as a particularly large demon entered the fray. It was an ashura, a warrior demon with six arms and each handheld a sharp sword. This monster came to Japan by way of India along the Silk Road. The ruddy-skinned giant grinned malevolently when he saw me. "Ah, *there*'s the shirogitsune! You will die for your insult, vermin scum!"

The ashura came at me in a blur, he was so fast! I dodged this way and that, felt the sleeve of my suit slice and tear! A sharp sting and blood welled from the wound, a graze. I had no time to worry about it. This monster was a dervish of death. I tried but could not land a hit. The ashura was like a blender! I could not get close! I took a few surface slices in the attempt.

I managed to maneuver into a clear enough space to vanish and reappear behind him, but when I made to hamstring him, he turned and repelled me! I flew backward and landed on my ass. The ashura towered over me! I rolled to the side as three swords hit the floor. A second slower and I would have lost my tail! I dodged and dodged, rolling and tumbling all over the damn place.

"Should have taken the deal, nogitsune! Now my Master will have your ears and tail!"

He swiped at me again as I ducked. Three blades whooshed over the place my head had just been. Had I not lowered my ears defensively, the pair of them would have been shorn off! Then a bullet wound appeared in his forehead, a sudden dot that dripped blood. The ashura fell back and thumped hard to the floor, its blades falling out of its lifeless hands.

Nani? I thought, confused.

I turned and saw Katashi. The tanuki nodded at me. Then I saw a flash of silver and sidestepped, severing my latest opponent's head. It fell and bounced across the floor. I glanced at my gory trophy's progress to see Chikako hiding under a table with huge eyes.

Damn it! She has to get out of here!

Nearby, Hiroko was clawing the face of some fool who had gotten too close to her or Chikako, likely thinking the ne-komata easy prey. Oh boy, was *that* stupid! Hiroko had a deep vicious streak, and she made use of it now. Apparently, she was the kind of kitty who liked to play with her food. She was covered in blood, and not a bit of it her own.

We fought for what seemed like an hour, but it lasted barely longer than the duration of the song. Then someone cut the sound off. The sudden loss of the music gave the immediate illusion of silence. But that was wrong. I heard screams of the wounded and dying, the shouts of battle cries. Katashi's guns.

Grimly I carried on, meeting opponent after opponent, cutting them down with my katana and my claws. Limbs were severed, blood spilled. Some I set on fire and let them run blind into their own comrades, who also caught fire. I was gratified to see my victims burn.

Somehow, I maintained my humanoid form throughout the fight. Other demons in rampage form called to the beast inside of me. Shiroi Uindo, too, wished to show itself and join the party. But I refused to let myself go that far. I think I managed it only because Chikako was watching. I could feel her eyes on me. I did not want her to see me that way.

But in spite of that, the monster felt reckless glee at the

clash of battle! I loved the feeling of felling my enemies. I whirled and cleaved, and took pleasure in the resistance of flesh as blood spattered and body parts severed! I was death's instrument! My face twisted cruelly with my enjoyment at the slaughter. The feral demon inside of me *loved* this!

That is not to say we did not have limits, however, Shiroi Uindo and I. The injuries I took throughout were having a cumulative effect in spite of my rapid healing factor. I was tiring.

Then the most beautiful and fantastic thing happened. A great azure dragon wound its sinuous serpentine curves above us, his hair and chin beard a flowing gold, mustachios longer than what I had done to Hiroshi's. Youta-sama himself floated above our heads, and it was impossible not to stop and stare. Then, with a deep inhale, he let loose a bellow of flame into the enemy.

Demons *shrieked*. Many fled on both sides. I stood and watched in awe. Youta roared his displeasure. The sound of it was a shockwave that jarred through my body.

After that, it was over. I heard shouts and transports driving away. There were pockets of flame as bodies smoldered. Smoke with the scent of charred meat drifted through what was left of our club. Somewhere I heard sirens in the distance, steadily coming closer.

"Chikako!" I yelled through the smoky haze, remembering her.

"Here!" I heard her cough.

I went to her at once. I knelt beside the table as she coughed again and gave her my free hand, awash in blood. After a moment's hesitation in which she peered cautiously up into my face, she took it and crawled out. I helped her to her feet. But the way she looked at me... one part admiration, two parts dread and fear. Chikako had seen my bloodlust and my darkness. There was no disguising how much of a yako I truly was, or that I enjoyed slaughter for its own sake.

"Are you alright?" I asked, worried.

She nodded. "Yes."

I sighed in relief and clutched her hard to me, katana still held fast in my right hand. She did not resist. We held onto one another in the midst of the smoking ruin. Chikako seemed to be in a state of shock. I could hardly blame her. Now that it was over, I felt numb. Kami-sama, what a damn mess the Ori was.

THE COPS CAME, OF COURSE. BEFORE THEY DESCENDED ON THE bombed-out ruin of our club, Youta and I burned the remaining dead. It would not do to have yōkai bodies examined. I summoned the wind to blow out the thick layer of ash covering the floor. Throughout this, Chikako bore witness to my powers for the first time, and I have to say that I enjoyed her wide-eyed gaze of awe.

The club stank of roasted meat and charred demon with the stench of burnt plastic and heated metal. The tanuki and I cast our illusions to cover the bloodstains. I watched as Hiroko went off to clean herself up. The next I saw her, she had put on a fresh hostess's uniform and waited with perfect calm. True nekomata right there.

The police were human to a man, paid for and owned by the oligarchy, although whether *they* knew that, I had no idea. They crawled all over the place, no more pleased by the mess and the hideous smell than we were. The higher ups in suits went to Youta's office. The uniforms took statements from the rest of us. To their annoyance, the information they obtained was vague at best, sometimes conflicting.

I cloaked myself deep in glamours to appear terribly ordinary. A typical lower middle-class Japanese man in a cheap suit, stained and frayed. My short, dark hair and thick glasses were askew. I played the part of one who had no means to fix such things as eyesight, a man from The Sprawl who commuted to an office complex every day. I gave my character an overbite and slight build, head drawn down into hunched shoulders.

Whenever an officer walked by, I bowed deeply and made myself look very humble. Chikako had to look away to keep from giggling at my act. Eventually a young, female officer approached me. "So, what did *you* see?" She bore the name tag 'Yoshimora.'.

I shrugged and pretended to be confused. "Nothing! I was in the bathroom when I heard a big, loud 'Boom!'"

"Yeah, seems a whole lot of you were 'in the bathroom' when this place blew," she said sarcastically.

I shrugged helplessly. "Lots to drink. I had to go. I'm so sorry!" I bowed meekly.

"Uh huh. Why were you here in an unmarked underground club, Mister...?" She was fishing.

"Friends from work brought me out for a wild night. Said I needed to loosen up and live a little. But they took me to *this* dive! Now I can't find any of my coworkers. What do I tell the boss man?" I bemoaned and mopped at my brow with a hanky.

Officer Yoshimora looked at me skeptically. "Tell him whatever you want. What was your name again?"

"Hey, Hanako-san," a male cop called to her. Reluctantly she walked away, but not without a backward glance.

"Don't go anywhere." She stared me dead in the eyes, although mine were cloaked behind my disguise. With a thoughtful frown, she turned to her fellow officer.

That was my cue. I immediately stepped back into the shadows and vanished from sight.

Chapter Seventeen

Akusho

The hit on our club was only the beginning. Hiroshi sent out a multi-prong attack unilaterally across the Sprawl, and by the next morning, more than half of Youta's illicit businesses were decimated. Everything that Youta legally held on record was destroyed. Many young demons were slaughtered, and humans, too, even those who had no idea for whom or what they were working.

The shockwave rippled across the Sectors. Bets were made as to how long it would take to round up the surviving fugitives of Youta Clan, myself among them. But the war was far from over. My master harbored a deep desire for revenge while the new and improved Cage was built several blocks east of its original location.

Youta wanted his next move to cripple Hiroshi's illicit businesses in the deep Sprawl. Our own coffers desperately needed the digi-cred. And the best way to do both in the world of criminals was to hit the brothels and the gambling dens. So, we started with the latter as September drew to a close.

"Hayate-san, you and Katashi will go into the tobakujou and undermine their wealth. Spread it around and do not take unnecessary chances, but always come out with more than you went in. Get the precise layouts of his establishments. Later, we will rob them."

"*Katashi*, my lord?" I asked, stunned. The tanuki only grunted, no happier about it than I was.

"Our tanuki is a most adept gambler and knows the dens very well. You can learn a great deal from him and I suggest you both lay your mutual animosity aside. This is business."

I was dismayed that I was being partnered with the one yōkai who hated my guts and would gladly take a shot at me to rid the world of one more kitsune! But I will say this for the old bastard: Katashi could set aside his baggage for a cause he believed in. All I had to do was meet him halfway.

"I don't like you, yako," Katashi said to me once we were alone, "and I will never trust you. But you're no snitch and you can fight. So, you know how to play mahjong or pachinko? Poker? Dice?"

I shook my head.

"Heh. Too pure bred for that kinda shit, huh? Not anymore, I bet." He laughed gruffly. I growled in warning, my ears fanned out low, eyes narrowed. "Oh, please! Think I didn't know?" Katashi snorted. "I'm over nine hundred years old, shirogitsune. I've known yako, hell I've *fucked* yako, and I know a broke-down celestial when I see it. Doesn't change a damn thing. You betrayed your god, didn't you? You'll betray us too one day. You just don't know it yet."

I ground my teeth and stared at him malevolently. He was wrong about me and I would prove it!

"But not today, eh? You're made of sterner stuff than most foxes, I'll give you that. Shove the self-righteous act already, kid. We ain't got time for it. I'll show you how to play and use your broadleaves and illusions to cheat without getting caught. So unclog those fluff-filled triangles on top of that thick skull of yours, 'cuz I ain't in the habit of repeatin' myself."

And for all that he was an insufferable bastard, Katashi did just that. Believe it or not, he was a damn good teacher! It helped I was a quick study, too, and what do you know? That old tanuki and I made excellent partners in crime. He taught me how to perfectly mimic cards and mahjong tiles, and make dice seem to go in my favor. With a few well-placed sleight of hand tricks and illusion spells, it was easy to make myself a winner every time.

Now for the record, gambling was strictly illegal in Japan. Regardless, this did not stop the dens from operating. Cops looked the other way, digi-cred changed hands, and no one said a thing.

Every racially segregated section of The Sprawl had its own Red Light District. The Japanese Sector, boasting the largest area and greatest density of citizenry, was in the best repair as the Japanese marginally cared more for their own natives. Obviously, these residents were accorded generally better employment, reflected in their income and housing. The Korean and Western Sectors were the two most run down areas in all of New Tokyo and considered especially dangerous.

Katashi and I did not discriminate. We went into a number of gambling dens across The Sprawl, always in a different disguise. It was difficult to track two shapeshifting saboteurs when they crossed Sector lines with no recognizable rhyme or reason. An enemy who cannot see the pattern of your strategy is at a great disadvantage. This was a game Youta played well.

In spite of our yōkai natures, this mission was not without risk. Tobakujou were predatory establishments, created to take money, not give it away. Win too much legitimately, and they were prone to condemn you anyway. They thought nothing of committing torture and murder to keep the digi-cred for themselves. The barest whiff of cheating was met with harshly. There were torture chambers for thieves and those poor fools who could not cover their losses. In the seedier establishments, men's screams were heard regularly from the back rooms. I could tell when someone lost a body part, for the sound became a long, strangled screech in a higher pitch!

One night, a group of strong boys ran out into the street after me, accusing me of being a cheat. I led them on a merry chase in the guise of a typical Sprawl rat, which is to say a fifteen to twenty-five-year-old punk who was unaffiliated with a gang. I ducked into a dark, dead-end alley, and like fools, they followed me.

There were no cameras back here, and the residents were too smart to peek. I allowed them to corner me, then shed my illusion in a whorl of shadow and mist before their astonished eyes. I grinned behind my mask and drew my katana, eyes gleaming with bloodlust. My fellow kabuki-masked demons silently materialized from the shadows to cut off their escape.

The concrete soon looked as if it had rained blood. With nowhere to run, they fought. But humans do not fare well against a pack of genuine yōkai. When our butchery was done, we dragged their remains into the shadows for lesser mononoke to feast on. The bodies were never recovered.

It took a full week for suspicions to arise, making it a bit harder to maneuver in this way. The tobakujou began beefing up security, and from the way the hired muscle scanned the room, it was clear they were looking for us. There were ways to trap and kill yōkai, and by now Hiroshi must have caught on.

To change things up, I went in as a prostitute on Katashi's arm. Man, was Katashi ever a jerk! He kept pulling me into his lap, randomly copping feels, playing with the hair on the back of my neck, and there was nothing I could do to stop it for the sake of appearances. The bastard was hard, too. Hate me he might, but he wanted me.

Disgusted and offended by his groping, I finally had enough. I made to stand and leave when he grabbed me in a bear hug and crushed me against him. "Ah-ah," he chided in my ear. "Look around. Is this how the little whores behave?"

Furious, I took in the young women in tight gowns circulating among the patrons. They were slathered in heavy perfume to drown out the stink of other men on their skin. They might not like the company they kept, but they suffered it in silence with painted faces and false smiles. It was a job. So was this.

"Good girl," he purred when I relented. He squeezed the underside of my breast. "You wear submission well. Relax and you might even enjoy it, sweetheart."

I decided there was only one way to turn the tables on that one-legged son of a bitch. I began teasing him mercilessly. We both knew damn well I was not going to let him to fuck me. I hated the way his stubby cock felt against my ass, but I flashed my inner thighs and wriggled all over his lap, with occasional soft murmurs.

I flustered that old tanuki so much he nearly busted his nut in his pants. Katashi scruffed my nape and slapped my ass with a hard, sharp *WHACK!* Men chuckled at my public humiliation.

"Stop it!" he hissed. "Whaddya think you're doin'?"

"But I thought this was how little whores behaved," I mocked, slipping a sharp pointy splinter from the table against his backside, and when he plopped his blue balls back down, boy, did he howl! That old pervert never molested me again.

When Katashi bitched about his sore ass to Youta-sama, I punched him dead in the face. "See what I gotta put up with?" he complained nasally, blood pouring down his lips and chin.

Our master waved his hand of the matter. "Enough, Katashi. We pay for what we take. Nothing is free," Youta said with a reserved smile, and that was the end of that. Youta-sama liked me better anyway.

"In any case, this game is now over." It had gotten too hot. Now was the time for flat out robbery. And in early October, we did just that.

The first establishment we knocked over catered solely to yōkai in the seedier side of the Japanese Sector. We might have had a fight on our hands, except Jūro brought a grenade launcher he got from our first mission together back in spring. It looked ridiculous, him bearing such a large weapon, but he lugged it around easily. He was ecstatic to finally be able to use it! And trust me: nothing is quite so intimidating as a monkey demon with a grenade launcher on his shoulder, backed up by six fellow great demons. We divested the establishment of its wealth quite easily despite the demonic clientele. No one said or did a thing. Even monsters are not so keen to die.

"Tell Youta he can go fuck himself!" the owner spat as we walked into the street, all his digi-chips in our possession. "Hiroshi-sama will have his bastard blue hide for this!"

Jūro swung around and let one of those grenades fly. *BOOM!* The vids always make it look like you can run away from shit like that. It's a lie. There were no survivors. That tawdry hole in the wall went up in a bright ball of flame.

"Ooops!" the sarugami cackled and that was the end of that.

We committed twenty robberies in a single night, giving Hiroshi's loyalists no time to prepare an adequate defense. The following night, we hit the brothels.

In a world where men controlled money, women sold their bodies to acquire some of it. Prostitution was a grueling business, hard and unforgiving. The average human Sprawl whore usually came to a bad end early in her career. Few made it out of the business alive, and those that did wound up on drugs, which tended to do for them where merciless clients and ruthless pimps failed.

As with the gambling dens, the tanuki was no stranger to this scene, either. He knew the location of every pleasure house in the entire megapolis, including the secret ones. I had no doubt that if he slipped out of his mask and robes, Katashi would have been recognized in an instant. And in one of the establishments, even the costumed get-up did not matter.

"What is this?" the Madame asked acidly when we stepped into her parlor. She was old, human, and cared not at all that we were yōkai. "A buffoon's parade? Wearing such nonsense in public! Have you come to dance the kagura for us, too?"

We had split into two teams, the better to cover more ground. Mine had Katashi, Shirou and Takeshi. The brothel grew silent when our party entered, all but this cruel old hag.

"I mean really, Katashi! I know it's you, thick old badger."

"You're one to talk about old, you prehistoric antique hooker," Katashi shot back. "Already acting the bitch. And here we came to make you a fucking offer, Ami."

"I heard Youta's making a bid. Stupid thing to do. Rocking the boat. Hiroshi-sama will put you all down like the rabid monsters you are." She looked at each one of us in turn. "Especially *this* yako," she said when her eyes fell scornfully upon me. "What the hell was that water snake thinking, taking this thing into his service," she sneered. "Where did Youta find the likes of you?" she addressed me. "Crawl out of a sewer? Hiroshi will –"

"*Fuck* Hiroshi!" Katashi roared, cutting Ami off. I had never seen the tanuki so pissed. "That son of a snake *screwed* me! Why do you think I went to work for the water dragon?" Now that was interesting. I had hoped to hear more about this, but the conversation abruptly changed.

"I don't give five farts in a windstorm why you left Hiroshi-sama's service. You have been a good customer, for all that I personally despise you, you fat old pervert. Get out and take these mongrels with you, and we'll pretend it didn't happen. I won't tell you twice."

Katashi drew his guns and Shirou his sword. That was enough for the soft meat creatures. The human customers ran out of the salon.

"This is shit, Katashi!" the Madame yelled in a chiding tone that made me want to claw her face. "Are you going into each room and dragging my customers out, too?"

"No need, Ami. They're our customers now."

"What a joke!" Spoke up an old yōkai with a whore on his lap. "Who do you think you are?"

"We are part of a dynamic enterprise that plans to absorb all such business throughout The Sprawl," Shirou said politely.

"You are thugs of Youta Clan!" called out a red oni, who no longer bothered to disguise his yōkai nature. Demons proliferated on both sides of this exchange. Nor were buyers and sellers exclusively mutual to species. Some clients had a yōkai kink, like the dastardly Miss Shizuka.

"Hai," I said, refusing not to have a voice in this.

"We know of you," the oni said to me. "Shiroi Uindo, is it? Ha! You are scum, *yako!*"

Now some people had a way of saying that word as if they were speaking disdainfully of an unwashed woman's privy parts. That was how *this* asshole said it. In response I sent a ball of kitsunebi at his head, which erupted in flames upon contact. He died shrieking in agony.

Women screamed. One vomited noisily. The ogre's body fell over sideways onto the floor, smoldering and slowly reducing to ash like an unattended cigarette. The room smelled of brimstone and barbecue.

"Next?" I asked, the drawl in my voice intoning my boredom as I tilted my head to the side.

The other yōkai clients stood. A small one made a run for the back door. Or tried. I launched four broadleaves from my fingers and flung them into his back. One exploded in snake vine and wrapped around his ankles. He lay whimpering where he fell, his claws scrabbling at the floor helplessly.

The others rushed the three of us. I did not bother to draw my sword. I slashed one across the throat with my extended claws. He fell back, hand clutching his throat as blood poured down his chest in a flood. Takeshi grabbed another demon by the head and crushed its skull between his hands! I had never seen the big blue oni do that before, but I admit, I was impressed.

I was less so when Katashi's gun rang out next to my head. His aim was great, but my ear rang for the next twenty minutes. Another found himself impaled on Shirou's blade.

"Hiroshi-sama will never stand for this!" the Madame yelled when her yōkai clientele were nothing more than messy corpses on her ruined carpet.

"Hiroshi no longer has any say here." I was far from the oldest, and the most recent member of the Seven to boot, but I naturally asserted myself with authority.

I stalked toward the crone, and I have to admit the old broad stood her ground. In a swift motion, I drew my blade and cut off her head. Women shrieked again as blood splashed across the screens. Her body fell with a thump. I picked up the head by the hair in my blood-soaked claws and held my prize aloft for all to see. *Drip, drip, drip...* This drew another round of shrieks and gasps.

"This establishment belongs to Youta-sama now," I announced to the room. "You there." My eyes landed on a woman made of sterner stuff than the others. This one was almost too old to stay in the industry much longer. She had seen it all, probably done it all. She had not cried out when her Mistress was cut down. "Swear your loyalty to Youta-sama, and this hen house is yours."

Her slight smile widened. "Alright. But we'll need protection, kitsune-dono. I cannot stand against armed thugs, let alone yōkai of your caliber." She gestured at the four of us, and the head. Case in point.

"Fair enough," I allowed. And it was done.

We did pretty much the same thing in nearly every red-light district all over The Sprawl in the next few hours. By the time we were done, Youta Clan had appropriated a goodly number of New Tokyo's pleasure houses. Oh, Hiroshi succeeded in taking back a few, but Youta's protection managed to secure the rest. Katashi stayed at the last one for the remainder of the night rather than head back to report in. Ami was right. He really was an old pervert.

This insult, as well as the robbery of the gambling houses, brought the Yakuza in against us. But Youta had a plan for that, too. And in short order, I was one of those sent to take care of it.

Chapter Eighteen

Night Flight

Tuyuko, Shirou, and I stepped onto the rooftop in our traditional kabuki masks and costumes. The city glittered around us in the artificial neon night. The cool October breeze blew through my hair, my robes billowing noisily. There was just the perfect amount of nip in the air. The gibbous moon rode high in a cloudless sky the shade of midnight blue. It was truly a beautiful night.

I stood poised in this moment, listening to the sounds of the Metropoplex below and surrounding me. Transport cars revving and beeping, people chattering, the giant holo-vid screens peddling state approved news and the latest products to improve human life. It was all just noise, but it made its own strange song.

This was my home, a concrete and glass forest of neon leaves and reinforced steel trunks glowing in a cold blue night. The air smelled indefinably like autumn to me. I savored it, knowing it might be the last time.

There was no signal. I lifted myself upward in the same moment as the yuki onna. The tengu expanded his large wingspan to embrace the air as he took a running leap off the building. Then the three of us were flying through the city, its bright lights and its glare. My native element embraced me as I flew, and I relished the sweet freedom of flight.

The windows of skyscrapers whisked past me. Fuyuko veered off sharply to the right, Shirou to the left, the better to confuse any radar or cams as we sped toward our target, the penthouse office of the Yakuza elite. Intel said they were planning a hit on Youta's investments later tonight. Our Master had a man on the inside. We three were being sent to bring the battle to them first.

I flew swift and sure straight ahead, past the huge vidscreens with advertisements and newsfeeds spouting the daily propaganda. Kanji signs flashed by in neon splendor. I dodged below a bridge span between two buildings, lifted myself above a traffic cam actively scanning the bright streets below, and twisted sideways past a delivery drone. I was like an arrow loosed at my target. My eyes always focused ahead in my snarling fox mask as I drove headlong into the wind.

Around the next building, suddenly Fuyuko appeared on my left side, and within two blocks Shirou winged into view on the right. They crossed paths in front of me and disappeared. More buildings blurred by. I diverted around a high rise directly in front of me and briefly saw my fierce visage in the mirrored glass. Then I was past it. Below spread a large, open plaza.

My masked compatriots appeared again to either side of me. We hurtled straight through empty air toward the upper floor of a tall, one-hundred story skyscraper. To my right,

Fuyuko froze the windows across the building. Ice crystals formed on every large glass surface, crackling as it spread. When it was coated in a fine sheen of white frost, I cast my lightning. Blue-white arcs danced across the windows, which shattered inward with explosive force. The lights cut out and the three of us soared in on a rush of autumn wind.

We stood in the center of the room, glass shards and ice powder glittering all over the floor. All around us confused human warriors blinked in a daze, stunned at the suddenness of the attack. Some had already been injured in our initial on-slaught. Glass daggers stuck out of armor and unprotected skin alike. And there we stood like statues in their midst, the frosty air whistling in through the broken floor length windows, the glass a jagged border around the frames.

A strong male voice gave the order. Enemy weapons were drawn. Although they had guns, the space was too confined to safely open fire. They were as like to hit one another as to riddle us with bullets. Shirou and I slowly and deliberately drew our swords and took stance. Fuyuko's ice blade glittered haunt-ingly beneath the moonlight in a wreath of mist.

Without a word we maneuvered ourselves gracefully so that we stood back to back to back. All was still and quiet for the space of an indrawn breath. An instant later, all hell broke loose. Fifty dark clad warriors converged upon the three of us on every side. What followed was a slaughter.

Armed and armored they might be, but they were not pre-pared for imminent combat and certainly not anticipating such a ruthless attack on one of their strongholds. Years of training and discipline made up for it, however. The first wave rushed us, and at least five came at me at once. I never felt so alive as

I did in battle, unless it was having sex. I grinned beneath my kitsunenomen and met the onslaught vigorously.

The clash of weapons was a song in my ears! I whirled, meeting this slash, dodging that thrust. I blocked a backslash and kicked the man backward a meter or so to give me the space to stab him. I withdrew my blade from his chest and cut another one diagonally across the lower torso. That one fell back screaming, entrails sliding out as I thrust up into the lungs of the man on my left.

I pulled my katana free and ducked a shuriken in the nick of time. I sent three broadleaves forth from between the knuckles of my left hand. One man was struck through the dead center of his forehead with enough force that it embedded into his brain. He fell over after standing stupidly for a few seconds, his body not recognizing the trauma immediately. The other two leaves went slicing deep into another man's right and left eyes, blinding him. He screamed as blood and fluid leaked down his cheeks. He could not close his eyes because my leaves were blocking his lids. I cut his head off and put him out of his misery.

Fuyuko froze the floor, a most effective defense against humans. One man tried to turn the momentum of his slide in his favor and lunged for her, but she grasped his wrist and gave him instant frostbite. His arm blackened beneath her icy touch. He yowled as her cold spread through him until he was frozen solid. When he fell to the floor, he cracked. Razor sharp ice snowflakes appeared in her hand and she sent them forth into her enemies with diabolical precision. Icicles followed, spearing into chests and throats. Her sword flashed cold and deadly in her hand, steaming with the blood that froze to the blade.

She blew her breath on another man and he became encased in ice as the water molecules in the air around him froze.

Shirou fought ten at once and never broke a sweat. He was sublime grace with his katana. I wish I could have watched. Shirou made a soliloquy of death. He was trained in the Hira Mountains, where his clan lived and practiced their mystic arts. Daitengu were warrior monks among yōkai kind. The crow was precise and controlled, no motion wasted. Limbs piled up with the slain.

As for me, well... with my demon's eyes glowing behind my mask, I savagely sliced and clawed my opponents to shreds. How good it was to be Shiroi Uindo the Demon Fox, bringer of death! I knew no fear, only wild joy! My white fur hanten was splattered wet with blood and gore.

Wave after wave of able human men rushed us, but I never tired. The few strikes that landed on my flesh scarcely hurt and healed almost instantly. I had fed well in anticipation of this battle, and my strength was worth twenty of these mortal weaklings! I was a great yōkai made to strike terror into the hearts of men, a furious battle machine born to kill.

It did not matter what weapon I faced. Staves, clubs, swords, yanyuedao, sai, it was all the same to me. One even came at me with tekko-kagi – the claws of death! He met with *my* extended claws in his throat instead and choked on his own blood. The bodies piled up in front of me, too.

Reinforcements from other floors, fresh and battle ready, flooded into the room from an open doorway and scrambled over the dead, screaming their human rage as they came. The minutes passed by in ethereal slowness, the seconds rushed past with the speed of a transrail. Time gets a bit hinky in battle. It lasted until every warrior was dead save we three.

I had to give them credit, though. Not a single man of them ran. Each and every one fought bravely to the death, knowing what we were, knowing they would die. It did not change a thing. Dead was dead.

When silence reigned save for the wind and the sounds of distant traffic, it saw us standing as we had begun. We were gods surrounded by sacrifices. They lay at our feet, mangled and in pieces. I held a bloody heart in my left hand, a parting treat from the last man I slew. Waste not, want not.

We left the dead where they fell, their sightless eyes staring in bleak accusation. A few of these were like to become yūrei or onryō. I could not have cared less. I had no fear of being haunted by the specters of those I killed. I was an energy vampire and could eat their incorporeal ghosts if I wanted. Without a word we vanished into the shadows. Fuyuko flew up to the ceiling, Shirou pivoted to the side, and I sunk down into the floor.

BACK AT THE ORI WE BOWED TO YOUTA, WHO WAS MOST PLEASED by our success.

"Good," our Lord Dragon said. "*That* will give the oligarchy pause before they choose to send anyone else against us. Let the council waste time deliberating on what to do next. This will frustrate Hiroshi. Lesser gangs will tremble to hear what has happened to the most elite. Soon this city will belong to *us!*"

"Hai, Youta-sama," we three answered in unison.

Upon our takeover of the brothels, Hiroshi declared all-out war on Youta. The oligarchy, in alignment with Hiroshi, actively plotted against us in their steel palaces. But the younger dragon had been quietly preparing for this for decades, and so he had safehouses, treasuries, and armories cached all over New Tokyo. He had inside men in every gang, at every level of government, and not all of them were demons, either. The Metropoplex was a human world. Many were in the water dragon's employ and not even aware of it.

Espionage was carried out secretly at the highest levels. Human gangs on both sides squared off on the streets. The Ayakashi War had spread to the world of mortals at last. There were no safe sidelines any longer, no neutrality. They fell in or they were trampled. Both sides mobilized now in a race against time, marshaling our forces as we sped toward the ultimate confrontation.

Since our new secret locker rooms were as yet under construction, I was still in my costume when I walked into my apartment soundlessly through the wards I had placed on the shadows. Instantly I noticed the air inside was warmer by comparison. The cinnamon and clove scented candles Chikako had bought were lit here and there, and my little shoji screen lamp by the bed was the only other light in my one-room. I breathed in deep. It smelled like autumn, and home… and her.

Chikako was reading her phone device, the blanket covering her up to the bosom. She was naked under the covers and waiting for me, propped up by the pillows behind her back. The nekomata shivered and looked up. She shrieked when she saw me padding towards her, her hand flying up to cover her lips. I stopped beside the futon, looming over her.

"That's *not* funny!" she declared angrily to cover her fright.

I laughed and tilted my kitsunenomen up high on the side

of my head, festival-style. Chikako pouted and sat up, the blanket sliding to her hips. I grinned lasciviously. How I so very much needed to fuck after that battle!

"Ah, but the evil nogitsune is back from hunting humans!" I purred playfully. "And now…" I leaned down to kiss her.

"Hayate!" Her eyes went huge as she got a good look at me and cringed back. Her ears twitched and planed out to the sides. I stared down at myself. I *was* a bit of a mess. I reeked of blood, was covered in it.

"Yuck… is that a bit of… scalp?" She plucked it off me with the tips of her thumb and forefinger, flicking it distastefully to the floor.

"Might be," I admitted, shrugging. I did not care. I smiled wickedly as I took in the sight of her curvaceous flesh. Just then that was all that I wanted.

"Gross!" Chikako wrinkled her pretty nose and shook her head. She was a gentle sort of creature for a yōkai. But for all that, she was turned on by me. I could smell it, the perfume of her arousal. I breathed in deep. "I swear, you are hopeless!"

I laughed, took hold of her elbows and pulled her to her feet. "Hopeless, am I?" I asked lightly, an arched brow raised.

She sighed and took the mask from my head. She looked at the evil thing, twitching her mouth in dismay before gently tossing it aside. That gaze softened exponentially when turned up to my face. "My yōkai samurai," she purred, "fresh off the battlefield. Beautiful and soaked with the blood of your enemies…"

My hanten I tossed in the air and set on fire, turning it to ash before it hit the floor. Chikako gasped, but smiled when I untied my obi, Kazuki's daisho landing noisily beside my feet.

She pushed my kimono off my shoulders and I took her in my arms immediately, kissing her hard. I pressed my naked arousal against her belly until she shoved me back roughly.

She grabbed my arms, spun me around and threw me down onto the thin mattress. My grin broadened as she pounced on top of me. I absolutely adored her wanton violence! She ground and slid her wet lips against my cock without taking me in, mewling the whole time. It drove me insane!

I rolled her in my passion, my hips between her legs. I delighted in the feel of the demoness pinned under my bare skin, one hand on the swell of her breast, the other on the gentle curve of her hip. I nuzzled her throat, nipping lightly with my fangs.

"You tease!" Chikako yelped, grabbing fistfuls of my hair.

She reached between us and guided me between her spread-eagled thighs. I slid into the silky, sodden sheath of her body. Kami-sama, what a sensation! There was nothing better than this after dispensing death for my daimyo.

"You belong to *me*," I hissed.

"Yes! Fuck me, dark heart! Take me hard, my warrior, my evil nogitsune!" I happily obliged. Immediately she began moaning, cursing and yelling.

I pounded into her, my knees up under her ass for leverage, tail wrapped around her leg. I took her as a conquest, holding her wrists down. The benefit of being with a fellow yōkai was that she was not so delicate as human women. She yowled and I grunted, and my mattress took its latest beating from our vigorous union.

Before it was over, she rolled me onto my back and slammed up and down my shaft, her claws gouging my chest.

I did not mind. When I took her yin energy in the moment of her pleasure, those superficial wounds healed immediately. She did not stop until she had milked me dry, the way I liked it. My world drowned in pleasure. It was bliss.

Afterward, she lay atop my body, the two of us still temporarily joined. I petted her head and back, running my hands through her dark hair and scratching behind her cat ears.

"Hayate?" she murmured, purring.

"Hmm?" I asked drowsily, content.

"What is it like out there?"

"Terrifying. Wonderful. *Alive*." I smiled up at her.

"You love it."

"Yes," I admitted.

"I saw that when Hiroshi hit the club. You were so beautiful to watch, but… The look on your face that night…" I felt her shudder. "It was pure evil. It scared me…" It also turned her on. She had trouble reconciling that I did not repel her. For all the warning in her heart, she was drawn to me as the moth to the flame.

"I know. The darkness is a part of me. I cannot help what I am."

I almost admitted I was Fallen right there and then, but managed to keep myself from it. Fortunately, the fit passed. That was not something I could entrust to any yōkai, especially not one I would one day betray because I could not return her feelings. I was convinced I was too far gone for such tender emotions as love. I felt kind of bad about it, so far as I could, but I did not know how to reach feelings I thought were forever lost to me, either.

"I know you can't, Hayate." She sighed and stroked my

cheek. "My beautiful white fox, so cold and cruel like a winter storm. How I wish..."

How she wished she could make me love her the way she loved me. Chikako looked in my eyes, wanting to see what was not there and never would be. "But you just can't, can you?" She looked so sad.

I closed my eyes and sighed. What could I say? I could not give her that which she most fervently desired. I did not have it in me. How could I love anyone, ever, or feel genuine compassion? So far as I could tell, the Hellfire had burned away my capacity for true sentiment and empathy. I believed these things implicitly for a long time.

"I'm sorry, Chika. I wish I could... I..." I fumbled for words. "I care about you more than anyone in my life," I said honestly after a long pause. My gaze did not waver from her eyes when I said it, my palm on her cheek and fingers in her hair. "I give to you all that I *can* give. Please believe that, Chikako."

She nodded. There was nothing else to be said. She rested her head beneath my chin and I wrapped my arms around her lithe body. We fell asleep that way, a nearly perfect end to a mostly perfect night.

Chapter Nineteen

Exposure!

Come on, already, I thought impatiently.

I peered into a dark room, lavish as only an abode of the wealthy could be. Blue moon shadows fell across the floor. It was full tonight and exceptionally bright, a brutally cold night for deep autumn. The master bedroom reeked of expensive cologne haphazardly applied on a sweaty, old, excessively obese human. My nose tickled and wrinkled at such odors.

The lawyer was staying up late with only his bed lamp and his holo-tab to keep him company. I watched him laugh at cat vids, the colors splashing across his face and chest. His striped yukata hung open to reveal the scars of previous heart surgeries. This man's flabby chest draped over his belly. And the damned pig was still crunching on seasoned corn chips at this late hour, crumbs spilling all over him and his bedding! He rubbed his fingers on his fine sheets, leaving yellowish smears and salt on the clean fabric.

I was... appalled.

This was taking too long. Youta was waiting for my return. I was feeling cagey, agitated. The longer I had to wait, the more I sensed I was being closed in on. Every instinct I possessed screamed at me to abort. Yet I could not. Was I not Shiroi Uindo, bringer of certain death, who never missed a kill and was hardly ever seen unless I intended to be? My reputation as an assassin of Youta Clan depended upon each life I took. This human was no exception. I *must* take his heart tonight for my daimyo.

At last the lawyer switched the damn holo-tab off and set it aside. He fell back against his pillows, adjusted numerous times, and immediately began snoring. Now I could do what I came for, this rare mission in which I was sent out on alone. I manifested into his room from out of the Shadow Realm. My vulpine shadow moved stealthily across the floor as I floated toward him, my feet never touching the ground.

But something must have given me away. Perhaps some instinct or the cold miasma my yōkai presence emanated. My prey awoke with a startled grunt mid-snore.

"Who's there?" the gruff voice asked as he sat up. "Kohaku, is that you?"

I did not answer him. After all, what did *I* have to say to the dead? I glided out of darkness into moonshine and back into darkness, silent and predatory. If my pale mask grinned with feral cruelty, it was no less than that which graced my own lips underneath. This was the moment I had come to love, the precious seconds of life before the kill. The scent of fear and the sound of terror.

It was even better when they so truly deserved their fate,

as this one did. This was the asshole at the top of the food chain who supplied sex slaves to clubs and brothels. Long had I dreamed of slaying this one.

His eyes snapped open wide. "I know you! You are Shiroi Uindo!" My skin tingled when he uttered my name. I drifted closer, my white hair weaving about me in the breezy wake I created for myself. He flinched away, his back thumping hard into the headboard. The scent of his fear pleased me.

"But why? I've done nothing! I am a lawyer, a business-man, an ordinary human being!" As if that made him better than the others whose lives I had taken. I drifted nearer still in my condemning silence. "I can offer you money, riches! Is it women you desire? You are nogitsune, yes? You must hun-ger for sex and violence! I can give you the best, Demon Fox! Clean, perfumed girls, young and beautiful; child virgins pure like lambs – whatever you prefer! Yours to fuck and shred as you will!"

I remembered the young victims in the Triple B, Aiko cov-ered in blood, and my lips curled. I would have killed him for his presumption on my nature and naught else, even if Youta had not already commanded his death by my claws. Children did not excite my appetites. Ah, but killing disgusting, twisted old fools who preyed on the innocent? Oh, yes. *That* was *fun*! Besides, what could *he* offer that I could not take for myself if I had a mind to?

"You need not to do this! They can use such a powerful creature as you, shirogitsune! It is still not too late to change your allegiance –"

Oh, but it was. Hiroshi proved that the last time we met. I did not fancy losing my ears and tail to The Dragon's vanity.

I pointed my yanyuedao at him and growled as only a vicious animal could. A throaty, masculine rumble purred up from deep in my chest and my tail lashed aggressively side to side. My fangs bared in anticipation, eyes glowing in the darkness through the eye holes of my mask, a deadly promise of my sinister intent.

"No! Don't! Stop! Please!" His eyes were wide, staring, his face filled with terror. The coward pissed and shat himself. It was sour, that sewer stench, but it smelled better to me than the overpowering cologne he smothered his rancid body in – *and* those garlic herb corn chip things. Kami-sama, but I *still* remember that fetid odor to this day!

I sliced his stomach up to his throat in a single, deft motion. Scarred, pallid flesh parted easily beneath the sharp blade. A spray of blood landed on his sheets and the wall. He gasped and gurgled on his own blood, then twitched and lay still, eyes staring in death. I knelt over my kill and ripped the partially mechanized heart from its cage. Hot blood welled beneath my claws, running in sticky rivulets down my wrist.

"Kuro? What is it? Did you have a bad dream again? You're not having another heart attack, are you?" a woman asked accusingly. "*Kuro?*" Her voice became worried. I heard the quiet rasp of a screen door slide open. "Answer me! Aki, lights on!"

My pupils slit into thin daggers against the sudden glare of light as I swiveled my head. His mistress stood in a floral robe, tousled and sleepy. I watched her expression become stunned. Her eyes grew wide as the scene before her sunk in past the layers of drowsy confusion.

The filthy lawyer for high ranking Yakuza *and* the corporate oligarchy lay dead. A masked monster in a theatre costume with the murder weapon in his hand was crouched over him, staring at her. And my left hand held his damaged heart in its blood-soaked talons. It spurted between my fingers as I convulsively squeezed.

Oh shit, I thought numbly.

The lawyer's mistress screamed. It was high pitched and painful, and It. Did. Not. Stop. Would that my hands were not so full, for I would have pressed them to my aching ears! Damn that women could emit such high decibels! All I wanted was to get away from that infernal sound.

I could not escape to the shadows, for there were no longer shadows deep or dark enough to retreat into. I had nowhere to go unless I went through her. And I cannot lie – I seriously considered it. *Anything* to shut that keening wail up and get away!

The first rule of my Code was 'Try not to harm innocents.' This woman was not on my list and I felt a bit bad for her if she had to cater sex to *this* disgusting asshole. So, I took the only option I thought I had available at the time. I shoved open the balcony door and leapt onto the railings. From there I jumped up to the peaked roof adjacent where the east wing met the main house.

The moon was bright, the shadows thin and too few. I had to get my bearings. There was no way I was going to risk another blind, long distance projection after the last time! A wooded park was not two blocks from here and I thought it should be visible from the roof. Once it was in line of sight, I would be gone like the wind.

I was rattled, not thinking clear. Never before had I been seen! This would be a black mark on my record, a great shame

I could not live down! I second-guessed myself for not killing the woman, was angry with myself for not being more careful.

"Baka, baka, *baka* kitsune!" I cursed. I ran along the roof tiles, my reclining moon blade held horizontal in my right hand, the rapidly cooling heart in my left. On the highest peak I stood silhouetted against the moonlit sky. The cold autumnal wind whipped through my hair and fluttered the white fur hanten, rippling the silk kimono beneath.

I had just caught sight of my jump point when a police transport-copter rose up behind me. I whipped around in the blinding spotlights. What a sight I must have made! My eyes glowed luridly through the black slits of my mask. My heart hammered, face numb and tingling. I trembled with adrenaline.

I should have killed the woman, or knocked her down and turned off the lights…

"Halt!" the loudspeaker called out in a voice of designated authority. "Remain where you are! Throw down the weapon!" The officer's voice boomed out again metallically, echoing across the night.

Idiot humans. They would not catch me, and they could not hold me. I was nogitsune! I swept the sickle moon-blade lance behind me and held the heart aloft for the men in the cockpit to see. I bowed to them formally, then fluidly turned like the demon I was and jumped out into midair. I folded space around me and landed in a tree in the park across the way.

I brooded as I watched troops of officers in heavy tactical assault gear run around the perimeter of the manse. They had been deployed *way* too fast in force. Someone must have known Murihito Kuro was next on the list. So why were there

no guards in the room? Or on that floor? Had Hiroshi sacrificed a piece to remove one of Youta's from the board?

Youta is going to skin me alive for this!

It would not be long before they came to the park to look
for me. Fortunately, the darkness was thick here. I leapt down
and sunk into a pool of thick shadows beneath the tree and
vanished completely into the Shadow Realm as the heavy
transport copter searched desperately for me in broad sweeps
overhead.

THAT NIGHT THE MEDIA GAVE ME A NEW NAME. THE KITSUNE
Killer. How 'imaginative.' I despised it. Unfortunately, it followed me throughout my criminal career in New Tokyo. Across
the Metropoplex, hundreds of giant holo-screens broadcast
images of a kitsune-masked murderer on that high-peaked tile
roof, clear in the full moon light.

Admittedly, I *was* terrifyingly sensational – a yōkai villain
come to life! With the heart dripping in my bloody hand and
then bowing to them before leaping out and disappearing into
thin air? I was iconic as hell!

"Metro-wide Alert in progress. Please remain calm. If
seen, do not approach this dangerous terrorist. Call the New
Tokyo Police Department immediately."

Where I had been the hunter, now the tables were turned
and *I* was the hunted. I had just become a notorious fugitive,
public enemy number one within a matter of *minutes*! They
wasted no time in blaring those few short seconds of my life
thousands of times over!

I fell to my knees before my master that night upon my
return without a word, head bowed low in my shame. The

screen in his office played the news footage behind him. That was when I learned how extensive the damage was. My ears pinned flat to my skull, my tail pressed tight to my leg where it wrapped around my knees in abject misery.

I was humiliated and nothing could change that. My immaculate record was broken. I was glad of the curtain of hair that shielded my stricken face. I could scarce hide how dejected I felt. The others stood in that room, my jury of six peers. Katashi, Fuyuko and Jūro were obviously experiencing a bit of schadenfreude at my disgrace, while the others frowned in consternation. I paid none of them any heed. It was Youta's judgment that mattered here.

I wondered if he would put me to death for my mistake, and if so, would he kill me himself or order me to do it by seppuku? In that moment I knew what those old samurai felt and, were it not for honor and to save face, I would have pissed myself right there as my life hung in the balance of my daimyo's whim.

"Hayate-san," the Dragon drawled softly after several nerve-wracking minutes of heightening terror with a side dish of raw despair. "What happened tonight?"

"I have failed you, Youta-sama," I said miserably.

"Failed? I am confused. Is the lawyer not dead? Is that not his heart in your claws?"

"Hai, Youta-sama! I cleaved him open and took his heart. I have it still if you desire to see it, my Lord." I held it out in my clenched fist. "It is... inedible."

"Lawyers, right?" The monkey demon laughed and suddenly fell silent. Youta must have given him the death glare. Believe me, a dragon staring daggers at you is damned intimidating.

"Why do you think you failed, Shiroi Uindo?" my master asked.

"Youta-sama, I was seen!" I confessed. "By human police!"

"Hai. I saw. You are on every vid feed in the city. The humans have given you a new name this night. The Kitsune Killer."

My heart dropped as I heard the name the humans pinned on me, and my posture lowered further towards the floor. A foxish whine caught fast in my throat. I bit my tongue before it could pass my lips. We foxes do not have much in the way of poker faces when we are this flooded by emotion. Like the animals we are, our bodies betray us every time.

"A frightening sight." I could tell by the pitch and direction of his voice that he was looking at the screen. "One to give the children night terrors…. and our enemies, too." He snorted. "They'll soon be selling kitsunenomen on every corner of The Sprawl until the oligarchy clamps down on it. Congratulations, my dear Wild Fox. You have just become an instant celebrity."

I dared to glance up. Youta was smiling at me. Fucking *smiling*! And here I was, shaking. *The Hell?* I thought, bewildered.

"You were only a rumor before, my White Wind. Now you are a potent message to all who dare oppose us."

"But, Youta-sama!" the tanuki exclaimed. "Hayate-san's blundering has endangered The Cause! Worse – the humans have the image of a real yōkai!"

The dragon stamped down on that swiftly. "They do not know that, and he has hardly harmed our cause! Shiroi Uindo has become the terrifying face of certain and swift death at my command. Hiroshi thinks himself clever to have exposed our fox, but Hayate's audacious theatrics turned the tables on that tactic."

Inside I was elated, if for no other reason than I would not die for my mistake! I was not ready to go to the darkest Hell in Jigoku or Yomi reserved for monsters like me. And apparently Youta was not ready to put down his pet Wild Fox. Thank goodness! I blew out a breath of hard relief and climbed to my feet.

"Sssooo, how did you get caaaaught?" the cold voice of the yuki onna spoke in wreaths of cold, breathy mist. Her arctic blue eyes fixed me fast.

"The job felt weird, but I would not shirk from my sworn duty. I obey what*ever* the personal cost." I glared at the tanuki. "I would not leave without taking the human's life. He stayed up late watching vid-feeds, and I wished to take him unaware so he could not call for aid. There was no interference, but the police seemed to be waiting for me on my exit."

"Why not slip into the shadows?" the tengu asked. "Or vanish into thin air like your kind do?"

"Murihito's mistress turned on the lights after I took *this* foul thing." Snarling, I tossed the cold, damaged organ on the floor. I no longer wanted to touch it. "She was sleeping in another room and cut off my only other avenue of escape. I regrettably chose to spare her life in that instant. There was only one other way out – up. I went to the roof to get a clear line of sight, which is rather important if I do not wish to find myself accidentally merged into something… or some*one*."

I let that hang in the air. Understanding blossomed in their eyes. I hated giving that much away about the limitation of my powers, to these villains especially, but it could not be helped in this instance.

"So that's how you got the side wound when you escaped

Hiroshi," Shirou correctly ascertained. "And that explains the pattern of your blood trail I saw that night."

I nodded. "I materialized around my barbell by accident." I scowled. Damn it, they did *not* need to know that!

No one held it against me for not coming forth with that information earlier and they squirreled the nugget away. I would have done the same. Only a fool openly admitted to the weaknesses in his or her powers. Yōkai and warriors implicitly understood these things.

"Hiroshi and the oligarchy knew we were coming for Murihito," Youta mused. "It could have been any one of you, whoever had been sent. It just happened to be Shiroi Uindo, much to Hiroshi's pleasure for your cheek, I am sure. It is said he has yet to appear where anyone but his closest can see." Again, that satisfied draconic smile. I shivered.

"Hayate did as he was instructed," Youta continued. "There will be no censure. *This*, my Chosen, is why we wear our masks. But we must move cautiously now in our haste. Our rival thinks this a clever ruse, and to his advantage over us. We will prove to him it is the opposite. And when the replacement is put in Murihito's place, Fuyuko will make certain he is already ours."

The yuki onna bowed, her face an emotionless mask save for the cruel gleam in those cold eyes. I did not envy Murihito's successor.

"Hayate-san, you have done much for us. I require you for my end game. I will not hesitate to bring you out as necessary, yet neither will I waste you for naught. So, until I say otherwise, Shiroi Uindo, you do not attract attention. No jobs and no club below. I will not have you make a scene should any be so foolish as to openly disrespect you."

"Hai, Youta-sama," I said despondently.

CHIKAKO WAS QUITE BESIDE HERSELF WHEN SHE RECEIVED THE news of my disgrace from the holo-vids above the bar. I found that out when I had a servitor send her word to see me in the employees' only area. Man, all the stares I got from the staff! That was really uncomfortable. Thank goodness Hiroko was off tonight. I do not think I could have born it from her.

"Are you alright?" Chikako's eyes were soft and wide.

"Yeah, except for my pride," I frowned.

"Everyone knows!" she exclaimed. Of course they did. "There's video... it's on all the screens! Our customers are glued to their devices, those that have them! The dancers are complaining that no one is looking at *them*!"

My face fell. "I can't come down to visit you for a while," I told her mournfully. "Youta-sama is isolating me, for obvious reasons."

She nodded, fretful and sad.

So the next week and a half did pass. Not being able to cop the occasional feel on Chikako until she came over to my place? Damn, that hurt. One time I grabbed her through the shadows when she was passing by and pulled her into a locked storage room. After being annoyed with me for taking her off the floor while she was technically on the clock, she unfastened my suit pants and took me into her mouth of her own volition.

Other than that? Life was so boring.

Even the stupid monkey came up and tweaked my tail over it. As in, he literally pulled my tail, the little bastard. I whipped around and extended my claws at him, but he only dodged away. "Hey, hey! Wild Fox got caught and can't play!

Nyah-nyah!" The sarugami stuck his tongue out at me and did a backflip.

I growled at him and made to lunge when Fuyuko walked in. The room grew very cold with the snow yōkai's presence, as if my miasma was not bad enough. "He only sspeakss the truth, yako. It doess not matter if it iss not precisssely your fault."

I stood straight and sighed, scowling. She was right, and so was the fucking monkey. I wanted to be out there, running against the wind! Fearless, powerful and free, hunting the night! It was all I could do not to gekker my frustration and whine piteously. I did neither. It would have made me look foolish to give in to my animal urges over such things.

"Ssoon, kitssune," she said, reading me easily.

"*Very* soon," said a deep voice I knew well. Youta. "I have a task for you, Hayate-kun."

I perked up at once.

"You and Shirou are to go to a local warehouse in the Japanese Sector. Under Hiroshi's direction, it seems one of the pharma corps has developed a nerve agent to incapacitate yōkai for use against *us*. The hack of the recipe is already under way. At the same time, I need you two to destroy the physical prototype. The containers will be in a stack of crates marked biohazard in an otherwise empty warehouse that most believe abandoned."

I was indescribably happy! I had been going stir crazy in my boredom. Foxes need things to do or we get into mischief. I suppose Youta-sama knew that and chose to loosen the leash a little. And besides, my kitsunebi made me perfect for destroying that nerve agent.

An hour later under the cover of darkness, Shirou and I padded through the shadows of the seemingly abandoned warehouse. On the ground floor was a stack of large shipping crates preloaded onto pallets, just as Youta said there would be. Cold drafts of seasonal air made the concrete building ice cold. There were a few overhead lights on, but only in the center of the room. The corners of the large industrial space were lost in empty darkness.

Human security agents sat up on the second-level metal deck beneath the lights, playing at cards. They had a space heater that muffled sound with its white noise and wore heavy coats. In spite of that they were shivering as they laid down their hands on a rickety old table. One of them cursed. I supposed he lost that round.

"Glad I folded. Time to make a sweep of below," another said with a groan. He stood, checked his holster, and clunked down the metal steps in his heavy boots.

"Another game?" the loser asked. "I need to win that back or my girlfriend is going to be pissed!"

"Baka! I'll take more off you," his fellow security guard laughed.

I nodded at Shirou across the way. With his red tengu mask and black kimono, he faded into the shadows. When the man making the sweep went past the scope of the lights, Shirou's hand darted out of the darkness. He grabbed the man from behind, his hand pressed firmly over the human's mouth, and pulled him into no-man's land before he could react. The security guard would never be seen again.

The stack of large crates was the only shipment in the room, just within range of the light. I came around the far back end and set the whole thing on fire with a summoned kitsunebi wisp. The boxes went up immediately in a whoosh of blue flame that burned bright and hot in the cold, dry air.

"Hey!" one of the men on the second level yelled. "We got a fire!" He ran down at full speed. Meanwhile, the winner of those card hands radioed in.

The one who pounded toward the fire made for an extinguisher on the wall of a pillar first, coughing from the thick, acrid smoke. Just as he reached it, I spun him, ripped off his protective vest and plunged my hand into his torso. It took only three seconds. He gasped, staring at the dread Kitsune Killer in terror, unable to speak or scream. When I pulled my hand out, he died. I backed into the shadows and lifted my mask enough to consume my prize. A thin wreath of fox fire boiled off the sticky blood from my skin when I was done.

"Hey! What's going on? Where are you guys?" I heard the last one shout. Now he ran down the clanging steps, too. The crates were already a smoldering heap of cinders and ash on the concrete warehouse floor. Kitsunebi burned hot and fast.

The guard saw his buddy lying face down in a pool of blood near the wall and ran to him at once. "Hey!" He rolled the man over. He had a gaping wound in his midsection. "What?" He stood and whirled around, just as the tengu stepped in with his drawn katana. The human fell down with a wheeze and died.

Shirou pulled a white feather from his wing and let it drift on top of his kill, his calling card. Without a word he stepped back into the shadows after we nodded to one another. Our work done, I gave one last glance around, preparing to follow my compatriot.

"Stop where you are!" a woman's voice cried out behind me. "Turn around, slowly! No sudden moves! DO IT NOW!"

Oh, fucking hell! What was this? Twice now? In a row? *Hayate, old boy, you are definitely losing your touch*, I thought to myself in recrimination.

I turned slowly. A young cop in beat gear stood with both hands wrapped around her gun, finger on the trigger, the barrel aimed at my chest. I recognized her by sight and scent. This was the woman who questioned me in the club the night of Hiroshi's attack. Officer Yoshimora.

"Holy – it's *you*!" Her eyes grew wide. "The Kitsune Killer! But, how? Why are you *here*?" I said nothing. "Put your hands up and away from those weapons! *Do it!* I will riddle you with bullets, I swear!"

I lifted my arms out from my sides gracefully, the sleeves of my fur kimono fanning out. I was not keen on getting shot tonight!

"What the hell do you think you are? A kabuki demon samurai?" she asked incredulously.

In point of fact, I was one. I tilted my covered face to the side, contemplating her. I must have looked a ghoulish sight in that theatrical mask made to inspire terror. I could hear her equipment rattle with her mild tremble, the smell of her fear beginning to take hold. I inhaled its scent. *Lovely*, the demon within purred.

"This is Officer Yoshimora," she said aloud into her comm link, a slight quaver in her voice. "I have a Code Red. Repeat! *Code Red!* The Kitsune Killer is here! *Looking* at me!"

She was so young and wanted to make me her first big ticket arrest. She was nowhere near *my* league, of course. Still, were

I human, she would have had me dead to rights. Too bad for her she was about to become the laughingstock of her precinct when I slipped away.

I summoned the cold wind and it blew at my command, rattling the docking bay doors, lifting my hair as it howled past us. Dry autumn leaves rattled across the concrete floor. The sound made the policewoman whip around with a shriek, her gun swinging away to the far wall. The second she turned her head, I disappeared in an outgoing rush of wind and darkness.

Chapter Twenty

Shiroi Uindo

They say war makes strange bedfellows, and that is undoubtedly true. Take for instance Officer Yoshimora's father, the Chief of Police for the entire Metropoplex of New Tokyo. You would think him in the oligarchy's pocket, a puppet for Hiroshi. And you might be right, except he chose our side to play ball with, having had quite enough of the old regime. Not every official in New Tokyo was happy with the status quo.

A headstrong idealist from a noble cop family that spanned generations, Chief Yoshimora played the game just enough to keep his family safe and his position secure. Otherwise, he was hard on crime, and unless the oligarchy directly intervened, he did not hesitate to punish those he found guilty. He was a law man, through and through. And yet he was fair, too. He despised yōkai, of course, considering we were responsible for the majority of murders and disappearances in the Metropoplex, and he could not bring us to justice.

He had been quick to see that the recent slayings this year were mostly gang related, and that included the ones attributed to the infamous Kitsune Killer. If the oligarchy, and by extension the media, were making me out to be an indiscriminate, lone wolf psycho-murderer, Chief Yoshimora knew better. After my run-in with his daughter, he decided to have a chat with Hiroshi's rival.

Youta, never one to miss an opportunity, promised he would regulate the criminal element to a stricter degree than Hiroshi ever had once he took power – and that included yōkai. Our dragon likewise vowed to keep a careful eye on the oligarchy, since Hiroshi cared little for human affairs except where his interests forced him to pay attention. Youta, however, had devised a clever plan for keeping the oligarchy on a leash decades ago.

Yoshimora listened patiently, and by the end of Youta's pitch, he was on board. But there were terms and conditions, and the safety of Yoshimora's family was paramount. That included my devoted huntress!

After our little 'face-to-face' in the warehouse, Hanako was determined to bring me in. She appeared at all of my crime scenes, asking questions. Soon she became aware of the other Six, too. I was certain she must have a friend in the cam-viewing-and-maintenance department of the NTPD.

Hanako was studying us. It was only a matter of time before she intercepted our paths again in person. Unlike me, my masked brethren would not hesitate to slay her – and neither would anyone working for Hiroshi. I might be sent to do the deed myself. Yet she was uncorrupted and innocent. I really did not want to have to break my Code unless I absolutely had to.

It was determined a line of communication must be extended to make Hanako understand what was at stake. Since I was the one she had fixated on thanks to my own stupidity, it was left to me to sort her out. And to do that, I was going to have to bend my Code beyond what I was comfortable with.

OFFICER HANAKO DRIFTED AROUND HER TINY APARTMENT IN tight, shorts-like panties and a sport bra, her uniform shirt carelessly unbuttoned and barely concealing her ass. She was thin, lithe, and muscular. A beautiful woman, in truth, now that I looked upon her outside of her beat gear. Twenty-two, tops, although I am admittedly a terrible judge of mortal age. She was too young and certainly too sheltered to understand how things really worked. That headstrong idealism of hers was going to get her killed.

Eventually Hanako settled in her chair and stared at her holo-tab for the next hour. Frowning, she ran a hand through her black, shoulder-length hair and scrolled through my rather extensive, if unenlightening, case file. I watched her swipe over to the footage from her lapel and goggle cams in the warehouse. She paused the video with a touch to the projected image right when the wind began blowing. Yoshimora shuddered.

"Damn, you're *seriously* freaky. But you didn't kill me. You didn't kill Murhito's 'caregiver,' either. Why?"

She pulled up other pictures. My masked compatriots were now on her screen, images she should not have access to. "Who are you bastards? Which outfit do you work for? What was in the warehouse that you needed to burn it? Argh!" She gripped her hair in frustration.

"Why make some killings look like professional hits, and

others look like something out of a ghost story? What do you freaks seek to accomplish with all of this kabuki samurai ninja shit anyway? And just… why the fuck now?"

Good questions. Damn, she was smart. Little did she know the answer to her last question stood in the shadows, waiting.

Every once and again she looked around, as if sensing my presence. Perhaps she could, at that. Cop instinct? Or that of the prey who knows she is being stalked by a hungry predator? A woman alone would be more apt to sense my miasma. I had her spooked, which was probably why she was babbling out loud to herself.

Kamaimasen, I thought to myself. 'It doesn't matter.' In the end, the result would be the same. The cruel demon inside of me enjoyed toying with her. I touched my tongue to the point of a fang.

She rubbed her shoulders and the nape of her neck, and suppressed a shiver. With a sigh Hanako flicked off the tab and the holographic display vanished. "Get a grip, Yoshimora," she whispered to herself.

Hanako stood and walked less than two feet to check her appearance in the mirror above her dresser. She flicked her bangs this way and that, frowning at herself. Without a sound, I glided out of the shadows in full costume. Her eyes widened when she saw my fearsome countenance reflected in the mirror behind her. She barely let out a gasp when I collided into her, rocking her furniture against the wall. I slapped a large broadleaf over her mouth. She was stunned at the swift violence of my attack, enabling me to grasp her wrists before she could react. Thanks to my ability to bend vine to my will, I bound her hands behind her back.

The girl writhed and struggled in my grip, her screams and shouts effectively muffled by my gag. Still clothed, I pulled her roughly against me.

Yesssss! Let this maiden feel our excitement, the demon hissed in my head. *The better for her to fear and submit to me!* The yako within shrieked for her.

No! I told it. *I am not here for that! Fuck off and settle down. This is a job, an act – got it?* Rule number two of my Code: No rapes. But to make her listen fast, I was going to have to threaten it. I reminded myself that I was ultimately trying to save her life.

I forcefully turned her toward the bed and tossed her so that she landed on the mattress face up, bouncing once. I pounced upon her immediately, pressing my weight down on top of her and between her legs. My clawed hand was at her throat, the snout of my mask hovered mere inches above her nose. I looked down into dark, terrified eyes, heard her frantic heart thumping inside her chest in terror. The scent of fear nearly maddened and overwhelmed my darkest demonic instincts.

I must have looked a nightmare to this fledgling cop who had been chasing me all over The Sprawl. Now here I was, in her home, and she had no idea how I had gotten in. So far as Yoshimora was concerned, I had come to rape and murder her. Sadly, the demon within me howled to do just that. I quelled it. I was a professional and no damned rapist.

"Are you done fighting me?" I purred, my voice loud in my ears but undoubtedly somewhat muffled behind the mask.

In answer she struggled valiantly beneath my weight, kicking me with her heels. She tried to head-butt me, but I simply let my claw points nick the soft flesh of her throat, and she sprang back before making contact with the mask. The weight of my body settled atop hers, my long hair falling forward. I leaned harder against her, only thin clothes separating our loins. My threat was implicit in my throbbing excitement. She squirmed this way and that to get away, but there was nowhere to go save to writhe beneath me like a frightened rabbit.

Pleasant as this sensation was to a male yōkai such as myself, I was not here to play. I placed my right hand before her eyes and extended my sharp, dark claws to their fullest length. Her eyes widened in fear and disbelief, and she sobbed. Officer Yoshimora's body went slack under mine. It was surrender.

"Gooood." My mouth wrapped salaciously around the word. "Now we can talk, you and I." Her eyes looked at me as if I were mad, her pupils constricted to almost pinpricks. "I am going to remove your gag. If you scream or cry out, I shan't hesitate to slit your throat," I said with soft menace. "Believe that, Hanako-san."

She looked at my claws with wide eyes and nodded. I removed the large broadleaf plastered to her lips. And such lovely lips they were, too. Pouty and full, but small like a little bow... I sighed internally.

Remember Chikako, I told myself strictly. *Yako or not, you will not cheat on a lover and you do not rape! This is just another job.*

Baka! the demon cackled. *Tell yourself that if you wish, ex-zenko, but this is still sexual assault. And upon an innocent, no less. What does your precious Code say about that?*

Unable to give a proper answer, I ignored the beast within.

"You know my name?" she asked.

"Oh, I know many, *many* things, Officer Yoshimora Hanako." I purred over the syllables of her name in grotesque pleasure.

She looked at me with shock before her outrage took over. "You are enjoying this!" she spat angrily. "You truly are a monster!"

I laughed, the sound hollow and wholly evil. "I am," I agreed.

"You take hearts –!"

"I do. And I *eat* them," I said, the wicked smile implicit in how I spoke my words. "*Raw.*" A gekkering pleasure trill quivered in my chest and throat.

Her upper lip drew up in disgust, wrinkling her pretty little nose. "And now you've come to eat mine!"

"Oh, no, baka onna. I have come to deliver a message, and I urge you to attend most avidly to what I say if you value your life."

"Yeah, right. Like I'm going to believe anything a masked freak says!" she declared with the remaining shreds of her defiance.

"Then as a gesture of trust, I will show you my face." I had no fear.

"NO!" she yelled. She squeezed her eyes shut and turned her face to the side. I suppose she thought it her death warrant to see me unmasked. Under normal circumstances, it would have been. But I was here to initiate her into my world. Tonight, Officer Yoshimora Hanako would become Sanctioned.

I took her chin in my fingers and forced her face to center below mine. "*Look* at me," I hissed fiercely as I drew the mask up over my head.

Her eyes fluttered open and stared wide as she beheld my true face. I could tell it startled her, for she went completely slack. She had not imagined so handsome a sharp-faced man was lurking behind that monstrous visage.

"Oh, I am *not* what she was expecting!" I smirked, unable to help myself.

It was my nogitsune nature to be beautifully alluring, while remaining fierce and alien to seduce my prey. I had no doubt she was physically feeling the pull now, even while she mentally denied my existence and was utterly terrified of my reality.

"Is your body growing wet for me against your inclinations, pretty one?" I asked haughtily. "Oh, but you *must!*" I grinned. Ah, the power I wielded over this woman! And how she *hated* me for it.

"You bastard!" she hissed, furious. Oh yes, this one had spirit! I am ashamed to say I enjoyed goading her.

"Not that you can help it. *Profound* desire is what I invoke in my victims. I could give you a night to remember," I promised, "if you would incline to be *my* lover, Hanako-san." It was a total bluff. I am not sure what I would have done if she had called me on it.

"This isn't real… it's just a dream! This has to be a really bad nightmare… Wake up, Yoshimora! Wake *up!*" Tears glistened in her eyes.

"Are you certain?" I swished my tail to the left side of her body and twitched the fur-covered appendage lewdly against the bare skin of her outer thigh. She jumped and gasped when she felt it, confusion clouding her eyes.

"What the hell is that? Stop! What are you *doing! Stop it!*" she squeaked, writhing to move her leg away. "*Please!*" Panicked, Hanako squirmed to see what was accosting her. In answer, I swished the white tip upright so she could glimpse it. I lashed it once and smiled broadly, my mouth open in a broad fox grin. It was proof that this was no costume prop. *I* was the genuine article.

"The hell?" she asked me, staring up into my face. "A tail? You have *a tail?* And your eyes…" She watched my vertical pupils dilate. "Those aren't fantasy lenses! What the fuck *are* you?" she asked, a mild quaver in that doll's voice. "A mutant? Someone's pet lab experiment? Or a madman in a mask good with cheap magician's tricks?"

I chuckled throatily. "Oh no, tasty morsel." I narrowed my eyes cruelly. "I am a *true* yōkai."

"Yōkai? There is no such thing! Those are just stories old people made up to scare children into being good!"

"Foolish child, those stories were meant to *warn* you, to protect you from the likes of us."

"The likes of what? A pervert?" Officer Hanako said bravely. She was trying to play for time, I could tell. But the eyes behind the vid-feed would not be sending aid.

"No one is coming," I told her. "And no one could stop me if they were. I can drag you into the shadows if I wish."

"Whoa! You're not faking… you actually believe that!" She was quite good at cold reading people. "Holy shit. What are you?" Her lips trembled, her body shook beneath mine. It was a good feeling.

"You *know* what I am, sweet virgin," I answered seductively as I sniffed her exposed throat. Oh yes, she was pure and smelled of woman. "*Say* it," I taunted, my eyes widening momentarily with my demand.

"Y-you think you're k-k-kit-kitsune."

I smiled again. "Of a kind. I am *nogitsune*." I felt her shudder at the word. As if I could be anything other than a filthy yako. Zenko kitsune do not behave this way.

She whimpered and pressed herself into her mattress to draw away. I only leaned in harder. She choked back a sob.

"Are you going to kill me like the others?" It was a little girl's voice. Finally. She was ready to hear me.

"That would depend upon the outcome of this conversation," I said as I toyed with the fine strands of black hair around her face. My claws flashed in her peripheral vision. She flinched away, then held very still. "As I stated before, I bear a most auspicious message and I suggest you heed it."

"What have you come to tell me?" she asked tersely.

"Ah, yes. That." I narrowed my eyes. "'*Back* off,'" I answered. "You cannot possibly understand the full scope of what is occurring. This is no simple gang war, but an armed uprising for supremacy of New Tokyo."

"What?" she asked incredulously.

"This upheaval has been underway for decades. The last stages cannot help but spill out into the mortal world. Of course, you do not understand. You have no idea who really rules this city."

"The government runs…" she began pedantically.

I shook my head and cut her off. "Your government is under the control of a plutocratic council of multi-conglomerate CEOs, who have imperial blood ties stretching back into the far past. And *they* are ruled by The Dragon."

"Wait! What 'Dragon?' That sounds like kooky conspiracy theory nonsense!"

I placed my right index finger on the center of her forehead. "Hush, human. Silence and attend." She frowned. I removed my finger and continued.

"The world you live in works like this: The Dragon rules the city, including the guys with the pedigree and the big bucks. They in turn buy government officials to act as puppets, who dance upon their strings in the time-honored tradition of greed and self-interest. The Dragon is also master of the local yōkai world that lurks next to yours, and *we* run the majority of the syndicates. We are the dark underbelly of New Tokyo since the earliest days of Old Edo. Why do you think they call it The Demon City, then as now? This basin was *ours* before there was ever a village here."

"But if that's true, then why don't people know about this?" she asked, bewildered.

"Some do. We call them Sanctioned. Until tonight, you called them superstitious or crazy. But the plain truth is, this is the Dragon's Law."

"You say 'Dragon' like you mean it for real."

"I do. I've met him, although I cannot say it was a pleasure." My lip curled. "But he is not the only one of his kind. My master is also a dragon, one with great ambition, and possessed of a bit more empathy for yōkai and humanity than he who now stands as king. Things are about to change, Hanako-san. You cannot stop it. In trying, you will only end up one more corpse in our conflict, a tragic waste we all agree."

She stared up at me, stunned. "If what you say is true, I've been looking at this all wrong. I..." I could practically see the wheels turning in her head.

"Our little shadow war is nearly concluded, and soon it shall be declared who will rule New Tokyo. When the contest is decided, all will settle once more. And what is lost, I ask you? Scores of yōkai and yakuza you never knew existed? Some cops on the take loyal to the old order? The boards of corporations and rich families so corrupt that they infest every level of government from the top down? And just so you know, that disgusting, sex-trafficking lawyer offered me *children* to spare his despicable life! And you have the gall to call *me* a pervert, mortal girl… Tchk!" I huffed.

"Well…?" She glanced between us. "But even so! Justice is for the courts to decide! The people –!"

I snorted derisively. "Do not give a shit, I promise you. This world is entrenched. Everyone buries themselves in escape rather than face the truth! That is why my master has taken matters into his hands, to change it." I smiled pleasantly and began my pitch. "*You* could stand to gain a lot from this, pretty one. All you need do is stay out of the way until the war is done. Who can say? You might just find your fortune in alignment with your purpose by war's end."

"But what you ask is impossible! I can't call off the hunt now! I've gone too far! My reputation! The honor of my family, the Yoshimora name, is at stake!"

I smiled with diabolical deliberation, showing her my fangs. "There is no need to abort or lose face. Simply do not pursue with such vigor. A cold winter is upon us, and your department will be the happier for not chasing phantoms through The Sprawl. You will find your 'killer' soon, and with his arrest, a great promotion and much honor will come your way."

"You'll turn yourself in?" She seemed so hopeful, if a shade disbelieving.

I barked out rich laughter at such absurdity. "*Baka!* Of course not. No jail of yours could contain me. But *you* could do a great deal of good in this world, as your father has done. He learned to look the other way from the shadows a long time ago. You should do the same, Hanako-san."

Her eyes widened again. "My father? What has he to do with this? He is a good man, an honorable man!"

I smiled slyly as I looked down into her eyes. "*Is* he? Perhaps. But even he understands his limits and his place. Do you know yours, I wonder?" I tilted my chin cunningly, looking down at the frail woman pinned beneath me.

"You're a liar!"

"What have I to gain from deceit in this matter? It is for your father's sake I am speaking to you thus. He does not wish you, his only progeny, harmed. It is for this reason alone you are not dead already."

"No! None of that is true!" She shook her head violently. "My father would *never* treat with a villain like you! Or this supposed 'dragon' of yours!"

I laughed again, a dry, throaty chuckle as I brushed her cheek with the back of my fingers. She flinched from my touch and whimpered, her bottom lip trembling.

"Oh, but he has! And he *does*." I insistently cupped her chin despite her displeasure. "Even such a man as he knows the importance of our war, as do the human syndicates. Badly needed change *is* coming, Hanako-san. Those who do not embrace it will be swept away with the tide. But you do not have to go out in the undertow where we sharks await. Not unless you *wish* to be eaten." I grinned wickedly, a promise I could – and *would* – do just that if she continued in her relentless pursuit of 'justice.'

"I do not believe it. I will not." But her voice quavered in doubt. "Not of my father."

"Yes, you do," I spoke softly, gently. "How else do you think he has kept you and your mother safe all these years? You have been in the Game long enough by now to know the rules, Officer Yoshimora. And now you know the price if you do not obey them."

Tears filled her eyes. I had just shattered her illusions. She had lived in that glass tower of good versus evil, where every decision was white or black, the bad deserved to be punished. Until now her father was the highest ideal of truth and justice she aspired to, her childhood hero. In an instant I had made him into a conspirator mixed in corruption so deep it was a fathomless abyss – which she herself would one day teeter into. She was on the verge of it now.

On top of all that, I had just proved to her that monsters were real, and we could attack her anywhere, anytime, even in the sanctity of her own home! There was nowhere she could hide, nowhere to run, no escape from the shadows blanketing her world. Only our 'benevolence' allowed her the delusion of safety.

I had stolen her naivety of the world, and more thoroughly than if I had simply violated her body and left. All her certainties, everything she held dear, destroyed in seconds. She was forever scarred by the knowledge I had forced upon her. I could smell the salt in her tears as they streaked her skin and leaked down into her hair. Her eyelashes were sticky wet, her nose red. She bit back a sob and looked to the wall, obscured by the curtain fall of my white hair.

"I hate you," she whispered, her voice weak.

"Tchk. I do not care," I said, meaning it. "Do not make me come to you again, Hanako-san. Leave the shadows where they lie and look not too deeply into them, lest you find *us* gazing back. My kind are not for such an innocent as you, and *you* most certainly do not belong in *our* world, human child."

With that I floated up, back and away from her on the currents of air I commanded with scarce a thought. My hair flowed out around me. Her eyes grew wide again and I thought that now perhaps she *truly* believed.

I reached down and pulled her up roughly by the shoulders. She squeaked in sudden fright. I turned her, slicing the vines that bound her wrists with a single swipe of my claws. I dropped her unceremoniously to the floor beside her bed with a thump. She turned at once and pulled a gun from under her mattress to aim at me, but I was already melting backward into the shadows, slipping my mask down over my face.

"What is your name, kitsune?" she called out to me in spite of herself, hand shaking around the handle. Yet she did not fire as I faded from view, the pale strands of my hair drifting slowly into the shadows until only the teal gleam of my eyes remained to stare out from the darkness.

"*Hah-yah-teyh*," I whispered wraith-like, each syllable held out breathily. My name echoed on a sudden gust of frigid, spectral wind. It was a final pledge of my good faith. Would she even know that? For her sake, I rather hoped she did. And then I receded fully into the shadows, leaving her and the scent of her womanliness behind.

HANAKO WAS SITTING ON THE FLOOR NEXT TO HER BED WHERE I had left her, knees drawn up as she wept into them. It was a violation to intrude so on her private moment, yet Youta and her father watched her through the camera's lens anyway. Just as they had watched me with her only a short time ago.

"You said you would *talk* to her, not attack her!" the Chief of Police spat at once, red with scarce controlled fury. I saw where Hanako got it from.

"I *did* talk to her. I was quite gentle, I assure you," I told Chief Yoshimora.

"You tossed her around like a rag doll! You threatened *to rape* her!" If looks could kill…

"I made her submit so that she would listen. I threatened to *kill* her if she did not back off," I said in irritation, crossing my arms over my chest. "I was never going to rape her."

"Leave it," Youta commanded the Chief of Police. "Hayate-san did good work. She is not harmed, and she will bend to our will."

"Look at her! How can you tell me my daughter is not harmed?" Yoshimora demanded.

I did look. Her head was on her knees, her arms wrapped around her legs.

"The world is a terrible place," I drawled, shrugging. "Do not blame me for helping your daughter grow up. This should have been your job, not mine!" I felt my lips draw back from my fangs. The Chief flinched as I narrowed my eyes, tail lashing.

"Demon…" he muttered.

"Enough, Hayate," Youta said sharply and I stilled at once. "You know what must happen next, Yoshimora-san," he told the Chief.

I watched Yoshimora's daughter sob on the holo-screen. No one could know how much internal distress this job had caused me. I was unsure what disturbed me more: that I had done it, or that I enjoyed it. Night after night I seemed to slip further into the impenetrable darkness.

Kami-sama help me, I truly was a demon.

Chapter Twenty-One

The Yokai Samurai

Chikako and I lay cuddled under a heap of covers on my futon. As predicted, my drafty converted garage with its cement walls and concrete floor at ground level was less than ideal in winter. This year was proving particularly brutal with record lows. Yōkai I might be, but even I felt the frigid cold.

With the war winding up, I found myself on mission quite a lot. My lover still spent most of her free time with me, which was little enough between her job and mine. I relished the days like one this where we could snuggle together for mutual warmth.

"Hayate?" Chikako asked out of the blue.

"Hmmm?" I asked sleepily. I had been dozing in that comfortable half-state.

"Who are you really? Where do you come from?" Her tone was reticent. I could tell she had to work herself up to ask. I blinked my eyes open as she shifted and rolled over to face me, still wrapped in my embrace.

"I…" I almost reminded her that I came out of the wilderness, but I stopped. After all these months with me, she deserved a better answer, not that it was much more informative. "I don't know." She frowned, trying to determine whether I was serious or not. "I do not remember," I added. Her expression became curious, questioning.

I sighed. I supposed I would just admit to it. "I have amnesia."

"What?" She blinked at me in surprise.

"I woke up in the woods a little over twenty years ago with a bad crack on the back of my skull and one hell of a concussion. I barely knew my name."

"Oh, Hayate!"

I shrugged. "I know it isn't the answer you want, but I scarcely remember anything before that. A beautiful forest, clean air and water, a planet and moons in the sky…" I trailed off. *The great shrine at dawn surrounded by mountains… the warm glow of my kami's grace…*

"Just impressions, mostly." I searched my mind for memories that simply were not there or just out of reach. It made my heart sore.

"And you don't know how you came to be there or what happened to you?"

"No," I answered honestly, returning to the present. "I tried to find my way home many times, but I couldn't. I'm stuck here. And the way it is outside the megapolis?" I grimaced. "I clawed my way into this city to survive."

"How long before you came to The Cage?"

"I went to Youta for sanctuary within hours."

"Oh." She was silent for a while after that and I drifted off again.

"Hayate…"

"Hmmm?" I asked drowsily.

"I… well… are you, or rather *were* you… uh…"

My heavy eyelids opened reluctantly. She was studying me intensely. And then… "Nothing. Never mind." That was one of those lies women made up when they had a lot on their mind but did not know how to broach it.

Instead of pressing, Chikako groaned and flicked on the vid-screen. "…-tsune Killer still at large. Last night two more bodies…"

Disgruntled, I rolled over and tried to tune it out.

"They're still talking about you," Chikako said, her voice anxious.

"I did not even make that kill!" I grumbled, burying my head beneath the blankets.

"The other one?"

"Yes," I admitted. "It was on orders."

There was nothing indiscriminate or balanced in what they were reporting. But that was the media machine. I mean sure, I was a bloodthirsty killer and a criminal, but my pattern spoke for itself. I was not breaking in and murdering random citizens. I did not even hunt genuine innocents! All of the hearts I took came from combatants and those who genuinely deserved to be put out of other people's misery.

"If seen, press the helpful police icon on your device. The authorities urge anyone who has information regarding this ruthless terrorist to come forward immediately…"

I took the digital remote from her hand and clicked off the vid-screen. I did not want to hear their lies. Her eyes were filled with worry as they followed my movements. "I am afraid for you, Hayate."

"They will not catch me, and they cannot hold me," I promised.

"But they *can* kill you!"

I shrugged. "We all die sometime, beautiful. Better in battle than in bed – unless it is with you." I smiled and wrapped myself around her with a contented sigh, burying my head against her shoulder. I loved the smell of her, the warmth of her body…

"Hayate?"

"Yes?"

"Why do you stay with me?"

What? Women…. I swear! Why did she require validation *now*? All I wanted was to cuddle and sleep.

"You're smokin' hot, for one thing," I quipped, snuggling into her. "And you are *amazing* in bed." I nipped at her neck.

She was unusually tense. "If that's the case, you could have anyone. There are a bunch of hot girls in the club and all over the Metropoplex."

I sat up halfway and looked into her eyes. I grew serious. "They do not have what you possess."

"What do *I* have?" She scoffed.

"*That*, right there."

"What?" she asked breathlessly, hanging onto my every word.

"Innocence. Of all the yōkai and most of the humans in this city, you are one of the rare few with it. So beautiful and precious..." I traced her cheek with my finger. "I want to protect it, and you." I surprised myself by meaning it.

Her eyes grew wide and softened, pupils dilating. Uh oh. She just fell harder for me. Oops.

"Is that why you never show your true form?"

My shoulders stiffened, ears flattening. "What? How did you –?"

"Hiroko told me." Of course she did. "She showed me images of nogitsune on the Metro Net. Is it true? Are you... really...?" Her eyes were full of horror. She wanted me to tell her it was not so.

I felt my face fall. "Yes." I looked down, uncharacteristically self-conscious and embarrassed. "I am," I said softly. I could only imagine her disgust upon seeing that, while Hiroko surely smiled. I knew the sorts of things the artists imagined of yōkai, and no matter how ghastly the rendering, they all paled in comparison to confronting the real thing in person.

"I am evil incarnate in that state." I winced. "It is hard to suppress the worst of myself, like when you are angry and wound up, and all you want to do is hit or claw something and never stop."

"Oh," she said quietly. "I see." I could tell she was processing my admission.

I looked down and away. I felt shame that she should think of me in that context. To be a yako was a badge of dishonor for one born zenko. She could not know this, and I was in no way willing to go into it with her. How I could explain? She was not kitsune.

"I don't like it," I told her honestly. "I try not to become that *thing*." My lip curled.

XANDER CROSS

"You know, it doesn't change anything. We all have our deepest demonic forms. I don't feel any differently towards you about it."

"You would if you saw me that way! I *never* want you to see me like that!" I shook my head emphatically. "A nightmare scarcely in control of its basest instincts? A vile *yako!*" I sneered, saying the word as if I were calling myself filth, because so far as I was concerned, I was.

She cupped my narrow jaw and I found myself looking into those big, beautiful cat's eyes of hers. "You are *not* vile, Hayate. You will always be beautiful to me." Then she kissed me.

Is she truly that naive? But I knew the answer. Of *course* she was. This was what I liked about her. In a world full of monsters, Chikako was a breath of fresh air, a rare, pure soul among yōkai. And I must admit, she kind of got to me right there. I cannot say I fell in love with her, but I felt more than I had since I buried Aiko and Kazuki.

I gently smoothed the hair around her ears. She smiled shyly and bit her lip, and well... What followed was the most gentle and intimate sex we ever shared in our time together. Her blind acceptance touched me deeply. I treated my lover as a precious virgin I was inaugurating into womanhood.

I had never played this game before, but I found it a refreshing change. Apparently, so did Chikako. She responded to my caresses, wrapped her twin tails around my one. After, we slept nestled together until the digital alarms forced us back into the flow of our nightly routines.

Such was life in the megapolis.

300

THAT NIGHT WAS BUSINESS AS USUAL AT THE ORI. THERE WAS A JOB later, of course, but until then, we put in our due appearance by our boss's side. We Seven had become celebrities in that club, myself especially. Humans feared me city-wide. Yōkai respected that.

It was because of me that a curfew went into effect from midnight until sunrise. Night employees were the exception, and they had to produce proof of work on demand. These measures were nothing to us true yōkai, but they convinced the populace that the authorities were doing something. Of course, between the street violence and the Siberian cold front, nobody went out who did not have to.

Before duty called that night, I went to look for Chikako, maybe get a kiss for luck. I had seen her drifting about in her slinky waitress uniform from my lofty perch. When I got to the lower level, I had difficulty finding her. I supposed she must be in the back filling an order and headed that way. Hiroko pulled me aside instead.

"What the hell do you want?" I asked tensely, annoyed to have to speak with her at all. This conversation was not going to end well, and I just did not need this before a run.

"What do I have to do to get you to back off from her?" Hiroko asked frankly.

"Why should I back off?" I demanded.

"Look, I know what you are – *you* know what you are! Don't you think she deserves better than you, yako?"

The truth was, Chikako *did* deserve better. But she was *mine*, damn it! Even the beast within agreed. Like hell was I going to give Chikako up! Not yet. Certainly not on this woman's authority!

My eyes narrowed dangerously. I was sick of this under-handed, conniving bitch! Every argument I had with Chikako inevitably contained some variation of 'Hiroko said' in it. I was exhausted of the constant drama.

"Who are you to judge *me*?" I growled. "You have been attempting to sabotage us from the first night! For months I have endured your interference in what does not concern you!"

"She's my baby sister! Her running around with a Wild Fox absolutely concerns me! I promised our mother I would look after her!"

"Chikako's the best thing I've got in my life right now," the only thing keeping me from turning full yako, "and you keep trying to take her away from me! I have had *enough*, Hiroko! Back. *Off*." I used my height as leverage to intimidate.

"Or what?" She glared up at me, holding her ground.

"Or I will make certain you lose your job," I said coldly, my kitsune eyes glittering dangerously.

"You're a lying sack of –"

"I'll go talk to Youta-sama right now. Then you can go peddle your ass in the street for all I care." I turned to go to Youta with a mind to do just that, I was so pissed.

"Wait!" She lunged and grabbed my arm, her eyes wide. My threat was not without teeth.

I shrugged her off. "Then leave us alone!" I demanded. "Or I swear," I growled, staring down into her eyes with the full force of my demonic aura. The monster bristled just beneath the surface, aching to come out. Her eyes grew wider and she cringed back. "I *promise* you, Hiroko, I will make you *suffer* for it." I meant every word I said.

"Hayate-sama? Hiroko?"

We turned our heads to see a bewildered and anxious Chikako looking at us. Yōkai in the immediate vicinity were watching. Man, did I feel like a heel. I took a deep breath and straightened. "Chikako..."

"What's going on?"

"We were just having a conversation, is that not so, Hiroko-san?" I shifted my eyes sideways at this pebble in my shoe.

Hiroko stood straight and glowered at me. "Yeah. That's right. A discussion."

I smiled pleasantly for Chikako's benefit and steered my lover away by the elbow. "I have to go out soon, but I wanted to see you before I left." And just like that I was smooth and urbane again.

"*Please* be careful."

I kissed her tenderly. "I will be." I embraced her. "I promise."

As I feared, she had fallen harder for me since our discussion earlier that day. I could feel it in the way she held me, see the soft way she gazed up longingly into my eyes. I understood why Hiroko was upset. I had won. I felt inordinately pleased with myself.

Once Chikako let me go, I kissed her hand gallantly. "I shall return before dawn," I vowed and left her mooning after me. On my way back to the upper level, I met the tengu halfway on the metal stairs.

"Yo, Hayate. I was just coming to look for you. Ready to go?"

"Shi-rou-san," I said with my trademark sly grin. "Hai. Just a little last-minute business I had to take care of."

"Need five extra, kitsune?" The crow grinned wickedly.

303

"Is that all it takes you, ten-gu?"

"Depends on the girl and the night," he said dryly.

I laughed heartily, my tension easing. "Probably longer than Katashi takes, eh?"

"I hear men who bear an overly-large testicular sack have premature issues with erotic stimulation," the crow quipped. "Hey, why don't you ask him?"

"I say we send Jūro to ask him," I answered snottily.

"Send Jūro to ask who what?" the short monkey demon asked suspiciously as we walked into the office. He frowned at us, knowing I was making a bit of a joke at his expense.

"Eh, we'll tell you on the way," Shirou said.

HALF AN HOUR LATER WE WERE LOOKING DOWN ON A BLEAK SHIP-ping yard. It was a large pit surrounded by high dirt ridges on all sides and a single road in or out. Transport containers were stacked up to five high in huge columns. Bright white lights were lit on tall poles and on the crane lift that set the payloads onto the back of transports.

A drug shipment was about to move to Seoul. It was still going to the original buyer, except Youta would be the seller. Money aside, the true intent was the loss of face Hiroshi would suffer. He would no longer be able to hide his insurrection troubles, further weakening his position.

Shirou pointed out the haul that was our target. The serial number on the side matched. I nodded. A few minutes later, we watched the crane pick up and lower the huge metal container onto the bed of a transport, heard the magnetized thunk as the metal made contact and locked in place. That was our cue.

I hit the cams with lightning, vanished, and reappeared on top of the payload. Shirou flew down to join me on those great black wings of his. Somewhere behind us, Jūro was supposed to be coming around the other side to sneak in and drive the whole transport out.

"Holy fuck!" one night-crew worker exclaimed.

"No way! Is that –?"

"It's the fucking Kitsune Killer and friend, boys," the yard manager said, unimpressed. "What are you assholes waiting for? Get them already!"

I wondered what four weakling humans could possibly do against two great yōkai, until I realized the guy in charge was not speaking to his men. The darkness between the stacked container units writhed and emitted predatory sounds. A horde of ink-skinned, lab-farmed yōkai came bounding out of the shadows and made a loping dash toward us! They were the same kind I met the previous spring in the shadows of Taka-hashi's office. No wonder there were no visible guards on site.

We stood atop the transport as the lesser demons climbed to reach us! Shirou and I drew our blades. We hacked and slew the first wave as they crested the top. Limbs, heads, and inter-nal organs flew everywhere! Black blood spattered.

Shirou cut the head off one, dodged another and slashed its back. He kicked it over the back end of the transport, spun and hacked down on the head of the latest one scrambling up over the side. He swept the legs off another demon goon. Its body landed in front of him, an impossibly long red tongue reaching for him between its serrated teeth. He plunged his katana through its maw, splitting its tongue into a fork.

At the same time, I hacked upward, a black arm went flying

into the yard. I arced down and cut off the other one. I kicked the ugly bastard out into open air as it screamed defiance at me. I severed the tongue as it reached for me before it fell. I began setting the little shits on fire and hitting them with lightning to destroy multiple targets at once! That made a goodly sized dent in the eyeless servitors. Unfortunately, the pyrotechnics tended to deplete my power faster, too.

Where the fuck is Jūro! I wondered as I slew.

There was an echoing BOOM! I felt a punch in my right bicep before I could figure out what happened. I looked down and saw I was bleeding, the arm of my hanten darkening with blood. I had just gotten shot!

"Damn it!" I swore. The manager stood with a shotgun below. "Mother *fucker!*" I roared. How did *he* happen to have a gun, anyway?

"I've got what's left of these!" Shirou shouted. "Get *him!*"

The yard manager was taking aim again, having just loaded the next round into the chamber. It was an old model weapon, but hey, it was effective. I nodded and jumped out into empty air, landing in front of him. I took his rifle by the barrel, ripped it out of his grip, and smacked him upside the head with the stock. I heard his jaw break on impact. He staggered. I dropped the gun and shoved my hand into his midsection, my claws shredding through his clothes. I took his heart and kicked the body savagely to sprawl on the dirt.

The other human lackeys put up their hands and backed away as I snarled at them. They hustled backward, then turned tail and fled. These were not warriors, just helpless men working to survive. I let them go. A quick glance showed Shirou killing the last servitor. That, then, was that.

I lifted my mask just enough to consume the heart. Immediately I felt its effect, healing my arm and restoring my energy. It was a rather empowering sensation. I wiped my lips and chin with the back of my sleeve and lowered the mask, then cleaned my blade with a white cloth.

Jūro came around the side of our transport, holding a bloody tanto blade, his hair matted with black blood. "I fucking *hate* those things! Couldn't risk my explosives in the yard. Too much flammable shit." Dramatically he thumped his back against the transport. "I need a better gig."

"Get in the truck and drive," Shirou commanded pragmatically. Jūro obeyed. I turned to look one last time around our perimeter, just in case…

And that's when I caught the tiny twinkle of light on yonder ridge.

"Coming, Shiroi Uindo?" the tengu asked.

"Hai. In just a moment. Go on without me. I want to check something out real quick."

Shirou nodded, spread his wings, and took off to fly above our stolen shipment. A bit of breeze brought a familiar scent to my nostrils. I smiled to myself and vanished to appear behind Hanako Yoshimora. She was not in uniform, but wearing black fatigues and a thermal coat without ornament. Interesting.

"Shit!" she hissed, lowering her binocular recording device and scanning the yard for me with her own eyes. "Where'd he go? How does he *do* that?"

I tapped the flat of my katana upon the back of her neck. Her body froze and she let out a little shriek. Slowly she turned to look up at me. Boy, did she ever look like a girl who had just been caught peeping in the boys' room!

"Hanako-san," I purred with the tone of a disapproving parent. I watched her shudder. "I believe you were told to stay out of this. Did I not deliver this message adequately?" I asked as if her disobedience grieved me, and it kind of did. I was trying to keep her alive.

How the hell did she even know we'd be here tonight?

"I am not here as an officer! I swear!" she exclaimed hastily. "I had to know – had to see for myself! I feel like I'm going crazy!"

I lifted my mask and tilted it to the side of my head. The wind gently tossed my hair. "I did warn you about looking too deeply into the shadows, mortal child." I pulled the sword away from her, but left it unsheathed.

She turned on her side to fully stare up at me, bloody mess that I was. I snapped the fingers of my left hand and held out my palm. "You know."

Reluctantly, with a look of defeat, she handed up her ultra hi-def vid recorder. I fried the technology with my kitsunebi and a bit of lightning just to make sure. Her eyes grew wide at such an effortless display of my powers.

"You – you just..." Her mouth hung open.

"Yes," I said simply.

"But that was expensive!" she cried out in dismay

I threw the molten metal and plastic on the ground. It sizzled with a whiff of acrid smoke. "I would not touch that. The radiation from the battery is not safe. Now run along, mortal girl, you try me sorely." I turned my back and walked away.

"Wait! Hayate-san!"

I halted and looked back. She laid still, staring at me in astonishment. She had not expected me to stop.

"Did you just say my name to see if I would answer to it?" I asked coyly when she said nothing else.

"Yes. I mean, *no*! I mean...." I could see the longing in her eyes for the strange mystery I represented. As afraid as she was of me, and rightfully so, she was also fascinated. I had opened a door into the vast unknown. Too bad there were monsters there.

I shrugged and turned away again when I heard her call out. "When your war is over, will you disappear for good?" I could not tell if she was hopeful or sad at the prospect.

A smile pulled at the corners of my lips and I turned my head back one last time to look over my shoulder. "Not unless I fall in battle. New Tokyo is my home, and I am my daimyo's yōkai samurai."

"Who the hell is your daimyo?" she asked aloud.

I adjusted my mask over my face and stepped to the edge of the ridge. I jumped out above the pit, turning my body lithely so that I faced her suspended in midair. My hair and robes whipped around me in a gust of Siberian wind. I saw her startled face gape at me as I sank. When I could no longer see her lying there on her stomach with those astonished eyes, I disappeared.

Chapter Twenty-Two

Hyakki Yagyo

Youta was a strategic mastermind, for which Hiroshi did not credit him enough. The old Dragon was by no means stupid, but he was arrogant and indolent. Youta used his aggressively to his advantage, and on the Winter Solstice of 2119, he took the war to a new level.

Japanese yōkai had an ancient and honored tradition called the Hyakki yagyō, the Night Parade of One Hundred Demons. At different zodiacal points of the seasonal year, demons of all species came together in celebration and made a grand procession through the streets of Japan. It was a grand spectacle beginning at midnight and lasting until the first light of dawn chased the shadows away.

The demon parade must never be glimpsed by mortal kind, and great misfortune befell any human who dared peek. Children were spirited away, sometimes eaten, else changed into yōkai or yūrei. Peeping eyes were put out. Adults were nearly always slain for their trespass into supernatural affairs. Occa-sionally some fool looked or stumbled out where he or she did not belong, and we dealt with them accordingly.

The Sanctioned were particularly keen on drawing the cur-tains tight and going to bed early when the Hyakki yagyō was abroad. Not even the oligarchy was so privileged as to wit-ness this wholly supernatural event. The cameras went dark throughout the Sector for this occasion.

We younger demons were not allowed to take part. It was for the older generations to participate, a great prestige to be selected. Originally this task was performed by the nurarihyon, an elite and exceptionally powerful yōkai in the form of a cat-fish-like old man. He traditionally led the Night Parade, except he had not been in Tokyo for over a century. No one knew where he went or why. Had there been such an entity leading and protecting the Hyakki yagyō, Youta Clan would never have considered the next step in our crusade.

It began at midnight on the dark and empty streets of the Japanese Sector. Many wore masks to represent their demon selves, while others put their full demonic natures on display. And what a sight! A few only had one eye in the center of their foreheads or had long necks. There were kappa and faceless noppera-bo, a variety of oni and kijo, bakeneko, inugami, and many more.

They were in high spirits, hooting and laughing, dancing, making mischief and merry. Some carried lanterns. Blue and orange onibi wisps floated among all manner of yōkai troop-ing down one street after the other in a long pack.

We Seven led a host of younger demons that kept distant

pace above, silent as ninja. I shivered with anticipation. It was rather empowering to be at the head of a demon vanguard! We stopped every few paces, letting them keep the lead, then ran for several more meters, leaping from rooftop to rooftop, crawling up and down slanted tiles. Stop, duck, watch, move. We loped like wolves under the waning gibbous moon. Slowly we closed our lead until we were alongside.

The fools below were so preoccupied with their pageant they never noticed us. As they rounded the narrow turn into the wide central bazaar, we leapt down on all sides with our weapons drawn. Young demons drove into older ones with fanatical zeal, howling for blood. What followed was a battle of epic proportions among demon kind, and accordingly, it was *nasty*.

Tonight, I wielded a nodachi, a Japanese long sword. My daisho was on my hip, but some nights I liked to play with different weapons I found in the armory. I chose this one for its visual ferocity and psychological impact. A weapon of such length, five feet, had limited use in close quarter combat, but it was most impressive in a full running charge.

And so it was now as I plunged into our enemy! Startled faces turned as we rained down hell upon them. They recovered swiftly, though. These were not young or incompetent monsters. Many were old and powerful, veterans of ancient battles, and they were not going to simply let us roll them over.

Blood splattered, voices howled. Claws, horns, fangs – it *all* came into play. Growls and snarls echoed between the buildings. We tore at one another like the savages we were! The scent and sight of blood created a yōkai frenzy. Those who had deeper demonic forms to shift into did so.

I was in the middle of it, no less caught up in the battle's thrall. My own inner demon howled to turn full yako and join in the fun! Somehow, I persevered. I was heartened by those like Shirou, who maintained his discipline. I reminded myself that I had fought in battles and never completely lost myself to the nogitsune. This was no different.

Stay in control, I told myself. *Stay focused.*

I took off the broad head of a hitotsume-nyūdō, a one-eyed creature that started out man-sized, but could grow into a giant. The key was to stare level at his eye to keep him small, because if you looked from his feet up to his face, he would grow as fast as your eyes could follow. I whirled and raised my blade, warrior's instinct making me move before I knew quite what I was doing. A sword came down on my nodachi with a hard clang. I came face to face with an inugami. Old dog demons like this one were strong and powerful, and he easily shoved me backward.

"Kitsune scum! Profaning our sacred rite! You will die for this outrage!!" he bellowed, swinging his katana at me with every syllable he uttered.

No, I thought, meeting and countering his strikes. *You will!*

But try as I might, I could not land a hit! We went back and forth, but he had more chi than I did, and had doubtless fought far more battles than I had ever participated in. This was only my first war, after all, and I could tell this old beast had been in *hundreds* of them. I needed a strategy or some trick to beat him, and soon! Strength, skill, and endurance were not in my favor!

For a few precious seconds I was holding my own. Then he got past my defenses and struck at my face, hard. The impact sharply cracked the snarling kitsunenomen in half. One side dropped away, the other lingering on my face for the space of a heartbeat the yako thrust me in the back and took over. My expression changed from momentary shock into a diabolically wicked fox grin filled with sharp teeth. Teal eyes gleaming, the demon within unleashed itself in its full glory!

My snout pushed the other half of the mask off. I became that bony, more fox than man horror, with its long talons extended from elongated fingers, all thin-limbed and wiry. I floated inches above the ground, my robes and hair billowing around me, dark miasma dripping from the sleeves of my kimono like mist. I was ghoul and specter both, a demon made of flesh as well as spirit. And it felt *good*.

In this form the full power of my yōkai self was unbridled and free! Until now I had never fully cut loose in it. But this night it at last took over as it had not done since the outset of my sin. I was evil incarnate without a care in heaven or earth. I had no empathy, no sympathy. I lived for wanton destruction. All who looked upon me were shocked by the sight of a former shrine fox, now defiled. These older yōkai understood the significance of what I was better than either myself or the younger demons fighting and dying beside me.

"*YAKO!*" I heard a female scream out in dire warning. Others took up that terrified cry. Quickly there was space as panicked yōkai moved to get away.

The old dog had not seen anything like me in quite a while, I could tell. He stared at me, mouth open, paralyzed. I flew at him. I disarmed my startled opponent, grabbed hold of the Demon Dog's head, twisted, and tore the thing off with my bare hands! I threw it like a ball, not caring where it fell, then plowed into a tight group of monsters. I shoved them back, knocking them down like bowling pins.

I rose up a meter and shrieked my defiance at the world, brandishing my bloody claws! I felt a tug and saw some creature – a bakeneko, maybe? – grabbing my kimono. I took hold of its offending arm and ripped it fee of its socket, whereupon I wielded my gory trophy as a club. All the while I cackled in malevolent glee!

When it had broken beyond any capacity to use, I flung the flopping limb carelessly aside, and was satisfied by a grunt when it landed on someone. No idea which side, mine or theirs. I did not exactly have a 'side' any longer. These things were prey, so far as I was concerned. I had no pity and no remorse. I was the embodiment of malicious evil made manifest in this world!

I randomly caught sight of Katashi's tanuki mask in the crowd and felt his hard stare. He knew what was happening to me, what it meant. Now that I had truly and fully given into the demon, I was a yako for true. This was always going to happen to me sooner or later. It was inevitable. If not for Chikako, it would have happened that night Hiroshi's men bombed our club.

At sight of me revealed, I found I had become a rallying point for Youta clan, and a terror for Hiroshi's loyalists. "*Shiroi Uindo!*" I heard a voice call out, followed by several more. It became a chant, a cheer! "*SHIROI UINDO!*" That was more like it!

Some of the weaker yōkai broke and ran. I shrieked my uncontrollable fury and let loose a wide swath of blue flame. Those it touched combusted. And the ones who ran as they burned stumbled blindly into others, who likewise caught fire.

Sadly, not all who perished were my enemies, strictly speaking. A few of our own got caught in the conflagration. I never paused to consider, and Shiroi Uindo simply did not care. They were casualties, nothing more. If they died, they deserved to. Survival was for the fit and the fortunate.

My violence fast became a blur. Someone stabbed me in the lower back. I descended on and shredded my attacker's face with my long, sharp claws. That was neat, so I shredded a few more. I called upon lightning to watch my enemies fry. And I laughed. And laughed.

"What fun!" I hissed out amid my dry cackles.

I saw a sparkle that led me to my dropped nodachi, although I did not remember losing it. I dove for it and began cutting heads off with the thing as soon as I floated back up. It was the best game in the world. How many could I get at one time in a single stroke? The answer to that question was ten, so long as I hit a herd clustered in full retreat and followed through.

Blood was everywhere and all of it black in the night. Limbs, masks, and shredded garments littered the ground. Some fought to the death, as lost to the slaughter as I was. I met one of those, an eight foot, red-skinned oni with long horns and tusks. We grinned and crashed together in the chaos. He broke my nodachi with his kanabo, but while he was locked in the momentum of his downswing, I sinuously twisted and wrapped myself around him, chewing out his throat with my sharp teeth while I clawed at his eyes.

I think I ripped his windpipe out and spat it on the street. It was rather surreal, like a dream. Kami-sama, help me, but I still remember the taste of flesh and blood in my mouth.

When the massacre was over, save for those few who

managed to escape, the majority of the Night Parade of One Hundred Demons lay dead in the street. I was disappointed it was over so soon. I was having such a delightful time of it, too.

"*Shiroi Uindo!*" My name was issued by well over a hundred demonic throats. They were cheering for me!

I swelled with pride. Was I not a splendid villain? So wanton, ruthless, and cruel? And how lesser yōkai trembled at such magnificence as myself! That was how it should be. Even the other Six were steering clear, but I scarcely saw them, let alone thought about them. I was lost in the majesty of myself.

I heard a scuffle and turned my long snout as nameless yōkai brought a human forward. Young, male, stinking of fear. I slavered, the drool dripping red and white from my long fangs. He cried out several times in his terror. Cackling, they shoved the man-thing to his knees. The demon who found him clutched the mortal's short hair, forcing him to look up at me. His eyes were wide and glazed in fright. He tried to scream, but no sound came out.

"Great Lord Kitsune! This human was lurking in an alley nearby. He *saw*!" the young yōkai declared.

"*Did he?*" I rasped. I grinned at the human and drifted toward him wraith-like, hair flowing in my wake. When I drew near, I sniffed him and he let loose a bloodcurdling scream. My maw opened wide in a fox grin. All that delicious fear! I could smell it, hear his heart beating rapidly in his panting chest. My tail wagged in anticipation! I cupped his chin in my long fingers, wet and sticky with blood. *"You know the penalty, mortal, for trespassing on our affairs?"*

"P-p-pl-pl-please," he whimpered in abject terror, shaking his head.

"The sentence is immediate death," I hissed. Innocent or not, this foolish mortal had seen what must never be seen. One who was Sanctioned would know this. Cleary this poor sod had never seen a yōkai in his life. He must have heard our battle and come out to see what the trouble was. It was a tragic mistake he would not live much longer to regret.

I seized him by the throat and tore out his heart without further preamble. I twisted the aorta, and delicately dipped the muscle into my wide maw, gobbling it down whole. The demon horde around me cheered. I casually tossed what was left of the human over my shoulder, where it was swarmed and eaten by the hungry yōkai who preyed on human meat.

After, I set the yōkai corpses on fire so that they would assuredly stay dead, their remains kept out of mortal hands. They burned fast down to ash, the smell of charred meat haunting the air. I stared at the remaining blue flames, *so* beautiful, hypnotic in the night…

"Aww shit," I heard a gruff, distant voice. "Kid's gone."

"What do you mean?" someone asked. Shirou, maybe. I heard, but barely registered the words, much less who spoke them. Instead I wondered what would happen if I set the buildings around me on fire. Would the whole city burn? And think of all the chaos if it did! People running, screaming in terror, trampling one another in herd panic!

"Feel the miasma building up? That's all him. Our boy's just getting started. I'm going over there before it's too late. If he kills me, run like hell back to Youta. If you have to make a stand, surround that yako and hit him with everything you got – and whatever you do, don't fucking stop 'til he's dead! Better wish me luck, though."

And all the while those beautiful blue flames! They would rage as I picked off whomever I wished! Swoop down out of the sky and pluck up the humans to drop and break! Rend and savage! My fingers convulsed in anticipation. Oh, yes! It did not have to be over! I could feast! And a woman…

Yessss, a woman would be nice…

"Hayate-san." It was Katashi's gravel voice behind me. I whirled, claws curling. What in the hell did *he* want? Did the tanuki not see I was engaged in my fantasy? A gekkering growl reverberated in my chest and quivered up my throat. I never did like this asshole.

The tanuki lifted his mask and stared me in the eye. "It's over, kid. Come on back now." I growled at him again. I drew my shoulders back, prepared to strike if he did not get out of my face. "Just look at yourself, shirogitsune," he said sadly. "Is this what you want to be?"

And something in the way he said it was… gentle. Concerned. That was not like him at all! In place of irritation, I suddenly snapped back into present focus. I blinked, and the consciousness that made me *me* was back in command. I shifted at once. It was like waking up out of a nightmare to discover it had not been a dream at all.

I felt something akin to shellshock as I stood there. I had never so completely and thoroughly lost control before. It felt so incredible! The sheer power, the strength, no fear of consequences… But what little of the zenko was left inside of me was horrified and afraid.

What have I done? Not to mention what I had been about to do! I shuddered and found myself shaking as I looked down at my bloody hands. My claws were caked thick with drying blood. And the scent of it…

Katashi read it all in my eyes. He nodded stiffly. "I know. Better than any of *them* do." He jerked his head at the others. "First time's a bitch, 'specially for you prissy types. You'll get over it, white fox, you'll see. But for now, suck it up. We gotta go."

He was right. I nodded, transfigured a new kitsunenomen out of a broadleaf, and joined the others to lead our survivors back to the Ori.

OUR ACTIONS THAT NIGHT SENT A POWERFUL SHOCKWAVE throughout the yōkai world. The name Youta Clan became synonymous with fear. We would stop at nothing to win. We had a cause, a need. And if we lacked the sheer, raw power of older yōkai, we made up for it in strategy and numbers.

The survivors spread the tale, and I featured large in the telling: the white Wild Fox who lived for slaughter. I was not just the Kitsune Killer, I was the Yako of New Tokyo, feared by yōkai and mortal kind alike. Those who had witnessed began to draw and circulate art of that ghastly event within hours. By dawn, the first images of Shiroi Uindo in the midst of the Hyakki yagyō carnage popped up on the Demon Net, a dark web for our kind. I became as iconic among the yōkai population as the footage of me on that roof was to the humans.

At the Ori, demons were partying in celebration in spite of our losses. We yōkai weren't much for grieving unless the death struck particularly close to home, and then we generally swore revenge. I was positive after tonight quite a few yōkai wanted to exterminate me. My celebrity had grown exponentially.

"Hey, Shiroi Uindo," someone called out. "*Boss* fight!" A fist was raised in Youta Clan solidarity. I nodded in that direction before turning face forward to find Chikako in front of me, spooked.

"Hayate-sama." She bit her lip.

I never intended to let the beast take over. It had been an accident. But I felt guilty, like I got caught cheating on her or something. Inside I was grimy, soiled, filthy...

"Hey," I said sheepishly.

"They're saying you turned into your full nogitsune form." For once she did not mince words.

"I did," I confessed, stricken. "I did not intend it. It...I..." I shook my head.

"And they say that you..." she trailed off. "They're calling it a slaughter."

"I couldn't help it. I tried! But... Are you upset with me?" The way she was speaking, I could not tell. Perhaps my own guilt was coloring things.

She peered nervously into my eyes. "No, but... Are you okay?"

In retrospect, I think she was asking if I was still *me*. Her Hayate. But at the time I thought she was referring to my feelings on what had just happened. I was quite the narcissist in those days.

I shook my head from side to side. "Yeah, I'm alright." But I was far from all right. So far as I was concerned, I had dishonored myself. I looked down and away, troubled.

"Oh, okay," she said. I could tell she did not believe me, and I did not have it in me to convince her. I could not even convince myself. "Still want me over later?" She seemed a little afraid.

I nodded, lighting up a little to know I would not be alone. "Please. I would like that."

Chikako saw my lapse of rare vulnerability. She lived for those. It was her only inroad through the invisible walls I built to protect myself. So she brightened to see me in this state, confused and out of sorts as I was. This was her big chance and she was not going to let uncertainty ruin it.

I saw all this, but I was too freshly wounded inside. I *needed* to be with the one person who kept that darkness at bay inside of me. I could not wait to get away from these monsters. All I wanted was to be alone with Chikako.

"I'll come home with you after work then."

I exhaled in relief. She smiled in return and squeezed my hand.

"Hey, Hayate!" Shirou called out. "Youta-sama wants a word." He jerked his thumb up towards the dragon's office.

"Hai, Shirou." I was so down I did not even do the cute pause in his name that I usually threw in. I watched him blink. He could tell something was wrong with me, but not quite what. Of course, he thought I had been born a yako. I did nothing to dissuade anyone of this notion.

I went up and let myself into Youta's office. I was in a total fugue state, my mind replaying what I had done during the massacre. Youta was not alone. Katashi was with him, and when I walked through the door, they both looked at me as if I might combust at any moment.

"Ah, Shiroi Uindo. A good battle."

"Hai, Youta-sama," I answered, but my heart was not in it.

Youta stared at me. "Katashi told me what happened. How are you holding up?"

I drew myself up and stood stoically before my master. "I am well, Youta-sama," I said at once. "I live to serve you."

I was a soldier, I told myself. It was just war, nothing more. I looked straight ahead and pretended to see nothing while images of black blood and blue flame flashed before my eyes.

I was going to… I was going… I trembled ever so slightly.

Youta studied me. At last he nodded. "Go home, Hayate-san." His deep voice was soft.

"I promised Chikako I would accompany her after her shift." I was not sure why I said it. When a dragon tells you to do something, you just do it.

"Take her with you," the water dragon commanded. "We will see you tomorrow night."

"Hai, Youta-sama." I bowed, leaving my master and the tanuki to stare after my departure. I wondered what they would say when I left, before deciding I simply did not care.

I TOOK CHIKAKO BACK TO MY PLACE A SHORT WHILE LATER, MUCH to her surprise. She did not question it, though. She simply smiled and spoke to her supervisor, then gave a quiet word to Hiroko, who disapproved of her sister's association with me more than ever. Under that was dread fear for her sister's safety.

Most would have thought me hungry for sex after that battle, and ordinarily I would have been. Chikako was prepared for it, if a bit hesitant, unsure of what sort of lover I would be this night. Considering what happened during the battle, I was surprised she was willing to be alone with me at all. Yako have a terrible reputation in this regard.

But once I was away from the others, I could not hide my dismay. I was too lost in my own head to get hard. All I wanted was to go into a dark place and disappear for a while.

"Hayate?" Chikako asked me as I slid out of my clothes, letting them drop carelessly onto the floor. I crawled onto the bed where I curled into a ball, my tail pressed tight around me. I did not even pull the covers over myself. I felt the cold draft on my skin, but I scarcely registered it. I knew I should answer her, but I could not make myself speak. Some part of me was dying on the inside, choking, drowning…

Chikako's mouth parted open, eyes filled with concern. She had never seen me like this, but I could not pretend to be strong any longer. I had sunk to a new low. I tried unsuccessfully to blot out the memories that intruded in non-sequential order, flitting across my mind's eye.

Without a word, Chikako turned on the space heater I had bought a few days before and aimed it at the bed. She stripped her waitress uniform down to her bra and panties, then sat cross-legged on the futon mattress by my head. She stroked the thick, soft fur inside my ears. I said nothing and enjoyed the feminine kindliness implicit in her touch.

"You really don't like being that thing, do you?"

"No," I said numbly. "But…"

"But?"

"What bothers me is how much I enjoyed it tonight. It was so empowering, I felt strong, limitless… It was seductive and heady, like nothing I've ever experienced." I stared blankly at the wall. "I have never lost it like that before, Chikako. *Never!* What I did tonight…" I trailed off as the images played through my mind again in their tawdry loop. I cringed into myself.

"Oh, Hayate." She brushed my hair from my ear. "Sweetheart, you are too hard on yourself. You *always* have to be in control, all the time. But sometimes that's not possible. Our yōkai natures catch up to us whatever we do. It's as true for nekomata as it is for kitsune. You've never seen me chase after a laser light."

I smiled a little at that adorable image. It faded as I remembered the things I had done not so very long ago.

"I killed a man tonight," I said, not knowing why. I never told her what happened when I went on a job, and yet the words tumbled out anyway. I needed to confess. "He wasn't prey or an enemy combatant. He did not deserve his fate. He was just unlucky and stupid to have been caught seeing when he overheard our racket."

"If one of the Unsanctioned mortals saw, he had to die. Every yōkai knows this, Hayate. It is our Law." She continued to pet my head gently, massaging the muscles behind and around my ears. It felt good, comforting. "Only grief comes of allowing them to live."

"I know." Boy did I know! "But I fed what was left of him to the horde. I just tossed the body like so much rubbish. And I felt... nothing."

"Then why be troubled?" Hers was the voice of an innocent.

"Because I have a Code," I answered.

"Like a Bushido Code?" she asked.

"Kind of." I shook my head slightly, unwilling to explain further. I had already let her in too far tonight. Chikako was a born yōkai. I was once the celestial messenger of a kami. How could she possibly understand my pain?

"My poor Hayate," she said softly.

I rolled over so I could look up into her eyes. She stared

down into mine. I reached up and tenderly touched her cheek. "I'm losing my ability to feel. I don't think I can fight what's happening to me any longer. I just lost another piece of myself tonight, a really big one. I am afraid soon there won't be anything left of me, and then... Who will I be, Chikako?" No, not who, but *what*. "I don't want to be... *that*." I shuddered.

If Katashi hadn't called me back, I would be Shiroi Uindo still, setting fire to everything, rampaging upon the helpless! Kami-sama, no wonder a yako must be caged or put down...

"I know you struggle against it. I see it every time we're alone together. What? Did you truly think I wouldn't notice? I know I'm naïve, Hayate, but I'm your woman and you are my man. I know you better than you think, my beautiful fox. I know you want to be better than the stereotypical nogitsune. You have an incredible amount of restraint. It's one of the things I... love... about you."

She blushed at her admission, eyes cast down in embarrassment. She never meant to say it. She knew I did not feel the same.

"I know, Chikako. I've always known, since the beginning. Hiroko is right, damn her. You deserve someone better, who isn't a heartless *yako*," I sneered in self-disgust.

"Hayate, please stop calling yourself that. You have treated me better from our first night together than any man has my entire life – and that includes my father! You are here when I need you, you never raise a hand against me or call me cruel names, not even when we fight. You buy me things, and no one's ever done that before! And they are things I like, which means you pay attention and care enough to notice." Actually, it was a sociopathic trait of mine, but anyway... "You're more decent than you give yourself credit for."

She smoothed the hair around my face, played with and fluffed my bangs so they would sit perfectly. She smiled. "You say you like that I am 'innocent.' Well, I like that you are wicked." She blushed again. "But what I love most is that at your core you are a good guy and a bad boy rolled into one. You are sexy, smart, strong... I feel protected when I am with you, because I've seen you fight. You put yourself in front of me against a horde of screaming yōkai! I *know* you won't let anything hurt me. You've proved it! I also remember you coming for me and holding me afterward. A lot of girls have guys who say they love them and won't even do half of all that!"

I could not argue her point.

"And then add that you do the most amazing things to my body that no one has *ever* done?" She smiled. "How could any gal resist you, my gorgeous kitsune? I am proud to be Shiroi Uindo's woman." She leaned over and kissed me on the lips.

"You are one of the reasons I fight so hard not to go completely under," I confessed when she came up for air. "Sometimes, when we are alone together, I wish I could be what you need me to be. I am afraid the best I can manage is to not be as bad as what I could become."

"I know," she whispered, nodding. "I do."

We crawled under the covers after that and shared intimacy, which she initiated. Some of it was sweet, some of it was raunchy, but it was just what I needed. For a little while the Hyakki yagyō went away and there was only her. Her warmth, her body, her devotion to me. I drank them in like the greedy vampire I was while she rode me for all I was worth.

I held my nekomata lover gently as she drifted off to sleep in the afterglow, my shoulder supporting her head, her arm draped across my chest. I knew one day she was going to want things I could never give her. Children, a place in the sun, a doting husband, perhaps the love she so dearly craved and I was incapable of giving or feeling. Then I would lose my Chikako. I wondered if I would be so far gone when I did to care.

But tonight, at least, she belonged to *me*. And I wanted her here. She had become my only security in a world gone mad.

Chapter Twenty-Three

Hanako

There were side effects from the Hyakki yagyō Massacre, as it came to be known. The first was discovered shortly upon waking the following afternoon. After a morning filled with joyous dreams saturated in blood and wanton destruction, I was sitting up in bed checking for messages. Chikako walked over from the kitchen with two steaming mugs of oolong tea.

"Hayate?" Her voice was tremulous.

I glanced up at once, concerned. "Yeah?" Chikako's face was a mask of anxiety. I tilted my head quizzically, brows knit. "What is it?"

She opened her mouth, but no words came out. She took a deep breath. "Your shadow..." Chikako was not looking at me. I turned, confused.

Writ large upon the wall was the shade of the Demon Fox.

My eyes widened in horror. "No..." Did this mean the

tattered remnant of my soul had changed over entirely? I tried to glamour it... but it stayed the same. My ears flattened and pinned back. The shadow's ears followed my movements, except we were not moving properly in sync. It turned its vulpine head sidelong against the light and grinned at me, tongue lolling between its sharp teeth.

"No! No, no, no...!" I stared at it. It stared back. And yes, it *saw* me. "Oh, please," I whispered queasily. "Not this." I was horror-struck and repulsed. It moved of its own accord without my consent! I swear it was introducing itself to me. I cringed back, closed my eyes and shuddered, turning my face away and drawing in on myself.

"I can't make it go away." My voice sounded vaguely child-like in my dismay.

Chikako put the mugs down and went to my side at once. "Hey, it's okay." She wrapped her arms around me and held me. I clung to her.

"It's *not* okay," I mumbled. I made one of those stupid fox whimpers in the back of my throat. My body trembled.

"Then it will *be* okay," she said in soothing tones.

I shook my head against her shoulder. It was never, ever going to be okay again! She kissed the side of my head.

"My poor baby." Even as she spoke those words of comfort, I knew she was looking at my shadow over my head. I doubt she could take her eyes off it. I did not know what *it* was doing, for I refused to look, but I could feel her tension, nonetheless.

Unfortunately, that was only the beginning.

I found myself increasingly drawn to bad habits. I acquired a taste for strong nihonshu, what westerners refer to strictly as 'sake.' It did not get me drunk, though not for lack of trying. My demonic body metabolized the liquor too fast. My new nature, on the other hand, demanded to go on a bender to see how much it would take to get well me and truly drunk. Trust me, living with that shadow was enough to drive anyone to drink!

I took up smoking a long pipe. I became a connoisseur of synthesized tobacco and opium. I loved the sensation of inhaling the smoke into my lungs and the steady release of the exhale. I also liked the feel of the stem in my hands, the way my clawed fingers curved around the brass and wood.

I certainly behaved more wickedly, my miasma atrocious. My jests were darker, crueler, and held the stinging whip of sarcasm. I tended more to that sly drawl when I spoke. My facial and body expressions followed suit. I played sleight of hand tricks for fun and to impress, a trademark smirk tugging at my lips. And if I had come to enjoy a bit of gambling, well… only an idiot would take me up on it.

The sleazy yako routine was no longer an act. I had Fallen into the ruin of a true nogitsune at last. I was more ruthless when I killed after the Hyakki yagyō. No longer merely inured to the pain of others, I *enjoyed* it. And fear! Oh, how Shiroi Uindo loved to inspire terror! I stopped being annoyed by the murders attributed to me that I had not committed. Whatever inflated my reputation, and by extension my ego, was just fine by me.

And my demon's shadow? It became my steadfast companion, revealing my true thoughts and feelings however stately my outward aplomb. It lunged and clawed at those I disliked, and sometimes it was grotesquely perverse to Chikako's poor shadow, much to my chagrin. I learned to live with the specter of my supercharged id, unable to do else. Occasionally I would talk to it, but only when no one was around. By its responses, I knew the shadow yako understood, and answered in its own silent way.

Chikako never spoke of it after that afternoon, or the darkening change in my personality. I could tell she was distressed, but she pretended nothing was wrong, and I pretended nothing had changed. I carried on as I had been with her, and she ignored my less savory traits as the most abysmally frigid winter on record settled in.

JUST AROUND THE STANDARD NEW YEAR, THERE WAS A BRIEF LULL in the war where both sides took stock for the final battles to come. The hellishly cold weather refused to budge. Winter dulls the edge on fighting, except for yuki onna. Fuyuko was ecstatic! But the ominous quiet was the calm before the storm. Freezing or not, the war was going to continue until one dragon reigned supreme.

Out of sheer boredom late one night, I decided to follow my dear friend Hanako around. I had thought about her a lot since the human I killed on Solstice Night. He died for the same knowledge Yoshimora lived with. Her life was held hostage to her silence. Granted no one was like to believe her, but she would die anyway. The police department never looked too closely at suicides, especially when a prominent family was involved.

It was a month until Asian New Year, and the sky was pitch black, nearly starless thanks to the light pollution. Shadows lay thick and heavy under the transrail overpass that soared into the Inner Metropoplex from this side of The Sprawl. I had participated in killing several human gang members down here a few days before. Their blood was frozen to the concrete. I supposed that was why Officer Yoshimora was here.

At sight of a cop, the few transients braving the remorseless cold scampered away. Homelessness was a crime in New Tokyo that resulted in workhouses for the most hazardous and menial labor – or exile beyond the perimeter if one was deemed too ill to work. Most were squatting in abandoned factories or hiding down in the sewers.

When Hanako was completely alone, she unexpectedly switched off her lapel cam and her goggle view. She lifted the hard plastic shield from her eyes and removed her tactical helmet. "I know you are there. I can *feel* you."

I lit my pipe with a whiff of blue flame and leaned against the concrete pillar. I stood upon the threshold between worlds, partially swallowed in the darkness to which I now belonged. She gasped when she saw me. Knowing I was there was one thing; appearing unexpectedly from the Shadow Realm was another.

"Hayate."

I smiled wickedly. "Some call me Shiroi Uindo." My name echoed weirdly in the night.

"I've heard. You have quite the reputation these days, Lord Wild Fox... Butcher of the Hyakki yagyō Massacre."

I inclined my head and sucked in a long, steady stream of smoke. The exhalation wreathed around my head in the dry, frigid air before dissipating.

"Are you following *me* now?" she asked, trying to sound more nonchalant about my appearance than she felt. I could see her anxiety, smell her fear. She was wondering if I was going to attack her again, knowing there was precious little she could do about it if I did, but determined not to act as prey.

"It is only fair. You have been following my kills all over this city. Tonight I was curious."

"About?"

"You." I inhaled another deep lungful of smoke.

"Well, *that's* not creepy or anything."

I shrugged. "I feel a little responsible for you." The smoke expelled with my words. "I *was* your first yōkai, after all."

"Ha *ha*. *Very* funny." And I thought I had the market cornered on sarcasm. She glared at me. She looked just like her father when she did that.

"Tchk. You know what I mean, girl."

"Yeah, I do," she said, frowning. "Are all first encounters with your sort so traumatic?"

"Usually. Consider yourself fortunate, Hanako-san. Not only did you survive our encounter with your virginity intact, you also retained your sanity."

"I'm beginning to wonder…" She pressed her lips together.

"You're not gibbering in a corner," I offered.

"I feel like I want to sometimes." She stuffed her free hand deep into her pocket and hunched her shoulders against the cold. "I'm seeing monsters everywhere now. It won't stop."

"No," I said sadly. "You are too good of a detective to deny the truth. And you should be more careful. There are worse things in the dark than me. Although I admit, I *am* one of the particularly bad ones." I grinned and lifted my narrow chin.

"Wonderful." She shook her head and cleared her throat. "I need to ask… Why are you doing this?"

"I told you, two dragons are competing in a game of power. The rest of us are dragged into it."

"Not that. I get *that*. I mean you personally."

"The reigning Dragon would have locked me in a cage and only let me out to kill and whore for him. And when he tired of using me, he would sell me to a new owner, to do with as *they* please. Or, more likely, put me down when my usefulness came to an end." I sucked on my pipe. "That is what gods and dragons do to kitsune."

She scrunched her face. "Oh."

I blew out a stream of grey mist. "My master accords me respect and grants autonomy outside of his command. Even yōkai have to make a living, you know. I barely escaped starvation out in the poisoned wasteland. I came here to survive, only to learn I would be hunted and captured as a trophy unless I found a protector. So I did. That was the night the Ayakashi War began," I concluded with a smooth air of melancholy.

"Because of you?" she asked.

"Yes. I was not given sanctuary out of an act of kindness, Hanako-san. I was the last piece to join the board. With a nogitsune in his elite menagerie, my master's years of preparation came to fruition."

"Shit. But what if your side loses?"

"Then Hiroshi will reclaim and restructure this city, and, in his desperate need to reassert his authority, he will become more of a tyrant. Otherwise, things will essentially go on as they have been. Yōkai like me will continue to find ways into the city, disrupting the delicate balance between our two worlds. Eventually the whole system will collapse. Dragons have survived worse than this. They do not care about the rest of us."

"And what about *you*?"

"If Hiroshi wins and I am captured, I will be tortured and raped every way there is before I am put to death. I expect I'll have my ears and tail cleaved off, to begin. I have given him too great an insult not to be made an example of.

"But if *my* lord succeeds, I am poised to become the new Dragon's right-hand enforcer of the Ayakashi Syndicate. I will wear expensive suits and be chauffeured around, live In-Met in a penthouse suite with a skyline view. I can hunt whomever and wherever I want, the healthy wicked being my preferred diet. Meanwhile, I get to have fun running amok to screw over the existing establishment!" I fixed her with my yōkai eyes. "*Why* am I doing this, you asked me? I ask *you*, Hanako-san, how could I *not*?"

"When you put it that way..."

"Ah, still the headstrong idealist, I see." I tsked. "Keep going on like this and one day this world will destroy it, or you. Maybe both. The way it already has me."

"Sage advice from a Wild Fox?"

"Hai," I said seriously, puffing on my pipe.

"As if you care," she shot at me, sullen again.

"It might be I do." The smoke wreathed around my head as I spoke. "I appear to have a soft spot for hard luck cases and protecting the innocent." I shrugged, perplexed with myself. "Go figure that one out."

"You? Protect innocence?" She shook her head in disbelief. "What in the hell do I make of that?"

"Make of it what you wish. In the end it's all the same. You will live and you will die, and this world with all its beauties and horrors will go on and on. Until it doesn't anymore."

Hanako frowned. "That's awfully pragmatic of you."

I thought so, but I did not answer. The silence stretched on as she stared hard at me. At last she spoke, and I could tell she had to gather her courage.

"I need to say this and I need you to hear me out, okay? What you did last autumn... You *assaulted* me."

"Yes, I did," I admitted at once. "Do you wish an apology? Should I throw myself at your feet and beg your forgiveness?"

"Yes!"

I shook my head sadly. "Then you shall wait a long time for what I can no longer give, Hanako-san."

She shook her head violently. "That's not good enough! No one has *ever* done *anything* like that to me!" Her voice raised in tone and pitch. "You... you *beat* me, bruised me, bound me, *threw* me around... I *felt* your excitement! You pressed it against me! I was terrorized! Traumatized! Then you... you took everything away from me!" Her voice quavered. "My trust in my father, my belief in how the world worked, every certainty I ever had! *Gone* in a matter of minutes that felt like a lifetime!"

Hanako took a deep, shuddering breath. "I – I cannot forgive you for what you did to me that night! Even *if* you begged!" Her tear-filled eyes were far away as she relived the memory in her mind. She ran a gloved hand through her hair.

"I neither expect nor desire your forgiveness, Hanako-san," I said gently. "Your censure means little and less to me. I no longer have the capacity to feel empathy as such. I did what I was ordered under the watchful eye of my master through your flat-cam. It was the only way to save you."

"*Save me?*" she asked, aghast.

"Of course. Most yōkai are not as patient toward such

meddling. Sooner or later you were going to run into something that was going to destroy you. The way you ran into me at the warehouse."

She stared at me open-mouthed. I shrugged. "I do not feel remorse, per se," I continued, "but if it helps, I did not find it amusing to damage you."

"Really?" She gaped at me.

"I take no joy in harming an innocent. I would never have come to you if it had not been commanded of me."

"Yeah, well you could have found another way, you know! Did you have to make me feel so weak, so helpless? So *vulnerable*!" Her shout echoed in the night.

"Yes. Answer me this, Officer Yoshimora. What would you have done had I walked up to you on the street and requested politely that you discontinue your ruthless pursuit of the Kitsune Killer? Hmmm? Would you have invited me for a conversation over tea?" I tilted my head.

"No," she said in the tone of a petulant teenager. "I'd have arrested you on the spot."

My smile suggested otherwise. "I needed you to hear me quickly. To get out of that sinister situation, you had to know what I was truly there for. And no, it was not your body." I gestured at her with my pipe. "You are a beautiful woman, Hanako-san, but I was never going to violate you for so small a thing. I have no stomach to go through with such an act." I puffed and let loose a stream of smoke that hovered ghostly in the air between us. "It was a bluff."

"A *bluff*!" That made her angry. "That was a damn good bluff! I was fucking convinced!"

I inclined my head. "Thank you," I said sincerely. "I had

to make you believe it. Once you were physically helpless, you had to use your wits to free yourself. And that meant..." I tilted my head again and pointed my pipe at Hanako to prompt her to finish the statement.

"It meant I had to listen. Instead of forcing you to submit to my authority, you made me submit to your will through strength and terror."

I nodded and saluted her with my pipe. "*Now* you are catching on." I smiled like a proud sensei.

She narrowed her eyes. "You're a psychopath," she spat at me.

"Actually, I am a *socio*path" I corrected. "Yōkai tend to sadism, you know. Among us monsters, the weak are prey, and to be prey is to die. It is not so very different among humankind. We are all animals, are we not?"

"So, you are what you are, and that's it?" she asked contemptuously. "I am supposed to just accept that?"

"Essentially. I was *forged* in Hellfire, Hanako-san. Can you imagine what that feels like?" I fixed her with my demonic eyes. "The pain and horror, the hungry darkness filling you, *changing* you into a monster, stripping everything away until there's nothing of you left..."

"Changing you?"

"Not every Wild Fox starts out feral. I have felt the greater portion of my soul ripped away. Soon there will be nothing of me left. The Darkness is taking me and I cannot stop it no matter how I fight against it."

"I don't understand." She looked at me as if I were mad. Maybe I was, to speak so to this mortal child.

"Is it so hard to believe I was a pure being once? A kind

and gentle spirit of the Light?" I laughed contemptuously, a sound both cold and cruel to match the winter's night. She shivered. "This foul world of yours poisoned me. Your kind finished me off," I said bitterly.

"Corrupted you? Finished you? What does any of that mean?"

I shrugged. "I am sure you will figure it out. You are a clever woman, Hanako-san. I respect you for that. And for your tenacity."

"I don't... I..." She shook her head, clearly confused, more so that I was praising her.

"We all suffer our little indignities in this life. I am no different from you in this regard. Do not let what I did to you define who you are. *I* did that, allowed the actions of others to twist me, and behold what I have become!" I lifted my arms in grandeur and leaned forward. My vulpine shadow crept out across the concrete, black as sin. Hanako stared at its freakish movements, then back at me, eyes wide. "Be stronger than I was, Hanako-san."

"You are a strange monster, Hayate-dono," she said, backing away a half step.

I grinned. "I suppose I am at that."

"So, I have to ask. That business over at the open street bazaar?"

"Oh, that? My friends brought me out for a wild night," I said, just as I had spoken the line to her back in September. I smiled as I saw her make the connection. She was quick, was Yoshimora.

"Wait! That was *you?* The little nerd?"

I laughed. "Hai. Clever girl."

"You son of a –!"

"Now, now. My mother was a fine vixen and not at all to blame for how *I* turned out."

"I cannot believe that was you!"

"That was a yōkai club. I helped incinerate the corpses."

"And that's why no bodies. Damn, you bastards cover your tracks."

"Of course we do. Old habits die hard and serve well."

"What about the kid who went missing in December?"

"Ah, him. Regrettably he saw what must never be seen. Worse, he let himself be caught. He had to die. It is our Law."

Hanako looked as if she might vomit. "Did *you* do it?"

"Hai." I saw no reason to lie.

She turned slightly pale. "Then why let *me* live?"

"We make exceptions for those chosen few who know how to keep secrets. We call you 'the Sanctioned.' Else, yes. Regrettably, you would have to die, and if my lord gave the order, I would in all probability be sent to do it."

She sighed in resignation. "Would you really find my death regrettable?"

"Yes." I said honestly. "I have become fond of you in my own way. I would take no pleasure in slaying you. But I would not hesitate, either. I know firsthand what happens when a significant group of humans believes in monsters. The innocent are always the first to pay that price."

I banged my wrists together and sent the little ember flying outward from my pipe chamber. It glowed brilliant orange for a moment, then promptly died as it hit the cold ground. It put me in mind of Aiko. A bright spark quickly extinguished.

Hanako watched its progress with her eyes and said nothing,

but I think she got the metaphor. My shadow watched, too, and put its hands over its eyes as though it were grieving. Of course, it might have been mocking our sorrow. It was impossible to tell.

"If it ever comes to that, I will make it quick and as painless as possible. I promise I will not desecrate your body or make it simply disappear. Those who love you will have the comfort of saying final rites for you."

"*Thank* you?" She was a bit aghast.

I inclined my head graciously. "You are most welcome." I felt I was being extremely generous.

She shook her head. "I wish..." her voice faded.

"You wish?" I prompted.

"I wish I didn't know about you or any of this. At the same time, I wish I was a bigger part of it... I..." Hanako hung her head.

"It will be over soon and all of this will fade. Oh, we will still be here, lurking in our shadows. But *you* can return to the light whenever you wish."

"You sound as if you envy me."

"Maybe I do a little. I cannot return to divine grace, for I am beyond all hope of redemption," I said, believing it. "But you... well... You need never Fall."

Hanako sighed. "I may be a child of the light, but I must turn my back to it and stare into the darkness to fight it, to keep the shadows at bay."

I shook my head. "Oh, my dear, you have it all wrong. It is light that casts shadows. What you see writ before you in the dark is only the silhouette of your true self." I inclined my head to her shadow, cast long from the angle of the light and feathered by other shadows of varying neon intensity until they trailed off into the night. Then I nodded to mine, which grinned open-mouthed, then melted back into my gloom-en-shrouded patch.

"In the end, the waiting darkness swallows us all no matter what we do, try as we might to fight against it. Even the stars will not burn forever."

"Then what's the fucking point of it all?" Hanako snapped angrily. "Well, senpai? Can you tell me *that*?"

I smiled. "There *is* no point. But hey, while you are alive, you might as well give it a go. What else is there to do? We are all just travelers passing through; memories in motion, ghosts who have yet to die. The stars which burn the hottest die in an explosion of epic proportion, then fade from all sight and knowledge out of time. So it is with us all."

"Wow. You must be *wonderful* company at dinner parties," she said sarcastically.

"I don't know." I tilted my head. "Shall I tell you when I start getting invited to them?" My lips spread into a wry grin.

She shook her head. "I am never going to hold an existential debate with a fox again."

"Very wise of you, I'm sure." I slipped my pipe inside the breast of my kimono and turned to go.

"Hayate-dono?"

I stopped and waited.

"For what it's worth, I kind of hope you survive."

I turned my head to look over my shoulder at her. "Thank you, Hanako-san. Such a polite child you are. Now go, and turn that cam back on before you are missed," I suggested. And with that I let the dark consume me from all sight.

343

Chapter Twenty-Four

The Last Raid

"ight there?" I grinned as I stroked in a short a rhythm. I was rewarded by Chikako's indrawn gasp.

"Uh huh! Mmmmmm..." She threw her head back.

"And how about *here*..." I shifted my hips and quickened my pace, short, fast, staccato. Yeah, *that* was perfect. An explosion of warmth flooded over that most sensitive part of my anatomy. She was liquid silk and pure heat.

Chikako cried out louder than before. "Yes! OH!" And then her words stopped making sense. My sly grin widened.

My further descent had one more unforeseen consequence. I was far more proficient at sex. You might think I would have become forceful, more rapacious perhaps. But that was not exactly the case. If I felt my lust more keenly, it also made me a bold lover. Ah, the games we were now beginning to play!

Chikako glanced over at my shadow plowing away on top of her silhouetted curves. Its long tongue licked between her breasts. I took her chin in my hand and forced her to stare into the dagger slits of my eyes.

"Don't look at that," I commanded, my eyes narrowing evilly as they bore down into hers. "Look at *me*," I hissed with authority. Her vagina flooded and began to quiver. I knew what that meant. She was just about there.

"Hayate-sama, *Hayate-sama, HAYATE-SAMA!*" She came harder than she ever had before. The energy burst was amazing, and so was my own orgasm in that sweet, undulating pussy – pun fully intended. Admittedly my ears pinned back before she was done, her screams hitting those decibels that *hurt*. But it was totally worth it.

I nuzzled and nipped at her neck, her arms thrown around me. "Wow..." she said, breathing heavily. "Just *wow*."

I sighed in mutual satisfaction. "Was that to your liking, my sweet?" My tone was a tad sinister, but playful. I smiled as she flustered a moment.

"Oh, yeah." She squeezed me, arms and well... you know.

I chuckled, itself a wicked sound. I rolled off and reached for my pipe. It was next to a pile of clothes on the floor beside my futon. My apartment had become an outrageous mess in the past few weeks. In a moment I had the pipe bowl stuffed and was filling the room with sweet, cloying smoke.

"Ugh!" Chikako fanned a wispy tendril away from her face. "I can't believe you've taken up smoking that thing!"

I glanced at my shadow, sight of which proved it was also smoking, putting the pipe to its long snout, its talons far longer than my claws. We shrugged. "Too stereotypical?" I asked in a bored drawl around the mouthpiece.

"Just a bit," she said, rolling onto her side and propping up

her head on her hand and elbow. She stroked the muscular outline of my abdomen with her other hand, her touch light and
deliciously feminine. Occasionally her eyes would dart to my
shadow and away again. We did not speak about it. Mentioning
it merely made it act out, and that was more disturbing.

I pretended I did not care. The truth was, I found it dev-
astating. I was horribly depressed deep inside, so lost to this
private despair that drinking every morning before bed became
a thing. I found it annoying that I was too powerful to easily become drunk, but at least that and opium took the edge off. And
so did killing, which I did nearly every night in my lord's service.

Winter or no winter, the conflict resumed in full. When
I was sent forth, men and demons died. Some broke and fled
at the mere sight of me in the kitsunenomen. I was renowned
for my mercilessness and... creativity. And I have to admit, I
really liked it. I was an upper echelon predator in my natural
place, the only kitsune at large in the known world; rare, white,
beautiful and oh, *so* powerful...

"You're going out again tonight." It was not a question.
Chikako's voice snapped me out of my cult of Self.

"Of course."

Chika pouted. "I miss you at the club lately. I like to look
up and see you."

I forbore to mention how dismally boring it was standing
up there. "If anyone lays a hand on you when I'm not there,
tell me. I will burn it off."

She grinned, but there was a touch of the queasy beneath.
"I know you would, and so does everyone else! Customers have
become most polite to me since..." Since the Hyakki yagyo
Massacre. "No one messes with 'Shiroi Uindo's girl,'" she said.

I shifted uncomfortably as she called me by the demon's name. The face of my shadow swung to her at once, ears pricked forward. She froze. I grimaced and sat up to block the view between them.

"Uh… yeah." I scratched at the back of my neck. "It can hear when its name is spoken." And so could I.

"Oh," she said in a small voice. She cleared her throat and changed the subject. "So the other night… a co-worker asked me if you had, you know… marked me yet." She suddenly looked shy. That was a hint.

It was my right to mark my woman, whom my Master had given to me. We were not only his employees, Chikako and I, but his property to dispose of as he saw fit. Ours was a feudal system, and I was higher up the food chain than Chikako. She could leave me if she wished, but that did not change that she had initially been turned over to my pleasure as a signing bonus.

If this seems barbaric, you would be right. This was the old way, *our* way, and yōkai traditions did not soften with human notions of good and evil, right and wrong. We evolved much more slowly over time, and we lived by fang and claw. It was simply the right of the strong to claim dominance over the weak.

I sighed and put down my pipe, the ember having gone out. I leaned forward and entwined my fingers into her hair. She leaned into my touch.

"I will when it's over, sweetheart," I swore. "If the worst happens…"

"Then I will have the scars to remember you by."

"You will have scars that identify you as mine!" And that

could be very bad if the other side won. "It won't be much longer now."

"I'm glad, but I'm scared, too."

"Hell, even *I* am scared," I admitted.

"Yeah, but it's different for you. You get off on the thrill of it. Me? I'm just worried sick all the time." Her anxiety showed plain on her face.

I gently tugged her to me and held her as she cuddled tight into my arms. She was right, I did enjoy the terror and excitement. Consequences were not something I particularly dwelled on.

YOUTA SMILED WHEN I FILED INTO HIS INNER SANCTUM WITH THE others that night. "No master could ask for more capable warriors than those I see before me. If we succeed tonight, there is only one battle left before us. You will go out in force and take Hiroshi's shining castle, the silver spire at the heart of the Inner Metropoplex, the center of his power in the mortal realm.

"The Dragon is attending to ablution for the Lunar New Year. He thinks his building sacrosanct even without his presence. Were we other than who we are, he would be right. This decisive hit will cripple Hiroshi. He will have no choice but to face me. Take the next two hours to study my plans and confer."

And that was what we did. Youta was good at masterminding these operations, and I learned a lot from his example. We memorized how each team was to get in, and where we would converge after sweeping through multiple locations at once, dividing the firepower of security.

At an hour until midnight we arrived at Hiroshi's center of

power in the mortal realm. It was one of the most beautiful and majestic skyscrapers in New Tokyo, soaring above all others. Two hundred stories of glass and steel, concrete and man-made materials, the graceful building reflected the city's neon brilliance in its mirrored surface. It was a magnificent fortress worthy of an emperor.

We could not get in through the shadows. Hiroshi had the entire premises warded against demonic and spiritual penetration. We also needed to be careful of any onmyōji or mages in Hiroshi's employ, as well as servitor demons and human security. My skin tingled, my muscles quivered in adrenal anticipation, high on the danger.

Fuyuko and Shirou flew to the highest point, where they would enter through a maintenance hatch. Their goal was to start at the top and work around to Hiroshi's main office at the topmost levels of the building, killing anyone in their path.

Taro, Jūro and Takeshi went in from underneath the tunnel network in maintenance uniforms and gear. They were to hit the vaults and destroy the server rooms, bringing down the wireless and Metro Net. Once all communication in and out of the building had been cut off, from there they were to haul ass to join us, removing any and all obstacles along the way.

Katashi and I went in through the ground floor service entrance disguised as two janitors. No one looked at our plain, ugly mugs twice. We rolled in with the bent posture and forlorn expressions of two guys who wanted to be anywhere else. I was the too-tall-and-thin, Katashi was short and round with big circular glasses. We looked like a poor man's comedy routine. Kami-sama, kitsune and tanuki indeed!

The keycards and DNA that some servitor had scored for

us worked. We got past ocular scans and keycard swipes without issue. Being trash collectors, we were beneath notice. Security scarcely looked at us when they scanned our badges and fingerprints. We were buzzed through without a hitch.

We walked slow and steady with our oversized garbage bin and cleaning equipment cart to the service elevator, which would transport us most of the way up to the office of the Chief Executive. Of course, we could only go as high as the one hundred and fifty-ninth floor, having no clearance to go higher. From there we would have to fight our way up the next thirty-nine stories, meeting Shirou and Fuyuko on the one hundred ninety-eighth floor.

The service elevator hummed along, each floor marked on the digital display. So far, so good. The doors opened on an empty hallway. I was just thinking how perfectly this was going when our fortune took a sudden negative turn. We rounded the bend on our way to the far stairwell and ran right into a woman wearing a sleek, navy blue skirt-suit with, oh, twenty or so armed guards surrounding her. We stopped and stared at the enemy, all of them human employees of Hiroshi.

The men seemed uncertain about being in full force for a couple of lowly janitors. We were just two lowborn saps with an insignificant job. They looked at one another doubtfully, then to the woman. I saw her innate glow intensify. I felt the brush of her energy ripple across my illusion. She glared at us with fierce intensity.

"No further, yōkai! I can *feel* your demonic auras!" The woman declared. This was an onmyōji from the ancient school of mages – the very best of their class. That she was Sanctioned was abundantly clear. Not so the guards, however, who wore expressions of frank disbelief.

Katashi put on a face as confused as theirs and held up his hands. "Pardon, ma'am. Don't know nothin' about demons, but me and my buddy here're just tryin' to pay the rent, ya know? Got trash need takin' out?"

"Your mouth is full of lies, bakemono! You cloak yourselves in glamours, but I will reveal you, and exorcise you back to Hell!"

The woman made gestures with her hands to direct the flow of her chi, the energy centers of her chakras glowing one by one from root to crown. I felt my skin prickle with electromagnetic energy, my hair and fur arose. And there was nothing I could do to nullify it.

When her spell reached completion a wave of light went out from her, invisible to the human guards' eyes, but clear to my own. And just like that, our illusions unraveled, revealing the tanuki and me for our masked selves, broadleaves on our heads. Well, there was no point in hiding now, I supposed. The time for deception was over.

There was tension in the air the second we stood revealed. Even the witch was astonished. Demons she had expected, but not two of Youta's Seven, and one of those the Kitsune Killer! The men should have been shooting at us immediately. They had us dead to rights. But thankfully humans freeze up at the most ridiculous times. A couple even lowered their weapons further.

"Is this for real?" one of the bluer recruits asked aloud.

If Katashi and I hesitated now, we were as good as done. We had to get through those guards and kill the witch before she could bind or exorcise us. Faced with such odds, there was no choice. In that split second, I let the yako in on purpose.

I did not turn into it, but instead, it turned into *me*. In the process another piece of myself broke away and surrendered to the darkness. The evil miasma of the nogitsune flooded my being and aura beyond. Its effect on those before us was immediately visible, for they moved back and away unconsciously.

I rushed headlong into the enemy *fast*, unsheathing and swinging my katana in a blazing arc of death! Assault rifle shots cut through the air as some of the guards finally did what they were hired to do. Katashi's gun boomed behind me, using my forceful assault and the rolling bin for cover. I ducked low as they shot, the rounds going over me, then I launched myself upward and sliced off the closest human's head. His body fell away to be replaced by the next to die. In this way I went down the line I maneuvered them into.

Men fell all around me before they could train their guns to follow my movements. They were in slow motion to my eyes, my speed inhuman. I was in so close among them that their guns became useless for their intended purpose. The rifles became blunt weapons instead, for all the good it did them.

I dodged a blow that went into the cheek of a comrade. I grabbed his arm and swung him like a dance partner into the guard beside him. Another one tried to bring his gun down on my head, but I moved to the side and it hit the shoulder of the man trying to tackle me from behind. It went on like that for a few seconds, and then I began setting fire to them. Ah, the screams! I was high on the power. It felt good to inflict so much damage!

I got shot once in the arm, barely felt it. I think it went right through the meat and kept going into the vest of his buddy, who was stunned by the impact long enough for me to pick him up and throw him into a wall, or rather, *through* the wall. That was satisfying. Somewhere in the background I could hear Katashi's gun again.

Then the woman was in front of me. Oh, the horrible things the yako wanted to do to her! I held it at bay, but it was not easy. Terrified or not, a new spell was on her lips and her chakra centers were firing up, starting at her pelvis and then her belly. I took her throat in my hand and tightened, cutting off her air. The energy reached the onmyōji's solar plexus and then abruptly vanished.

She made strangled sounds as I lifted her so that I could look directly into her eyes when she died. She looked down into mine in distress, her hands locked onto my pale wrist in a feeble gesture to loosen my grip. Her feet rapidly kicked me. I shook her violently first to one side, then the other. Her neck snapped, her head slumped over, her glow extinguished. I dropped her and she fell bonelessly to the floor among the other corpses.

Katashi whistled. "*Damn*, son." He shook his head and waddled down the now empty corridor, the gears in his leg obnoxiously loud. "Just out of curiosity, how many tails did you have before you Fell, shrine fox?"

"That is none of your business," I hissed through gritted teeth, following.

"Definitely more than one."

I did not say a thing.

"More than two. But I'll lay odds you're too young to have acquired four before you turned yako, and I'd bet double *that* wasn't long before you came to us. So, three, then." My tail lashed hard and my shoulders stiffened. He laughed gruffly.

"Damn, kid! You were one of those loyal and true whiteys, too." He looked me up and down in his raccoon dog mask. "So how did you end up here like this?"

My answer was a long, cold growl with a bit of gekker in its timbre.

"That good, eh?" He grunted. "You're still holding back, you know. You've only scratched the surface of what you can do. You don't even understand half your powers on this side of the line. But as you embrace the demon, it embraces you. Heh, you gotta know by now you can't fight it forever, shirogitsune. There ain't no salvation on *this* side of the street. The Darkness will swallow you up, and then all you'll be is a vicious predator, a lowly anim– *yurk*!"

I grabbed him up by the throat and slammed that fat old tanuki into the wall. Plaster cracked around him. "Let. It. Drop." I let him go and he rubbed at his throat, contemplating me for a moment as I walked on ahead.

"What did you do, Hayate-san?" He rasped softly. "How did you Fall?"

I stopped and turned. "*I* ate the heart of an *'innocent'* human child," I said in my slyest, wickedest tones. "That is all *you* need to know."

His eyes bore into me. "See, I just don't buy it. Not *you*. That's not all there is to it. Doesn't matter, though. You're all the same." He knocked on his robotic shin. "She did that to me."

"Did you rub your cock all over her ass, too?" I was a shade bitter this mysterious kitsune had failed to rip his dick off instead.

"Still sore about that? First hard-on you ever felt beside

your own, huh?" He laughed again. "Won't be the last. Trust me on that one, kid. You'll experiment every which way there is. *She* sure as hell did. Anyway, that's ancient history. I might even tell you about it one day if we survive this mess. Then you'll know why I want to bring Hiroshi down so bad, and how I know better than to trust *any* kitsune. *Ever.* No offense."

Katashi shot the lock from an emergency stairwell door. We climbed the remaining floors, much to the old tanuki's whining sorrow about his fat old ass and bum robot leg. I ignored his bitching and kept an ear out. But his words had done more damage in a few minutes than any wound I had taken in Youta's service thus far. He had gotten to me, the wily bastard, his words running through my head on a ceaseless loop. I curled my lip and kept my anxiety to myself.

Out of our elite group, only Katashi could get to me like this. He knew me better in some respects than I did myself. Until I had become a yako, I did not know anything other than bare facts with which to hunt and kill Wild Foxes with. This tanuki had known such creatures for centuries. Perhaps I was only using a part of the power I had acquired, but I was not about to ask *him* for pointers. I would never indebt myself to the raccoon dog in this way!

We made it to our destination without further incident, which we would later learn was in no small part due to Shirou and Fuyuko's handy work. Out of nowhere we felt the rumble of explosions from far below. Sirens inside the building blared and a steady blinking light flashed down the length of the corridor. A woman's mechanized voice calmly told all non-essential personnel on site to please leave the premises via the nearest exit. That meant the other five would be joining us soon.

The office slaves working late on this floor surged past us toward the steps. "Another drill?" I heard one mutter.

"At this hour? We'll be stuck here all night into tomorrow morning!" They walked around us in spite of our sinister appearance. Theirs was almost a brainwashed conditioning to leave the building. A few looked at us in confusion as they went by, especially at me, splattered with blood. Most gave us a wide berth, looking down at their devices only to start when they realized they were about to collide with someone.

"Sick joke, man," one of them said in disapproval.

When the tide of the least necessary swept past, Katashi and I followed the corridor to the main office on this floor. This suite belonged to the highest-ranking human in Hiroshi's organization. And just outside the huge glass walls, complete with dystopia art deco, were a dozen men dressed in dark ninja outfits.

A ninja death squad? Really? I thought.

But yes, really. And some of them were cybernetic *and* genetically enhanced. I saw the reflective lights of their robotic eyes and heard the hydraulics and electronics inside their limbs. Bionic mutants! The flexes and poses might have been laughable… if there had not been twelve of them.

I shoved my kitsunenomen to the side of my head as Katashi reloaded his antique pistols. "Kid! What the hell're ya doin'?"

I grinned. "Swaying the odds in our favor." I took the form of Shiroi Uindo in a black swirl of miasma and blue flame. And it was an unbelievable rush! All his power and strength! My training and intellect! Upon embracing my demonhood this way, yet another piece of me fell away into nothingness.

Perhaps if there was a bottom to this pit, I would be impaled upon the jagged shards of my own heart.

"Better hold onto it this time, kid," Katashi muttered in a low voice.

As Team Ninja launched itself at us, I swept an inferno of kitsunebi at them. The lucky ones scattered and leapt away at the last minute. The not-so-fortunate littered the silvery grey carpet with their ashes and melted plastic-metal limbs. Well, that was three, anyway.

I felt a foot connect with my muzzle and reeled back with the momentum, but in this form, there was much greater resistance to pain. I scarcely felt more than the thump of impact. I reached out and succeeded in grabbing the leg of the foot that kicked me. I twisted and spun, sending the ninja flying into one of his friends, and both of them subsequently crashing through the glass wall display when I let go. I reached down, twisted, and yanked hard. A robotic leg came out of its socket in a wash of blood and a fringe of shredded muscle. It was like winning a prize!

I whirled and clobbered a ninja over the head with it, and whipped it upside the head of another one. Man, I *loved* this game! I blocked a thrown knife with the leg, which stuck fast in the fleshy material. Suddenly shot after shot rang out behind me. A ninja went falling back past me with a perfect bullet wound in his head. Say what you will about Katashi, but that fucker could shoot! Meanwhile, I dodged a thrown knife, which embedded itself in the wall. I did not dodge another, which I yanked out of my left forearm and threw into the throat of a different ninja than the one who aimed it at me.

My wound was already sealing itself when I pulled out a

fistful of broadleaves from inside my kimono sleeve and sent them whirling around me in a vortex. Grinning like the specter of death, I sent the leaves hurtling at two more with the wind speed of a typhoon. The missiles struck their eyes and cloth-covered faces. Ah, the screams! More shots rang out from Katashi's gun, and then abruptly there was silence.

Around us the warriors clad in Hiroshi's livery were dead. I floated above the dozen bodies that littered the floor along with cubes of jagged glass, admiring my work in particular.

"Way to go, kid. See if you can stay in control of that hellbeast a bit longer. And grab a heart from one of these assholes, would ya? A recharge never hurts, and neither will a little demonstration."

I did as he recommended, cluing in at once to what he was about. Katashi stepped over the corpses and stomped his older-model bionic leg down on the face of one who was mostly dead. The skull exploded like a melon. Then the tanuki waltzed into the office like he owned it, and I drifted in his bloody wake.

Within were a core group of five men and three women desperately attempting to shred documents and upload data. Katashi shot the ceiling and it all stopped. Jaws dropped. Two of the women gasped and shrieked when I floated in behind the tanuki. The bloody muscle in my claws dripped a steady *pat-pat-pat* on the bleak, grey carpet.

The scent of fear was a maddening ambrosia. I breathed in deep, my head turning toward a woman as I took in the odor that was individual only to her. She was particularly heady, that one, in estrus. She screamed as my eye fell upon her, my lips pulled back into a predator's grin that revealed my sharp teeth.

"The Kitsune Killer is a real kitsune." The Chief Executive said numbly. The human came bravely out of his office and stood in their midst. That drew my attention back to why we were here.

"Worse," Katashi said. "He's nogitsune. I've seen what he does to humans, boss. Rips your hearts right outta your chests and gobbles 'em up whole." He made a slurping noise. "And this Demon Fox here's damn hungry."

I held the heart above my head and lowered it delicately into my long jaws grinding it popping and squelching between my teeth. The crowd reacted with the appropriate level of fear and disgust, which I found most gratifying.

"You might want to reconsider your current position with Hiroshi if you'd like yourself and these fine people to survive this night," Katashi said as if it did not bother him either way. "Otherwise…"

The human gulped as I growled. With all of my claws to their fullest extension, I drifted ever so slightly toward the man in charge. Before he could react, Taro crashed through the wall in Devil Bear form on the opposite side of the room. He stood on his hind legs, his roar shaking the walls. There was an explosion, and standing in the dust and debris stood Jūro with the huge blue oni and his great iron kanabo. The size difference between them was terribly incongruous.

Humans shrieked, some fell to their knees. A few panicked and tried to make a run for it, but Shirou arrived and intercepted their path, his katana bloody. Fuyuko was with him, her hands filled with swirling vortices of icy power. Snowflake shuriken hovered in the air around her.

"So what's it gonna be, boss?" Katashi asked over the

sobbing of the mortals. "And remember, what goes for you goes for the rest of these fine folks, too. Choose carefully." He cocked and pointed his gun at one of the suits, never taking his eyes off the head exec.

The human in charge gave up with no further resistance. Hiroshi's shining castle was ours. The emergency system was shut off and we took the humans with us through the Shadow Ways, open now that all spell slingers on the premises were dead. As it turned out, there had been two that night, ours and a young man Fuyuko had done for with her icy kiss.

Youta had servitor yōkai take our captives into the bowels beneath the Ori, while we stood before the dragon in his inner sanctum. It was very elegant and had only grown more so as his wealth and prestige increased.

"Well done. I congratulate you on your success, my champions. Our struggle has at last come to its ultimate conclusion. Auspiciously, tomorrow evening is the New Year by the old calendar." New Year in Japan was adapted to January first in accordance with the Gregorian calendar, but we yōkai kept to the old lunar cycle from before the Meiji Restoration period, as did the various Sectors of The Sprawl.

"We meet here at ōmagatoki, the hour of twilight. I have already invited Hiroshi to our final battle, and he will, of course, accept. We will meet him and his remaining Nine after nightfall."

"Hai, Youta-sama!" we shouted in unison, bowing.

"So, this is it, huh?" Shirou asked when we were on the upper deck. Below us, demons watched dancers and drank, some of the patrons were moshing in a pit made for that. Business as usual. It was like the world was about to come to an end and no one knew or gave a damn.

I nodded. I was still reeling from embracing the yako earlier. I could feel myself becoming worse, more twisted inside by the moment. Hell, I only felt alive when I was fucking, fighting, or killing. Otherwise, I was numb, and the only part of me left that could feel was trapped within an amber chrysalis of deep pain.

"Almost can't believe it," he said.

Chikako looked up, smiled and waved at me. I smiled in return, but mine was a trifle sad. She gave me that questioning glance, but then a customer got her attention and she was gone.

I was not sure what to think or feel. If I survived, it seemed like my life would be set for the foreseeable future. If I died, I would go to Yomi a yako. There could be no redemption then, however slight the odds. I would lose any chance of seeing my people, my ancestors gone before me. I would never see my mother again in any world. I threw my life around so casually and rarely thought anything of it. But just then, the enormity of what I was gambling struck me hard and shook me to the core.

"What's that look for?" Shirou wanted to know.

I shook my head. "It means I am going to get as drunk as possible before dawn," I told him.

I WENT BACK TO MY APARTMENT THAT LOOKED LIKE A BOMB HAD gone off inside it. All of my inner turmoil was on display around me. I pulled out several bottles of the strongest, most highly polished nihonshu sold in the Metropoplex and sat on a cold pillow at my short lacquered table. The apartment was freezing, the alcohol was practically refrigerated! I poured the first cup from a shuki set Chikako gifted me.

Fucking tanuki.

Katashi had really gotten in my head. I was pissed about that. I knew one day I might turn into nothing but an animal, a demon out of control of itself. It scared me worse than I ever wanted to admit! I needed the demon to survive in this world. But the old raccoon dog was right about something else. I was not quite as evil as I pretended to be, although I felt that I was becoming so.

I was a complete wreck. I felt alone, isolated, hunted, and lost. I thought about Kazuki, how desperate I had been when I first met him. Then I remembered that most of his students had ended up criminals. I looked at his katana and wakizashi on their stand across the room and sighed.

"Sorry, Kazuki," I said to his memory. "I guess I became another one of your boys to go into a gang." I wondered if I would die like them, too.

I examined the clear liquor in the otchoko, tilting it this way and that to catch the light. It was genetically modified to be extra strong. I wondered how much it would take to get me well and truly plastered. Well, I had the time, the motive, and ten more bottles in the cabinet besides the three I had set up on the table in front of me. I endeavored to find out.

My shadow and I toasted one another, then we threw back the first cup one-handed like a shot.

Chapter Twenty-Five

A Brief Interlude

Two hours later, Chikako came home. And she was not in a good mood. "Where were you tonight? I'd thought you'd stick around at the club after you got back."

"No need," I slurred. There were empty six bottles on the table. I was on the seventh, and that one down to the dregs. I poured what was left of it into the tokkuri and stood the empty bottle alongside its fallen brothers.

Her eyes grew wide. "Hayate! You've been sitting here drinking *all this time*?"

"*Hai!*" I toasted her and drained my otchoko. "I finally imbibed enough to get properly drunk. Come pour me another. Or, why don't I pour one for you? Come and sit, onna!" I waved her to the table. "The dawn is nearly upon us, and by tonight we may all be dead!" I said dramatically. Then I laughed.

"Hayate!" She sounded angry, her tone chiding. I wondered if I was in trouble, and if so, why? I looked at her serenely as she dropped her purse and coat. She reluctantly came to the table and sat across from me with her arms folded over her chest, pointedly looking away.

"It's going down after sunset," I said seriously. I poured the sake in the tiny cup and set it in front of her, then drained what was left directly from the flask.

Chikako's head snapped up. "You mean...?"

"Yeah." I wiped a rivulet from the corner of my mouth with the back of my hand.

She drained the liquor in one gulp, then coughed. "But... we were going to watch the fireworks..." Her face fell.

"I know. The Lunar New Year is why this is happening tonight. Listen to me, Chikako. You need to leave. Get out of New Tokyo! Today!"

She shook her head.

"No, listen. If we lose-"

"But you won't!" she shouted.

"Chikako, please! *If* we lose, Hiroshi will take the Ori in less than an hour. You can be IDed as mine on sight. If you're lucky, Hiroshi'll just kill you. But..." I looked her up and down in her sexy waitress outfit. Damn, she was hot! "He's not going to waste merch. I wouldn't, if I were him. He'll peddle your ass in the streets of the Korean Sector, Chika! Humiliate you for belonging to me, the yako who cut off his stupid mustache thingy."

"Hayate..."

"Shh... shh... Just listen to me..." The last thing I wanted was for her to be drugged and raped into oblivion simply because she made the mistake of loving me. The very idea of it twisted a sour knot in my belly. Kami-sama, why had I not thought about this before tonight?

She shook her head. "It doesn't matter." Why was she not listening to me? Did she not understand?

"It *does* matter!" I slammed the table with an open palm harder than I intended, making glass rattle and thump. Chikako jumped, cringing back. "It matters to me!" I bulled on. "You *have* to get out. I have traceless digi-cred, been saving it. Go see your mother in ŌsaKyoto, or fuck! Go anywhere! I'll get word to you when it's over. I swear."

"I'm not leaving," she said adamantly.

"No. You have to. I can't protect you. Just like I couldn't protect her."

"Hayate, what are you talking about? Protect who?"

I felt woozy. The room spun. "I'm not losing you to assholes, too. So, *leave. Please.* Stay safe."

"If what you said is true, it's probably too late already. Hiroshi will have every outgoing train and transport watched. I'll be a bigger liability if I get caught."

"Well, that's true," I conceded. "But you should go to ground. Pack light and get out of that apartment. Dye your hair, fur, everything." I blinked as my eyes blurred in and out of focus. "Whoa." I stared at my hand in mild fascination.

"I will," she said calmly. "I promise. But right now, we need to get you in bed."

I leered at the mention of my futon. "Is that because I've gotten better at it since I became more evil?"

"Hayate..." She blushed and looked away.

"Were you surprised, beautiful? *I* was. You know, every time I level off, I think to myself, 'I can't Fall any lower than this,' but I'm always so fucking wrong! I am beginning to think there's no bottom to this abyss. I just keep Falling and Falling down into the... a big, *black* hole..." I looked down at the table as everything went dark and fuzzy. I started to fall forward and only snapped back when I heard her voice.

"Hayate, baby, let's get you into bed. You can barely sit up!" She got up and began helping me.

"Ah, so you *do* want me in bed," I grinned up at her, showing my teeth

"Not like this! Hayate, *stop* it! Please! You're scaring me!" She *was* scared. Her heart rate was up, her breathing fast, eyes wide. That made me stop acting the asshole immediately.

"*Whoa.* Hey." I softened and let go my hold on her arm. I had not been aware I grabbed her. I backed away into the table, bumping it hard enough to knock the empty bottles onto the tatami mat behind me. Glass clinked sharply and rattled as they rolled. "I won't. I'm not *that* far gone." I scrubbed my bangs back from my face. "Inari-sama willing, I never will be."

I grew angry in the next instant and crossed my arms over my chest. "Not that Inari-sama ever answers any of *my* prayers anymore!" I said with all the grace of a peevish five-year-old. "That's why I'm *in* this position!" I snarled.

Chikako gaped at me.

"I was Chosen, Chika! *Chosen!*" Where was *this* coming from? "Before I spent over twenty years abandoned in that poison forest, cut off, hunted and alone!" I pointed at my apartment door to indicate 'out there somewhere' even though it was not the right direction. "I prayed and prayed, I called out... but Inari-sama did not answer me! I do not know what I did to earn this punishment!" I looked up at her in distress. "I cannot remember." I touched the back of my head forlornly.

"I wandered for years, but I could not get back home!" I

babbled heedlessly. "All the earthly shrines stood derelict, and no one from the great shrine came for me." I felt so lost and alone admitting that. "Kami-sama dumped me in this hellish world and left me here to die." My face crumpled, but no tears came. There was no way to release the pain. I turned my face away. "And I do not even know why," I lamented.

"Hayate…" she whispered. Her face swam in my vision, sad but rapt.

"I tried so hard to stay good! I wanted to! It did not matter. I lost practically all of my *soul*!" I tugged on my hair, clutched where the bell once hung. "My hoshi no tama torn away, just…" I wriggled my fingers and gestured up to the ceiling above us, "Whoosh! Gone. All because of that little *bastard*!" My lips curled back away from my fangs and my hands clenched into fists. Chikako's mouth dropped open. "I wish I could kill him again!" I growled in a gekkering staccato.

"That was when the Darkness came for me," I said forlornly. "I had three tails before the Hellfire burned two of them off!" I held up three fingers… no, oops, that was four. Or was it supposed to be two? I used my other hand to arrange my fingers and fixed it. "*Three*." I held my hand toward her and nodded staunchly. "It hurt *so much*, Chika! You don't know."

Her hand flew over her lips… and were those *tears* in her eyes?

"And now look at me!" I gestured at myself. "Ruined! A disgrace to my kami, my people! Just a *yako*!" I snarled the word in self-contempt. "A filthy yōkai…" I buried my face in my hands. "My kyuubi mother would be so ashamed. She would weep to see my shadow and what has become of me. If

I die tonight, I will go to Hell a Wild Fox, and be only a demon lost forevermore..." My voice trailed off dismally.

I felt Chikako's hands on my upper arms as she gently guided me out of that position toward the bed. She did not try to help me stand, knowing it for a lost cause. She had a lot of experience with drunks.

"Don't let the fuckers break you, Chikako," I burst out. "You're better than they are – better than *all* of them! And you're stronger than you know. Your innocence is your strength!"

"Okay, Hayate." I could tell she was humoring me, but I needed to say it anyway.

She helped me crawl to the futon, which was a bit of a trial because I kept scuffling onto and pulling my hair. Once I yanked so hard that my forehead hit the floor with a clunk. "Ow," I pouted, sprawled face down. So much for dignity. I would have passed out and spent the day there if not for Chikako.

She giggled at me and got me moving again with a motherly hand. "Come on, sweetheart. Just a little further, you can make it." She lifted my hair and held it back and up like a leash as I ambled forward awkwardly on my hands and knees.

Thankfully we managed to get there in the end, and she helped me under the covers, which was another trial because my tail got caught on the underside. The layers got all turned over and twisted about. I cannot work out exactly how that happened, but there you go.

Somehow, she got that sorted out and then I was surrounded by softness. Within moments I felt snuggly warm. I curled into a ball beneath the blankets and let go. Oh, how good it was to not move! I felt her hand on my head, petting my ear. "That's it, baby. You just lie there and I'm going to clean up a little." Chikako kissed my forehead. "Go to sleep, my poor, beautiful angel." She smoothed my hair into place with a final, gentle touch.

It called forth a hazy memory of someone else doing the same thing. My mother, I think. I felt like a child again. I smiled and sank into a deep sleep accompanied by the clinking of sake bottles as she picked them up and carried them to the sink.

I FLOATED IN A NIGHTTIME FOREST. I DID NOT KNOW WHERE I WAS or how I got there, but it did not seem to matter. I had no idea where I was going, either. I was searching for something, but I had forgotten what. It was precious to me, and I fiercely wanted it back. If I could just think, remember…

Ahead of me I saw a light, bright in the darkness. *What is that?* I started toward it, slow at first, then faster… faster. It was brilliant and beautiful! I was excited to see it!So close now! The light turned into a child's shape. A girl. I slowed and drifted closer, curious. She turned…

"Aaaaiiiiko?" I rasped, my voice rice paper thin in the dark wood. It had to be! It looked like her, smelled like her, *felt* like her… I was so happy. I missed my friend so much!

Aiko screamed.

I drifted back, confused. Why was she afraid of me? I saw the extension of my muzzle apparent in my lower field of vision, and I knew.

Ashamed, I drifted backward and hid behind a dead tree trunk. There I curled in on myself in the worst misery. Her rejection cut like a knife. I hated myself for what I had become.

I whimpered and rocked, covered my eyes, keening in place of the tears that would not fall. Good thing, too. A demon's tears were poison.

It was the warm glow that caused my eyes to squint open between my claws. Silently Aiko stood before me. Her eyes gazed into mine, wet tears streaking her cheeks. "Hayate? It is you, isn't it? What happened to you? Where is your hoshi no tama?" Her face crumpled and she sobbed.

I stared at her, afraid to reach out to see her shy away. I was this thing because I had slain her brother and eaten his heart. I deserved neither her pity nor her compassion. I earned my fate.

She reached out to me and petted the top of my muzzle. Her hand was warm and soft. "Hayate." Such a sad, tremulous smile. It broke in a fresh burst of tears. "I promised I would save you if this happened," her voice quavered. "And I will."

Everything went dark, except for the light of her soul. Then she, too, faded as the darkness swallowed my vision whole.

Chapter Twenty-Six

The Final Battle

blinked. Everything was still and quiet. The bed was empty. I was used to waking up next to Chikako, the sound of her breathing, her warmth. I wondered what day it was. The position of the light told me it was mid-afternoon. I groped blindly for my device until my hand plopped down on it.

Chikako left a message for me on my hand-held, and in my hazy state I read it. I do not remember it word for word, but the gist of it was that she had to go to her place before work and did not want to disturb me. Something about taking my warning to heart and seeing me tonight when it was all over. Oh, and best of luck. Please be careful. Love, Chika. Kitty face. Heart. Heart.

I tossed the phone-and-everything-else device on the bed and sat up in my rumpled clothes. I *never* slept in my clothes. I looked down at my disheveled appearance. I groaned and ground the heels of my palms into my eyes, which felt good, but made everything blurry as fuck for the next couple of minutes. My mouth was dry. I had to piss so bad I stumbled blind into the toilet and nearly tripped. Relieving myself of seven bottles of alcohol took two minutes longer than I wanted it to. Man, did my piss stink.

I forced myself immediately into a hot, recycled-water shower until the world became less surreal. Then I combed and dressed into something halfway respectable, and finally made myself a mug of tea before I headed out. I did not need the caffeine, but it gave me a moment to collect my anxious thoughts.

Chikako had cleaned my place, I noticed as I leaned back against the counter. All the clothes and towels were picked up and put in the laundry, some of it already done and neatly folded. The sake bottles were in the recycling unit, a practice which was strictly enforced by law. The counters were wiped down, the sink was sparkling, everything vacuumed...

It occurred to me then that she had not even slept! She must have cleaned for at least two hours and gone home. The entire space was immaculate as it had not been for the past six weeks. I had always been fastidiously tidy before the Hyakki yagyō, but looking at my apartment made me see it all clearly for the first time.

I resolved never to let it happen again. A yako I might be, but I would not be slovenly. Maybe if I kept things organized, I could keep myself from straying too far off my path.

I had an epiphany right there and then. Yes, I would continue to Fall, but I could control the speed and momentum with which I Fell, and the trajectory. I had a Code, made by me to suit me, and this was my source of inner light in the

Darkness. Demon or otherwise, I had the right to determine who I was going to be.

Try not to hurt innocents. No raping. Do not kill kids. Hunt only those whose deaths will make the world a better place. Take no trophies. Leave no arbitrary corpses. Do not cheat on your lover and never beat on your girl. Repay your debts and fulfill your obligations. Do not steal from those who cannot afford it.

There was nothing in my Code that said I could not smoke and drink, fuck and kill, or take my demonic form when it suited me. That included letting it off the leash when it was necessary to my survival. If I died, so be it. That was the life of a warrior.

And just like that, I felt better.

THE DATE WAS JANUARY THIRTIETH, 2120. TONIGHT WAS THE BE-ginning of The Year of the Dragon. The auspiciousness grant-ed by a whim of fate was not lost on me. Ah, but to which Dragon did this new year belong? I am certain Youta and Hiro-shi each thought it would be them, but I was not half so sure.

There was no question I needed to hunt. The battle would call for me to have a full store of power. Sex was off the table with Chikako absent. So, in the wan glow of the wintry after-noon I prowled in various disguises through the narrow back alleys of The Sprawl.

It had apparently snowed while I slept, and the air was frig-id. That did not stop revelers and tourists from taking to the streets enforce. It was a yōkai buffet! Nor was I the only one hunting as the shadows grew long. I scored three hearts before the muted colors of a frosty pink sunset forced me to go to Youta in preparation for what lay ahead.

At sundown the fireworks began. Music shook the lantern-lit streets and over a billion voices added to the cacophony. Humans, particularly in the Chinese Sector, loved to dress in symbols of their birth-year, so there were tigers and dogs, rats and rabbits, pigs, horses, and oxen walking abroad. Multi-legged sheet dragons danced in brilliant display, sparkling fireworks cracking off around them. A whore dressed as a cock – the rooster, not the body part – called out to me as I passed by. I smiled, waved, and kept going.

I rounded a corner near a local hot pot shop and gave a most precious parcel to one of the alley dwellers who crouched in the shadows thereby. A loathsome fellow I had recently become aware of. "Happy New Year!" I told him jovially, waving. "Enjoy, my friend." I smiled at his staring eyes and went on my way.

I joined the others on the roof of the Ori soon after. The sky was a deep, clear blue, the winds mild, but a thick blanket of white clouds was moving in on the distant horizon. We were all attired in our most elegant costumes, standing tall in our fierce masks. There was an air of unspoken tension. One or more of us would doubtless die tonight. We stood in a semi-circle around Youta, who faced us, looking at each of us in turn.

"My loyal Seven," he said with pride. "We go to face Hiroshi and the last of his enforcers. I am confident we will rise to the challenge. You are the elite – not just in my own employ, but in all of New Tokyo! Perhaps Asia! I chose you Seven because Fate sent you to me, each one. You are the pride of your races, and we will do what we were born for! Tonight, we take New Tokyo from Hiroshi! Now come. History awaits."

In strident formation we came out from under the long shadow of a bare-limbed tree, embraced by freezing winds that

374

stirred our hair and garments. The snow that had fallen earlier blanketed the rooftop garden atop the high skyscraper. It was perfect in every detail, crisp and white. There was even a little bridge and a stone lantern to complete the effect.

Fireworks lit the sky in loud bangs and bright sizzling colors that reflected off the snow. Yet it was serene, the air whisper soft with the occasional shrill whistle. It was a beautiful place to die.

Hiroshi stepped out of the shadows across the way with his yōkai elite in tow. The Dragon's mustachios were much shorter than appropriate for such an old dragon as he. Youta's were longer than his. It was doubtless embarrassing. There was venomous hate in the ancient's eyes when he looked at me, and it was not hard to guess why.

"Is *this* all you have, Youta-kun?"

"I do not need more," Youta boasted. "My Seven are more than formidable enough."

"As to that, we shall soon see. Have you any last words?"

"Only this. I came to you in peace one hundred years ago, and requested an audience many times since, Hiroshi-san," Youta said as an equal. "But you would not listen. Things have grown direr in the ensuing years. You left me no choice."

"You are an idealistic fool. Water dragons are, by nature. Whatever your reasons, there can be no compromise." The old dragon glanced at me, smoke wreathing from his thin nostrils. "And one more thing. If you chance to win this night, Youta-kun, do yourself this boon. *Destroy* that thing at once. Lock it away, or better yet – kill it! But never let a nogitsune run loose. Put your Wild Fox down or he shall be your death one day. Is that not accurate, Katashi-san?"

A cheap shot. The miserable old beast smiled knowingly at the tanuki. Katashi said nothing. I stared hard at Hiroshi through the eyeholes of my mask. Youta turned his head to look at me.

"Shiroi Uindo is my concern, Hiroshi-san." My Master smiled benevolently and faced the fire dragon, his tone light and bemused. "Only bother yourself over him if I die and he does not."

There was no more to be said after that.

Hiroshi called out the order and his demons stood at the ready. Likewise, did we Seven prepare. Fuyuko took stance, ice katana in her hands, snowflake shuriken hovering around her and sparkling in the city light. Katashi drew his guns, Shirou and I our swords. Takeshi shifted his big cudgel from his shoulder, holding it out in front of him like a baseball player at bat. Taro took Devil Bear form, black fur rippling across his mass of muscle. Jūro placed his hands in his pockets where his explosive rounds waited, and crouched, ready to leap.

Hiroshi called out another order, and his Nine drew their weapons. Then Youta and Hiroshi both lifted from the ground and transformed into their huge, serpentine bodies with deafening roars. The two great beasts slithered on currents of air, coiling together like a caduceus and tearing at one another's scales with their talons. Their heads dove in to bite each other's throats. The red dragon latched onto the blue as a terrible roar went up from Youta's upraised maw. Broken scales fell around us like flower petals, translucent on the snowy ground.

Without warning the yōkai in front of us attacked as a unit. For the space of a short breath it all slowed down to my eyes and I saw everything clearly. One of them was a bear demon and he crashed chest to chest with Taro, their growls and snarls thunderous as that of the dragons. The two onikuma ripped and clawed at one another savagely.

A crow tengu flew at Shirou, wings spread, and for the first time ever I saw my friend transform into his demon self. He became beaked, his eyes large and black, the mask shoved up onto the top of his feathered head. It was in answer to the other, for the two morphed in the same moment. They shriek-cawed at one another, razor sharp beaks open!

Fuyuko was confronted by an evil version of a kodama, or tree spirit, except this one was vile, its skin was a dull grimy brown-grey covered in pestilential fungus. When it made to extend its long, thorny finger limbs to skewer her, she hacked the poisonous digits off with her blade and blew her icy breath mist on the plant yōkai. It froze, coated in ice. A humanoid white moon rabbit dressed in glowing silver armor jumped over the immobilized kodama. When their blades met, hers shattered.

Meanwhile, a weasel yōkai launched itself at our blue oni with short handled sickles in either hand. I heard iron strike iron, then explosions from Jūro, although I could not see what was attacking him. It was probably the kijo in the hannya mask. Whatever anyone else was doing became unimportant as *my* opponent stood opposite me.

I suppose it was only fitting that I face the Dog Demon. His stance was pure aggression, the miasma of bitter hate. He wanted to kill me.

"Kitsune," he growled derisively from beneath his own mask, represented as feral as my own."You murdered my father at the Hyakki yagyō, vermin yako!"

"I recall. I tore his head from his shoulders and threw it in the market square."

The dog growled and bristled, shivering in pure adrenal rage. Since an inugami may be summoned or created by cutting off an old dog's head and burying it near a crossroads at midnight, my act was extraordinarily offensive to this creature.

"Do not fret, puppy," I drawled slyly. "I will send you to him soon."

He growled at me again, a deep, menacing sound. My own hackles rose in response. "I will *eradicate* you, wicked fox! Prepare to face eternal torment!" His miasma flared with his righteous fury, his stance that of the avenger facing evil. For of course I was. There was no question who the villain was here. Me.

By some unspoken signal, the dog and I flew at one another without mercy. He took the offensive at once, and such was his prowess that he pushed me back a few feet before I recovered. I summoned Shiroi Uindo to join with me in perfect synchronicity and faced the inugami, feet planted.

We dodged and wove around one another, occasionally meeting blade to blade, our movements a blur! Even my motion sensitive eyes could not entirely track how fast we were moving! Our swords sparked whenever the metal struck and scraped to block and ward the other away.

The son might not be as strong as the father, but he had the raw energy of hate. His reserves would not last forever at his present level of ferocity. I simply had to endure. I defended against his raining onslaught until the little signs of his impending weariness became apparent. He stopped swinging quite so hard or as high. His momentum slowed, his maneuvers increasingly reckless and predictable.

I met him stroke for stroke as the sound of embattled demons tore across the night. We locked so close we could see one another's eyes behind our masks. His were filled with contemptuous aggression.

I summoned a bright blue flame between us, startling him. Temporarily blinded, he hastily jerked away from my kitsunebi. I used that opportunity to beat his sword out of the way. He stumbled backward and tried to get his katana back up, but I batted it down again. He slid on a slick patch of snow.

Never one to miss using an opponent's mischance against him, I cut his arm off at the elbow. Limb and sword fell to the ground in a torrential outpouring of blood. I swiftly turned three hundred sixty degrees in a sweeping, fluid motion, katana fully extended. My white fur hanten and blue-flame kimono rippled in the wind, my hair flowing around me with the momentum. A few seconds later, the Demon Dog's masked head fell off of his shoulders. The body joined it on the snow-covered ground seconds later.

A mighty roar tore the night to pieces. I looked up, unable to help myself. Flames were pouring from Hiroshi's eyes. Youta let him go and the great red beast fell with the groan of a dying leviathan. Like a kite that had lost the wind, Hiroshi sank tail-first in sinuous waves down into his own shadow, never to be seen again. It was a terrible and sad sight, the demise of such a magnificent creature. We all watched in awe. I will never forget it.

Youta landed gracefully, retaking human form as he touched down. My master looked battered, his skin bleeding and raw where his scales had been raked off in dragon form. It took a moment to process. The war was truly over. I felt both elated and stunned. We had won! But not without cost.

Jūro lay dead. Taro's face bore four claw marks over his right eye, which itself was a ruin. Takeshi had sickle slices all over his limbs. He lost his kanabo, handed down from father to son for long generations, and his expression was forlorn as he stared at what was left of it in his meaty hand. I wondered how the thick end of the heavy iron weapon could have stove in like that. Damn.

Shirou's feathers were ruffled in every direction and more than a few had been torn out. Fuyuko had a slice on her arm, another beneath her breasts, but she had frozen the blood. I only then realized I had likewise taken slices and grazes, scarce felt at the time. I was already healed.

None of the other side still lived. It was a testament to our strength and skill that we six and Youta had survived. I wiped and sheathed my blade.

"Shiroi Uindo," Youta ordered. "Destroy the evidence and meet us back at The Cage."

"Hai, Youta-sama. But… Jūro," I said, looking at the corpse of the sarugami. Did Youta expect me to burn him here like the rest? He was one of ours!

"Jūro was an excellent warrior and he died fighting with honor this night," my lord confirmed. "His sacrifice will not be forgotten. But we can leave no trace behind for the humans to find. See him cremated on the battlefield, Hayate-san."

"Hai, Youta-sama." I bowed my head and shoulders as the Dragon of New Tokyo turned away. My compatriots retreated into the shadows behind him.

The night fell silent save for the whizzing pops of distant fireworks. The slain seemed so quiet and peaceful in eternal repose, brilliant lights washing over them only to fade and bloom again. I made my way to the sarugami. Looking down on his corpse was eerie. The monkey demon was covered in blood, his torso made into a pin cushion. Judging by his expression, he died painfully. His eyes had all the consciousness of empty glass.

I knelt down beside my fallen brother. We were not friends, the monkey and me. In fact, I hated him. We were rivals in trickery and the little bastard was always pulling my tail, mocking me. But we worked well together in spite of that.

This coldness did not sit well with me. I thought he should be brought back with us and given proper funeral rites, not burned beside our enemies without ceremony. Alas, our only worth was in the skills we wielded for Youta while we were alive. In that, our dragon was no different from the tyrant we just deposed. I felt inexplicably naive. Heh. I did not know I could be so since Aiko had died. Such was my conceit.

Baka kitsune.

I closed Jūro's eyes and clapped my hands together twice in quick succession, held prayer-like in front of me. "Inari-sama, you no longer answer me, so I do not know if you can hear. But please, I call upon your divine grace on behalf of another. If you have any influence, please see this sarugami to a peaceful afterlife."

A golden shimmer in the shape of a monkey emerged and floated free. It hovered before me for an impossible second and then it was gone, soaring upward among the celebratory explosions. I smiled sadly.

"Farewell, Jūro-san," I said as I stood. "May your next life be better than this one, and twice as fun."

With the pang of dissonance heavy in my heart, I walked to the center of the garden among the corpses. I felt nothing for any of them. I had little in the way of a soul left and could not find it in myself to lament those I would never miss. The formerly pristine snow was disturbed and stained with blood.

I could feel her watching me even now from a different set of shadows, hear her young heart beat strong and fast. I had smelled her when I stepped out onto the terrace before the final battle. I was quite amazed the others did not, or maybe they had not cared. I made a show of inhaling her scent and was rewarded by Hanako's unique blend of woman and adrenaline. Such delicious fear, too. It was near making me slaver.

Hanako did not come out, hoping I did not know she was there. This certainly had never been meant for her eyes, nor those of any mortal. I wondered how she had known to come here. Always the clever girl. And yet, in spite of her presence I did what my master commanded of me. I secretly relished that the policewoman would see. I decided I was going to make this special for her, a parting gift.

Amid the carnage I shrugged off my fur hanten and removed the kitsunenomen. I stared down into that snarling face for a moment, then dropped the fox mask on top, the fur ruffling in the icy breeze. I stood exposed, buffeted by the wintry air. My large, furred ears rose fully from out of my thick hair, and my tail lashed from side to side very slowly. I turned in place to look at them all. Finally, I breathed deeply, stilled myself and gathered my chi for the funeral conflagration.

I lifted my arms and called forth the winds. Immediately I rose above the ground, lifting the bodies of the slain with me lest I set fire to the building. The cold wind whipped the long tendrils of my hair around me. I was rewarded with a soft feminine gasp and could not help the slight upward tug at the corners of my lips. It was rare to display oneself to a mortal so fully and let them live, but oh *so* satisfying.

I wove my pale hands and arms in a fluid, martial arts dance, summoning my kitsunebi with my chi, every movement beautiful and controlled. With each pose a new wisp was born to heed my bidding, and floated next to the head of each corpse. When the appropriate number of small, blue flames danced around me, one for each cadaver, I transformed behind a screen of shadows. A stick-thin monster caught hideously between fox and man, I was more frightening than the mask I had worn. Smoky miasma rippled off my sleeves and hem.

That earned me a short scream and a whimper from my human observer. I imagined she must have clamped a hand over her mouth from the way the sound cut off. Hanako-san was right to be afraid. *I* was Shiroi Uindo, demon of fire and lust, wind and rage!

I unleashed the blue dancing flames upon the corpses with a deafening shriek. They all went up in a brilliant flare of blue violence and charred stench. I hovered at the center of this maelstrom of my creation, the small inferno surrounding me in its nimbus of lurid, azure light. The slain demons were quickly consumed, their dust encircling me in a blustery cyclone. I sent forth a nimbus of blue flame outward, scattering the ashes to the winds in every direction.

My task completed, I lowered myself down onto solid ground and shifted back. I draped my left forearm casually over my daisho, palm open on the pommel of my katana. I started toward the shadows, then grinned. I turned my torso toward the sculpted evergreen bushes. My triangular, finely furred ears pricked upright.

"Do you understand now?" My voice purred into the darkness, my left ear flicking toward her while the right remained upright. I tapped a finger on the tip of my nose. "I have your scent, Hanako-san. I know *well* the tang of *your* fear." I grinned.

I could hear the transport copters cutting the air some distance away. My fire had burned bright and they were coming. There was not much time.

"You will find your killer on the street outside the hot pot shop on the corner of Omato and Yuri in the Japanese Sector, hunting his next victim. The human believes he is a yōkai in his madness and has taken to eating the innards of young women. Quite a shame, too." I sighed and shook my head as if despairing. "He has no finesse whatsoever. Your quarry should be easy to recognize. Someone gave him a kitsunenomen, the poor fool." My smile was extraordinarily sly.

"I would go *now*, Officer Yoshimora, if you wish your promotion... and to spare a life this night. Perhaps you will spare many lives in the dark nights to come. Sayonara, human child. And Happy New Year." With that I turned and walked into the deep shadows, vanishing without a trace.

Before I went to The Cage, I watched Hanako step out in her police uniform, cautious as a mouse. "Sayonara, Lord Wild Fox." I personally approved of her polite etiquette.

There was a slight smile playing over her lips, the sort made by one who has just seen wonders come to life and survived them. Hanako stood over my discarded assassin's costume and knelt. She made to pick them up, but at once they dissolved into autumn leaves and November dross in her fingertips. I heard her gasp aloud as the sodden, leafy mess crumpled in her hands. Then she was running.

I suppose she heeded my instruction, for the next day she was on the news receiving accolades for apprehending the dreaded Kitsune Killer, who was none other than an ordinary, deranged man with a penchant for cannibalism. He happily confessed not only to his own fledgling murders, but to many of my kills as well.

Upon his capture, Hanako got her promotion to detective. If the deceit troubled her, it did not show when the medal was pinned to her chest. Her father smiled lovingly as he shook her hand and patted her shoulder for the media cams. It was the beginning of a stellar career for young Officer Yoshimora. One day she would take her father's place as Chief of Police. Youta's reign was especially good to her family.

The Kitsune Killer became another artifact of history. He who bore my title died in his shadow-strewn cell late one night before his trial. A suicide, they ruled it. There was no way in or out, no one on duty heard or saw a thing. In the end, nobody cared, and the human world found new distractions to fascinate itself with.

Chapter Twenty-Seven

Takeover

Supremely pleased with myself, I stepped out of the shadows onto the upper deck of the Ori. I was thrumming full of elation, and so was everyone else in the joint. Wall to wall yōkai were celebrating everywhere! The noise was deafening.

I spied Chikako on the floor below, bobbing her head to see over people. Her expression was writ in anxiety, her hand clenched in front of her heart. I smiled cavalierly when I saw her and swaggered the short distance to look down over the rail. She exhaled in relief and ran to the stairs.

"Hayate-kun," Youta called out. I went to him at once. A samurai did not deny his daimyo for even an instant.

"My Lord?"

He gripped my shoulder. "Good work, tonight, and this past year. None of this would have been possible without you." It was true. I was indispensable.

"It is my honor to serve you, Youta-sama."

The Dragon smiled. "Take thirty minutes. Sport." He nodded at Chikako struggling through the crowd to climb the steps, desperate to reach me. She was having a tough time of it with so many demon supplicants of higher rank waiting to see and offer their sycophantic support of the preeminent Dragon.

"Come back to my office after. We're not done, you understand. We've only just begun this night. In the morning when we break down the High Council's doors, they will have no choice but accept us."

I understood implicitly. "Hai, Youta-sama."

"Go, have fun. We will see you shortly."

I turned and saw Chikako stalled halfway up, unable to break through. Her face was a mask of feline frustration as she jostled this way and that to no avail. Smiling, I went down to her regally, yōkai melting aside for me.

"I heard someone died!" She yelled over the booming music. "When you didn't come back right away, I was afraid it was you!"

"Hell no!" I grinned and took her in my arms amid the celebratory pandemonium. "It was the sarugami who fell. I had to stay behind to burn the evidence."

"Oh! I am so glad you are alive!"

She buried her head against my chest. I could feel her tears against my skin where the kimono parted open. She touched my sliced sleeve and fingered one of the blood-encrusted gaps open to see. I stroked her hair and made her look at me. Her eyes were shiny and huge.

"Hey, beautiful. Everything's going to be okay now. Believe me?" She nodded and I kissed her lustily in the middle of the loud music, and the hooting, screaming, and howling. She melted against me.

I took my woman by the hand and led her down onto the floor, through the revelers and into the cage dancers' dressing room. There were two on break inside, a pretty bakeneko boy and the long-necked rokurokubi stripper, who was smoking a vapor pipe. "Out," I ordered them, perhaps a shade belligerently. I did not have the time to bother with their paltry feelings.

"Hayate-sama?" Chikako asked me nervously, her hand gripped in mine.

"*Out!*" I told them again, my miasma flaring. "Now!"

They grumbled, particularly the feline fem-boy, but they went.

I slammed and locked the door, turned and lifted Chikako onto the dresser counter, pressing her legs apart with my hips and shoving her miniskirt up. Her mouth was on mine in an instant and she pulled me into her embrace, her thighs spreading wide for me. I grabbed her desperately, apparently needing this more than I knew!

She pulled my kimono apart and I ripped off her panties with my claws. I went into a near frenzy when I felt her wet lips against the tip of my dick. Then I was inside of her, and I felt her open around me, her legs wrapping tight around my waist to pull me in deeper. She gasped. "Oh! Oh, Hayate!"

"We won," I breathed huskily.

"Do it," she said, squirming against me. "Please..." She flooded.

I sank my upper and lower fangs into her flesh. By this act I proclaimed Chikako mine. She held my head to her throat, shoved my kimono off my shoulders, and bucked hard into me in a mad frenzy, jostling my daisho, which made things a bit awkward. Not that I cared.

"Bite harder!" she screamed. "*Harder!*" I pressed my fangs deeper in and rammed her hard. She dug her fingers into my scalp. "YES! My fox! My wicked, *gorgeous* kitsune! I'M *YOURS!*" She began that ululating wail I knew so well, flooding me. I almost lost it inside her right there.

The door beside us banged as a fist pummeled against it. "Hey, in there! OPEN THIS FUCKING DOOR! *RIGHT NOW!*"

I growled and unlocked it, wrenching it open, my cock still buried balls deep inside Chikako, whose mouth was a perfect, startled O, her legs and arms locked around me. We both looked out at the hairy manager, a kejōrō. Not an inch of skin showed beneath the tangled mop of long, matted black hair.

Behind her, other yōkai bobbed and peeped around her to try to get a look at us, including the rokurokubi. Some were scowling, others grinning ear to ear. There were a few whistles and catcalls. One of the fem-boys gave Chikako a high thumbs up in the air above the kejōrō's head.

"This is not a brothel!" the kejōrō proclaimed.

"I don't care what the fuck it is!" I snarled, my ears fanned down and low aggressively. "*I* need a little privacy before I go back out," I demanded haughtily. "Now – Fuck! Off!" And I slammed the damned door shut in her face, or what I supposed was her face. I had never seen under a kejōrō's tresses. The wall rattled violently.

Chikako giggled into my chest as I relocked the door and resumed thrusting into her. "You're horrible!"

"Hai!" I grinned.

"Are you really going back out?"

I stopped moving and looked in those liquid golden-amber eyes. "Yeah. This is an intermission. We have to tighten the fist by morning or risk throwing the entire Metropoplex into chaos. We seize this opportunity or lose it. I don't have much time..." I looked at her desperately and she nodded.

I lapped the light seepage of blood from her shoulder while nuzzling her neck and that quickly reignited the mood. With a masculine, throaty growl I declared her "Mine!" and bit roughly into the holes I had already made.

"Hayate-sama!" she screamed and yowled her head off, grabbing fistfuls of my hair, and the intensity resumed as if we had never been interrupted.

I opened my eyes to see my monstrous reflection gaze back at me in the dressing room mirror. It was beastly, yet strangely alluring, this ghoulish thing that was my yōkai self. I found I no longer feared it. For better or worse, the demon and I had made our peace. I watched the Demon Fox bang my girlfriend in fascination for a time, or more to the point, I watched *myself* grind into her as the White Wind. But I came looking into her eyes, her blood on my tongue, and she never knew a thing.

TEN MINUTES LATER I LEFT WITH CHIKAKO IN TOW BEHIND ME, MY hand on her wrist as I pulled her along. She followed passively in a state of euphoric bliss while I wended us through a crowd of curious, grinning yōkai. Some of them clapped and whistled for our performance. There was no one in that hall outside who could not hear my Chikako. I was pretty smug about it.

The large demoness covered in long, black hair stopped us.

"Hold it. You can't just kick my dancers out of their space to have a quickie with a server!" the manager complained.

"I can tonight," I said matter-of-factly. "Want to come up with me and complain to the risen Dragon of New Tokyo?" I paused to let that sink in. It did.

"Damn kitsune," the manager mumbled.

I smirked triumphantly and walked past her.

"And if there is any penalty or repercussion against this woman, I promise you Youta-sama will hear of it – from *me* personally!" I called back over my shoulder.

I dragged Chikako behind me again, while she apologized over her shoulder for my bad behavior. "I'm so sorry! He gets like this after a battle. Sorry! Oh, hey, Kiko! Look! He *bit* me!" I think she squealed.

I never looked back. I was Shiroi Uindo and I had nothing to apologize for and only Youta to answer to. Before I went back up, I turned at the stairs and took both of Chikako's hands in mine. "About this morning... I am sorry I scared you." I meant it. I could not remember much, but her fear and my deplorable behavior stuck out. "I wouldn't have hurt you, I promise." I straightened her tousled hair affectionately.

"I know. You're not like that. It's okay, really."

I shook my head. "No, it isn't. As soon as matters are settled with the Syndicate overnight, I swear I will make it up to you. That bed is damn cold and lonely without you in it." Chikako smiled and got that sappy look on her face that I had come to adore. "And thanks for cleaning the place up. I noticed, and it is appreciated. I won't let it get like that again."

Chikako smiled brightly. "You're welcome, my gorgeous ange- uh, fox. I just wanted to help. I'll be waiting for you in the morning when you come home." Ah, 'home.' What a nice word that was.

I smiled my coy little grin and kissed her forehead, then the back of her hands before reluctantly letting them go. "See you then," I said as I backed up the stairs. She was smiling, that lovesick expression plastered on her pretty face as she gingerly touched a feminine hand to the wounds I had made. I glanced over to see Hiroko watching us, her frown turned into a full scowl when she beheld what I had done to her baby sister.

She's mine, Hiroko, for as long as I want her to be. Remember that.

Smiling in supreme satisfaction, I went back up to Youta's office to receive my next orders. I joined the other five. How odd that seemed. It was like someone had gnawed off one of our fingers.

Youta studied us. Shirou had smoothed his feathers, and a medic attended to Taro's blinded eye. Takeshi still looked like someone sat on his favorite china tea set.

"Victory seldom comes without sacrifice," he said at last. "We all might have died this night." That was true. Even he still looked bedraggled after his epic struggle with Hiroshi. "Yet we who stand here are alive! We faced our enemy and beat him. If we are to make good on all we have struggled to achieve, we cannot rest to lick our wounds. Our sacrifices must *not* be in vain," he urged. "We will now go forth and take this Metropoplex in hand, and when we go to the Oligarchic Council at break of dawn, they *will* submit to our rule!

"Hayate, Fuyuko! Go to the Yakuza. A new leader has risen to claim ownership over their ranks. Kill him and replace him with this one." He showed us a face on the holo-vid screen. "He's already ours. Here is the location. Our man will be ready. And make a show of it. Prove to the humans we are *yōkai*."

"Hai, Youta-sama," Fuyuko and I said in unison.

"Shirou and Takeshi, you will go to this man." Another face appeared on the projection. "He is poised to join the oligarchy as soon as one of the members retires or meets an untimely demise. He will get his call today. Prepare him for his new station… and ensure his loyalty to us."

"Hai, Youta-sama," the tengu and the oni said as one.

"Katashi and Taro, make certain the brothels and tobakujou know who their new master is. Do not hesitate to be loud about it. Whoever protests, dies."

"Hai, Youta-sama."

The Dragon nodded. "Return an hour before dawn. We go together to face the human rulers of this city with the strength of the underworld behind us." And that is just what we did.

We walked through the shadows, Cold Fury and White Wind. We could have been siblings striding side by side. She was ice and I was fire, but we were both ayakashi. Nothing and no one were going to stand in our way.

Fuyuko and I emerged into the midst of the Yakuza, who were arming themselves in their headquarters. We were both dressed in crisp suits, hers white and I in a pale, almost metallic sheen of blue. All activity stopped at the sight of us. The one Youta had stipulated as the Dragon's chosen successor was there, as was the human who currently held the command.

"If it isn't two of the three who broke in and killed many of our brotherhood last October," he said. "You will die for that affront, yōkai bastards!"

Fuyuko remained as frozen as ever, those azure ice eyes glittering. That meant violence was imminent. I smiled in a most friendly-type fashion.

"So sorry, but you have it all wrong," I said congenially. "You alone will die, and your men will pledge to Lord Youta their fealty as befits the reigning Dragon of New Tokyo. Else they will soon be joining you in Hell."

Without further ado, Fuyuko sent her icicles hurtling at him out of thin air and pinned him through the shoulders and thighs to the wall. He stared at us in disbelief, then at the ice spears that emanated a cold mist. Blood welled around them. The other Yakuza stood in shock or disbelief, depending on the individual.

"Hiroshi is dead!" I decreed in ringing tones. The humans stood stunned.

"Is that true?" I heard someone ask.

"Lord Youta slew him in righteous combat this evening. A new Dragon is risen. You will swear to Youta-sama or you will die," I said with The Dragon's absolute authority.

"Do you want him, Ssshiroi Uindo?" Fuyuko's breath misted the air as she spoke.

"If you're offering, certainly. Arigato gozaimasu." I grinned.

"Shiroi Uindo?" one of the men asked.

"*This* is the White Wind?" asked another.

"That means *he* is the Kitsune Killer!"

"*That* pretty boy? Heh! Not likely!"

The hushed muttering fell to silence when I morphed into my darkest self, complete with the blood-soaked kimono I had worn when I first turned into this thing. I rejoiced in the gasps of terror I elicited from the mouths of grown men. Many moved back and away as my baleful miasma flooded the room. Three ghostly balls of blue flame flared to life. My wisp attendants accompanied me when I floated wraith-like over to the injured man, who watched my approach in mute shock and pain.

I ripped off his armored vest with a single swipe. No one lifted a finger to stop me. I plunged my claws into his soft meat belly, reached up in that warm, wet cavity, and ripped loose my prize! I held the heart aloft in blood-soaked triumph and ate it before the witness of them all. Fear, disgust, anger, horror... all these things I elicited from those men. One noisily threw up. And he called himself Yakuza... Heh.

With that act, the Ayakashi Syndicate under Youta's leadership claimed authority over the human syndicates from the top down. He whom Youta had chosen now took command of the room quickly and bid the others to stand down, although no one was exactly volunteering to run forward and have a go at me or Fuyuko.

He pledged his faith to our master through us. Only then did I transform back, much to the relief of everyone present. The humans looked at me warily afterward while I licked the blood clean from my fingers.

The other teams did as had been bid of them as well. By dawn, Youta had the entire criminal underworld in hand. Now there was only one thing left to do.

As ANTICIPATED, THE HUMAN OLIGARCHS CONVENED. SHIROU AND I were sent in first to prepare them. We kicked the doors in hard, the lock broke upon impact, and the heavy wood swung inward, half splintered. The crow and I each shoved one of the double doors out of our way as we walked in briskly side by side.

"What is this?" demanded the older gentleman sitting at the end of the long table. It was one of those sleek, black jobs that showed the council members' mirror images like an inky pool. The leader of this human wolf pack stood halfway out of his custom ergonomic throne. "How dare you!"

I laughed with sheer evil reverberation. "Oh, we *dare!*"

Shirou and I each grabbed two dumbfounded underlings at the far end of the table and threw them out of their seats. Mine hit the wall and slid down in a daze. I may have used a touch too much force, but I was used to dealing with heavy hitters, not soft suits. Like hell I was going to apologize for it, though. Shirou's landed hard on his ass and then ran out.

"You do not belong here," the chief exec in charge continued. "Get out! Immediately!" He pressed a button on his console.

"No can do," Shirou said smoothly. He wore a coal black suit with a crisp, white shirt, the front of his long dark hair swept up into its usual high topknot. I chose shark grey that morning with my own hair wild and unbound. We both sat in the empty seats we provided for ourselves and put our feet up on the table, leaning back like a couple of assholes. "My associate and I have most urgent business to attend to with you."

"The very same that you are already here to discuss, as it happens," I added slyly. My wicked eyes looked at each member of the oligarchy, taking note of their faces and their scents.

One man among their number stared hard at me and met my eyes without flinching. He did not look upon me as an enemy, either. Something in his gaze was thoughtful, piercing... considering. It was as if he recognized me, although I had never seen this human in my life, I was sure. It was an effort not to shiver. I stared back, eyes narrowed warily, but it was I who broke first with a sidelong glance at Shirou when he spoke.

"Our master, and now yours, will be arriving shortly," the tengu said. "We respectfully advise you remember your manners in Youta-sama's presence. Dragons can be touchy creatures about their honor, as I am certain you are well aware."

"I said for you to leave," the old human said, brusquely.

"Now, that is not a proper way to begin," I drawled. "Do you agree, tengu-dono?"

"Quite, kitsune-dono. The Dragon will be most displeased by such blatant discourtesy."

"Hmmm," I answered thoughtfully. "It is never wise to get on a dragon's bad side." I shook my head.

"See here –!"

"Ah, but wisdom can be taught," Shirou said lightly. We both heard the approach of our master and the other four. "And I believe the lesson is about to begin."

We stood at once and bowed low. Youta strode in and up to the edge of that solid black pond, and faced the Corporate Council. Shirou and I backed away to join our comrades in line behind our daimyo.

"Hiroshi-sama warned us about you, Lord Youta. Do you really think you can just barge in here with your menagerie of freaks and disrupt –"

Katashi pulled a gun and shot the President of the Council. And just like that, the most powerful mortal in the known world fell facedown upon his shiny table. Blood pooled from his forehead, liquid bright and reflective as the dark surface it puddled upon. I stared in demonic fascination.

"Hiroshi is dead," the Dragon announced. "Per the old

laws, his empire now belongs to me. You all seem so glum to receive this news. I am certain you have been told nothing but vicious lies about me. Did he say I was attempting to overthrow the old order? Replace you all? Tchk…" he scoffed. "Nothing could be further from the truth! Indeed, I would prefer to *benefit* us all!

"I present to each and every one of you a new era of prosperity befitting the twenty-second century." There were holo-vid projectors embedded into the table and they began beeping. The startled members of the oligarchy turned toward the sound warily. The projectors displayed data and financial figures before their astonished eyes.

"Here is an outline of my agenda. I think if you peruse my proposition, you will find my endeavors are not at all in conflict with your own. I will make us all individually wealthier than we are together currently, and I will do it in three years or less. Hiroshi hoarded much of the incoming wealth, and so did his accomplice." He nodded at the corpse at the other end of the table. "Both were short-sighted as to what we and our city can accomplish together.

"So please, friends, let me do what a benevolent water dragon is supposed to do, starting on this most auspicious day as we enter the Year of the Dragon. I promise, you will curse Hiroshi's name for an old, blind fool who robbed you by the end of next year."

"And if we disagree?" asked the suit who sat closest to the President.

"You must discuss what you wish to do amongst yourselves and come to a consensus, of course. But you are more than welcome to send any inquiries to me through one of my associates here." We loomed deadly dangerous behind the Dragon, the six of us great yōkai, silent and implacable. To dissent was to die, of course.

I extended my middle claw to its fullest length and picked a bit of the heart I had eaten earlier from my teeth. I speared the dark muscle on the point of my grey talon and slid it onto my tongue between my sharp set of fangs. I gave them my cruelest smile and tilted my head sideways. One man looked as if he would be ill. No one said a damn thing.

"Very good. I look forward to my future dealings with your esteemed Council. Good Morning." Youta turned his back on the mortals and we parted, then followed him out.

Before I left, I grinned lecherously at the lone, middle-aged dame who sat among them and gave her a wink that promised a wicked good time. She flushed and looked away. My sly smile broadened. I turned to leave when I caught sight of that man again, the one who did not fear me. He stared and stared as if I were the only thing in the entire world he wished to acquire. Even when Youta was in the room, this man had eyes only for me.

The thin line of my mouth hardened, my exposed demon's eyes glittering in silent warning. I promptly turned my back on him and followed the others out into the hall. I did not look back, but as the last to leave, I felt his eyes boring into me until I disappeared from sight. I ignored it, but it made my back itch right in the center.

Fucking *creepy*. I was the one supposed to be creeping *him* out, not the other way around! The hell…

WITH THAT, OUR LITTLE WAR WAS WON! THE COUNCIL COMPLIED,

of course. Youta offered a sweet deal, and a protracted war would have been costly and risky. Common sense and self-interest prevailed, and we were all the richer for it. At the epicenter of Youta's innovative renaissance, New Tokyo grew in prosperity. Life was good for those of us on the inside, especially for the fabulously wealthy.

I crawled into bed nude less than an hour later and snuggled in tight with Chikako's naked, sleeping body. I admired the wounds I had made upon her exposed throat and kissed them. She smiled in her sleep, clutched my arm and drew it more tightly over her, and I could have sworn she murmured something that sounded suspiciously like, "My dark angel…" But then she always did like to call me sweet little names. I did not trouble myself over it and drifted off to sleep in short order.

The first new moon of spring proved a true herald of the season. Once the little rebellions were put down, it was like a dream. On the last evening of January 2120, I awoke to a new world order, one in which I was to play a critical role. I became a top demon enforcer in the Ayakashi Syndicate, feared throughout New Tokyo. Eventually all of Asia and beyond would know the name Shiroi Uindo, the Demon Fox.

And as for Youta Clan itself? For thirty-five years I served as one of the Dragon's chief lieutenants, an assassin *par excellence*… until one day I stopped. What happened, do you ask? Ah, *that*, my friend, is another story.

Glossary of Japanese Terms

(in Romaji)

abayo (ah-bah-yo) - goodbye

akusho (ah -koo-sho) - a dangerous road or place, usually in reference to a red-light district

arigato gozaimasu (ah-ree-gah-to go-zah-ee-mah-s/u/) - formal thank you

ayakashi (ah-yah-kosh-ee) - medieval term for yōkai

baka (bah-kah) - stupid, foolish, idiot

bakemono (bah-kay-mon-oh) - shape changing spirit

-chan (chahn) - a diminutive attached to a name to denote a young child, particularly a girl

daimyo (dy-my-oh) - feudal lord

daisho – (dah-eesh-oh) – "big-little," the combination of katana and wakizashi, generally worn in the *obi* by a samurai

daitengu (da-ee-tain-goo) - greater crow goblin, known to live like monks in the mountains

gaijin (guy-jin) - non-Japanese; a foreigner

hannya (hahn-ee-yah) - a demon mask specifically representing an oni, particularly the female kijo

haori (hah-oh-ree) - a short kimono worn as a men's formal outer garment

hitotsume-kozō (hee-toh-tsoo-may koh-tzo) - a one-eyed yōkai that takes the appearance of a boy around age ten

hoshi no tama (ho-shee no tah-mah) - a kitsune's spirit ball

hososhi (ho-so-shee) - a ritual exorcist

Hyakki yagyo (hi-yah-kee yahg-yoh) - the One Hundred Demon Night Procession, a gathering of a large group of yokai who troupe in ceremonial procession throughout urban streets

Jigoku (jig-oh-koo) - the Buddhist conception of Hell

kabuki (kah-boo-kee) - type of theater

kami (kah-mee) - a Shinto god

kamikakushi (kah-mee-kah-ku-shee) - to be spirited away, a mysterious disappearance

kamaitachi (kah-mah-ee-tah-chee) - sickle weasel yōkai

kanabo (kah-nah-bo) - the iron cudgel frequently utilized by oni

karasu tengu (kah-rah-soo tain-goo) - crow demon

kawaii (kah-wah-ee-ee) - cute, adorable

kejōrō (kay-joh-roh) - type of female yōkai covered in long, black hair

keukegen (kyu-keg-ehn) - a hairy little yōkai that feeds on filth *kijo* (kee-joh) - type of female oni, one usually who was human to begin with and transformed into a yōkai

kitsune (kee-tsoo-neyh) - fox

kitsunebi (kee-tsoo-neh-bee) - fox fire; a manifestation of spirit fire generated by a fox: a will-o-the-wisp

kitsunegaochiru (kee-tsoo-nee-gow-chee-roo) - to be freed from fox possession

kitsunenibakasareru (kee-tsoo-neh-nee-bah-kah-say-ray-roo) - to be deceived by a fox

kitsunenitsumamareru (kee-tsoo-neh-eet-soo-mah-mah-eh-roo) - to be bewitched by a fox; confused

kitsunenomen (kee -tsoo-neh-noh-men-/u/) - fox mask

kitsunetsuki (kee -tsoo-nee-tsoo-kee) - fox possessed

kitsunewootesu (kee-tsoo-neh woh-oh-tay-soo) - exorcism of a fox spirit from a person

kodama (koh-dah-mah) - a tree spirit

kotengu (koh-tain-goo) - lesser crow goblin

-kun (kuhn) - an honorific attached to a name to affectionately denote one of lower rank

kyuubi no kitsune (ky-uu-bee no kee-tsoo-neyh) - nine-tailed fox

mononoke (mah-noh-noh-kee) - an older term for a spirit or yōkai

Nani? (nah-nee) - What? What is it?

nekomata (neck-oh-mah-tah) - two tailed cat demon

nihonshu (nee-hohn-shoo) - Japanese word specifically for rice wine

nogitsune (noh-gee-tsoo-neyh) - evil fox spirit/demon, a wild fox, field fox; malevolent, mischievous, a sexual vampire; a fox spirit from the Kyushu Region capable of demonic possession.

obi (oh-bee) - a sash that holds a kimono shut

oni (oh-nee) - an ogre or horned demon, usually red or blue in color and depicted wielding a kanabo

onikuma (oh-nee-ku-mah) - devil bear

onna (oh-/n/-nah) - woman

oniisan (oh-nee-sah/n/) - big brother

otchoko (oh-tcho-koh) - cylindrical sake cup

rokurokubi (roh-ku-roh-ku-bee) - long necked woman, type of yōkai with extended, snake-like neck

ronin (roh-ni-n) - masterless warrior

sake (sah-keyh) – liquor, refers to any alcoholic beverage

sakura (sah-koo-rah) - cherry blossoms; a cherry blossom tree

-sama (sah-mah) - an honorific attached to a name to denote one of a higher social status

-san (sah/n/) an honorific attached to a name to denote politeness, such as Mr., Mrs., Ms., etc.

sarugami (sah-roo-gah-mee) - monkey demon

shiroi (shee-roh-ee) - adj. white

shirogitsune (shee-row-git-soo-neyh) - white fox

shuki (shoo-kee) - sake set

tanto (tahn-toh) - a dagger or knife 11.93 inches or 30 cm long worn by samurai.

tanuki (tah-noo-kee) - a raccoon dog (or badger) yokai known for casting illusions via broadleaves and its overly large testicles

tatami (tah-tah-mee) - straw floor mat

tenko (tayn-koh) - high ranking kitsune of at least one thousand years old, nine tailed

tobakujou (toh-bahk-oo-joh) – gambling den

tofu kozo (toh-foo koh-tzo) - tofu boy, a yōkai that manifests as a boy offering tofu on a rainy night; depending on the legend, the tofu may create a nasty mold in whoever eats it

tokkuri (tohk-koo-ree) - sake flask

tsukumogami (tsoo-koo-moh-gah-mee) - an old household object that has transformed into a yōkai

tsunami (tsoo-nah-mee) - a large and destructive tidal wave

uindo (ooh-een-doh) - wind

ushi oni (ooh-shee oh-nee) - a chimera yōkai with the head of a bovine and the body of a spider

wakizashi (wah-kee-zah-shee) - a short sword/long knife of 30 to 60 cm or 12 to 24 inches with a shorter grip, worn with a katana by samurai. The combination of both is called *daisho*, or "big-little".

yako (ya-koh) - a demonic kitsune or nogitsune, a wild/field fox

yōkai (yoh-kai) - spirit, ghost, demon, or faerie

Yomi no kuni (yah-mee no koo-nee) - Shinto underworld/spirit realm, akin to Hell

yukata (yu-kah-tah) - lightweight kimono generally worn in summer

yuki-onna (yoo-kee-oh-/n/-nah) - Snow Woman, a frost yōkai that takes female form and freezes her victims to death and drinks in their potent life force.

yūrei (yoo-reh-ee) - a human spirit, ghost or specter

zenko (zehn-koh) - a celestial fox, divine messenger usually of the god Inari

About the Author

Xander Cross lives a quiet life with his spouse and cat. He holds a bachelor's degree in History, which he unapologetically uses to write his paranormal fiction. A lifelong enthusiast of Japanese culture and folklore, Xander cosplays as a kitsune yōkai on occasion, and photographic evidence can be found on Instagram and Pinterest under @ayakashi_fox. He has also published a short novella as an adjunct to The Atlas Dystopia Apocalyptica series, entitled "Come by Night" on https://www.wattpad.com/user/ayakashi_fox.